THE
DISSENT

THE
DISSENT

LEAH VERNON

47NORTH

Text copyright © 2023 by Leah Vernon

Published by 47North, Seattle

www.apub.com

Amazon, the Amazon logo, and 47North are trademarks of Amazon.com, Inc., or its affiliates.

ISBN-13: 9781662500374 (paperback)
ISBN-13: 9781662500381 (digital)

Cover design by Mike Heath
Cover image: © Krakenimages.com, © NatashaRamenskaya / Shutterstock

Printed in the United States of America

THE
DISSENT

Chapter One
AVI

A pale worker girl with sapphire eyes floated past. As she spread her arms, her body exploded in sapphire flames. A deep-blue fire that resembled viscous waves engulfed the nuptial dais. Where Father was. The General of the Union of Civilization. Our divided region, where Black Elites forced Europes into indentured servitude.

My eardrums reverberated, battering violently against the canals after the first explosive detonated. Had there been one eruption? Multiple, perhaps? I was having a hard time recollecting the specifics. Thoughts raced every which way, clamoring over one another, only to stumble back to the beginning again. A marathon that never ended. Insanity.

"Father," I murmured. Or had I only imagined that I'd whispered it?

An excruciating high-pitched static remained as I squirmed about in the aisle like a slug, drowning in the dense, bejeweled matrimonial gown that Parade had designed. My eyes remained pinched because in the depths of my being, I knew that when I opened them, nothing would ever be the same again.

Time felt slow and thick like honey.

The girl with the sapphire eyes. Like the flames. Like the ripples in the sea during golden hour. Like Liyo's. The Europe boy who I'd fallen headfirst for.

Was solidarity even attainable when both sides kept at each other's throats? This mutiny by the workers would set us back once more.

My head hurt. Among other things.

Pea, who was the lead worker in the Citadel but also secretly a part of the uprising, had been feeding me intel, but I had to stay obscured. That was the plan. To not make a move until I got confirmation that Saige, an Impure who'd saved my life, and Liyo were alive. The confirmation had never come. What was I supposed to do? I'd made a conscious decision to wait it out. I'd thought that the Lower Residents and I could work together. With no more violence. That was the arrangement, in exchange for my assistance.

The rebels had gone back on their agreement.

Open your eyes. It was Saige. Her voice. So rich. So certain.

Her light-brown eyes with orange and green specks were fearless and sure.

Was I dead? Was she dead too? Was that the only way that I'd be reunited with her?

Open your eyes, Princess.

I gasped as if she had breathed life into a cadaver. I then sprang into a seated position, smearing beads of blood that trickled along my cheeks from my ears.

Blue flames sprouted among tables in the once-grand decorated hall like dazzling wildflowers as guests fled, stumbling over one another like tumbleweeds. I witnessed the cries but still could not hear them fully. Just that same monotonous ring as before. The full moss garlands, and the velvet walls, and the massive white caged centerpieces all charred. Live birds had escaped from their decorative enclosures. Flapping their wings to go somewhere, anywhere but there. I didn't blame them. I'd want to get away from us too.

Holocams hovered over my and Phoenix's forced matrimony. Or at least what was left of it. The green lights in the middle of their domes systematically blinked. Indicating that we were indeed still live for all Subdivisions to observe. Some remained stationary in the airspace while others zoomed to catch guests who took cover underneath scorched tables or tried to climb from the enormous picture windows.

The migraine in my head pulsated, causing me to sway.

Get up, Saige's voice commanded. The voice had been closer before, and now, it was distant. She was leaving me once more.

I found the strength to stand as the ornate gown continued to weigh me down. I unfastened the bottom half of the skirt and immediately felt relief. My hearing returned little by little, and I soaked in the surroundings. There I stood in the middle of the Great Room as Lower Resident workers attacked Upper Residents. An all-out insurgency had befallen us.

I looked to my left and noticed that the main entrance was barricaded. Watchmen banged on the other side of the gateway.

The uprising had been carefully planned by the rebels. It just had to have been.

"Stop this madness, at once." I managed to peel an Upper Resident's grip off a worker's throat. "Stop fighting each other!"

I ended up with an elbow to the mandible and stumbled back into yet another match. I was caught in a net of arms and then tossed onto the ground like common waste. I spat out a wad of red phlegm and wiped the corner of my mouth on the delicate lace hem.

"Elite scum," an unrecognizable voice bellowed.

I was tackled from behind. His full weight crushed my lungs as he pinned my arms at my sides. I writhed on my stomach, but nothing made him budge.

He scooped his hand underneath the back of my head and took a fistful of my halo braid. Pulling my head back, he fixed a small blade to my throat.

"For the Brotherhood," he announced.

"Get away from madam!" Pea thumped the assailant in the back with a curtain rod almost twice her size.

On impact, he fell sideways. The knife skittered.

She pulled stray hairs of her wiry brown bob from her mouth. "Are you okay, madam?"

"I'm fine, Pea." She assisted me to a standing position. "Gratitude."

Pea gripped the weapon so tight that her whitish fists quickly turned as red as cherries. "Be careful, madam."

I nodded and knelt over the man. He was a worker that I'd never seen before. Or perhaps I had, and his pallid face just hadn't registered. His once-toughened expression turned apologetic. His yellowed teeth chattered. "I ain't know you was—I woulda never. We was only spose to go for da General."

"You are *never* to touch her," Pea fumed, using the rod to prod him in the chest. "That was the deal."

"The General—my father." I clarified the man's word. "Who sent you to do this?"

"Your—" His pupils dilated.

A laser ripped a precise hole in between his brows. The tenseness in his body released as if he'd been struck with peaceful sleep.

Jade stood there with that superior smirk that I loathed plastered on the bottom half of her face. My younger sibling, if one could call what we had a siblingship, had a long face and fawn skin and wore an obnoxiously short bang that dusted the tops of her bushy brows. She was Father's female copy.

"You're welcome," she said as watchmen slashed through workers as if they were hanging branches.

She aimed at Pea. Pea dropped the rod, trembling.

"Madam?" she muttered.

"Jade, are you insane?" I stepped in front of Pea.

Jade cracked her neck. "How do I know that she wasn't the orchestrator of this attack? How do I know that she hasn't been a mole this entire time? Living among us, secretly gathering intel to take back to the rebels. Perhaps you two did this stunt in collaboration. Sister, I know how much you hate your own kind and how much you entertain honks like her."

"Elite Jade—" Pea's voice softened.

Jade's finger rested on the trigger too much for my comfort. "Do not address me, honk."

I guided Pea farther behind me. The holocams all seemed to have found a better story angle and zoomed in on the sisterly spat.

"You don't have to do this." I motioned toward the holocams.

Jade pulled the trigger. The laser whizzed past my ear, past Pea's face, and ended up in a worker instead.

Half the holocams zipped past to get a close-up of the now-fading subject.

A very tall worker in a nude bodysuit saw an opportunity and grabbed Jade from behind. Her gun clattered to her feet as the worker placed her into a headlock. Pea didn't budge. She didn't charge at him with the ferocity she'd had when I'd been in danger. I'd never seen her with a look so satisfied as Jade clawed at the man's thick biceps as it tightened around her throat, her face.

The Union would be a better place without Jade in it. That was an unspoken truth.

Holocams lingered on me. On Jade. Even if I had wanted to let it play out, I couldn't. I was not going to meet her at her level of savagery. Everyone deserved grace.

I grabbed the rod that Pea had dropped and struck the attacker. His hold relaxed. Jade took the chance to crouch down and strike him with an elbow in his abdomen. I was satisfied with him being incapacitated, unable to attack anyone else until we could figure out how to put a stop to the disorder. No matter what happened, I was not going to kill, but Jade couldn't let it go. Her ego, her passion for vengeance, was too heightened.

On top of him, she began hitting him in the nose and jaw. I tried grabbing her, but she shoved me away with the viciousness in her eyes of someone who had gone completely mad. The bones in his face began to crack as he moaned through a mouthful of shattered teeth. Her knuckles and face were covered in blood. Jade grabbed his collar and brought his head from the ground, examining her work.

"Beasts," he said weakly and spat in her face.

"A beast, indeed." She pressed both thumbs into his eye sockets. The man yelped in agony, and she took solace in the torture. She continued as he thrashed until he stilled.

Silent tears streamed along Pea's face while her fists were balled tightly at her sides.

Another quarrel collapsed into me. More bodies dropped, more guests were stabbed, and random shots were fired across the space of the Great Room.

A familiar wail cut through the fight. Mother. She was in danger. Together, Jade and I mowed through forms until we got to her. Mother's voluptuous body was adorned with a soft cream bodysuit, and a velvet cape swathed her shoulders. She sat on the backs of her thighs and pulled Father's head into her lap as he wheezed. The inhales sounded like whistles, as if he were trying to take breaths through a congested straw. Black and flesh-colored boils the size of plums covered half his face, oozing with buttery pus as his cabinet surrounded him. Physicians and medbots were already on the scene with their digital equipment and mechanisms.

Why was everyone just standing there? Observing? Why weren't they doing something?

"Father?" Jade howled from her core as she shoved through the bodies to be by his side.

The physicians had already removed his signature gloves, which he never went without. Jade took his large hand and brought the fatty part of his thumb with the puzzle-piece-shaped birthmark to her cheek. I'd never seen her so gentle before.

I approached sluggishly. Still in shock. Afraid, perhaps. Not fully understanding the attack as an actuality. Perhaps it was all just an outlandish nightmare. Perhaps I'd been asleep the whole time and I hated the idea of an arranged matrimony so much that I'd created a landscape where the oppressors were punished.

My legs had an agenda of their own. They carried me beside Jade and forced me to kneel, overlooking the mess that we'd created. Mother's stream of tears tumbled along her dark skin. The tears were so continuous that each fell onto Father's forehead, then rolled off to the sides, mixing with his own.

Father tried to speak, but the words emerged only in wet, ragged coughs.

"Rest, my love." Mother placed her face on his. "They are going to figure this out."

Physician Pike, the same person who'd secretly contacted Father when I'd tried to gather information on lethal Lower Resident injections at the Health Department Headquarters, was now the only person who Father's life depended on.

Physician Pike manually worked on Father's lesions after the lasers from the medbots failed. The wounds would not respond to the procedures. Bots continually scanned his body, monitoring vitals, but the signs kept declining.

"No method is yielding surviving results," Physician Pike said.

Father began to cough violently. His body flapped like a trout's on the end of a hook.

The medbot continued to read the descending numbers as lower-tier physicians began to step away, making room for the cabinet. Jade yanked one of them back. "Do something!"

7

"W-we have tried all we can," he offered.

Physician Pike was the director of the Health Department, top of his graduating class, and revered in the field of science and medtech. And if he couldn't revive Father, then no one could. He shook his head. "The injuries aren't receptive to our tech, nothing. That flame is no ordinary flame. The remnants of it just keep spreading, destroying his organs. We don't have the medical resources or know-how to halt it."

Jade looked like she wanted to terminate Physician Pike right there. "Imbeciles," she spat. "All of you! You are going to just linger like you are at some performance while the General, your General, my father, dies?"

Mucus trickled down to her quivering lip. She buried her head into the crook of Father's arm. Jade hated when people witnessed her being emotional. Ever since she was little, she'd find a corner or a hiding place to let her sentiments loose. I hadn't seen her do it in so long that it felt almost like an act.

"Father, I have failed you." Her voice was muffled in his thick-plated bodysuit. "We have all failed you."

Father's eyes were expansive then, and they remained fixed on me even as Jade spoke. In my entire existence, I'd never seen the man fearful before. It rendered me uncomfortable to even witness. Father was a leader, a warrior who'd always demonstrated strength.

Although we hadn't agreed on how the Union was run, he stuck to his beliefs. This couldn't be how it all concluded. I had planned on breaking the proverbial shackles, demonstrating to Father that we could live cohesively with the Lower Residents. A new beginning was what I dreamed of, but not this way. Not with his death.

The medbot beeped more methodically, reminding the room of his imminent demise. The hard truth was that he'd never get to experience a new reality, to see the possibilities of hope. But I'd just been betrayed by the very people that I'd thought unity could be achieved with, so perhaps there was less hope than I had initially believed.

Father had taught me that every action had a reaction. How could I solely blame the rebels? We could all glower at all the aggressions we'd inflicted on them for the past millennium. We'd enslaved them over a thousand years ago, as they'd done to us prior. The recent attack was retaliation, but also change was never easy, and things would get bad before they shifted. I had to keep reminding myself so I wouldn't become one of the forlorn.

There were always losses in conflict. Father knew that better than anyone.

His unblinking brown eyes stared deeply into mine. I knew that in his last minutes, his life flashed at record speed before him like an ancient malfunctioning projector. I witnessed dread mixed with satisfaction plain as the night was obscure. Fear of his sealed fate, death, and proud bouts that defined him as an honorable man. I was reliving it, feeling what he was feeling with him.

Father never showed fright because he was invincible. Perhaps he was afraid of what we now faced without him. That he hadn't done enough. That the people he'd mistreated had been his ultimate demise. How cruel and twisted the world was. How poetic. No one was safe.

It was the first time that I saw him as human and not just the great, grand General Jore.

There was so much that I wanted to confess. I wanted to tell him that I forgave him for all the things he'd done in the name of duty. That I understood that he truly believed there was only one way to tackle our world. That he'd instilled in me perseverance, strength, and never giving up on things you believed in. He'd taught me survival.

Somehow, I knew that he heard, felt my sentiments, in some celestial way.

He managed to take his hand from Jade and laid it ever so gently on mine.

I'm not sure why the tears hadn't come yet, like they had for Mother or Jade or the other cabinet members surrounding us. Perhaps I knew Father disliked it when we cried. Perhaps he would finally be able to rest. He had worked so hard taking care of others, his family, and it was his turn to take the road less traveled.

We didn't believe in the afterlife. We were a people of science who believed in what we could prove. Religion had been used to enslave us once before, so we'd rebelled against it. We assumed that once you were no longer around, you became one with the universe, returning to the earth, from where you'd originated. Once you decomposed, your soul went nowhere. But who knew, really? No one had ever come back to tell us how it really worked.

"Your." He struggled through a raspy voice. "Sister."

I felt Jade's eyes burn a gaping cavity through me. Instead of focusing on Father, his last words, his last swallow, she couldn't take her attention off me.

His hand went firm as it slowly slid from my knee like a teardrop. It landed softly beside him. His eyes remained open. Unoccupied, though. He had made the transition. Mother kept repeating his name as she was gently pulled away. Moaning filled the space from the guests who'd survived the uprising. Watchmen had finally subdued the rebels and even the workers who had just been at the wrong place at the wrong time.

"You!" Jade's voice didn't sound like her own.

I heard the soft drone of holocams positioning themselves closer.

The area went silent after that.

"You. Did. This." Her upper lip twitched as her palms dug into Father's unmoving chest.

How could you say something like that? was what I thought I'd replied, but the words hadn't left my thoughts. She was looking for someone to blame.

"You haven't shed a tear." She hoisted herself up. "Has she? Tell me that I am dishonest!" She motioned to Physician Pike and Admiral Butler.

"Jade, I—"

She pointed. "You empowered these scum, these so-called rebels, to do this. You gave them permission to come and murder your own. You aided and abetted two fugitives of the Union and weren't even apologetic. Even when he gave you chance after chance after chance. You hurt Father to his core, and you've betrayed the Union. Once again. You aren't fit to lead a herd of sheep, let alone the people."

Instructor Skylar, Father's right hand and head of watchmen training and tactical guard, stepped forward. "Jade, enough!"

"Not enough. This is just getting started." Jade spoke to me again. "If you think you and your army of honks are going to run us into the earth, it will be over my decayed remains. I will gladly lie right beside Father to stop you. To end this." She motioned to Father's corpse.

She stopped talking for a moment. I wasn't sure what she was trying to muster during the long pause, but something didn't feel right. It seemed almost staged.

She knelt beside him and picked up Father's gloves. She examined them as if it were the first time that she'd laid eyes on them. She sank her face into them. Afterward, she slipped one on and then the other. They fit loosely on her hands. Her fingers flexed as if a power had transferred. She adjusted her bodysuit, stood taller as if she'd grown inches, and jutted out her chest.

"This was your plan all along. Wasn't it?" She pointed at me with a gloved finger. "To get rid of him so that you could take over and be with your honk lover boy."

"Enough, Jade." My nostrils flared and my body stiffened at the mention of Liyo. She had no right to even allow him to cross her brutish mind.

11

She chuckled impishly. I figured that I'd given Jade exactly what she'd wanted.

"Do you all see? She just can't seem to control herself," she said to the holocams, to the people. "I want the entire region to know that I will not allow blood or anyone else to ruin what my forefathers, my father, have built. I *will* be the next succeeding General."

All eyes that had been on Jade before were now hyperfocused on me. Boring into me like beams. Thousands. Perhaps millions of them. Searching for reassurance. Trust. Safety. Some grand speech like Jade's. They wanted me to show my newfound General strength and top her. Or at the least challenge her. What could I have promised to the people to make them see me in a better light? What could I possibly say that would make them believe in a region-wide equality doctrine? That wasn't what they needed to hear right now. They needed hope. And I wasn't the one to give it right then.

I retreated within myself as I always had, where I was comfortable. I was not brave that day. I allowed Jade to dig a grave and lob me in.

My silence sent rifts through the ballroom.

Jade's voice interrupted. "Prepare his body for the bereavement ritual."

Each member carefully grabbed a different part and lifted his body from the platform. Watchmen and the battered crowd gathered in the center. The members lowered him onto a bed of raised arms. Hundreds of them created a path. Father's limp form floated across the floor. Farther and farther away.

Jade balled her fist and stuck it in the air and repeated the slogan that Father had used right before he rode into battle. "Long live the Union of Civiliza-tion."

The people pounded their chests before balling their fists and throwing them into the empty space above. "Civiliza-tion. Civiliza-tion. Civiliza-tion."

Chapter Two
SAIGE

Visibility was moderate that day. I stuck my tongue out and allowed a snowflake the size of a cotton ball to dissolve on its slimy surface. The air smelled crisp, pure. Small white clouds drifted from between my lips with each exhale. I lay flat on my belly, well concealed in a snowbank. I had on so much felt and fur that the cold had nearly no effect on me. I could've been out there for more hours and been fine. After the escape from enslavement of the Southern Region, I'd integrated quite well to the north's excessively low temps.

In a thick mitten, my hand rested on a handmade spear. I'd done the best I could with what I had in the mountains. I'd like to have thought I was doing better than most in my predicament. I hadn't died. Just yet.

Liyo was in front of me, crouched in the white abyss much closer to the prey—a medium-size elk with meat that'd last us a while.

I was being the bigger person, allowing Liyo to prove himself. He kept begging me to take him on a hunt after he'd gotten better. I kept making excuses. Telling him that he was far too sick to leave his corner of the cave we called home, but he got better at some point. Stronger.

He'd threatened to go alone, if not with me.

So, there we were. Together. My least favorite pastime.

I'd laid out the ground rules before, though: (1) always follow my lead, (2) no talking, and (3) absolutely no using his powers. He had the ability to move things. I wasn't sure from where or from what, though. I didn't know who—or what—exactly was out there, and I wanted it to remain that way.

Every so often the wind would pick up and cause a halo blizzard effect. The snow dancing around in a vortex. Blowing the soft fur of Liyo's massive hood to one side. That was the only way I could tell he was even still there. He blended well.

Every time the elk would move a little, we'd get on our hands and knees and crawl a bit nearer. I'd been tracking that particular one for the last couple of days, and today was the day.

As long as we stuck to the plan.

We'd been out there for a while—I could tell by the light from the sun hidden behind the clouds—but I didn't mind the wait. Even though Liyo was around, this place was my peace. I hadn't known what to expect when I'd plotted my escape from the Elites, from bondage, but the life far away from it all was everything that I'd wanted. Quiet. Mostly safe as long as we stayed under the radar. It was the safest that I'd ever felt, which was an unfamiliar thing. At first. But still something I had to get used to.

Every day, I'd wake up and repeat, *No one's going to take this from you.* It was how I stayed centered. Present. How I stopped myself from slipping back into the dark memories of what I'd seen before. Kids' ribs poking through the skin. Workers dying from injections. Impure babies being tested on in labs.

The Union believed that our very existence was a virus that needed to be contained, eradicated. That was the original plan for us workers after the Elites banded together and destroyed the systems back in the early 2000s. Europes were only supposed to rebuild the Union for a period of time when they took power.

Now, here we were a thousand years later at each other's necks.

"What the fuck are you doing?" I mouthed as Liyo crawled way too close to the animal.

The elk lifted its head from foraging, ear twitched a bit, and began to move in the wrong direction. Liyo got to his feet carefully and pursued. It took everything not to throw the spear right into his thigh.

I followed close behind, unable to call out for him to hang back.

The animal picked up speed, and so did Liyo, weaving through all the trunks and tangled branches. He was chasing it into another territory. One that I hadn't crossed yet. I was very careful to make sure I explored and hunted only in a certain range of the mountain.

Liyo had entered a wooded, much denser space, going downhill. The flakes became thicker, wilder. It was getting harder to see more than a few arm's lengths ahead, to keep track of the elk, let alone Liyo. The snow got deeper too. It was a struggle to trek and to even stand upright.

"Liyo?" I whispered harshly. "Liyo!"

A branch cracked faintly in the distance. I gripped the weapon and spun in a full circle, surveilling my immediate area as far as I could see.

I saw no one, but it felt like someone, something was watching me—us.

I moved forward again. Battling the high wind as it pressed me back.

It was too quiet.

Someone was there.

I wasn't going back to what I'd been in the Southern Region. If it was my time to die, then it was time, but I'd never be a slave again. Never. People like me, who were born of both races, Impures, were at the bottom, usually killed before they could even make it past infancy. Ma had decided to keep me and had paid for it with her life when Head Gardner had given her the lethal injection. The Union had snuffed her out like a flame on a match's tip.

I finally spotted Liyo not too far ahead. The elk was in front of him as he held a spear in one hand and raised the other, palm facing forward. The elk was struggling against an unseen force. It grunted and then began a hollow-sounding bark as its front hooves lifted off the ground. Its rear dragged across the ground, and the antlers swung as the animal's agitation grew from it being manipulated. Liyo pulled the creature forward with his abilities.

So that was all just a ploy to see if he could control a beast over five hundred pounds? I felt myself wanting to injure him once more. I had a clear shot.

As I got closer to the spectacle, ready to go off on him for being so reckless, so stupid, a nimble body jumped from one branch to another.

The second I pivoted, they dropped down, and something thick clunked me in the face.

❖ ❖ ❖

When I woke up, I was alone in an armored bodysuit; the Union's red triangular emblem was embroidered on the left chest plate. I wore gloves just like the General's. I opened my palms and then closed them into fists that cut off the circulation. When I pounded my chest and then raised my fist, a Transmega as big as a building and an army of watchmen appeared. Faces, all hues of black and brown, surrounded me. We were in a straight, disciplined line.

The General stood at a podium. They all chanted.

I chanted.

The Union of Civiliza-tion. The Union of Civiliza-tion.

I wanted to say it too. It spilled from my lips with surety. Dignity. As if I was one of them. And not a filthy Impure.

My body was not my own. It was theirs again. I was his pawn. Unable to resist.

The General called out. I floated toward him. I didn't hate him, but something told me that I wanted to.

Daughter, he said without saying it. It came from his mind. We were connected.

I was of his blood. Elite running through me. We shared the same birthmark. His firstborn hidden from his people. Avi's lost sibling.

I was now in a rickety kitchen that'd been messed over. My helmet busted. There must've been a battle. I was wounded. The wounds felt too real.

A trail of warm blood smeared the floor, leading into the hallway. I followed, already knowing what I was going to find. What I always found behind that same old door. I started to sob as my body propelled me forward.

The door led to a high-tech lab. Underground. There was a patient being tested on. Physicians surrounded the specimen. I could smell the sterileness of the operating room. I felt like a ghost. Light and airy. I floated above the operating table. There was an infant. Being poked with needles and grabbed with silver tongs held in hungry, gloved fingers. A scream. I rushed down to save her, but as soon as I touched the skin, I ended up becoming the specimen myself.

I was stuck to the table. Why couldn't I move? I needed to get away.

A physician with blue eyes leaned in and slipped the surgical mask from his face.

"Remember me?" He ran a nasty tongue over his tan teeth.

The man I murdered for the General to gain his trust so that I could escape. Be free. One had to suffer so the other could survive.

The laser wound in his forehead vomited congealed blood.

He dug his finger into the flesh hole. "You!"

I pinched my eyes shut so that I could wake myself. I shook my head back and forth and wiggled my toes and fingers so that I could jolt back.

"Your fault." His breath was hot in my ear, sour smelling, like death.

I mumbled, "Don't hurt me."

He moved one of my wild ringlets and tucked it away. "You do such a good job at it yourself."

He pulled out a gun and shot me in the head.

I hated going to sleep.

❖　❖　❖

I was tied to a sturdy bed. Soggy with sweat.

Where the hell was I? I did a quick scan of the area. Looking for Liyo. Any obvious exits. Weapons for when I escaped the restraints. I was surrounded by timber panels and a curved wood ceiling with strings fixed from wall to wall. From them hung colorful papier-mâché lanterns. There were long brown shelves, layers of them, holding cloudy jars of who knew what. A fire crackled nearby, filling the room with the sweetness of burning hickory. That homey feeling that I never got to experience in the Southern Region quickly dissolved once a man entered the door. He had a triangular tattoo on his forehead. The people of the north that the Union had warned us about. He carried a tray of scalpels and rusted scissors. He set it down beside me as if I weren't even there.

I lurched at the savage with a throaty grunt. He was unfazed.

He hummed a foreign tune and scooped water from a basin, then brought the deep spoon of water to me. I hesitated. He placed it farther along my lips, forcing me to drink. I took a gulp, swished it around, then spat it back at him.

The savage stared down at me with black eyes, the irises so large they took up most of the whites. The eyes were full of concern, disbelief, and annoyance all mixed in one as the water and saliva dripped along his long dark hair and humped nose. I eyed the thick twine restraints on my ankles and wrists and then looked back at him, but with narrowed eyes. He knew what it meant. I wanted out.

The man that I had spat on grabbed a smooth wooden bowl engraved with squiggly looking symbols. He ground some kind of dark-green paste with a pestle. He then scrambled through shelves looking to find something specific. Once he got it, he added it to the concoction and ground some more. It had to be some kind of seasoning that they mixed in order to make flesh tasty. Where I was from, they told us that they were cannibals.

He scraped some off the sides with three fingers, tasted it, and then brought it to my view. I threw my head back. I wasn't going to allow him to season me without a fight.

He huffed as if I was the most disappointing thing he'd ever dealt with.

"Stop fighting," he finally said. His voice sounded as smooth as grease.

He spoke my language.

He pointed at my forehead. A second later, blood began to trickle.

I was getting woozy, so I finally laid my head back and accepted his help for a wound he'd inflicted. But after that, it was on.

He gently rubbed the paste on the gash. I winced. Afterward, he cupped the back of my head like I was a newborn as he wrapped the wound. I couldn't stop outlining the highness of his cheekbones and the plumpness of his face and how his tattoo was an outline, but this one had two other triangles inside of the larger one. I'd never seen anyone with features like his, not of a worker but not of an Upper, but of something different. He caught me watching, so I looked away. But when I found him focused on something else, I just stared again. Although his game face continued to carry no emotion, his eyes said something else.

He laid my head back down and returned to a stool on the other side of the room. I kept my face to the ceiling, but I could feel his eyes. It took everything not to look back, but I had to resist. Despite him patching me up, he'd struck me, so he was the enemy.

"I would ask your name, but I'm sure you won't give it." He almost sighed.

He was right. I wasn't giving him anything. I didn't know what he would do with the info. I didn't know if he had Liyo or if there were others like him lurking about. There were too many unanswered questions.

My mind was moving a bit slower than normal, but I chalked it up to the concussion.

Out of nowhere, he said, "I'm Miah. Medicine man in training."

Like that was going to get me to trust him. Offering his name. He must've dealt with the weakest of hostages.

"I know you don't trust me," he continued. The words coming from his mouth slowed down. "Yet you were the one lurking on our territory with a boy that lifted a beast with no machinery."

My head snapped in his direction.

His face was open, welcoming even, but his tone didn't match. "You can see our predicament."

I'd already seen the predicament from kilometers away.

He finally stood and walked so lightly over the wooden planks that they made no sound with the shifting of his weight. He lingered. Not menacingly. That time I didn't look away. Nor did he. A visual tug-of-war.

"It's peaceful here. And we want to keep it that way." I could hear his breaths and his heartbeats. They pumped so loudly that they sounded like drums in the next room. "I'm not sure what you're doing here, but I know—you know that you don't belong in this colony."

I sucked a tear back in that threatened to kill the whole badass-hostage front I was playing. He was right. I didn't belong in his colony or even mine. I was a drifter. A nobody seeking refuge on someone else's turf.

"I can tell that you're running away from something, fighting against something." I noticed that he stopped himself from reaching out and instead balled his fists. The heartbeats became stronger, louder in the base of my ear. Were they mine or his? "Maybe if you talk, tell me what's happening, I can be of some assistance."

Tuh! I'd never trusted a man, and today wasn't going to be the day I started.

He looked embarrassed. "I see."

The room began to tilt, yet he remained stationary.

"What did you do to me?" I grabbed his wrist even through the restraints.

Miah watched me struggle.

"I need to know the truth." He gently unpeeled my grip. "Don't fight it."

He'd mixed something up, and it was affecting my mind.

And just like that he left me and the snapping, fiery logs alone.

For what seemed like hours, I tried my hardest to get out of the restraints. My wrists had rubbed up against the rope so many times that they were raw.

You aren't escaping this time. Avi appeared with that jaded look on her face. A short thing with pecks for tits, the deepest toffee-colored dimples that gave her a doll-like appearance, and her usual braided crown with tiny curls draped over the tops of her ears.

She took a seat beside me; I even heard the bed frame creak beneath her. I thought I must've passed out again.

Avi crawled on top of me and rested on my chest like a pet. She sighed as she looked up at me with those hopeful brown eyes.

Avi giggled. *He is a looker.*

"Why are you even here?"

Because you want me here, big sister.

The words made my jaw clamp. I thought my teeth would shatter.

What?

"I left you behind."

21

Avi's ghost wrapped one of my almost-knotted coils around her finger.

"I'm a coward." I laid my head back down. "Always running from anything and nothing."

She eyed me.

"At first, I thought I'd found something out here away from the government, the General—for a moment, I really thought I had, but look at me." I twisted my hands in the restraints. "Back in shackles. Maybe there's truly no place in the world safe for an Impure."

Saige?

The voice that came from her wasn't her own, but that of a man.

I gasped awake.

Miah hung over me.

I slammed the back of my head into the bedstead. How much had he heard?

"You drugged me."

He didn't deny it.

"Are you just gonna fuckin' stare or what?"

"I needed to know that you had no ill intentions on this colony," he said matter of factly. "A precaution."

"Precaution my ass" was all I could get out.

Colony? As I suspected, there were more.

He looked pained. "I'm sorry."

I sucked my teeth. "You don't know shit."

"You've had a hard journey."

My nostrils flared.

"No one should have to go through what you've gone through."

He heard everything. Knew everything. At least the bulk of it.

"Untie me."

He started with the ankles. At first, I thought it was a ploy, but he kept untying. Once I was freed, I'd grab a scalpel and slit his throat. Take my furs back and find Liyo.

Miah kept his eyes on mine as he carefully undid the knots. I stayed still. He held out a hand. I stared it down. Then pushed myself to a sitting position. In the next moment, I had grabbed the blade and pinned him against the same bed he'd tied me to. It was too easy.

I breathed out hard as I waited for a punch to the ribs or a knee to my lower regions. Instead, he did nothing. He didn't even beg me not to or ask me why. I dug it deeper into his throat.

"You've been on survival mode for so long."

I dug it farther, not wanting to hear anything he was saying to me.

"You have choice."

What the hell was he talking about?

"Are you not tired of running?" he asked.

Yes—I meant no. I needed to go. I knew that he'd stop me from leaving. There was no choice. I never had a choice.

I pulled his hair back, exposing more of his neck, but he never broke eye contact with me. I wanted to so bad, but I just couldn't do it. I dropped the scalpel, then backed away.

I wanted him to retaliate so I could say *I told you so*. So that I could have a real reason to off him. But he only approached with his hand out.

"You don't have to run."

Was that why my legs were heavy, my body lethargic—because I was tired of running? Was it telling me to consider my options, options that I'd never had access to before?

"You have no idea what you've just invited onto your land."

"I've invited a person who had the choice to kill and run but chose otherwise."

"You don't know what I've done."

"We've all done things, but that doesn't mean that redemption doesn't exist."

"Not for people like me."

Miah came too close. "You are welcome to stay until you figure that out."

The medicine man's herbs were still working on me, allowing him to somehow be reading my mind still, and I didn't like it at all. Maybe he'd been watching Liyo and me struggle the entire time up in that mountain crevice or had his colony cronies listening in on our rare conversations between long stretches of awkward silences. Either way, with that simple question—*Are you not tired?*—he'd hacked away the walls I'd built around myself and exposed a once-hidden core. I had to admit that running was my thing, but maybe it didn't have to be.

Chapter Three
LIYO

The power I possessed, whatever it was, surged through me in a way that I'd never felt before. It felt more controlled this time as I held the elk steady. I'd been cooped up in that cave sick for so long that I'd forgotten what it was like to be human, a man.

I knew Saige was going to be mad. She was always mad anyway, so what would more mad matter? I heard her call my name through the whirling flurries, but I was focused on getting our feast. She'd be okay. She was always okay. She didn't need me for anything, and she always made that very clear.

My face turned as red as a beet, my beard was covered in bits of ice, and my white hair stayed tangled on my forehead as drips of sweat began to roll along my temples. When I thought I lost the connection, I brought it back to the center, breathing heavily like I'd just sprinted in a marathon. Nostrils flared with each inhalation as the animal writhed and stomped midair.

With a flick of the wrist, I snapped its neck. The beast went limp. I laid it down gently like a baby into the powdery blanket of snowfall and grinned from ear to ear.

"Saige," I bellowed, trotting over snow mounds to get a closer look at the fresh kill.

I got on my knees and ran a hand over its stomach. Still warm.

"Saige?" I called out. "Come take a look at this."

I expected her to come up from behind spewing curses about how I never listened and that she'd never take me hunting again. Or her favorite, a grunt followed by the silent treatment.

Neither came. I turned and looked out into the white abyss. She wasn't there. I scrambled to my feet and trekked back to where we'd come from, where I'd last heard her calling my name.

Nothing.

The wind picked up; the flurries became more violent, covering any tracks.

I'd lost her. Or maybe she'd finally lost me.

The entire time we'd been in the north, she'd never just disappeared, but Saige was unpredictable. I'd known her for longer than anyone else, yet I still hadn't *known her* known her. Or at least that's what she wanted. To keep that dam up so that no one could get in. That was her safe place.

I returned to the cave. Hoping to see her there, angrily tossing wood into a hearty fire. Instead, it was barren and cold. She had never come back. One of the rules was to always be back before dusk. Nightfall had already hit, and I was worried.

I paced back and forth, trying to figure out the next move. Should I stay and wait like she'd want, or should I track her down in the night? I huffed hot air into my hands and rubbed them together as I weighed the options.

She was either hurt or someone had taken her.

I hadn't thought of it before, but we'd been in the north for some time and never come across any camps, but we'd also never trekked into unknown territories. We always stayed within the perimeter. Maybe they'd been watching us the entire time, and today they finally decided to act.

I grabbed an extra fur and wrapped it around my shoulders. The temps had dropped below zero. I took a light orb and made my way from the cave and into a region unknown.

❖ ❖ ❖

The jelly in my joints began to harden and sting. I'd lost feeling in my face kilometers back. I kept the light orb off and only brightened it when I heard rustling in the bush or an animal huff. Other than that, I used the brightness of the round moon to illuminate the path. There was still no sign of Saige or anybody else.

I was too far away from the cave but also too far in the middle of nowhere to turn back. I could've started a fire, but that would make me stick out. Also, I had to keep moving. I'd been stupid enough to allow all my attention to stay on that stupid elk. I'd been so bent on showing Saige that I was strong and useful—that I wasn't just a burden—that I'd lost focus.

When we were kids, my family was a part of a small rebel compound led by Mama Seeya. Saige had come in alone as an orphan. It was a long time before the Union found us hidden somewhere in the Outskirts, but when they did, my parents were executed by Head Gardner and her watchmen. Mama Seeya fled. Saige and I had gotten separated on the way back to the Southern Region to be added to the slave labor force. I'd left her back in the city before and hadn't seen her since.

We were all we had out there. I had to find her. I was *going* to find her.

As a young man, I became tired of slaving on the Farmlands picking produce in the blazing sun until my skin blistered to feed the Elites as my people withered away. I couldn't take it anymore. I had to protect

Uncle Tate and his daughter, Eve. So I joined the rebels again. Met back up with Mama Seeya. She had a plan. My powers would carry us into salvation.

Instead, my powers had led me to being alone in an empty forest in the north as my people still toiled in the fields. I'd lost everything. Little Eve, who favored me. Saige. Avi, the Elite I'd fallen for. The one I thought about before I passed out on that cold rock each night and the one I thought about when the sun warmed my face. I'd never been treated like a citizen by an Upper before until I met her. With her, she didn't see the color of my skin. She just saw me for who I was.

And I'd run away from my duties in the south. Leaving her to pick up the pieces while Saige and I hid. It wasn't fair to her.

I hadn't known how to describe what we had, what we'd shared. The Union had erased any connection between us and them. Love wasn't allowed to exist between races. Integration of any kind meant death, and if there was a child that came from the mix, it meant death for them too.

That rule, that fear, had always lived free in the back of my mind when I'd imagined anything other than something cordial with her, but we'd gone past cordial, knowing the risks.

Something came from my eye. It started out as a tear, but due to the temperature, it quickly turned into an ice droplet.

The cold had gotten to me when I'd least expected it. I collapsed like a corpse. I knew that I was freezing, but my body had started to feel prickly and hot. Hypothermia. I relaxed my fist, and I thought all my fingers would fall right off the knuckles. I willed the energy to engulf me. Static began bouncing around my limbs and inside my sockets. I allowed the electricity to warm me.

I wasn't sure how much time passed or how long I was knocked out from exuding so much energy, but there was a familiar whirring sound.

The trees began to rustle, and a cyclone of wind hit me. Beams of light flashed underneath many crafts as they all passed overhead. There was a loud thump when they landed in the distance. Hovercrafts from the south. I tracked them to a clearing, then climbed a tree to get a better look. Huge outlines circled the outer banks, animals maybe, but I wasn't sure. A watchmen hive. They must've discovered us. The time had come that I would have to face them again. We'd caused a commotion before we left. We added to the rebellion. We made the impossible possible for workers and Impures alike. Our escape was too high profile, and I knew that they'd never stop looking for us.

The General couldn't just let it go. He needed us back to make an example. And I needed to go back to save my people, to save Avi, finish what we started.

The torture—filling us with deadly injections, aborting our babies, starving us—was going to end when I killed the General.

"You have no right to be here." An unknown figure spoke to the stationary watchmen with weapons plastered to their large chests. I wondered if the Union was still genetically altering them to be even beefier than before.

I couldn't get a good look, but there were five facing the hive wearing light-gray fur parkas with heavy hoods concealing their heads. They had to be the savages. They were the only people who lived in the north, according to the Union. Saige had probably been taken by them.

"Well, we are straddling martial law at this point." I recognized that voice. "See, the thing is that we have a couple of really big issues."

A path was made for Head Gardner on cue. She was shorter than all her men, thicker in physique. Four heavy braids trailed along her back. She wore a matching black armored bodysuit with a red triangle embroidered on the left shoulder. The Union's sigil.

"What's the issues?" Head Gardner asked herself to mock the savages, who remained steady, silent.

Head Gardner barely dipped her chin, and on command a watchman shot a laser into the savage standing next to the one who had spoken initially. The body dropped in the snow, face first. Something on all their foreheads shimmered blue, but I thought my eyes were playing tricks on me in the dark. One rushed over to survey the wound as the remaining savages raised their weapons.

A shake of the head confirmed that the person was dead.

The remaining approached with hostility as Head Gardner began talking. "Blue flame. The honks had access to it and created quite a bit of havoc on our side." She clasped her gloved hands behind her back as she marched closer without fear. "Now, where would they get such a mineral? A mineral that is solely mined here. The treaty states that—"

"—no tribe shall interfere with another's territory," the savage finished, surveying the men who'd gunned down their member. "We know the words of the treaty very well. Our ancestors created it for reasons like this."

Head Gardner chuckled. The sound of her joy made the back of my neck itch.

"A lot of things just seem coincidental. The flames. The fugitives of the Southern Region just up and disappearing. Nowhere to be found. And what better place to get lost but here in the north."

"You don't strike me as one who beats around the bush." The savage asked, "What do you want?"

Head Gardner made her way over; each step was careful, deliberate. I imagined flames flicking in her eyes as if she were an ancient evil incarnate. She placed her face uncomfortably close to her prey's. "Tell me that you aren't hiding any fugitives of the Union. That would cause our treaty to dissolve into a finely grated powder, because if I get an inkling, the tiniest feeling, that that is the case, oh, I will take pleasure in pouring down a lightning storm on this entire colony. I will scorch you and your people into a white dust to be forgotten by even your history scrolls."

"Why would we interfere with your dictatorship now after all this time for a race of people who wronged us?" The savage spat on the ground and added, "As far as we're concerned, you both can finish each other."

"Sounds like motive to me." Head Gardner clapped.

"For what?" they retorted.

"Motive to assassinate the General, of course. Cut the act." She poked her own head. "He's dead."

I almost choked on my own tongue. The General was dead? How? When? I was supposed to—dead?

My thoughts raced over one another as I tried to wrap my head around how it had happened. Had Mama Seeya's plan worked without me? Had things gotten so bad where they had to take him out?

Someone had beat me to it. I couldn't help but feel upset. I wanted to be the one who ended him. I wanted him to look me in my eyes as I unleashed on him everything that he had on my people. I wanted to stand over him as he took his last breath. That moment replayed in my head in that cold cave each and every night. Me ending him. Ending his reign. Ending his regime. Taking back what was ours. That revenge fueled me. Made me stronger. Gave me hope.

Avi. I knew that she wouldn't have agreed with me offing her father. She probably would've even tried to stop it. She was good and just. She always believed the best in people, but I knew that's not how people won in life. I was like her once, but now I believed in sacrifice. And I had sacrificed too much to allow her people to wipe us out.

Avi wanted us to cohabitate, but her people were too far gone to ever consider it. One of those people was her father. He wanted to euthanize us. I was glad he was dead. I hoped he rotted. I hoped that with every breath it was a pain he'd never experienced before. I didn't care about the consequences anymore. If she truly cared for me, then she'd know why I'd have to do it. And now that he was out of the way, it was time to mow down the other Elites because even with Avi being the next General, I knew that they would not be down for assimilation.

I had to get back to the south.

Snow crunched beneath the savages' boots as they made their way back through the forest.

"What now, Head Gardner?" Admiral Butler inquired.

"They're here." She slid a helmet over her head. "Set the entire colony on fire."

The admiral pointed forward, alerting the hive. They advanced, their laser guns humming as they loaded.

I slid down the tree trunk and sped up to catch the savages. I kept my distance, though, tracking their footprints and the drips of blood from their deceased. They were going to lead me straight to Saige.

They cut through what seemed like abandoned outbuildings. I ducked behind fortifications and ancient-looking wagons. Still no sign of anyone. It looked like a deserted town, but I knew there were more of them.

The group disappeared.

I moved in between small dwellings and peeked in windows. Still no sign of her.

The smell of a barn drifted. Maybe they had Saige tied up there. I pressed my back against the outer wall and listened for movement. There was movement but not of a human.

I slid inside. There were lots of stalls lined in a row. Thick clouds emerged from each. The animals grunted, snorted. The same beast that I'd seen circling earlier in the clearing. It was built like a carriage. It was maybe half-canine, half-bear. It was thick and meaty with sharp silver claws. Its eyes almost looked human as they locked on mine. Its fangs bared, and it snarled. Saliva dripped from its teeth. The thing was much sturdier than an elk.

I wouldn't be able to hold it off. I held my hands out; electricity appeared.

I prepared for it to ram the meager stall separating me from it, but instead of shredding me to pieces, it approached warily and sniffed my hair like a domesticated pet.

I opened all the stalls and allowed the animals to roam free. The diversion prompted all the hidden savages to leave their dwellings and gather the herd. I noticed that no one had exited out of one particular dwelling. When the coast was clear, I burst in the door.

Saige. She was facing a man with a marking on his forehead. Before he could react, I tackled him. We crashed into a table. I placed him in a chokehold. The tattoo glowed blue just like the ones in the forest had.

"Liyo!" Saige said. "Stop."

I wasn't listening.

"You're killing him."

"So what?" I spat.

"Let him go," she growled.

I didn't even have to see her face to imagine how serious she was. I released him but then grabbed some rope and tied his wrists.

"You're welcome." I got in her face.

Saige didn't look happy to see me, or even relieved, for that matter. There was no pleasing her.

I waited for her to say something, but she only stared with those striking eyes.

"They're here." I cut the silence.

"Who?" She finally spoke.

"Watchmen." I peered through the window. "They're about to burn the place down. We've got to go. Now."

"What?" The man stepped forward. "I've got to tell the colony."

I put my hand out and allowed the power to jerk him back. The back of his head hit the wall hard.

Saige rushed to his side. "Miah!"

She knew his name. As she checked his head, she glared at me. I glared back.

"You will tell us how to get out of here. How to get back to the south," I explained.

Miah looked at Saige for some kind of confirmation.

She walked to the far part of the room. I followed.

"Were they really watchmen?" Her eyes darted.

"We're outlaws," I told her. "How long did you think all this was going to last?"

She grunted.

"We've got to get back to the south. Finish what we started. Find Mama Seeya. Find Avi."

Her demeanor changed when Avi was mentioned. She stayed in deep thought, going over the information, the options.

But her process was cut short when the dwelling shook so bad, knocking urns and jars from the shelves. An explosion detonated nearby. We peered from the window again.

Watchmen had arrived.

"It's not safe." I took her wrist. "We've got to go." I motioned to Miah. "And he's our only way out."

Chapter Four
AVI

Father's naked body had taken on an unnatural hue of grayish black. He was surrounded by a cold vapor as he lay peacefully in a cryotube. He was on frost until the bereavement ritual commenced. I wanted to wrap him in a heavy blanket. He must've been freezing.

Jade had allowed the broadcasts to set up a live stream so that the region could be reminded of what happened when we wavered from our principles. Her last words to the region before she receded into whatever abyss she'd spawned.

It felt wrong to have him on display like that, but I didn't have the energy to oppose her. Not yet anyway.

I'd monitored the same image of him, his body for—I wasn't sure the duration, but my eyes were sore and raw. Yet they stayed flayed open. It was the least I could do. I couldn't take my attention from him. Not for even a moment. There was still a flicker of hopefulness that perhaps the physicians could pluck another life from anywhere or grow one in their labs and transfer it into his vessel. At that point in life, I'd seen a boy move things with sheer will of the mind, no gimmicks or threads attached, so nothing was impossible.

Leah Vernon

I wished Liyo were there. I would've never asked him to help Father because I knew how much pain Father had caused him, but I just wanted someone to cradle me for a moment.

I had to scoff at myself at that preposterous idea. Elites and workers weren't allowed to mix. I knew that the offense was punishable by death. It hadn't stopped us from sharing bits of intimacies, though, but look what damage so little had caused. Father had imprisoned me in my quarters, and the Union had almost cost Liyo his life. Perhaps it had. I hadn't heard from him since.

The entrance to the quarters slid open, but I didn't care to see who it was.

"Leave me be," I ordered without visual acknowledgment.

"Elite Avi." A droid approached carrying a polished tray of decadent fruits, pastries, and an array of floral teas. "It is teatime."

Scheduled teatime. Wherever I was in the Citadel, the droid always found my whereabouts and served me. Perhaps Father had placed a tracking device in my arm at some point without my knowledge.

The droids resembled us. Dark skin and woollike tendrils. Wide noses and thick lips. The mannerisms were much smoother than before as it carefully placed the platter down. Scientists had worked diligently on releasing the betas after the first launch of the silver malfunctioning models that had Elites scrambling back to retrieve their chattel workers.

We were now at a 29 percent droid-to-worker ratio in Elite homes, and the plan was to extend it to the rest of the region sooner than later. Father wasn't going to allow his original plan of slowly killing off the Lower Resident population by poisonous injections masked as vaccinations to fail. He just found another way to do it.

The droid remained idle, waiting for its next command. Something about the eyes was off. They were dead like Father's.

I raised from my slump, still in the frayed bridal attire.

I reached out and touched the back of its hand. Its skin was made of a firm gelatinous substance. Warm too.

"Can you feel that?" I inquired.

The eyes narrowed as it observed the patch that I caressed. "Affirmative, Elite Avi."

"What is emotion?"

Its pupils zoomed in and out, like a real being thinking of a response. "Emotion. Noun. 'A natural instinctive state of mind deriving from one's circumstances, mood, or relationships with others.'"

"Do you feel emotions?" Tears streamed along my cheeks like rivers. Father created this—this thing—with the hopes of euthanizing an entire people.

"Negative," it replied. The expression turned empathic. "But I am programmed to handle emotions of humans as well as creatures. It appears that yours is grief. Would you like for me to provide comfort by way of an embrace?"

There was a commotion outside of the entrance. I turned to see Pea scuffling with watchmen. She breathed heavily, and her hair was damp at the ends.

I ordered the guards, "Release her at once!"

They obeyed, reluctantly.

She fell into my arms, barely able to get the words out. "Madam, there's been a message."

❖ ❖ ❖

We'd been using a covert underground tunnel in the woods between the Citadel's grounds and the Farmlands for workers to smuggle antiviral serums into the compound. I rejected the idea that it was the same tunnel that had been used to traffic the blue flames that had killed Father. Was it my fault, like Jade had suggested? If I had put a stop to this point of transport earlier, then perhaps Father would still be alive.

The tunnel was many kilometers long, tight in some spaces and wide in others. It was winding and dark and framed with uneven brick, earth, and rigid rock configurations that protruded from the ground like stalks.

Pea tugged at my wrist as I struggled to keep up. Her legs seemed to double in speed as the tail of her cloak flapped in her haste.

"Where are we going, Pea?"

She pulled me through a hole and dusted particles from her shoulder.

"Drake." She tried but failed to unplaster her bangs from her forehead. "I got a message that she has information for you. For us."

She began to walk-run again. I stayed behind. She spun around and doubled back when she discovered my absence. "Madam, we must go at once."

"My father just died. Was killed." I hugged myself tighter, reliving the moment. "I don't think it's a good idea for me to be out here. Alone."

"You are not alone, madam." She touched her chest. "You have me."

I mustered a smile. "I know, but—"

"But you think we—you think I had something to do with the attack?" She looked like she'd just lost something of value.

I opened my mouth, but only a huff escaped.

"Madam?" She wrung out the fabric of her cloak. "Do you trust me?"

"With my life."

"Then you'd know I'd protect you no matter what." She held her hand out. "You are like—no, not like, are—a sister to me."

I felt horrible for thinking that it was all a ploy. Pea had never done anything to betray me. She was more blood to me than Jade, and it was not the time to start doubting her.

I took her hand, and we continued our journey to a place called the Underground Apex.

❖ ❖ ❖

Pea adjusted the hood I wore to cover my face. We wouldn't know who we could trust until we spoke to Drake, a liaison for the rebels—and she'd also saved my life once. There were no chances to be taken.

"Spare nutrition. Spare nutrition." An elderly man wearing a discolored nude bodysuit trailed passersby with an outstretched hand with long ribbed nails that resembled old timber. He was a Disposable. A person no longer profitable to the Union due to age or disability. They usually became beggars or thieves.

Workers kept their heads bowed and continued on their ways, shoulder checking him when he got too close. He wandered into a posted watchmen hive struggling to subdue a woman with swirling eyes who was having a bad Glitter trip. The man was visually impaired. Another watchman couldn't care less about the Disposable's disability and struck him in the face. He tripped into a wobbly bench and just lay there. People around just kept going, stepping over him as if he was a minor inconvenience.

We'd made it through the chaos aboveground and stopped in front of a rickety door in a Lower Resident cube in Subdivision Four. Pea banged twice, hard, and then spoke through the crack. "Daffodil green."

After a few beats, the cube's door was unlocked. The man inside said nothing as he shoved a slumber pod to the side, revealing a passageway underneath.

Pea flicked on a light orb and then lowered herself in. I tailed her.

The man sealed the hole once more, covering us in complete obscurity.

"Stay close," she mentioned. She didn't have to tell me twice.

It was too quiet. Too damp. The walls were tacky and narrow, and it reeked of mildew and earth. We shuffled toward one direction. Hopefully the end.

I thought about Father. Was it that dark where he was too? Was it the same darkness that had engulfed him as he spoke his last word, took his last breath? Would he be forever there, wandering through space with no end?

The longer we trekked, the more my mind wandered into the depths of the unfamiliar. Into fear. Perhaps Pea was tired of being my worker, a sidekick. Perhaps the whole thing with Drake wanting to see me was a guise to get me far away from the Citadel so they could dispose of me. We were in the perfect place to do so. No one would know.

"Are you pleased that Father is dead?" I asked.

I couldn't measure her expression in the dark, but I felt her hand tense in mine as if a swift shock had gone through her.

She shone the light in my face. I shielded my eyes; the brightness was painful.

That was intentional, and I deserved it.

"Now is not the time to take note of my pleasures or displeasures, for that matter." A hint of light sliced the rock in the void. She said, "Come on. We're almost there."

The muffled music became more pronounced as we lurched into a full-on celebration. A festival of sorts. The colors were bold and sparkly and striking. It reminded me of the parties we had in the city's Square. Beads were being thrown from the tops of shops by men with painted genitals. Women gyrated; breasts bounced about. I wasn't sure what the nudity signified, but I was taking mental annotations of their cultural customs.

We meandered through bare bodies, trying to reach Drake. Pea was on a mission and clearly not fazed by the partiers encompassing us.

A girl with golden teeth and swirly eyes pulled me back, separating me from Pea.

"Madam?" I heard her yell as the crowd urged her in the opposite direction.

"Such purdy skin." Her tongue whipped like a snake's as she grazed my cheek with her lengthy, bedazzled nail. She touched her own, which was caked with copious layers of foundation trying to conceal the craters that the drugs had produced.

"Gratitude," was the only word I could gather.

"Oh, she be usin' dem fancy Uppah words." She lobbed her head back in a fit of laughter.

She dug her head into my shoulder, continuing to chortle. When she saw that I wasn't, she grabbed my chin, squeezing hard, but not hard enough for me to create a scene. I had to play it smart, not reckless. I'd learned that in watchmen training.

"I'm glad he dead and gone." She got close to my ear and sucked on the lobe. "Long live the Brotherhood, sweetie."

Pea grabbed the back of the girl's hair and tossed her into the throng of partiers. "Madam, are you okay? Did she hurt you?"

I hadn't noticed before, but behind Pea were huge holomonitors overlooking the midpoint of the Apex. I hadn't even known that the Underground could receive live streams. In the center monitor was Father's body in the cryotube. In the surrounding screens were clips of Father being blasted with blue flames. Some had added comical commentary to the clips, while others created cartoon versions and GIFs of my mother's wails. They remixed songs to his labored breathing. Jade and I were a part of the mockery too. My family's pain had been turned into some farcical act.

Men on top of floats wore poorly made armored bodysuits and gloves and wore makeup resembling Father's peeling flesh after his skin had been scorched. DIY blue flames made from papier-mâché erupted from the float's flooring.

I felt the urge to blow it all to smithereens. The druggies. Their children. The grinning faces. The decorative trollies. All of it. I wanted them all gone. To propel them into the chasm that was in the pit of my chest. The one that Father was in.

I felt acid arise in my throat as the absurdity became worse and worse. They just couldn't help themselves. Gaining pleasure from pain.

I had extended my hand, my life, to helping these people, and this was how they showed gratitude? Could they really change? Were they just something worse than animals, like Father had said? Was that the group that I was fighting for?

Pea took my shoulder. I flinched.

"Why have you brought me here?" I barked.

"I—I had no idea that they would—I swear it to you."

"Liar!" My head was getting lighter as I tried to hold it all in. The tears. The anger. Tried to not turn into Jade when I really, really wanted to.

"We've got to get to Drake," she reminded me. "This is urgent. We need to stay united. For the future. You told me that. You made me believe that we *can* coexist. You did that."

For some reason, her regurgitating the information that I'd said in the past angered me even more.

"Avi? Say something."

"You address me as *madam*," I ordered.

Pea lowered her head. "Yes, madam."

❖ ❖ ❖

I felt gutted. In more ways than one. I was too wrapped up in my feelings to care much about Pea's resigned demeanor as we finally made it to the Vixen. I didn't want to be there. It was the first time in a long time that I wanted to return to the Citadel.

The club was dingy, dim, and gaudy. It reeked of old rugs and tobacco smoke. However, I was pleased that it was much more subdued than the streets. Dancers twirled on a shiny silver pole onstage. Old currency flew as girls opened their legs into splits and made their thighs jiggle rhythmically to the beat. Glitter was everywhere. On the tables and on bar counters. Empty vials rolled on the carpet.

"We're here to see Drake," Pea notified the bartender.

He dried a cloudy glass with a stained towel that had seen its better days and then pointed ahead.

Drake was one of the next dancers in the queue. She carried a fake laser gun and wore a provisional watchman's suit. It was much tighter and had cutouts for the chest, waist panels, and buttocks. She played with her red locs as she sauntered toward the pole, inviting the hungry audience to the show. She seductively aimed the weapon at the people. She broke out into a front flip followed by a backflip and then landed in a half split. She bent her long back leg and touched the crown of her head with a pointed toe.

We made our way to the front of the section to get a closer view, hoping that she'd notice us. We stepped over legs and bumped a few knees until we made it to two vacant seats. Two girls removed their tops and slingshotted them into the swarm and began twirling their breasts like hovercopter blades. More money rained on them in reaction to the gimmick.

The bralette landed on a man's face not too far away. When he removed it, he clutched it in his large palms and then buried his nose in one of the cups, sniffing in deeply as if it were going to get him off sooner than later.

When the ecstasy of the scent began to fade, he raised his face, noticing me noticing him. It was one of the graduating watchmen from my class. Watchman Doucet. His features always reminded me of an ant's, but he made up for his insect-like appearance with a muscular body that put the other watchmen to shame. His eyes expanded with what I observed to be humiliation, perhaps dread. He quickly dropped the article and dashed into the standing crowd.

Drake's raunchy performance came to an end, and a man named Silver called up the next set of dancers. Pea and I took the opportunity to sneak behind the curtain. We stumbled into a dressing room full of girls rushing about in outfits no thicker than twine.

Drake scooped me in an embrace. She hugged Pea too. I noticed that it lingered a little bit longer. "Let's go someplace quiet. We don't have much time."

Drake rushed us down a short hallway. In passing, she said, "Aye, Tony B. These two want a private dance. Lap Room Five's occupied."

"Girl-on-girl action." His grin was crooked, and his chin had a long gash across it. "Can I watch?"

Pea stopped and looked up at him—he towered about two feet over her—and replied matter of factly, "I'd rather you not."

Drake shut the door behind her and locked it. She paced the length of the modest room. I'd never seen her so tense. "You two should take a seat."

I rested carefully on an unbalanced stool and placed my moist palms on my knees. "What's so urgent that you needed me to come here right after my father's murder?"

"I knew that you'd think it was us. That we were behind it all." She crouched down and took my hands in hers. "I swear that the rebels had nothing to do with this. Someone's trying to frame us."

"Can you garner proof?" I asked.

She turned away. "No, but I've heard some things."

I leaped from the stool. "About Saige? Liyo? Are they alive?"

Drake shook her head. "No. I still don't know. There's been no word from them since everything went to shit."

Why had I even gotten my hopes up only to be disappointed once again? "Then what information do you have—because I can't keep the Union from launching a full-on attack after Father's bereavement ritual. Jade, the cabinet, will want blood. Who has done this?"

Drake kept glancing over at Pea. Like they shared a secret beyond me.

"Answer," I almost barked. "Who did this so that they can be punished?"

"My source said that someone from within the Citadel gave the order. Supplied them with the tools, the flames, and the exact place where the General would be."

"That's not true." I grabbed her shoulders before I could think. "You are trying to cover for someone. One of the rebels transgressed. Didn't they?"

Drake shoved me into the wall and then put a blade to my throat. "I. Saved. You," she hissed. "Pulled your frail little ass out of that rubble when your own people blasted us from the sky. Remember? Let me jog your memory, Princess. If I wanted you dead, I would've carved you up a long time ago."

I knocked the knife from her hand and headbutted her in the mouth until she fell. I grabbed the blade from the ground and jumped on top of her. I placed the blade where she'd placed it on me. I had no intent of using it, or that was what I told myself. They all thought I was a weakling who couldn't hold her own. I wasn't the girl I was last year. I'd evolved. Perhaps in the worst ways, because I wanted Drake to pay even if she hadn't been the cause of what'd happened.

"You gonna use that?" Drake guffawed, sucking the blood from her busted lip. She brought her face closer to mine. "It would be my pleasure to be taken out of this miserable life that you've created for me."

The blade dropped from my grip with a *clank*.

I hugged my knees into my chest. How quickly I transitioned from being a renegade to that same girl that I'd been prior. The truth was that I didn't know how to save anyone. I couldn't even save myself. We were just going to continue to kill each other out of alarm and retribution. I wished Saige was there. She was the strong one. I was the one pretending to be someone I wasn't. It didn't matter how much watchmen training I'd had; I was still that same Avi.

Drake rested beside me. "I saw what Jade did on the broadcast, what she said. She's trying to pin this crime on you. She's trying to get the public on her side so that an election will occur and you're voted out. You can't let that happen. Do you hear me? If she becomes General, the rebels won't uphold the treaty anymore."

The treaty was that if I was able to assist them in smuggling antiviral serums, then they would hold off on the terrorist attacks. That came down from Mama Seeya herself.

"Mama Seeya told you that?" Pea asked.

"Yes," Drake confirmed.

Pea slumped back in the chair. "We're screwed."

"There's only two options," Drake said. "We need to prove his own offed him or, you know, kill Jade."

"No one is *killing* anyone else," I protested.

Drake flexed her jaw. "She has the most to gain from his death."

I looked at Pea for reassurance, but she only looked away. We both knew that Jade had tried to rid herself of me once before, so it wasn't the most far-fetched notion. But Father? It seemed implausible. He was everything to her. She'd tried her hardest to please him since as far back as I could recall. Made sure he witnessed her excelling and doing better than me at every point.

"Mama Seeya wants to assassinate my sister but hasn't had the decency to tell me in person?" I asked. "Where is she?"

"You know I can't tell you that."

"I want to see her," I insisted.

"It's not safe for her to just rush to the summons of an Elite, especially one that has a region-wide bounty on her head. So please forgive her caution." There was venom in her words.

"We are on the brink of a complete genocide. Is that not serious enough?"

"A genocide of who?" She entered my space again with overt aggression.

Pea placed her body in between us, sensing the abundant tension. "Madam, we should get going before someone finds out we're here."

The Dissent

We took our usual route back through the subdivision. Dodging patrolling watchmen and Disposables loitering on the streets. We'd found our hidden crevice and made sure no one watched. When it was clear, Pea entered the hole. We walked along the path, taking rights and lefts as needed to return to the Citadel. We both trekked in silence. The heaviness of what had just occurred weighing on us both.

I slowed the pace, sensing something abnormal, but Pea kept moving before I could alert her. I saw her being snatched by a cluster of watchmen. Someone grabbed me too. The watchman pinned my limbs in his armpit and tightly cupped my nose and mouth with a gloved hand.

Chapter Five
AVI

The watchman and I were well hidden in a recess. From the gap in the tunnel's barricade, I witnessed watchmen surround her. Next to little Pea, the gorilla-size watchmen circled. One backhanded her as the others held her slender arms from resisting. Another punched her in the abdomen. Her head sagged. They allowed her to tumble to the ground like a puppet cut from strings. On her hands and knees, she wheezed. One stomped on her back. With each blow, my body jerked as if I were the one being beaten. Tears trailed my face but then were absorbed by the fabric of the captor's glove. I stopped struggling to get out of their grip because I realized why they held me back when Jade plodded into full view.

Pea lay in a heap on the gravel, coughing up fleshy blobs. My sister used her foot to shove her onto her back.

"Dear little honk, what have you gotten yourself into?" she said in a singsong voice. "I suspected your transgressions early on. I just wasn't able to prove it. Also, it was hard to get to you, you know, being my sister's mangy pet and all. Always following her around. Tending to her every need. Knowing that the only significance in your meaningless life has been being her chattel."

She knelt beside Pea and brushed hairs stuck to her face. Pea wept between labored breaths.

"If I were you, I'd be fearful too." Jade surveyed the tunnel, then motioned to a watchman. "There. Fetch me that."

A timeworn hatchet.

Pea's body loosened as she tried to scoot backward, but Jade was too quick. "Aht, aht," she said, laying the head of the weapon on Pea's chest. "Who were you down here with? I know you weren't alone. Confess and I will spare you."

Pea's lip trembled as the weight of the blade dug farther into her chest cavity.

"Is my sister down here?" Jade searched that space comically. "Oh, Avi. Come out of hiding. Spare your old slave girl."

I began squirming again, but the person behind me had me in a death hold.

Jade allowed several beats for me to reveal myself, but they didn't allow me. Or perhaps deep down inside, I knew that I couldn't allow myself.

"A coward as always," Jade spat. "To be expected."

Pea turned her head to the side. I wasn't sure if she could see me. Jade placed the tip of her boot on Pea's wrist, steadied her left arm, lifted the hatchet over her head, and allowed it to linger. "Last chance, honk," Jade offered.

But Pea remained still, ready to meet whatever fate awaited her.

"Guess not." The cleaver came down at Pea's elbow. But it didn't go all the way through. Jade continued hacking away until the arm was in two pieces.

My cheeks puffed, and I held my breath until my face felt like it would explode. I didn't recall what happened next.

Jade's eyes were pools filled with swirling, glossy tar. She rose above me. Taller and taller. Her body stretching like rubber. Her tongue split into two. It flicked.

I couldn't move. I screamed her name to remind her of her humanness, but my mouth didn't stir, or perhaps she just didn't hear me or didn't care.

A hatchet appeared overhead. Panic set in.

She allowed it to drop on my neck. I felt it slice. The jolt brought me back to consciousness, screaming and clutching my throat.

"Avi?"

I fell from a high place and scrambled backward, knocking into unsecured objects.

Hands grabbed at me, but I swatted them away.

"Calm down. It's me." Instructor Skylar lifted me from the ground. "You're freezing."

"Pea." I felt hotter than ever. "Where is she?"

He opened his mouth to speak, then closed it. That was all the confirmation I needed.

"It's my fault." I shivered, finally experiencing the chill that he felt.

"I must return to the Citadel," I announced.

"And do what exactly?"

"Well, I—I will—"

"Confront Jade. Hmm?" He clasped his hands like Father used to. "And tell her that you were strolling through a secret underground tunnel? One that may or may not have been used to smuggle in the very matter that killed your father?"

"Watch it," I spat. "We aren't in watchmen training any longer. I am still your superior."

His mouth slowly turned into a toothy grin. "Ah, there she is."

I'd graduated from watchmen training only recently. Father had been proud. He'd thought it was the most patriotic thing I could do, especially since I'd created such a stir with the Union by empowering the rebels. He'd thought that we would battle the opposing team, side by side. I remembered the look on his face when my name flashed across the holoscreen in the Great Room. It was the proudest he'd ever been of me.

In his eyes, I saw him envisioning his daughter planning battles and leading the charge as I cut down any rebel in our way, but that was never going to happen. I'd still allowed him to believe it, though. I'd had to play the game, his game. He'd always taught me strategy. This delusion of his allowed for me to not remain under heavy surveillance as I had been before. I'd had to gain his trust back after being charged with causing the insurrection with Saige and Liyo.

At first, I decided to plow through the rigorous training because I was tired of being called weak, being fragile. I wanted to gain control of myself. My life. I wanted to experience what Saige had when she was in the Cube, a place all graduated watchmen had to go through for testing.

There were times that I wanted to give up in the levels. The Union's game makers watched on as men perished. I watched them drown, fall into pits of lava, get shredded by cyborg beetles. The Union had created something horrific in that contraption, but I had to survive it to make a point. I had to survive in order to reset the region, because no one was going to do it but me.

Encrusted in the blood—my own and others'—I made it out alive and victorious.

I was reborn that day.

But what had any of that mattered, when I still wasn't strong enough to save Pea from being chopped apart? Clearly, not enough.

"What were you and Pea doing down there?" the instructor inquired.

I wasn't sure what the safest answer to provide was because I didn't know how far he'd followed us on the journey to meet Drake. I trusted him more than anyone else, but I wasn't sure how far that trust could go. He was still a part of the Union's cabinet.

"Why do you suppose?" I countered.

Although the sides of his hair were tapered, the middle carried fresh ear-length locs. The whites of his eyes and teeth were the same brilliant color. I always compared his smile to that of a light orb. It was truly infectious and overtook entire ballrooms. If I hadn't seen him as an elder brother, I would've fallen over him like the other girls and boys had.

He cupped my cheek in his balmy palm. "I want you to know that I will always protect your best interest. You can come to me with anything in this galaxy and even beyond that, and I will find a way to support you." His voice cracked. "I—I made an oath to the General, your father, that I would protect you with my entire being, and that is an oath that I will never, ever break. Do you hear me?"

Through all of it, I had forgotten that he was not just a soldier, Father's right-hand man, but family. We were all hurting. Grieving. His death still fresh.

"Gratitude." I sighed. But I still couldn't expose the truth about my connection to the rebels. He wasn't ready for it, and I couldn't risk it.

"Whatever it was that you were doing down there, you need to be careful." His voice turned grave. "You can't give the Elites, Jade, any reason to discredit you. Right now is a critical time."

I nodded. I knew that in between his words was something much more, and that he was keeping secrets of his own.

❖ ❖ ❖

The slumber pod hissed open. I had programmed it to the maximum amount of rest hours allowed. It still wasn't enough to sleep away all that had occurred at the matrimonial ceremony.

And Father wasn't coming back.

I heard the entrance to my quarters open. I rushed to the doorway but was halted by disappointment midway. It was not Pea. Instead, the same droid that had offered me condolences entered.

"Morning saluta—" it began.

"Get out," I ordered. "And do not come back."

Its head bowed. "As you wish, Elite Avi."

I observed myself in a reflective holoscreen. My eyes were sunken, my usual braid disheveled, and my lips discolored and cracked.

"Incoming call from Elite Phoenix Chi," a computerized voice announced.

I kneaded the tension from the back of my neck. "Answer."

Phoenix's upper body filled the screen. His hyena-like face carried concern.

"I've been trying to get in touch with you all evening," he said. "I even contacted Jade."

"Why would you do that?" I slammed my fist against the counter. The thought of her, her name even, caused a reaction that I'd never felt before. That was how she must've known that I was not at the Citadel.

"I—I was just checking to see if you were okay."

"Okay?" I imitated. "Does it look like I am remotely *okay?*"

He stuttered, "This is hard on you—on me too. He was like a father to me."

I crossed my arms over my chest and mumbled, "More like a political status increase."

He frowned. I watched him try to find an appropriate comeback. He sat straighter and puffed his chest. "I'm going to let that go. You are hurting. But you will learn to respect me. I am an Elite, a man, and your partner in matrimony."

I'd never wanted to wed Phoenix. He repulsed me in too many ways to count. He was sly and arrogant and unkind. I'd been forced to marry because of Elite lineage customs. I hadn't even kissed the boy prior to the ceremony. Was he that stuck up his own sphincter?

"Even with Father's death, all you can think about is fulfilling an archaic rule that forced me to be a part of an arranged marriage?"

He showed disgust at my argument. "The Union needs this. They need to see that Elites are united. It's what *he* would've wanted."

"Ha!" I exclaimed. "Well, it's never what *I* wanted. Want now, or ever."

"It is bound, Avi." A thin line of sweat slicked his upper lip as he steadily lost control of his temper.

I turned my back to him. "Nothing in this life is bound, Phoenix. You and I both know this to be true. Moments are precious. They aren't unlimited, as many of us privileged choose to believe. I refuse to spend another waking moment with you. Let alone a lifetime. I will never voluntarily marry you as long as my mind is sound and the sun sets to the west. You will have to locate another means into the position you want. You have Jade's number. Last time I checked, she is of marrying age. End call."

Not long after, Lanah and Bres, Pea's workers, arrived. They appeared shaken.

"I'm so glad to see you." I embraced them both. "Have you heard from Pea?"

Lanah began sniffling. "I—"

Bres hurried to her side, shielded Lanah's mouth, then murmured, "Remember what she said. You can't speak. Not even a peep."

"Who said that to you?" I asked.

Bres looked both ways as if she were about to cross a busy avenue, but only one eye moved with ease. The other was cocked from a beating with a former Elite family. She peeked at the corners of the ceiling like the place was wired with surveillance. She took my hand and guided me to the bathing quarters.

When the door was sealed, she said in a low voice, "It's Jade. She's gone mad."

"I know." I recalled the violence in the tunnels.

"Oh, madam." She bit into her knuckle. "She threatened that if any of the workers speak, make a sound, she will take a hand or foot. I

54

can't afford AI limbs like the Upper Residents. I won't be able to work, provide for my family that way, madam. I'll become a Disposable."

I wanted to provide comfort, tell her that she mustn't worry about Jade and her antics, but I had witnessed the butchery, and Jade meant every threat she uttered.

I rested my hand on Lanah's lower back. "It will all be over after the bereavement ritual. After I take my official position as General. She will have no choice but to abide by my rule. Until then, keep your head down. Spread the word."

"You are the one who helped us get the serum. You saved so many of us." She took my hand and squeezed. "I trust you, madam."

❖　❖　❖

Trust. The word lingered. Left a gritty taste on my palate way past being bathed by Bres, past Lanah carefully sectioning thick parts of hair and braiding the long tresses until the ends met and curled like springs, past being fitted in a black armored bodysuit with the Union's red sigil. The taste became even more pungent as cabinet members and guests filled in the spread-out lawn—any one of them having motive to take Father out—each lowering themselves to hug and offer condolences to Mother and me.

I caught a glimpse of an old friend and Academy mate, Reba, who I'd last seen at a private Marco Grant show. Amid Saige and me trying to escape watchmen and Head Gardner, we'd ended up ruining the party and tearing apart the club that she'd personally invited me to. Afterward, her parents forbade her to have any contact with me. I understood and didn't blame her. No Elite wanted to be attached to anyone who would make them look bad. She caught my stare and then darted away from my eyesight.

The Administrator from the Academy that I'd attended as an adolescent made eye contact with me over the dozens of heads, and I quickly turned away, hoping that she wouldn't take the connection as an invite. From my peripheral vision, all I witnessed was her very monumental hair, which resembled one of the grand buildings in the Square, cut through mourners like a shark's dorsal fin through the sea. She was the tallest and widest Upper Resident I'd ever seen and flounced about as if she owned everything and everyone in her vicinity.

She was a rude woman and didn't want to wait her turn to speak as she bulldozed through a family of guests to garner the attention of Mother and me. Other than her ridiculous hair, the next thing I noticed was the size of her exposed breasts. They were like two infants squished together and perched very high.

"It's so good to see you, Vivienne." Her attention and greetings went to Mother first. "I'm so sorry that it's under these circumstances. He was a great, great man, indeed. And he will be sorely missed."

The Administrator puckered her lips at me in disapproval, twisting a ruby-encrusted ring on her index finger. "Avi."

"Administrator," I said with a minute head dip.

She huffed under her breath and moved aside, revealing Blair and Grandmother Gardner. Blair and I studied in the same year at the Academy. Her skin was a chestnut color, and she wore tight curls that cascaded along her back. I was her archnemesis and for good reason. She was progovernment, derived from one of the wealthiest heirs in the region. Their affluence came from the privatization of the prison system.

Grandmother Gardner sat in a high-tech AirChair suspended six inches from the grass. She wore a short salt-and-pepper Afro. Her eyebrows were thin and dark and appeared as if they'd been tattooed on ages ago. Large fat deposits weighed down the skin under her eyes.

I raised myself as a sign of respect for an elder. Blair I couldn't have cared less about. She'd made my life a living nightmare during our Academy years, and I still hadn't forgotten how she'd shoved my head into a commode with her little friends.

I took Grandmother Gardner's veiny hand and kissed the back of it. "My child," she offered. "I still cannot believe this day has come." "I know." The words barely spilled out.

Her eyes were a grayish, faintly blue color from cataracts. "You will do the Union justice just as your father had."

I sniffled and laughed once. "I surely plan on achieving that."

She pulled her hand back. "And promise me no more of that silly egalitarianism prattle you were spewing. I almost thought for a moment that you were never going to fully fill your father's boots."

My pleasant smile faded as her words seared through me like hot iron. Blair twirled the ends of her hair, taking the utmost pleasure in my reaction.

One of their family members unknowingly interrupted the stiffness by ushering her and Blair to another waiting conversation.

"Well, if you need anything from my family, we are always here," she said over her shoulder.

Mother returned to her seat and I to mine. Jade's seat remained empty, and I wondered who she was terrorizing during her absence.

Mother viewed the people mingling as she clutched a damp embroidered handkerchief. Instead of sitting in anger at the ignorance of Grandmother Gardner, I washed it all away and focused on Mother. She was a timeless beauty. I used to pine for her smooth coffee-colored skin. She was a curvy statue of a woman who'd made a career modeling as an adolescent and would grace covers of fashion dailies. But Father's death was physically taking its toll on her.

Like Father, Mother lived in her own multiverse. She saw a version of me that had never existed. Out of politeness, I participated in her activities. Each proving how little she actually knew me. Even though she didn't have a malicious bone in her body, she wanted me to stay in line. Participate in an arranged marriage, as she had. She'd told me that I would become accustomed to Phoenix. That I needed to give it a chance. She told me to stop being stubborn. It was unbecoming of a lady. A wife. And it would be to my detriment one day. She loved Father fiercely despite the arrangement. A love that she'd deeply wanted for me. One that I wanted for myself one day. One that I had found with Liyo, but I knew that she'd never accept it as valid.

Commander Chi and Phoenix approached. As our parents engaged in conversation, Phoenix hovered over me, sizing me up, as he always had. I always felt like a cut of meat when I was around him. The old Avi would've broken the gaze a long time ago, afraid of silent tension, any tension really. Instead, I squared my shoulders and stuck out a hand. He hesitated, then shook. Keeping up false appearances of cordialness was an important Elite trait.

More people clothed in different shades of black amassed. I lost count of how many shoulder grips and condolences I received. When I should've been grieving, I was preoccupied by looking for evidence during interactions with cabinet members in order to pinpoint who could've been involved in the assassination. If Drake was telling the truth, then the killer was in that very place.

They weren't going to get away with it.

Instructor Skylar excused himself from Admiral Jemison and Admiral Butler. He then motioned for me to join him off to the side.

"How are you feeling?" he asked.

"Better." I wasn't in the mood for deep conversation. I'd save my emotions for another day. I scanned the area, trying to pick up on anything out of the ordinary.

He slid in my frontal view. "What are you looking for?"

Droids ushered guests to their places, and I noticed that no workers were around. What had Jade done to them?

"Where are they?" I said. "The workers?"

"They probably aren't allowed at this point on the account of the whole situation."

"Doesn't that seem odd to you?" I said. "Father had been cracking down on worker population before; why kill him now and not before?"

"Wait a second." He pointed. "I know that look. Whatever you're thinking, whatever you are planning, don't."

I shot him a look. The one that stated that I couldn't make any promises.

"Avi, we talked about this. Don't give them a reason. Not one reason."

Over his shoulder, I caught of glimpse of Jade strolling in, and no sign of Head Gardner, which I believed odd. One would think because she'd always been by Father's side that she'd be at the front pew to give her respects.

"Head Gardner," I asked, "where is she?"

Instructor Skylar and I watched Jade slither through the rows.

"Good question," he replied.

Holocams immediately zoomed from each direction to capture Jade's entrance.

"I wonder who she's wearing," I overheard a woman draped in stiff diaspora print ask another about Jade's ensemble.

Lights flashed; people called her name as if she were Marco Grant herself. I knew Jade; she was adoring the attention. It had always been about me, the firstborn, leaving her overshadowed often. When we were younger, I'd tried my best to share the light, but everyone wanted to harp on the fact that I was the next General. I watched Jade excel at everything, rising to the top of her class. Jade was fierce, never took no for an answer, but the person she'd become—I didn't recognize.

Father was the last dangling piece keeping her human. Now that he was gone, I feared for not only my safety but that of others. What would she do when I was officially placed into power?

"Sister." Several lenses pointed at me as Jade pulled my shoulders toward hers. I was taken aback by the gesture.

"Have you seen Pea?" she mentioned in my ear. "I heard she was in the worker's infirmary."

I closed my eyes so tight, remembering what she'd done. "I swear—"

"You won't do a thing, dear sister." She shoved me away so lightly that only I'd notice.

She positioned herself beside Mother.

The bereavement ritual commenced.

Don't give them a reason. Instructor Skylar's voice repeated over and over again in the base of my mind. Jade was trying to get a reaction, cause me to act out of character, and sadly, it was working. It took everything in me not to yank her from that chair. All I saw was red when I glanced at her.

I wanted to end it. If she was dead, then it'd all just stop, in theory. Drake's offer still stood. I wouldn't even have to get my hands muddy. All I had to do was give the word . . .

Mother took my hand, sensing the shift. She smiled a weary one. I closed my eyes. Warm tears flowed along them. What was I thinking? Murdering Jade. That's exactly who I didn't want to be. Killing was not the answer. I had to control my emotions, myself. Father would've said something along those lines. I had to look at the bigger image. It wasn't about Jade and me. She was only an obstacle to a means. I didn't have to become merciless like her to beat her; I just had to be cleverer than her.

❖ ❖ ❖

People spoke. Performers performed. Nostrils and faces ran with excretions. Then his body was burned. Simple. The flames danced along his shroud, engulfing him completely as his society surrounded him. Cries could be heard from the distance. Thousands were in attendance to witness the great General Jore's final achievement.

The fire was so high and so fierce that it almost created a blockade. I watched as Jade lurked closer. She seemed to be in a trance. Then I saw the slightest grin. It was ever so minor. She'd always had that same look when she'd gotten away with something.

My heart dropped, and it took everything to keep from folding. She had done it. She murdered Father.

Jade spun around as the blaze roared behind her. She created a steeple with her gloved fingers. "Citizens of the Union, let us not take the death of the General as the end, but as the beginning. He will never be truly gone. *He* is in all of us. That unwavering spirit, that fight, is in us all."

A few people sopped up their tears and nodded in agreement.

"My people, hear me when I say that we have come so very far." She scanned the crowd. "From kings and queens of the diaspora to chattel for the Europes to the systematic slavery of capitalism to the ruins of the Revolt and now, the resurrection."

More than half the gathering made an uproar now, hanging on to her every word as if it were the Union's original doctrine itself.

"I want to lead this nation into a new era of Black brilliance." She paused. "But in order to do that, we must disturb, disrupt the standard that we've fallen prey to."

Fists started to pump midair. Bellows thundered in anticipation of her next statement.

"I—we—cannot allow the Union to backtrack into devastation." She paused for effect. "So, I will be running against Avi Jore for the position of General over the Union of Civilization."

The crowd went ecstatic.

"This is preposterous, Jade." Commander Chi stepped forward. "This is a private matter to be discussed with the cabinet. The coals are still smoldering!"

"This *is* my right." Jade's voice rose so that all could hear. "And, when I win, all of the old will be cleared out, and in with a new, competent cabinet. Your old ways have stifled the Union for far too long."

The crowd began to chant her name as they pumped their fists.

People rushed forward to get closer to Jade. I was jostled around as if I didn't exist. Instructor Skylar pulled me away and guided me against the hyped crowd. "We've got to get you out of here."

Jade had planted her seed with the people, and her master plan had just sprouted its first leaf. She'd just sealed my fate.

Chapter Six
SAIGE

"The Union is here?" Miah hollered. "I've got to alert the colony."

As Miah tried to get up, Liyo pushed him back, harder than he had to.

Miah stared, waiting for me to interject. When I didn't, he said my name, but there was a pain, a betrayal behind it. "Saige?"

Liyo looked repulsed.

We had brought the Union to the north. It was our fault. The Union would go to any lengths to retrieve their property.

Liyo pulled me to the side and spoke so only I could hear him. "What's going on?"

I didn't like open-ended questions.

"Are you even listening?" His agitation grew. "We need to get out of here, and he's going to take us. We've got to get back to the south. To Mama Seeya. Avi. It's not safe here anymore."

"What about his people?" I massaged the stress forming at my temple. "We've led them straight here."

"We can't save the world right now." Liyo sighed. "We aren't any help if we are captured or, worse, dead."

I checked on Miah with only my eyes; he seemed to be in deep thought.

"What if we went farther north," I said. "I know it sounds crazy, but it's worth a try."

"That's insane. We have no idea what's out there. And besides, this isn't our home, Saige. We don't belong here."

I didn't belong anywhere.

I knelt in front of Miah. "We need your help."

He only stared, as if he hadn't understood any of the words.

"Can you help us?"

He wouldn't take his eyes off Liyo.

"Miah, we need to help each other," I pleaded. "The Union won't stop until they find us."

He turned his face away.

That was enough for Liyo to grab him by the collar and pin him against the wall again. Electricity cracked around Liyo's body as bombs were let off outside the hut.

"You will take us to the exit, or you die. You choose."

Miah was still defiant until Liyo began to use his abilities to crush his throat.

I watched, unable to move, react. I didn't want to die, but I also didn't want Miah to get hurt.

Before I stepped in to stop Liyo, Miah gasped, "I'll do it."

Liyo let go.

The door flew open, exposing a winter dystopia. Lasers crisscrossed over one another from overhead, lining the ground like a rash. People in gray furs and fuzzy boots scattered, almost knocking into me. Weaving through stalls of hanging dried meats.

Hovercrafts emerged from the mists. Black figures began to rappel down like spiders in tactical groups. I knew how they rolled.

Another explosion. Blue flames gushed.

A bell dinged, originating from somewhere, but I was too absorbed in it all. Liyo yanked me out of the way of several riders on sleds being pulled with great speed by massive beasts. That kind of animal I'd never seen before, but they ripped apart watchmen like they were dolls. The things were thick and meaty and almost moved like a crossbreed on steroids.

"Where do we go?" Liyo jerked Miah's restraints.

"There." The wind blew through his dark hair like silk on a clothesline as he led us to a barn.

Most of the stalls were emptied.

"What is it?" I asked when we came up on one that was sleeping. Its hulking arms curled up underneath it.

"A PolarWolf." Miah whistled. It came to life, stretching, yawning, and finally shaking out its fur.

"This is your plan?" Liyo was getting impatient.

"Do you have a better one?" Miah hissed.

"Hey!" I yelled at both of them, and then I turned to Liyo. "We don't have a lot of options right now."

Miah shot him a look of triumph.

Liyo rolled his eyes. "It better work."

Miah was able to wrangle one other PolarWolf that was seemingly smaller and much more energetic. He told Liyo to get on that one.

"I don't trust you."

"You are going to have to," Miah replied.

"Liyo, it's okay," I said. "I'll keep him in line. Just stay close."

Liyo begrudgingly mounted the smaller one. I got on the back of the one with Miah and hung on.

We charged through the exit and past watchmen burning down silver-paneled structures with small windows and shooting lasers into anything that moved. We had done that. We'd brought the mess to his people. I clutched onto Miah tighter and closed my eyes as the cold wind rushed past us.

An explosion happened, and plates of ice swelled in front of us, causing the PolarWolf to leap. Miah and I flew as the beast skidded sideways.

I couldn't see anything through the snow cloud.

A watchman dropped in from above and right in my path. I tackled him, both of us landing in a snowbank. Another arrived, and I kicked them in the stomach. Then a third form came from the rear and placed their forearm around my neck, lifting me from the ground.

I tossed my head back, striking them in the helmet. Their grip released, and I dropped into a horse stance. Their gait became off balance. I took an arm and twisted it behind their back, then kicked them in the spine. The watchman fell headfirst into slush.

Another descended. Then another. Sandwiching me in the middle. They just kept multiplying.

The adrenaline was so high that I was using strike combos that I didn't remember learning. Legs and arms and fists and elbows were thrown, becoming an entangled blur as I fought for my life.

I held my own until two more entered the match. I took a blow to the chin, which knocked me loopy. That jarred me to the point where the punch that I threw didn't hit the target. I tried to recoup with a cross, but before it even fully extended, one of them drove their knuckles underneath my jaw. The hit nearly lifted me to the sky as I plunged into the sleet. I tasted warm metal, hoping my tongue wasn't sliced in half.

"The target has been acquired," a watchman said through his wrist-com as he dragged me across the battlefield by an ankle.

"Let. Her. Go!" Liyo raised my captor into the air. With the flick of Liyo's finger, the watchman was chucked into the side of the hut.

I watched from the ground as watchmen got into a U-shaped formation. The ones from the sides charged, and Liyo moved his arms to a rhythm, a music that I couldn't hear, almost like a dance, as he picked each one off, sometimes two at a time. Figures were flipped and tossed about with an invisible force. Liyo was stronger. He'd clearly been tapping into his abilities.

Watchmen from a distance fired lasers at Liyo as he held off the ones closest. I thought he was going to be chock full of holes. Instead, he cocked his head, and two of his fingers went erect. Laser slugs froze, floating. He reversed them and refired back toward the hive. As he disarmed the last of the watchmen, another landed behind Liyo. He must've sensed it, because he spun around and lifted them. The watchman's body vibrated at first, then shook violently. The next thing I knew, the helmet had collapsed on their skull.

He was out for vengeance.

Liyo grabbed my arm. "Where's he?"

I tried to locate Miah through the bodies, but I couldn't find him. Liyo didn't even wait for confirmation and began running.

I followed him into a large see-through globe, where people of the colony tried to seek shelter, but Liyo was too fast, and we got separated.

One last watchman rappelled down the line. I got closer to the barrier to get a better look. They hoisted themselves dramatically and then unlatched from the connection. The shiny helmet mirrored the ugliness around us. They didn't seem to be in a hurry to chase anyone or dive deeper into the town like the others.

This one had locked their attention on me. One of the fugitives of the Southern Region. Maybe they wanted the reward of bringing me in.

They finally removed their helmet. Head Gardner shook out four long braids, never breaking eye contact.

Déjà vu. I was transported back to when she executed Ma right in front of me. I remembered the look of contempt, pleasure on her stupid face as Ma convulsed in that cold metal chair after Head Gardner instructed physicians to inject her with the execution serum. I watched through the holoscreen as she squirmed in those restraints, as blood trickled from her eyes and mouth and colored her teeth crimson.

Head Gardner lifted her hand, palm side up, and slowly motioned for me to meet her. The only thing separating her and me was the glass-like wall.

I accepted the invitation.

I sprinted toward her, ready to burst through like Liyo had with his abilities. I didn't really care about the logistics. I just wanted to get to her.

Liyo seized me midstride by the waist, while also holding onto Miah, dragging us both. "We need to leave."

A half grin grew on Head Gardner's lips as she raised a muscle-bodied weapon that I'd never seen before. She pulled the trigger, and blue flames swelled from the nozzle. She was burning a hole in the barrier.

The material melted like wax.

The wall dissolved, and watchmen began to pile in like cockroaches in a kitchenette when the lights went out. They blasted into the crowd, in our direction, hitting fleeing people in their backs. People burned; I could smell bubbling skin and charred furs.

Liyo, Miah, and I finally got out, floating along with the frenzied crowd as the Union continued the massacre.

❖ ❖ ❖

Miah told Liyo to head southwest, follow the curved path through the tundra until he saw a misshapen sapling. There he'd find the exit. He wouldn't divulge anything else after that.

Liyo threatened him once more and then tugged on the rope restraints that bound his hands. Miah's restraints brought up some emotions that had been holed inside me. I'd been collared before by watchmen like an animal. And there we were buying into the same method.

I caught up to Liyo. "Is this necessary?"

"He just tried to get away." Liyo didn't bother looking my way. "You tell me."

I slowed my pace and rejoined Miah. I didn't have the guts to make small talk. I was his captor now.

I trekked quietly as we got farther and farther away from the madness. We'd left a city in the clouds behind. It wasn't as high tech as the Southern Region, but it was something out of an imaginary land. Now, in the tundra were long stretches of grayish ice sheets and blankets of snow covering mountain pockets ten times the size of the Transmega. Angled rock formations that resembled upturned fingers stemming from the hardened ground shot up into the sky as if they would take a handful of cloud in their palm. So high that each peak was missing in the haze.

It was getting colder. The sun was setting lower. There was no sign of the sapling. And it wouldn't be long before Head Gardner tracked us.

Liyo figured it out and stopped. He hadn't turned around yet, but I could hear the crackling of electricity. Before I could get to him, calm him, he shot Miah into the air, throwing him several feet back. He landed hard.

"Liar." Liyo stomped forward.

Before Liyo could get to Miah, I threw my body over his and held my hands out.

"Get out of the way." Liyo looked crazy.

"What are you going to do?"

"I'm going to make him talk." His lips barely moved.

"Oh yeah, and how's that worked so far?"

"Move, Saige."

"No."

"Move, or I'll make you move."

We had a stare-off. After a few beats, I hadn't felt anything. I wasn't sure if he'd run out of steam or he'd just given up.

The electricity in his eyes subsided. "You'd rather die out here, then?"

"No, I wouldn't. I just think we can treat him like a human," I explained.

"We don't know what these savages are capable of."

"If he wanted to kill me, he'd have done it."

"We don't have time for this."

"We?"

He rolled his eyes. "Saige, this isn't the time for—"

"For your show of stupid masculinity?"

"You know this is the most you've talked to me since we've been here." He swiped the snot dripping along his cupid's bow, chuckling to himself at my audacity. "What? Would you rather stay with them than me? People you don't even know. Savages? I really never thought you'd be that stupid."

I stepped back, farther away from him.

"Why don't you ever just trust me?" His voice almost became whiny.

In a monotone, I replied, "I trust myself."

"And here I thought that being out here would make you less of a selfish prick."

That hurt. Bad.

We stood silently hurling curses at one another until I noticed a form appear behind Liyo holding a sleek bow with a trio holster that held vertebrae-spined arrows.

Before I could react, she let the arrows soar. Liyo was fast, pausing them in midair with one hand and with the other tripping the assailant on her back and dragging her closer. The arrows hovered over her head, prepared to rain down.

She pulled back her hood. The girl appeared younger than us, short in stature. She was wide, with a round face and stout nose. Two long fishtail braids cascaded along her back. An upside-down single outline of a triangle tattooed on her forehead.

"Elu?" Miah called out.

"If you harm us in any way, I'll never tell you where the exit is," Elu said.

Liyo's eyes searched for something as he weighed his options. We were at their mercy. He dropped the weapons all around her. They were left sticking upward in the snow like a makeshift fence.

"Let's go," he said.

Elu crawled over to Miah, and they both embraced, touching foreheads. She cut the restraints from his wrists and checked over his body for wounds. I wondered if that was his girl.

Once she'd gotten confirmation that Miah was fine, she spun around and began crunching through the snow. "This way."

Chapter Seven
LIYO

The savages were leading us to who knew where. One of them had already wasted our time and led us to a dead end. They couldn't be trusted. They had the information that I needed, but I ultimately had the upper hand. I didn't care what Saige thought about it, but she was acting strange. I never thought I'd hear myself say it, but where was the cutthroat Saige that pulled the trigger and asked questions later, if even that?

Had she gone soft? Lost sight of why we were even there in the first place? She'd gotten too comfortable in the north. She'd had a home, a family. It probably wasn't the one she wanted, but it was the one she had. We all had to deal with the hand we were given. Saige would have to understand that one way or another. She'd have to understand that we were a team. And that I knew her far better than anyone else, whether she cared to admit it or not.

The savages walked ahead of us almost in unison and in very close proximity, like some invisible force held them together. Saige and I kept a distance from one another as if we repelled each other like matching magnets.

"Hey!" I yelled at them. "How much farther?"

"It's just ahead," Elu replied.

I shortened the distance between Saige and me. "Stay ready."

She cut her eyes at me like a teen raging with hormones.

"Saige, I'm serious," I said. "We can't trust these savages."

Elu was faster that time. A blade flew with the speed of a laser past my head, and the tip wedged itself into something behind me. When I touched my ear, I found a thin slice had been made in the skin; a streak of blood slowly surfaced and colored my fingertip.

"We are *not* savages." Elu huffed like a bull ready to charge. Her chest visibly rose through the layers of furs. "That is a slur made up by southerners to depict us as fiends."

The triangle on her forehead glowed. Her dark eyes became much wilder.

"We are a native colony of the Northern Region," she said. "And while you are here, on my land, you will not bring your vulgar ways, your slurs. You may have powers, but so do we. If death was what we wished upon you."

As she spoke, I grappled with the idea of tossing her around like a wet rag.

Elu calmed down, then scoffed, motioning to the slaughter we'd just left behind. "Seems like we aren't the ones you need to worry about."

As we trekked through the winding frosty paths, we came upon another city. I took in all the one- and two-story silver buildings. Everything was so flat and simple in comparison to our region. There were formations that looked like thick mists or smoke frozen in place. The daylight rays recoiled off the snow, almost blinding me. It was like looking into the sun directly.

The farther we went, the more the atmosphere changed in a way that I couldn't understand. The energy shifted. The coarse hairs on my forearms began to rise. Along the path were massive trees with attached vines for the trunk the size of muscly giants' thighs, and the branches twisted every which way, creating a sphere as the crown. They seemed to almost glow with an unreal cobalt hue. The temple was at the end and almost misplaced in the icy metropolis.

"What is this?" Saige asked as she tried to catch a blue fleck that floated around us like pollen.

"The heart of the colony." Elu stopped in front of the temple.

It looked like a religious place. I'd never seen one in real life before, since the Union only believed in science and struck down anything related to God. Although workers always found a way to keep and practice their silly beliefs on the low. Like the Union, I'd stopped believing in the creator when they allowed us to be enslaved. What kind of God was that?

"Let's go inside," Elu said. "We need supplies."

Together, we stepped over the threshold of the stony pyramid structure.

The inside was very angular. It looked like a difficult geometric equation. The scent of old incense still held strong. On the wall, an older woman adorned in a colorful beaded poncho with thin, fully white hair that was braided in a heap atop her head carried a thin stick with a flame on the end. The painting was so real that I could count the veins in her hands.

Both of them bowed their heads and whispered something under their breaths. I tried to see if their markings would glow again, but they were facing the center of another smaller pyramid that floated above a dais. Inside was blue-flame matter. It was like water sloshing around, but it also looked like fire too.

Something inside me wanted to be closer to it.

"You can feel it inside your body, inside your marrow," Elu said, answering my thoughts.

I remained mesmerized by the suspended twirling blaze.

I heard Saige call out, but her voice seemed farther away than it actually was.

I could've sworn that the painting of the old woman moved. Somehow. And, then it was as if someone, something held my mouth shut and pinched my nose closed. Something foreign had entered me.

My eyes fluttered. My head lurched, and my back arched like I'd been possessed. I began to float, and not by my own doing. Someone clawed at my dangling feet. Light beams came from my hands, my mouth, my eyes, and I couldn't help but to cry out.

I fell flat and then rolled off into a limp puddle by Saige's feet.

"What did you do to him?" Saige checked my pulse.

No answer. Just odd looks.

"Liyo?" She cradled my head and smacked my cheek. "Are you okay?"

I saw flames in my own eyes. After a few blinks, they went back to normal.

I got to my feet and shook myself out. My gait was a little unsteady, but then I was fine.

"What the fuck was that?" Saige was angrier than I was.

I was still trying to understand.

Elu acted like nothing had happened at all, and then said to me, "Come, we've got to get supplies."

"Right," I said.

She threw us several slimpacks and led us to a storage room with dried food and waterskins. As I grabbed what I thought I'd need, the girl kept staring. Maybe whatever plan they were conjuring was making her nervous. Her pack was barely filled with items. Looked like she wasn't planning on going far.

I snatched it from her. "Planning on leading us to another dead end?"

"Of course not." She snatched it back. "I'm a woman of my word."

I grabbed a pack and sniffed it. It smelled meaty. "Yeah, well, sorry for my apprehension, but nothing comes for free."

"You outsiders all sound the same." She swiped her mouth with her arm.

I picked up another pack and sniffed. It was so pungent that I gagged. The girl couldn't hide her sniggers.

Elu took it from me. "Dried durian." She stuffed it into her bag. Maybe Saige was right that I had to be a little nicer.

"Ask me anything. I'll answer truthfully. I swear," I said.

She zipped the bag and then tossed it over her shoulder. "Why did you risk being killed by us to leave your home? We have every right to execute both of you for breaking the treaty."

"Bad things are happening in our region. To the Lower Residents. To me. The Elites—they tried to poison all the workers. They no longer have a use for us. They have been testing on us. Shooting us down in the streets." I took a deep breath. "They even killed my parents. When I was young. We had no choice but to take our chances here. Get far away."

"Elites. Still at it again. They never stop." Her expression softened for a split second, but then she put back on a tough one, remembering where she was. "This is why the treaty was created. To keep them and us separated. For a thousand years, they've caused havoc, and we wanted no part of it. Their lack of faith and greed is not the way of our people."

"Then you understand why we have to return to them." I doubled down. "We have to get back so that we can help them fight the Elites. End this once and for all."

Her face scrunched. "And then what? Who will take over the region? You? The workers? What will happen to the innocents on the other side of your never-ending wars? Your people will eradicate them as they tried to eradicate you. How you've tried to eradicate the other since the beginning of humankind's conception."

I leaned back. "I can't think about casualties right now, when my people are suffering."

"Spoken like a true opportunist." She wore a weak smile. "Whoever is on top will always do absolutely anything to remain there. Haven't you people learned that by now?"

She had a point. What would happen if the plan worked?

She sucked her teeth. "And you people call us 'savages.'"

I cleared my throat. "I'm sorry."

She grunted. I took it as she'd accepted the apology.

"We have a seeker who travels to the Union every odd year to make sure that the treaty is still upheld as well as to deliver goods," she stated. "The Union's mediator visits on the even years and does the same."

"How is that possible?" My mind raced, thoughts tumbling over one another. The Union told us that they'd cut off all communication from the north. Why was I even surprised? Another one of their tricks. I wondered how the people would feel about this piece of info.

"They proposed a new trade not too long ago. They wanted to mine near the Border, but they wouldn't say why." She shook her head. "We had a virus that was spreading like wildweeds. People were dying off at high rates. None of our holistic medicines worked. We became desperate. They offered us a cure in return. The colony had no choice but to take the offer."

"What were some of the ailments?" I asked.

She grimaced. I knew that look. The look of recalling something painful. "Coughing blood. Fatigue. Grayish skin. Seizures. Always ended in death."

I knew that it was the same illness that the Union had inflicted on us, and they had somehow infected their colony.

She twirled a turquoise ring on her thumb.

"You made a huge mistake by allowing them to slither in and attach their tentacles to your resources. They're a disease that needs to be destroyed at the source."

Elu stiffened, visibly bothered. "So what do you propose?"

"We combine forces, and together we destroy the Elites and who-ever else gets in our way. Us working together for a greater good."

I proposed a war of all wars.

"Hypothetically." She chuckled. "If we band together, what's to say your people won't try to enslave us again. You must've forgotten your own history. Your kind doesn't have a good track record, historically speaking."

"I can't speak for my ancestors, but I can speak for me. Right now. I can guarantee that after it's over and done, we can live separately again. Return to the original treaty in place."

She backed away, shaking her head. "No. We will not interfere with southerner wars."

"Then you are more naive than I thought," I said. "They *will* come for you."

"We will take you to the exit and then part ways." She left to join the rest of the group.

We grabbed spears from the armory that were made of obsidian, tips as sharp as talons. They had lances and whips in there too. We loaded and strapped them to our backs and hips and across our chests. If we needed that much defense, I could only imagine the journey to the other side.

Suddenly, Miah stopped and put his finger to his lips. He scanned the armory, then threw his body over all of ours. At that moment, there was an explosion, caving in the ceiling and wall. Watchmen dove in through both craters. I lifted as many as I could and tossed them to the side, trying to create a pathway. The stragglers were stabbed with spears as they tried to stop us from moving forward.

"This way!" Elu motioned.

We followed.

There was a stained glass ceiling of blues, reds, and greens. The sunlight created a beautiful kaleidoscope on the ground below. Life-size engravings of their people holding spears and bows were carved into the walls in a dusty red clay. The same carvings were on tall pillars, but instead of people it was PolarWolves and other animals like whales, ravens, and eagles that had long gone extinct in the south. The hall was lined with clear cases displaying ancient weapons, tools, decorative pouches, and etched urns and jugs. It was a museum.

Elu led us to a secret passage with many steep steps leading into darkness. "Get in."

Miah went first. Then Saige. Me. Elu was last.

Watchmen were in pursuit. Shooting lasers that pinged off rocks. The stairwell got tighter the farther we got. My ears started to pop. I tried my best to hold them back, but they just kept coming.

We finally got to a trapdoor. It was ancient. It craned upward, getting stuck at the halfway mark.

"This is your exit," Elu said. "Go."

Miah stood next to her.

"Thank you," I said.

Saige wouldn't budge. "You can't fight off all these watchmen."

"We'll make it." She looked like she was almost in tears.

"No, you won't."

Lasers started to ping. We all ducked.

"Saige," I yelled. "Leave them."

"No."

Miah finally spoke. "Go with him."

Saige shook her head. Defiant. What was wrong with her? Watchmen were getting closer. Lasers were flying. So I made an executive decision.

I caused the entire stairway to implode on itself.

"You!" Elu shrieked. "Let us out."

"I can't." I was too weak from creating the implosion. I was dizzy, and soon after my face met the ground.

❖ ❖ ❖

When I awoke, all three of them were huddled together. I still didn't possess enough energy to join. Although I was quite sure they wanted nothing to do with me, we needed to figure out a way out. If Saige had just stuck to the plan, then we wouldn't be in this jam in the first place.

It seemed as though she was bent on doing the opposite of everything I said.

"I had a bird's-eye view of the battle raging below." Elu's voice shook. "They all looked so small from where I was. I was so far that I couldn't tell which were the watchmen and which were the colony. Flashes of lasers. Muffled screams were all that remained.

"Suddenly, I saw the watchmen being transported back onto their crafts. Just zipping up by the hundreds. Why were they retreating so fast? I thought to myself. They were winning.

"That's when a bulky silver figure the size of at least twenty of their crafts jetted from the skies and slammed right into the center of it all. Trees shook and splintered at the sheer force."

The Union had completed their monstrosity. The Transmega.

"It had a wide screen for its eyes that turned a glowing red color. It raised its palm. The light in the middle swirled like a tornado. Once the energy was full, one single blow was discharged. The shock desecrated the entire forest, Miah, for miles, destroying every person and beast in its wake."

She began to whisper. "The area looked like a singed desert in the middle of the tundra. There were no survivors left."

I cried silently because I felt for them. I understood them. How the Union just came and picked us apart like the seeds on a dandelion. I tilted my head to face them.

"I knew that we would die back there." She looked at Miah. "I'm sorry. I just thought that if we died, then at least we'd be together. With those who were lost."

Elu buried her face into his shoulder.

"We're going to figure this out," Saige assured her.

I finally got the strength to get on my feet and join them. Elu looked up at me. Her eyes weary, puffy.

Before I said anything, she beat me to it. "Gratitude."

I was surprised. A minute ago, I was bad guy number one.

I nodded.

"From here on out, we work together," I said. "First things first, we need to find a way to the other side. Then we find Mama Seeya."

Saige scoffed at the sound of the name.

I ignored her. "She will know what to do next."

"I can't believe that I'm going right back to where I just escaped from. Ain't that a bitch." Saige shook her head.

I couldn't ignore her ignorance any longer. "This was never supposed to be forever. Have you forgotten? Our place is back in the south. With our people. Mama Seeya. Avi."

Avi's name made her flinch. "*Our* place or *your* place?"

"You don't get it, do you?" I said. "You are still only thinking about yourself. You don't care about anyone else or who you hurt to get what you want. I keep making excuses for you. You think you have it so much worse than everyone else. That it's only you who has suffered!"

She took a swig from the waterskin like it was Fire. Her jaw flexed as she tried to keep it all bottled. Saige hated looking soft in front of others. She did what she did best. Gave the silent treatment.

"Why did you bring me over here?" I whispered, wiping tears away. "Why didn't you just let me die?"

She only stared.

"Answer me, Saige. Stop being a heartless coward who runs away from everything for once."

Nothing.

"You never talk to me. You act like I'm not even here," I confessed. "Tell me that I matter to you. Tell me that you need me like you did before."

She came really close. "I never wanted this. Any of this. The only reason you're here is because I made a pact to keep you alive in exchange for the protection of Avi. Nothing more. Nothing less. You're a pawn for the rebels. Always have been. Being used to further someone else's agenda. You hide behind this wholesome Brotherhood act, but you're lost. Just as lost as I am. The only difference between you and me is that I'm real enough to accept how ugly I am inside."

I looked at her real hard. The tears had dried, got sucked back into the ducts. She always knew how to strike a nerve. Say the most awful things to get a rise out of me. It worked. Instead of throwing her across the tunnel, I said, "You think you have all the answers, huh? You think all I do is think about me? I'm not like you. I take care of my people. I want to protect my people, including you. The reason why we need to go back to the south is because the General is dead, and Avi is next in line. She's going to need—"

Saige staggered back as if she'd been hit with something heavy. "What did you just say?"

"The General is dead. I heard Head Gardner tell the colony. She thinks that they had something to do with it. Either way, someone beat us to it."

I expected for her to jump up and down. Shadowbox the cold air. Howl in joy. I mean, we knew deep down the General dying wasn't enough to sway the system. It would live on past him, but instead she appeared almost heartbroken.

I saw it in her eyes. She fell on her ass. I moved forward, and she swatted me away.

When her lip started to quiver, she just covered it with her hand.

"Are you not happy?"

She wouldn't say anything. She was stuck.

"What are you not telling me?" I became more insistent.

"He's my father," she said meekly.

I repeated the same stumble and fell on my ass too. "This can't— impossible. Why—how? Wh—so Avi is—"

"This is my attempt at not being a *heartless coward.*" She lifted the waterskin and offered a cheers.

We sat in quietness while I absorbed the information she'd just dumped. Why'd she kept it a secret the whole time? Had Mama Seeya known? The fact that she hadn't trusted me to share this bit of information messed with me. That even after all that we'd been through, she still treated me like some nobody. Some stranger. Instead of harping on it, I had to bury it, give her a pass like I'd always done.

The Union couldn't have known either. I figured that the General would have done all he could to keep it under wraps. If it got out that he'd fathered an Impure, the whole system would've collapsed.

Not only was she mourning her father, but Avi could very well be mourning the fact that her father had tried to get rid of her sister. If she knew, then it was even more urgent that we go back.

"We can't stay here," I said. "We have to return. Now that the General is gone, the next in line is . . ."

"Avi." I hadn't heard her say her name out loud in a long time.

"Yeah," I said.

"She's going to be in danger." Her eyes hadn't left the light orbs.

"The Union isn't going to allow an egalitarian to rule." I added, "Head Gardner said the Union was blaming the colony for the General's murder. Said that they supplied the workers with blue flame."

I looked to Miah and Elu for confirmation. "We know nothing about that," Elu said. "Nothing that comes out of the Elites' mouths can be trusted."

"You can't trust anyone in the south." Saige stood, finally coming back to reality. "You were right." She said to me, "We've got to go back."

The stakes had just gotten much higher for her. Her sister.

"But don't expect me to join Mama Seeya's rebel group. I don't know her, and I don't trust her."

I wanted to ask her why she was so anti. Why she had a vendetta against Mama Seeya. But I left it alone. She'd just agreed to return to the south, and that was the most she was going to agree to.

"And one more thing." She looked me deep in the eyes before moving forward. "This whole General thing stays between us. Got it?"

I nodded.

Chapter Eight
AVI

The cabinet had been in complete disarray ever since Jade called an election. They all gathered in Father's former study in clusters, quarreling with one another like hens. His study used to be a magical place to me. He had some of his greatest think tank moments there. He'd always reminded us how powerful we were in numbers.

As I shut out their voices, I took in the room's grandeur. Suspended above the chaos was a shimmering solar system ranging from the wild sun to the glacial Neptune. Asteroids orbited and moons shone an intense gray as cosmic snowballs of luminescent blues and purples zipped by. I mentally cataloged the most notable ones: the Pleiades, or the Seven Sisters; Alpha Gruis; Epsilon Pegasi; and my favorite, the North Star.

Members encircled the same counter that Father conducted his tactical meetings at. His chair at the head remained unoccupied. I shrank farther into my seat, hoping that it would swallow me entirely. A true-born General would've taken that chair, his chair, without hesitation. Made the entire room silent with just one look. Jade would've if she'd been there. I hated to admit it, but she had the natural qualities of a leader but also those of a tyrant. As for me, I'd never possessed those kinds of merits. I saw myself as more of a diplomat.

The room went silent, and not because I'd morphed into an authority figure but because Head Gardner strolled in as if she owned the place after having been missing from the bereavement ceremony.

She relaxed into an empty space and crossed her legs. "I'm here as an appointed liaison on behalf of the future General, Elite Jade Jore."

Had they lost their intellects?

"Where's Jade?" Commander Chi leaned forward with haste. "You tell her that her presence is requested right now. This is not some adolescent's game."

Head Gardner scoffed. "Did you not just hear what I said, you hoary crustacean? She is *not* coming."

The board erupted in disagreements again.

She leaned back into her chair as if the arguments were melodies. I rose, not even making it halfway, and Instructor Skylar seized my wrist.

"Not worth it," he said under his breath.

I lowered myself back down.

"I'm assuming you came here to do something other than be a shallow annoyance." Instructor Skylar's voice quieted the room. "So, spit it out."

"My friend, I thought you'd never ask." She perked up, whipping her braids to the back. "After great consideration and deliberation, Jade has graciously offered to take back any members who'd like to join the new regime. Abandon this pathetic attempt at supporting Avi. We all know this honk supporter will never truly rise to the occasion of filling the former General's position. So, let's make this quick, shall we? Jade is the obvious choice for the betterment of our society."

My blood boiled over as I tried to keep myself calm.

Commander Chi spoke. "You are asking us to break custom, tradition. One that has been in place for over a thousand years for some infantile sibling rivalry?"

"You are much more senile than I thought." She waved him off. I'd never seen him move so fast. Commander Chi leaped over the table and had a blade to her before Head Gardner could exhale. "I am sick of you ducklings underestimating the veterans of this Union." He dug the blade deeper, causing her discomfort. "While you were still suckling, I was in battles carving people like you. Do not make me regress, child."

He holstered his weapon and climbed down in one motion.

She wiped her neck, spreading the blood. Afterward, she readjusted her bodysuit. "Well, according to the Union's election bylines, voting takes place when the challenge is publicized. In twenty-four hours, the results will be announced."

A young woman named Kai, who wore thin trifocals, added, "That's not enough time to create a campaign."

"A byline is a byline." Head Gardner almost sounded as if she were teasing the girl. "We all know how this is going to end. This is your last chance to join us. Salvage your positions and reputations now. Jade is a merciful ruler. Avi will not win this. We all know it. Leave now with your dignity and your jobs."

The legs of chairs began to scrape as many pushed back not long after she'd finished her spiel. With lowered heads and eyes that refused to meet mine, over half the members followed behind Head Gardner.

"Cowards," Commander Chi spat. "Every one of you."

Kai slid the frames farther up the bridge of her nose and began tapping a reader. "We have less than twenty-four hours to create some buzz around Elite Avi. Really get people to see her as a great leader. Any suggestions?"

A man wagged his finger. "Well, we could drive the fact that she's the rightful General and that it'd be breaking tradition if we deviated from that. Maybe that the General would be rolling over in his grave if customs broke."

"I like that. Good angle." Kai typed vehemently. "The older population of the Union would definitely buy into that. We just have to find some way to stimulate the youths. Any more ideas?"

"Maybe we could create a new dance craze." The same man snapped his finger. "I got it! We could get Marco Grant to endorse her."

Kai added more proposals to the reader as the suggestions became more and more degrading. It all left a bad taste. Using Father's death and a pop star to get votes. That wasn't how I wanted to win the seat. I didn't want to employ gimmicks and trends in order to sway constituents. I wanted to win the election fair, with actual feasible systems put in place, creating real changes, not just surface ones.

I finally spoke. "I will speak to the people. From the heart. I will tell them that Jade is not a good choice for our future, and I may not be, either, but I can learn. I'm learning to fill Father's position, but they must be patient with me, with us, as we move toward a better future."

Kai's mouth gaped open. "The people don't want to hear that you will *try* your best. They want to be taken care of. They want to know that you will lay your life on the line for the sanctity of the Union. This is *not* the Academy, Elite Avi. This is real life."

"Oh no," the man with the bright ideas said, covering his mouth. "We've got to come up with something quick." He expanded his reader screen for us to take a gander. "Look at these stats."

The tallies were imbalanced. Votes were already pouring in, and Jade was very much in the lead.

❖ ❖ ❖

Commander Chi tried to prevent me from leaving the assembly. He urged that work needed to be done. That time was of the essence in catching up in the polls. I told him and the rest to do as they wished, but to do it without me.

Jade had caused irreparable damage to my character. She'd already turned the Union against me the day Father took his last sip of air. She'd been plotting this grand scheme for a while now. I guessed she thought if she couldn't get rid of me physically, she'd eradicate my image instead. How clever she was, but something told me that it wasn't only her who had crafted the conspiracy. Head Gardner was in on it, too, but it still wasn't clear to what extent.

Instructor Skylar cornered me before I stepped into the hall. "You're just going to give up, then?"

Kai maximized the volume on the holoscreen. There I was, in a political smear commercial. Grainy footage of Saige and me rappelling from cables when we stole the serum from the physicians' headquarters for the workers. "Is this the General you want leading your nation?" a strong male voiceover asked. "I think not."

"Vote for Jade Jore for next General elect." A clip of Jade pumping her fist wearing Father's oversize gloves played. "Your future depends on it."

I stalked off into the corridor. I'd had enough. Instructor Skylar moved in front of my path once more. "Give me something. Anything that we could use against her."

I wanted to tell him about the theory I had about Jade murdering our father, but would he even believe me? Would he think I'd just stooped to her level and would do anything to beat her? Perhaps he already had a hunch and was waiting for me to second it. Either way, I needed proof, and I already knew Jade had wiped her prints clean.

"I don't have anything I can prove," I replied. "I must go now."

Against his intuition, he allowed me to leave.

❖　❖　❖

I took a hovercraft to the Farmlands, where workers toiled in the heat to harvest the fresh produce that nourished Upper Residents and Elites. The workers were a lot dustier, darker, and tougher than the ones who worked within the Citadel. As the craft soared over the landing deck, dark-red workers veered up from the rows of cornstalk, shielding their eyes from the dust and sun. Their limp hairs flying about and their gummy frowns noticeable.

Liyo's uncle, Tate, met me at the rear of the hatch. His skin was like worn leather. His appearance had far surpassed his actual age. I couldn't help but feel remorse as I stared into his weary gray eyes. I was probably the last person he wanted to see. The last time he saw me was when I was with Liyo and he'd ordered me to leave his dwelling and return to the Citadel, where an Elite belonged.

I deserved whatever outburst he chose to issue.

He stepped forward. It appeared as though he would leap; instead, he embraced me. Tate stepped back, wiping the mist from his eyes.

"I just wanted to say gratitude for the serum." He dug his hands in his pockets with the shyness of a boy. "You didn't have to do that for us. But you did. You saved a lot of us. Gave us another fightin' chance."

I couldn't even find the words to let him know how happy I was that I was able to assist, so I just nodded.

"What can I do ya for?"

"I need to see Pea," I said with urgency, "in the worker's infirmary."

His face turned grim. "All right, this way."

Jade had relocated the remainder of the Citadel workers to the Farmlands in order to put a spike in the rebellion. Immediately, I was able to sort which ones were from the grounds. They each took turns approaching me, asking how long it would take for them to return home, back to the Citadel.

"I'm working on it," I'd reply each time.

Some retreated with disappointment, while others held a flicker of hope that my words were stone.

Tate led me along rows upon rows of med stations, and I got to see firsthand the suffering workers resting on low cots through the enormous infirmary tent. So many injured from Jade's exile. There weren't even enough beds to house all the patients. Many had to double and triple up on the beds. Some even occupied the floors on blankets. As we got deeper, the ward changed. It was the area where the critically ill were stationed. The smells became more rancid so that I had to breathe slowly through my mouth.

He pointed to one of the half-tubelike beds. "There she is."

Tate's daughter, Eve, was assisting one of the medics. Although still small, she'd grown a few inches. Her skin was smooth and pale like ceramic, her hair white and stiff, and she had the same blue eyes as Liyo. The mutation must've run in the family's genes.

As soon as she saw me, she zoomed in, almost knocking me clear off the floor.

"It's really you. Oh, dear, how I've missed you." She rambled on as if we were the oldest of friends.

"What a lovely young woman you've become." I took her hand and spun her around like a dancer.

Her cheeks turned pink, and she smiled, exposing a missing front tooth.

"Have you talked to Liyo?" Her eyes widened with hope.

My voice broke. "No, no. Not yet. But I know that wherever he is, he's fine and thinking of you." I tapped the tip of her nose.

"Come on, Eve," Tate said. "We have to get back. Ever since we've had this influx of workers, there's just not enough help to go round."

I grabbed his elbow. "I *am* working on a solution. You have my word."

"I'm sure you are." He mustered a lopsided grin.

I watched Eve hand in hand with her father, skipping along the pathway. Pea, still unconscious, lay nearby. Half her left arm missing, the rest bandaged in thick wrappings.

"Oh, Pea." I collapsed over the side of the tube. "Forgive me."

I caressed her cheek. It was lukewarm to the touch. I watched her breathe softly for what seemed like hours, until I found myself drifting.

The Dissent

"Madam?" A soft voice nudged me awake.

I lifted my face. "Pea?"

With the hand that still existed, she stroked the top of my hair.

"You don't have to call me madam anymore. Just Avi," I said gently. "If we want to truly level the playing field, it starts with the things that we've normalized. My body, my life, is no greater than yours."

Pea turned her face away. It turned redder as she choked on her feelings. Workers were programmed to keep their emotions concealed. Especially in front of Elites.

"What Jade did is inexcusable, and it will never, ever happen again as long as I stand."

She nodded. "I believe you."

A medic from the back pointed to the glitchy holoscreen and yelled, "Turn it up."

All eyes were forward, awaiting the results. The timer counted down the last few seconds until the official vote was in. I had fallen asleep for so long that I hadn't even noticed the time slipping away. I checked my wristcom. Numerous missed messages from Instructor Skylar. I tapped on the latest one.

"Avi, it's not looking good." He rushed through his words. "Where are you? You need to call me back. Immediately."

The timer burst into digital confetti, and Jade's face filled the screen. She had won by a landslide.

"Maybe if we had voting rights in this hellhole, Avi would've won!" a patient perched on a cot grumbled.

Others concurred, but it didn't matter at that time. I had lost.

On-screen, Jade was surrounded by each cabinet member who'd deserted me as well as some new ones.

"Congratulations, General Jore," a reporter gushed. "Do you know where your sister is?"

"Probably somewhere brooding." She shrugged.

91

Another reporter asked, "What's your first line of business as the nation's leader?"

"The first thing is to elect a fresher, stronger regime." She announced, "The new appointees are as follows: the Administrator and Elite Blair Gardner."

Of course, she'd choose them. The Administrator was a tyrant over the Academy, and Blair was a baby tyrant in training. Her family owned prisons that housed wrongly accused workers and then executed them. All their wealth had been derived from systematic murders. Neither believed in anything other than disposing of all Europes. The Union was going to fall even harder with the dynamic trio in charge.

Jade had more to spew. "Commander Chi will be succeeded by Head Gardner as the newest head of Defense and Security. Instructor Skylar will be succeeded by Admiral Butler as head of Watchmen Training and Tactical Guard. Effective immediately."

Reporters erupted with waves of inquiries. Lenses zoomed in on the shock of the crowd. Instructor Skylar stepped down from the dais with his hands behind his back; holocams followed as pesky reporters stuck microphones in his face, attempting to get his reaction. Commander Chi lingered motionless as the news soaked in. He had just been stripped of a coveted position that he'd dedicated his entire life to. One that Father himself had appointed.

"And what about the workers? What's in store for them?" a reporter inquired.

Jade smiled. "I have many things in store for them. The first is that all Citadel ground workers will be removed and pushed back into their respective Subdivisions. I can't have them interfering, plotting as they've done before. But, in time, we will share the entire proposal. For now, I want them off my father's estate."

Pea had pulled herself into a seated position. She began snatching off wires pasted to her chest.

"What are you doing?" I tussled with her. "Sit back—"

A worker whooshed in, his nude bodysuit soaked in perspiration. "Run!"

Pea's eyes narrowed. "They're here."

It was too late: a soft purring sound was followed by a missile tearing through the top of the dome and exploding, sparks and fragments soaring. Instinctively, I snatched Pea and threw us both to the ground. Another blast hit, causing jagged pieces of furniture to come flying. Everything was sped up, blurred. Sounds of mixed bedlam echoed as I pulled Pea in tighter. Together, we watched injured people high off adrenaline scatter like mice.

After the bombings ceased and most were injured or dead, watchmen marched in to finish off the remaining. Lasers flew, hitting targets in backs, heads, and chests. Kill shots. I watched as watchmen hunted anything that twitched.

A mother who had been pinned under part of the collapsed dome tried to claw her way free. She kept pushing her son away before watchmen arrived. One took the boy by the hair and yanked him. The other watchman stayed perched over the mother.

"Run," the watchman ordered the child.

His mother nodded, urging him.

When the boy got a quarter of the way across, the watchman mowed him down with a single shot to the back of the neck. He dropped. The mother wailed, reaching out. The other watchman placed one in her temple.

Detonations, sobs, and lasers became a vile symphony.

Pea was crouched over, her head between her knees.

Predisposition rebooted itself. I was just as much of a watchman as they were. "We've got to get to the hovercraft," I told her.

She looked up at me with sad eyes and nodded vigorously.

"Stay down and stay close." I plopped on my stomach.

Watchmen had already fully infiltrated the interior, leaving few exits unmanned. We belly crawled over shards and bits of fleshy unidentified parts.

"Almost there," I called. "Pea?"

When I didn't hear a response, I rolled to my back. A watchman had taken her leg, trying to yank her back into the madness. Pea fought him, but she was no match. He lifted her entire body with one arm and marched her to an exit. My body tensed as I could hear the pulse pounding in my head.

I wasn't leaving without Pea. I crawled double time to make it to the same exit without being deterred. Outside was an identical calamity. Workers running into the cornfields. Watchmen rounding up clusters of would-be escapees at gunpoint.

"Pea!" I called for her.

Then I found her.

Her bare legs dangled from the edge of a harvest collection bed. A watchman ripped the fabric of her infirmary gown and then tried to fight his way between her thighs. She screamed, and he placed his hand over her mouth. She bit him, and he recoiled, surveying the mark. Out of fury, he struck her. She stopped moving then. I found a shovel and gripped it so tight and glided across the dirt like a banshee. With all the strength I could gather, I swung it against the back of his skull. He tumbled, disoriented.

Watchman Doucet scooted backward, and I pursued.

"Avi?" He'd realized who'd struck him. "What are you doing out here? Everyone is looking for you."

My hands trembled as I brought the blade of the shovel above my shoulder. "What were you just doing?"

"I-I—" He couldn't take his eyes off the weapon.

"Answer!"

"I w-was enjoying the spoils," he stated matter of factly.

"Spoils? Rape, you mean? You rape them?" It felt like my eyes were going to pop out of the sockets.

"W-we all do it." He shrugged. "They aren't real people."

I came down over his face with the heavy metal. Then I brought it up and came down again. The bones in his face were cracked; he coughed blood from some unrecognizable orifice. I tried to strike him once more, but Pea touched me. The shovel stayed suspended over my head as I was taken back to a time when Phoenix had attempted to do the same to me. Saige had saved me, but I knew she wanted to slash him, see him bleed out. I wanted the same for the watchman.

I lobbed the shovel aside and swiped his guns, tossing one to Pea. We then took shelter behind a cluster of wagons. Other women were hiding there, including Eve. A few women gasped at our arrival, but Pea assured them that I was on their side.

I gave Eve a once-over. "Are you hurt?"

She shook her head quickly.

"I'm going to get you out of here." I looked at the entire group. "All of you. Just stay calm and keep quiet."

One had an infant strapped to her chest, but it stirred.

"Please, shut that baby up," an older woman said.

"I'm trying." The mother wept softly. "Shh-shh."

"I will shut 'em up permanently if you don't." The woman advanced.

Pea stepped in between. "You will do nothing of the sort."

"That baby's going to get us all killed." She pointed repeatedly.

The opening I was waiting for cleared. "I have a hovercraft stationed less than a kilometer headed east. We cut through the fields." I knelt. "Pea will take the front, and I'll cover the rear."

The women all bowed their heads.

"Stay together," Pea said, moving first. The rest of the women followed one by one. I helped the woman and her child, and together we dispersed into the stalks.

The infant's soft cries turned into harsh screams that started to echo like an alarm in the expanse. The women's faces held desperation, as we'd just become watchmen targets.

"Shh, shh," she whispered into its ear.

"Leave them," one of the women suggested.

The mother seized the collar of my bodysuit. "Please don't. I'll make her quiet. I swear it."

She placed a trembling hand over her tiny mouth, but it was too late.

Lasers flew, and one hit the mother in the eye. I caught her before she fell forward on the child. Blood dripped from the hole.

Pea returned fire. "Avi?"

"Just go!" I unwrapped the baby from her carrying sack with one hand and shot into the distance with the other. "Get them out of here."

I sprinted with the girl tucked underneath my arm like a football, zigzagging in an attempt at dodging lasers. My chest constricted as my legs pumped harder and faster through loose soil.

Pea helped the women climb through the platform one after another as I sped to the control panel and activated the thrusters.

"Autopilot," I said. "Get us out of here!"

Watchmen fired at the craft from afar. The autopilot sensed a threat and began to hover. I aided Pea in pulling in bodies as fast as I could, but three were left dangling over the edge.

"Don't let go," I grunted.

"I don't want to die." The old woman wailed, seeing how high we'd gotten.

Pea was able to get another woman in. The third one couldn't hold her weight, so she slipped and was swallowed by the clouds.

"Pea?!" I screamed. "Help me. She's sliding."

All the women banded together to assist, holding her suspended body.

"Pull!" I instructed. "Pull!"

We managed to get part of her torso onto the platform. Then her body convulsed. She gurgled and then spat blood. A barrage of lasers tore through her frame.

Pea and the other women jumped back, trying to take me with them.

"Let go!" Pea wailed. "She's gone. We have to close the door."

They peeled my fingers from her corpse, and I watched her plunge. The hatch was sealed, leaving only me and the survivors hyperventilating on the deck.

I wasn't sure when, but the baby had been placed in a compact storage hangar. I heard her start to cry once more. Eve held out her hand. Currents sparked around her fingers and palm, and her eyes lightened to almost a pearl color. The metal drawer opened gently, and she scooped the child from its container and floated her to her arms.

I beamed, remembering when Liyo had been comfortable enough to show me his abilities.

Eve comforted the child, cooing and pinching her cheeks. "I can only manipulate small things. For now. But one day, I'll be strong like Liyo."

"And that you shall."

It was more important now than ever for me to move forward with an equality policy. It wasn't going to be easy. Yet another obstacle had been placed in my path, and I had run out of people to turn to. I couldn't be certain where Liyo or Saige were at in the region, but I had to travel onward. Make things right.

The hovercraft zoomed through the air for a period of time. We all thought that we were finally safe. Then we heard loud bangs stemming from the outer shell of the craft. I sprinted to the control room. Hovercrafts were in the vicinity, attempting to shoot us from the sky. The hovercraft I borrowed didn't have the proper firepower to take down all the armored watchmen crafts that surrounded us. I hadn't planned on being in a full-fledged cannon fight.

There wasn't much time for me to absorb what it all meant, but if this was the day that was written for me to perish, then I would leave the planet taking out as many of them as I was able.

"Pea." I glanced over. "Strap in."

"Yes, mada—yes, Avi."

I powered the autopilot off and began steering the craft through billows of clouds, crisscrossing and dipping to bewilder the enemy pilots. I caused two to smash into each other. Angered that they were outsmarted, they fired with all their artillery power. Our system began to blink red. Levels critical. The shields weren't going to hold for much longer. I turned the craft around and shot back.

I felt my face contorting, teeth grinding, and sweat rolling down my back as I plucked as many as I could from the sky. I took pleasure in watching their crafts explode. Knowing that I snuffed out all the people that would kill their own because of what? Nonconformity?

I just hoped that my demise lit the spark that the rebels needed; the people of the Union needed to understand that no one was safe. The Union would do what they needed to whoever they needed to remain on the top of the chain.

The last hit disabled our cannons. I stood solemnly, closing my eyes, feeling every hit the craft was taking as if it were my own body being bludgeoned. The Union was relentless, and they were never going to stop until I was eliminated.

I waited for the cabin to be engulfed in flames or for us to lose balance, spin out of control, and then be engulfed by flames.

Instead, the attack just stopped.

"What the—?"

We floated idle in the sky like a globe. I walked forward, ready to meet my demise. Perhaps Jade wanted to see me before she snuffed me out. The hatch lowered. I waited for Jade or even Head Gardner to step on the craft and finish the rest of us. I wasn't going to give them the satisfaction of cowering. I would allow them to kill me as they had Father: with dignity.

The form steadily approached. Then removed their helmet.

It was Mama Seeya.

Chapter Nine
SAIGE

The General was dead. Gone. And so was I when we got back to the Southern Region. Because I didn't believe that the Union had stopped hunting me. That they had just forgotten. I was living proof of the General's indiscretions. By merely existing, I had made a mockery of everything they prided themselves on. Me being alive threatened their whole existence, and anyone who was around me would always be in danger. They'd just torched an entire colony to show how serious they were.

My father was gone, and I'd never get the answers I wanted. Needed. If I wasn't spiraling then, I was spiraling now. He'd held the key. To everything. And my chance had just vanished.

I hated the part of myself that clung to the hope of being part Elite. It made me sick.

That ending never even came as a possibility. The General had burned into all our skulls that he was invincible. Immortal even. I'd just known that if I was executed, it'd be at his hands. This wasn't supposed to happen. He'd won all battles with only wounds to show. The Union wouldn't let us forget it. Their almighty and all-powerful propaganda even had me convinced that no one could touch the man.

I wondered when—how it had happened. If it was sudden or slow. If he was surrounded by his family or if he was alone. Had he thought of me? Had he even known about me? I massaged the matching birthmark that we shared.

I replayed over and over again in my head how his face would twist when I confronted him about us being connected. It was the most impossible scenario, but I would be lying if I said I'd never imagined it.

My feelings were all over the place, so much so that I fucked up and allowed the others to see it and ask questions. Then out of sheer stupidity, I shared the secret. That was a mistake. Showing that I was upset over the death of a dictator was a mistake. I wanted to feel nothing. Instead, I felt everything.

That man didn't deserve my sympathy. But why did it keep arising?

I shoveled the feelings into an empty corner and thought about the larger effects of his death. The Union was probably in disarray. Avi was next in line, but I had a feeling that it wouldn't be so simple. And even if she had resumed the post, she wasn't safe.

Avi. My sister. I had also shoved the memories of her into a corner because it was too painful to recollect. I'd left her to fend for herself in order to save myself. I hadn't really thought about her like she'd deserved. How alone she must feel. I knew what it was like to lose a parent, and in that way, I could empathize, but there was another part of me that was glad it was over.

Our father had looped a collar on me like a beast, almost had me killed in the Cube, and made me kill a man to prove my loyalty. But even with all of that, there was a very distant part where I mourned the fact that I would never have a chance to see what it was like to have a father. In some fucked multiverse, maybe Avi was the daughter that was shunned and I was the coveted child. In that life, I was maybe happy.

I was messed up in the head.

As Elu and Liyo worked on getting us out, Miah stared at the side of my face as I tortured myself with crazy thoughts. I wanted to say something to him, but it wasn't worth it. I wasn't worth redeeming. I'd tried to tell him before, but they never listened.

I was happy when Liyo caught the lever, and the wall on the other side ground and lifted. Cold, fresh air whistled through the fracture, and a sliver opened just enough for us to squeeze through. Liyo was wiped out once again.

"Let's get out of here," he said.

I stepped forward. "You should lay—"

"No." He wobbled. "We've been here long enough. It's time to get back."

He leaned on Elu, and Miah scooped his arm over his shoulder on the other side.

"You lead," Liyo told me.

I nodded. "Eyes open. Weapons up."

❖ ❖ ❖

I knew that Avi needed me, and I knew that I had to be there for her, especially since the General was gone. She was kind of like me in a sense. No real allies because we went too far in the other direction. People either loved us or hated our guts. But there was something in me that didn't want to return. With each step we took closer to the other side, a familiar sickness twisted in me. I guessed they would've called it anxiety. It'd been flaring up lately in a way that made me want to throw up stomach acid.

It all just felt like a trap. One that I couldn't seem to escape no matter how damned hard I tried. It was the first time that I was afraid of what was to come. For all the reasons, I hadn't seen it ending well. Especially for me. I was returning to the hole. Liyo was so bent on seeing Mama Seeya as an ally, but allies became foes under the right kind of pressure. As far as I was concerned, I wanted nothing to do with her or her minions. She hadn't showed her ass in almost a decade.

Never showed when I'd needed her the most. She'd left me floating. She probably didn't even know if I was dead or gone. That didn't sound like a mama to me. Or at least a good one.

I knew it was dumb, but in order to keep from breaking down, I thought about a scenario where I'd stayed in the north. Maybe with Miah there too. How different life would be. If only the watchmen hadn't come and killed everyone.

I could feel Miah boring into the back of my head. We hadn't spoken to one another since Liyo had barged in. Maybe he was ignoring me, or maybe I was ignoring him. I mostly wanted to apologize for bringing that mess into his home. We were the reason that he'd lost everything.

We didn't deserve their help.

"A question for a question?" Elu proposed to Liyo.

He'd regained some of his hearing. "Deal."

"Your abilities." The questions seemed to tumble from her lips like a hyper adolescent's. "How? Why? When?"

"I wish I knew myself. They said I was special. That I was sent from God himself to deliver them from harm, from evil, but now I just feel like I bring the things that I was sent to protect them from." He chuckled. It sounded sore.

"Hmm," she said.

There was an uncomfortable pause. The only sounds came from our boots scraping along the dirt and gravel.

"There's a loose prophecy in the north about a mage with great powers that would come from a faraway land that would bond the nations." She continued, "Although most of the colonies have strayed from prophecies of the older nation. They want to live in the here, the now."

"Colonies?" Liyo perked up. "There are more, then?"

Miah and Elu made quick eye contact. Then Elu raised a brow. "Is that your one question? Choose wisely."

Liyo truly laughed that time.

"The blue flame. I'd never seen it before until today. They mined that in the north? I thought that the Union cut the north off in the last century."

"We were too desperate to see through their deceit." She looked like she was going to explode. "We couldn't have fathomed that they would use the blue flame to . . . we had an illness that we couldn't contain without their serum. We had no choice."

"How convenient that a sudden illness plagued your colony, and how convenient that they had an antidote," Liyo said. "You were duped. Just as we were. That same thing they tried to use to kill us off with is the same thing they used on your side."

"There." I pointed up ahead where artificial light came through the cracks of the foundation.

"We're in the south," Elu said.

I knew that's where we were, but hearing her confirm it made the hairs on my arms grow.

"What part?" I asked her.

"Near the outer perimeter of the Square."

"Fuck," I said under my breath. "The place will be swarming with watchmen."

"We can't stay in here," Liyo almost pleaded.

"I know." I paced back and forth for a few, building the courage to slip out of the small opening back to the other side. "Stay on guard."

The city bustled with sounds of crafts zipping above and the hover-tram's door chimes. The four of us stayed low behind a short brick wall. Luckily for us, it was night. We'd use it to our advantage. I popped my head up to scope out the scene. A watchmen hive was in the distance. Closer to us were workers in nude bodysuits shackled by their wrists and being siphoned into waiting hovercrafts.

Liyo saw it too. Electricity overtook his eyes. I grabbed his arm. "Cool it," I mumbled. "You'll blow our cover."

He cut his eyes at me.

Guards from the hovercraft surveilled the area. It was only a matter of time before they found our little hiding spot.

I ducked. "You two take Liyo and head that way."

"And you?" Liyo asked.

"Someone's gotta stay and"—I looked back at the guards—"create a disturbance."

"Saige."

"I'll be right behind you. Promise."

"Your promises hold about the same weight as a watermelon seed."

I laughed. So did he.

"Don't die," he said.

"They're coming. Go."

I placed my attention back on the hovercraft. Someone grabbed me. I thought it was Liyo.

It was Miah. "You heard what he said."

"What?"

"Don't die."

I became shy out of nowhere and then got shyer because I was shy. After what I'd done to him in the north, he still cared about my welfare. I hadn't expected it. I never expected anything from anyone, but I wasn't going to lie to myself and say that it didn't feel good.

When he let go of my hand and hurried to meet the others, someone tossed a high-frequency noise detonator at my feet. Instantly I dropped, clutching my ears and rolling in the dirt. The watchmen knew we were there . . .

Although muffled, I heard boots stomping nearby and the whir of laser guns loading.

If hell existed, I'd be seeing dear old Dad very soon.

I thrashed my head around, trying to find some sort of relief, until a pair of arms scooped me from underneath and dragged me away from the sound.

The person kept slapping my cheeks until I came to. It was a red-haired worker wearing heavy-duty earmuffs. I wasn't sure who they were or where they'd come from. They gave me a welcoming smile. "I saw you on the broadcast. With Liyo. You came back to save us."

In the next moment, a laser went through the back of their shoulder. Their weight fell on top of me. As I tried to roll them off as they bled through their bodysuit, I heard chains rattling, and men grunted. When I finally got up, I saw all the workers wrestling with the guards as best they could.

"For the Brotherhood," one of them yelled.

"Protect Liyo!"

They knew he was back too.

Elu and Miah took Liyo farther and farther away.

I loaded the bow from the colony, and when I released, a trio of arrows zoomed across the field like lightning and pierced watchmen. I kept doing it with speed and ease as I backed up, going in the opposite direction. I had to lead them away from the others.

"You are much cleverer than I thought you were." The familiar voice spoke. "For a mutt, that is."

Head Gardner appeared with a pointed weapon. Her helmet off. A smirk painted on her mouth as if she were a child who'd done something disobedient.

It felt like I'd gulped a whole doorknob. I'd run out of arrows.

"I thought for a moment that maybe you'd died in that crash." Her head tilted in curiosity. "But there wasn't a body. So, I said to myself. Yes, Head Gardner. Where else could she have run off to?"

My eyes searched for weapons nearby that I could use to disable her with. Kill her with as she continued getting off on hearing herself ramble.

"Ah, the north," she answered. "You made them break the treaty. So, we had to break them. How does it feel to have caused more deaths, well, you know, other than your dear ma? Isn't that what you called her? Ma?"

My stomach twisted as I held down bile. "Do. Not. Speak. Of. Her."

"Oh, she's arrived," she said in a singsong voice. "I thought you'd gone flaccid on me."

"She never left."

"Now that's the Saige I want to see . . . for the last time, of course." Her finger rested too comfortably on the trigger.

"Remember that day in the ring." I played into her game since she enjoyed them so much. "I had challenged you to join me, but the General, you know, your controller, commanded you to heel like a pup in training."

Her smile faded into a sneer. She tossed the gun aside and fished a blade from her ankle, tossing that too. "I want this to be a fair fight—for you, of course. I want to tell my children and my children's children about how I took great pleasure in ending the Union's rotten impurity."

I found myself drawing nearer to her as she to me.

"I don't have regrets in life," she said as she put up her fists. "But the only nagging one was that I couldn't personally take your mother's meaningless life with my own bare hands. I really hate using that execution serum. There's really no fun in that kill."

I howled and charged. Her body tensed on impact as I carried her through the air and then slammed her into the earth. She let out an audible moan as the breath left her body.

She brought her elbow across my chin. My head jerked to the left. I bit down on my tongue and tasted milky metal. I bore down on her with my weight and tried to pin her arms. She headbutted me, then popped her pelvis. When she got enough space, she rolled over to the side and then hopped on my back. She grabbed fistfuls of hair and began banging my head against the ground. My brain shook with each thump as she attempted to crack my skull like an egg. Ripping braids from the follicles, I brought her pinky finger down to my mouth and bit to the bone. She wailed. Her hold loosened. I twisted my torso and hit her in the side of the ear with a back elbow.

On her back, she surveyed her trembling half-severed finger. When I approached to strike at her lowest point, she swiped at me with a blade, slicing into my stomach. As I was hunched over, she did a kip-up to a standing position.

We circled one another with our hands up as mayhem proceeded around us. We both went in for the kill once more. Someone wasn't leaving the situation alive. I was able to wrestle the knife from her. It skittered over the ground. A series of kicks and hand strikes landed; some missed. She beat the hell out of me, and I returned the beating.

I leaped in the air and drove my knee into her chin. I felt something crunch as she flew backward. She twisted and landed flat on her stomach. She tried a meager attempt at crawling away from me as I drew nearer, preparing to stomp her head in until brain matter spilled. I grabbed her boot, and she twisted her torso and tossed something in my eyes. It felt grainy underneath my lids. I rubbed my face and stumbled over the redhead's body in the process. My eyes watered bad as I tried to rub the substance out, but it was too late. With one blurry eye ajar, I watched her loom nearer.

She managed to get on top of me.

"I win." She placed her hands around my neck. "And you, well, you lose."

I clawed at her wrists, tried to rip them off. Her grip tightened around my throat, her thumbs dug into the base of my neck, my legs thrashed, and my face contorted as she slowly crushed my airway.

In and out of grayness. One image was of Ma. The next was a blurry one of slobber darts spewing from Head Gardner's mouth as she used all her might to void me out. Grayer. The dark sky. Dissipating clouds. Crazy eyes. I couldn't breathe. My breath.

A weight lifted from me. Like magic. I gasped. Choking on air. At least I had air to choke on. I grabbed my neck and took in deep gulps of oxygen.

The red-haired girl must've gotten Head Gardner off me because even though she was injured, she fought her best she could. But Head Gardner was too strong. The redhead gurgled as Head Gardner stuck a blade in her back.

"Get up!" Head Gardner made the girl get on her knees as she positioned herself behind her.

She aimed the torcher.

I staggered to my feet with not much energy left to defend myself, to run.

I was a dead woman standing.

Just as I was going to collapse, a force halted me. I rose inside a transparent bubble.

Liyo was taking me away.

Head Gardner watched in wonder as I floated like a feather in a gust.

Head Gardner pulled the trigger, and I watched from high above as flames consumed the girl who'd saved me. Her entire body was lit up. She rolled around, shrieking, but then she just stopped as the fire continued to consume the skin, hair, everything.

Head Gardner tried to light me up next, but the blaze couldn't reach. She stood over the burning corpse. The flames flickered in her eyes. She pointed and mouthed, "You're mine."

By that time, I was as high as the tops of the trees, high as the hovercrafts perched above transporting human labor as I watched Head Gardner and the other watchmen execute every worker that was still in restraints.

I felt myself being gently guided to the ground by many hands.

Elu's round face was very close to mine.

I felt Liyo's fingers frantically moving over my body to check for wounds.

Miah riffled through his pack and began crushing dried plants.

"Stay with us," I heard Liyo say from far away, even though he was near.

There was no more trying. Maybe I didn't want to stay anymore. Like she said, she won. And I lost.

❖ ❖ ❖

Someone peeled my lid open and shot a blinding light into the pupil. When I came to, I grabbed their wrist with one hand and with the other, their collar.

"Ah!" We both squealed in unison from the pain.

Liyo rushed into the room and stripped my grip from their bodysuit.

The Europe man with a buzz cut and pale eyes grimaced. He stabbed at me with two fingers. "If that mutt's going to act like that, then she can leave."

"Don't ever call her that again." Electrical currents jumped in Liyo's eyes as he comforted me. "She's just woken up to a strange person handling her. Give her some damn grace."

The man straightened his posture, then laid a hand on his chest. "My apologies. It won't happen again, Savior."

"Where are we?"

"A safe house. For fugitives." He adjusted the collar of the nude bodysuit that I had wrinkled. "Name's Gabriel. My worker status is medic for the Lower Resident ward at the Physician's Headquarters. They don't want to treat us, so they trained us to treat one another."

"So, you were the ones injecting us with those poisons." I swung my legs over the side of the table.

His too-smooth face turned downward. "I did."

"Let's go." I hopped off. "He can't be trusted."

"That is why I opened this space." Gabriel motioned around us. "If the Union ever found out about this, they'd surely execute me."

"What do you want? A cookie?" I spat.

He moistened his slender lips. "No, not at all. But I would like to help the Savior in any way that I can."

"Stop calling him that." I stormed out of the room, pretending that I wasn't in agony.

I didn't know where I was or where I was headed, but I had to get out. I was back at square one, back right where I'd left off. What kind of shit was that? All my life I'd fought and schemed and killed to be free, and just like that, I was back in the imprisonment of the Southern Region. I couldn't bring myself to believe that I'd just survived all that only to be a slave again. The region was hopeless. Backward and superficial. A place where conviction came to expire.

There was no saving it.

The halls reeked of mold and ancient cement. With each step, dust was kicked up, and the particles stuck to my shins. There weren't many lights. And especially no sunlight. We were somewhere deep, deep underground in a flat mazelike structure with narrow passageways. There were nooks everywhere. Some stopped right there, while others led down other pathways. It was definitely a good hiding spot for runaways.

I stumbled upon a crevice of an entrance with a drawing of a girl figure scribbled in white chalk above it. I slipped inside and wiped the crud from the fractured mirror with my sleeve. I lifted the parka and surveyed the stab wound that Head Gardner had left. It was still sore, but whatever old med equipment they'd smuggled had done the trick of at least lasering my organs back shut.

I twisted the knob on the faucet. Water sputtered from the spout as the pipes groaned like a group of old men getting up from low seats. It was brownish. I stuck my blood-coated hands underneath and scrubbed the grime away as best I could.

The monotonous task of rubbing my fingers together, the sound of the water plopping in the rusted tub, caused me to detach. I slapped myself hard, leaving a wet, red mark on my cheek. I needed to wake up. I pinched myself. Smell reality. I was still there. Life was suffering.

My head dangled over the tub as dirty liquid began to fill to the top rim. I watched as the streams trickled over the sides and pitter-pattered on my boots. I lifted my head and gazed into the blur of the mirror. My face distorted. Broken into three segments.

The General's face appeared over mine like a freak creation. I gasped, touching my lips—his lips—smashing my nose—his nose—from side to side. I closed my eyes so tight that I almost crushed my own eyeballs. When I opened them again, it was just me, but still shattered.

The General was inside me. In my skin. In my veins. Inserted in my DNA.

Half of me had burned those workers. Half of me had killed them all. The way they'd burned. It just kept playing over and over and over like a broken slideshow.

I was to blame.

I stuck my head deep inside the water. I screamed, but it came out only as low hums and gurgles. Bubbles flitted past the edges of my mouth as I screamed some more until all the air in my lungs ran out.

Take a deep breath. Allow it all to devour you. Let it be over.

I was grabbed by the back of my hair and yanked the wrong way. I fell onto another body into the brittle tile. I choked as water rolled along my chin. I peeked at Miah through a moist eye as he sat on his butt in a puddle.

I took a few deep breaths. "Life's a pile of shit."

He flicked excess water from hands. "Do you believe in reincarnation?"

"They don't believe in anything here." I wrung out the ends of my braids.

"I didn't ask about them," he said firmly. "I asked what *you* believe."

"What does it matter what I believe?" I leaned back against the dilapidated wall and faced the ugly ceiling.

"We believe when we all depart, if we were good and noble and helpful to the people around us, that as a reward we'd be reincarnated as something we admired in that life," he explained.

It sounded like a comforting thought, but I didn't believe it.

"How's, ugh, Elu holding up?" I felt embarrassed trying to make small talk.

"She's trying." After a few beats, he stood and then grabbed me upward. "Was that all you wanted to ask?"

I scoffed. "Wh-what are you talking about?"

He stared, giving me a chance to do the right thing.

"I'm sorry that we brought chaos to your colony. I'm sorry for not standing up for you. I'm sorry that everywhere I go, I just fuck things up. I seem to just bring madness. At this point, I'm not even sure why people—"

"Stop punishing yourself," he said. "The Union would've come sooner or later."

What was wrong with me? Tears began to ride along the curvature of my cheeks. I couldn't hold them in. I was really, really tired. I'd find a time later to beat myself up about showing weakness in front of a stranger.

Miah tried to reach out.

I turned my head away. "Don't." I didn't deserve comfort. His comfort.

"You are sad, hurt," he said.

I sniffled and wiped my face. "No, I'm angry. Okay?"

"Hmm."

"Why do you keep staring at me like that?" I asked. "Why are you even here? Don't you have something else to do?"

My theatrics didn't faze him. He kept a calm, warm demeanor. "I found you with your head submerged in a tub of water. I think you are the 'something else to do.'"

"Yeah, well, no one asked you to come after me."

"Is that why you did it? So you could die?"

"What's it to you if I did or didn't?" My eyes burned again. I talked fast so that he wouldn't answer that. "Why does everyone keep trying to save me? Maybe I don't want to be saved. Maybe I don't want any of this. Maybe I just want to . . ."

He stood, perched over me with those big black eyes. Miah wiped a tear before it could travel too far.

I let him that time. His caring without wanting anything from me was starting to eat away at my walls. I was used to transactions with men. Miah scared me. And I was afraid of who I was becoming around him. I wasn't a soft one like the other girls. I was hard through and through. Men were often scared of me, and if they weren't, then I made them scared.

Miah was unusual. I was drawn to him. I both hated and liked it.

"Why are you being nice to me? You have no idea who I am, what I've done here. What the General made me do. I'm not good."

His expression softened. "We've all done things, Saige, that we are not proud of. Every human has a past, a present, and a future. You can't dwell in a form of you that no longer exists. You have a chance to start anew here. *This* is your narrative. One that you can write from here on out. So take control of it. Yes?"

I nodded, my face becoming lower and lower with each nod. "Yes."

"You didn't strike me as such an agreeable person," he said with a boyish laugh.

His mouth. His smile. He smelled of ginger and cedarwood oil. I leaned in. He leaned in back. I could taste his breath. I wanted to taste him fully.

Elu knocked once, then flung the door open. We both sprang back as if opposing magnets were placed in between us.

"Am I interrupting?" She eyed us both.

We both shook our heads vigorously.

"Good," she said slowly. "Liyo needs us."

❖   ❖   ❖

I plopped down on a bench across from Liyo, still dripping. Miah, who was also damp, took the spot next to me.

"What happened to—" Liyo's face scrunched.

"You've dragged me all the way back to this dump to hide among moles. What's the grand plan now?" I asked.

The moles—Lower Residents—sat around in a decayed common room all staring at Elu, Miah, and me like we were some kind of spectacle. I noticed their discomfort and confusion as they observed each person. I got it: they'd never seen someone who looked like them and barely someone like me before, but it was working the last nerve that I had left.

Liyo explained the next move, but I couldn't focus on anything but the conversations of the pales around us.

"What are they?" I heard a woman ask a man with a dirt-smudged face.

I scoffed.

"Dunno." He sucked his teeth. "Maybe a mutt like dat one next to 'er."

I wanted to jump the table. Interrupt their conversation. Cut them up a little. But my knife was gone.

"Saige?" Liyo snapped his finger.

"What?" I hissed.

He was taken aback by my displaced anger. "I know you don't want to be here, but we're here. We've got to get to Mama Seeya."

I groaned. "And what the fuck is she going to do? Save us from the Union? Save me from these people? Make us integrate and then kumbaya?"

His eyes narrowed. "These people?"

"Why do you act so oblivious to the fact that. They. Don't. Want. Me. Here?" My voice rose so the others could hear. "They call me mutt, Liyo. Just like the Uppers. They look down on Impures. The only reason they let Mama Seeya lead is because she's the only one who's gotten them this far. And you look like them, so you don't see it. You sit on a throne of ignorance. Delusion. These are *not* my people!"

"I *am* your people." His fist was engulfed in currents, and when he slammed it into the table, it broke in half.

The muscles in his face tensed as he surveyed the damage. Elu and Miah kept their cool, staring at his sparking hands with not fear but curiosity. As for me, I remained seated and unfazed as if nothing had happened. I'd noticed that ever since the temple, his abilities were much stronger, more volatile than before.

"I am *not* your enemy." He emphasized each word. "I'm doing my best with what I have. And we can't do this without muscle. Mama Seeya has muscle. You know that, and you still find reasons to defy me, defy her."

I sat back, crossing my arms over my chest. I was itching to tell him that he sounded like an Elite, but I had had enough of his electrical outbursts.

"If you have any other viable options for us, then I'm all ears." Liyo stared.

The others did the same. Waiting for something viable to hang on to. The truth was that I didn't have any options. No plans. Nothing. My plan was to never go back in the first place, but there I was. Avi wasn't an option because there was no way to get to her without tipping off Citadel cronies.

The same worker with the dirty face ogled me. I glared back. He didn't even try to hide his disdain for me.

"How can you trust these people won't rat us out?" I didn't break eye contact with him as I spoke to Liyo.

"I trust this network."

"This network is full of criminals wanted by the region. There's a huge bounty on our heads, and they'd do anything to be free. Trust me, I'd know."

Elu cleared her throat. "Saige is right. I think we should start heading to this Mama Seeya as soon as possible. We should keep moving."

Liyo bowed his head. "Then we leave at nightfall."

Chapter Ten
AVI

Mama Seeya conveyed to me what I needed to do. The task was not an easy one. The stakes were high, and the chances at succeeding were low. But I needed to get to Saige and Liyo. I needed to show Mama Seeya that I was an asset and not a liability. The only way to show my allegiance to the rebels was to do exactly what she'd requested.

I returned to the Citadel as if it were just another day. As if I hadn't just survived an attack on the Farmlands. As if I hadn't just manned an entire hovercraft through flying watchmen hives. As if I hadn't been spared by Mama Seeya herself.

The Citadel was quieter than it had ever been since Jade had all the workers removed and replaced with droids. She had really done it. Adhered to Father's forthcoming aspirations. I wondered if he would've been proud of her feats by any means necessary and scolded me for what I was about to partake in. Who was I mocking? I knew Father would've never wanted us to fight one another. I also knew that Father wanted to extinguish the Lower Residents too. In my mind, I had tried to believe that Father hadn't hated them. He'd just wanted to fulfill what the Union of the past had wanted for the future. He'd been caught in groupthink and archaic traditions like the rest, but I still couldn't let go of the slight optimism that had he been alive, if I had shown him another viable option to live among the Lower Residents, he'd have listened.

That was the plan before he'd perished. Now, things were much more complicated.

Jade wasn't salvageable. Father had retained part of his humanity. Jade's was completely void. I had lied to myself that she could be reasoned with. That if I used baby-sister mitts on her, allowed her aggression to sort itself out, then over time she'd become logical. How idiotic on my behalf that I ever thought she could adjust. She'd tried to have me banished once, and I'd almost died, and now she was onto larger schemes.

We came from the same womb yet experienced the world from opposite ends. *Bound by blood,* Father would always remind us during tiffs. I snorted to myself at that one. Blood meant absolutely nothing. We bound ourselves to people who were worthy of that connection. It was that simple.

Jade was not of my blood anymore.

Father was the last piece holding us together, and now that he was gone, I was alone.

I no longer fit in with my own and hadn't fit in with the Lower Residents either. That's what Saige must've experienced. That kind of isolation was the norm for her. At least I was fortunate enough to have known what it was like to belong. She had never had the opportunity.

The life she was dealt was not of her own doing. The system we'd created automatically allocated it to her. No Impure or Lower Resident deserved that.

It had to break.

Jade perceived Lower Residents as parasites that needed to be exterminated. Perhaps it was us who needed to be removed from the equation.

Images of watchmen trying to eliminate me earlier kept replaying. Their own. If Mama Seeya hadn't intervened, I'd be long gone. I was the last fragment impeding their means to a purified region, and they were willing to eradicate me to further their objectives. Father would have never approved. Stooping so low as to harming his own kin.

I was done with their politics. Jade had to be removed for the region to flourish. And as for Head Gardner, her positioning could only go so far. She would never be General. I was the heir. That held power that she'd never wield.

If I didn't go through with the deposition, Jade would destroy the entire Union. At what level would the tyranny reach its peak? Would she begin blood testing the remaining Upper Residents to see who had the most melanin-rich lineage? Would she begin to color caste—darkest being top tier?

Individuals like Jade couldn't be trusted with influence. She'd only been elected for a short period, and she'd already painted the grounds red. She had to be stopped.

❖ ❖ ❖

Mother rested in a heap of Father's bodysuits and armor on the deck in their grand closet. She'd torn apart the once-tidy area and had probably collapsed right where she lay. A droid casually sorted through the items on the outer edges of her frame and began placing them back on their respective mannequins.

Mother was sprawled halfway on her side, clutching one of his jackets underneath her chin.

I had to see her one last time, but I wasn't expecting it to be in that form.

I got to my knees and rolled her limp body onto my lap. She was too weak to protest the movement. I'd never seen her so disheveled.

Mother was the epitome of affluence, composure. Now, she appeared to be a shell of her past self.

Her usually slicked-back hair was tousled. The bejeweled signature brooch that was passed down to all the firstborn women, which she wore clipped in her high bun, was crooked.

"Here." I tried my best to center it.

Fixing her reminded me of when I was younger and she was always stuffing me into uncomfortable ensembles for the holocams and motioning for me to smile with more teeth instead of gums. I hadn't ever thought I'd miss that version of her.

My arm brushed against her eyelashes, and she blinked intermittently until her eyes just closed completely. I noticed that her nose was inflamed and her lips cracked. Had she eaten since the bereavement ceremony? Jade was so caught up in her tyranny that she had forgotten about Mother. Why hadn't she checked on her?

Why hadn't I?

"Water," I commanded the droid.

When it had fetched it, I brought the spout to Mother's lips, but she turned her face away in revulsion.

"Mother," I cried. "Please. Drink."

She looked away—so very far away from where we were in the Citadel. Perhaps she had transported herself to wherever Father was. Perhaps we were wrong about the higher powers; perhaps we roamed about after death. Perhaps there was something more than the theories we could prove.

I rocked her. My tears dropped onto her chest and absorbed into the material. I wanted to confess what I had done, what I had planned to do. I wanted her to console me, tell me that I was making the right decision.

But I knew that she couldn't give me what I needed. That she couldn't give herself what she needed. She was heartbroken, grieving, and deteriorating in front of me.

I planted a long kiss on her lips. I looked into her swollen eyes once more, then softly laid her head back into Father's wardrobe pile. I sat there watching her stare into nothingness until the droid stepped in front of me. Its eyes turned blank, and its body stiffened. Only the mouth moved. Jade.

"Sister." Her voice was laced with superiority. "Please report to the study."

What did she want? I hadn't concocted a plan yet to get in her presence, but this was my chance. It was time to set the plan in motion. I looked down on her once more. "Salutations, Mother."

❖ ❖ ❖

Watchmen guarded the outside of the study. My hand hovered over my weapon just in case. When I appeared, they gave me a once-over and stepped aside. I was still cautious of a sneak attack. I thought it was a possible guise. Perhaps they were onto me. They'd known about the meeting with the rebels. I remained on defense.

The Administrator had an extinct lion's head draped over her shoulder, and Blair, with a look of loathing, stared me down as everyone else ceased their chattering. I approached the table. The same table where Father had carried out tactical meetings. The cabinet was filled with a few different faces, with the former members who'd betrayed me mixed in. Jade positioned herself at the head, in Father's chair, with her fingers interlaced and her feet propped up.

"You look like you've made death your confidant." She swung her legs back to the ground and then leaned in. "You can stand down, Legionnaire." She motioned to my hand on the hilt of the laser gun on my hip.

"Legionnaire?" My finger twitched.

"Hmm, do you like it?"

I scanned the rest of the faces to get insight on what new amusements Jade partook in.

A group of official-looking Impures strolled in without notice from any of the cabinet members and positioned themselves behind Jade's chair.

"These are my little insurances." She noticed the curiosity. "What Father was cooking up in the labs. Demonstrate."

One of the Impures pointed two of her fingers at me, then slipped my laser gun from its holster. It hovered for a bit; then she laid it carefully in front of her leader.

Jade rolled her wrist and waved to the seat next her. "Sit."

It was the only vacant place.

There was surely a detonator embedded in the cushion, leading to an explosive, but if she were to do that, the blast would injure her as well. I slowly made my way to the spot so as to go over all the ways she could slay me. Poison prick? Blue flame like Father?

I pulled out the seat and hesitated. She patted the center. It didn't detonate. I rested on the edge, sitting up square. Ready, prepared.

"While we wait for the brief, I just wanted to notify the members that I'm letting bygones be bygones." She confessed, "I haven't always done the right thing. I'm human like the rest. Imperfect. But I only want what's best for the Union. And I think—no, I *know* that Father wouldn't want us quarreling. He'd want us to do this . . . together."

She was filled with so much dung. I wondered how it was possible to even contain it from gushing from her orifices.

"I've created a new role for you, sister." She was so proud of herself. "Lieutenant Legionnaire. Your duties will be making sure new laws are being abided by as per the new regulations. You'll work directly beside me."

I loathed her like never before. I hadn't even thought it was possible. She had the audacity to rip away my title, then keep me as a lap companion.

I mustered up the most earnest expression that I could. Like Mother had said, smile with your teeth, not your gums. I thought about all the good things. Liyo's kiss. Marco Grant concerts. Decadent chocolates. I had learned from Jade that in order to succeed, you had to outperform the rest. And in my case, many lives depended on it, including mine. I thought about all the horrific moments too. Seeing her take Pea's arm. Losing Saige. Father's death. Tears rolled on cue.

Jade tried hard to hide her bewilderment. "There, there." She patted my shoulder like a droid.

"I-I'm just so honored to have a position beside you, my sister." I sniffled through a sob. "The great General Jade Jore."

She couldn't hide the disdain. Her face held no expression as she tried to figure out the move I played. At that moment, I took great pleasure in knowing that she didn't have an inkling.

"Then it's settled." She cracked her gloved fingers. She always had done that when we were playing a game that she was possibly losing.

Her wristcom chimed.

"Head Gardner has arrived." She glanced at it and then addressed the rest of the meeting. "Are there any other trepidations or queries that I can answer? Before we commence?"

Phoenix raised his hand. Amid the sororal tension, I hadn't even taken notice of his presence.

Her eyes narrowed at the sight of him. "I don't recall assigning you a position in the cabinet."

"You didn't, General." Phoenix raised himself; his muscles flexed through his bodysuit. "But I came to offer to you my hand in matrimony."

Jade lobbed her head back. "You? Me? Matrimony?"

He contracted a little, embarrassed, but continued his proposal. "Your father knew that a robust man needed to accompany his daughter in order to lead the Union into a brighter future. He chose me before, and even in his absence, I know that he'd choose me again. General

Jore, allow me to be that partner, your equal. Together we will create a better, stronger Union."

"Now that right there"—Jade slow clapped—"took heart."

Phoenix's confidence rose to peak level. I imagined his head swelling to fit the entire space, but I knew Jade. Her kink was tearing alphas apart. It would not end well for him.

"An equal, you say?" She cocked her head sideways. "Someone with a flaccid organ between their thighs will never be an equal to me."

He puffed his chest, trying to maintain his masculinity.

"You XYs seem to think that women need you to thrive. That a woman's sole purpose in life is to please you. Submission is what you all desire. Equal? Equal! You don't want to be equals with me; you want an easy path to rise above the rest because you are a privileged, mediocre muscle who will always slink in the shadows of his father at best."

His ego had taken a blow from Jade, but he knew that he couldn't push his limits with her being the General. Watchmen would incinerate him before he even laid an extremity on the fabric of her bodysuit.

"The reason Father chose you to be with Avi is because she's weak and you're imprudent and easily swayed. He knew that you could be controlled if needed by Commander Chi if any decisions needed to be made."

"Enough!" He pounded the marble.

She flipped open a knife. "I wonder how much of an equal you'd be if you were castrated."

Head Gardner burst through the doors with a gaggle of battered watchmen.

"The fugitives are here!"

Jade's face ignited as her attention moved from Phoenix.

My stomach plummeted. The room spun and crashed against me like surf. How was I still upright? Had she found one of them? Both? Were Saige and Liyo imprisoned on the grounds, or had she already executed them on the spot and brought their corpses for show? I grasped the edge of the table to center myself. *Stay focused, Avi. You can't assume anything.*

After I tucked the anxiety away, I went over their tactics. Jade wasn't that great of a performer. She hadn't known about their arrival—dead or alive. Head Gardner was more complex; perhaps it was all a guise. Perhaps she knew I was going to be present and wanted to see how I'd react to the news. Her men were injured, though, and so was she. Someone had given them a worthy fight.

"Tell me where they are, and I'll have the Union's entire fleet rain down on them in a glint of an eye." Jade was hungry.

Head Gardner limped forward. She gazed over me and sneered at the sight.

"We can't send an entire fleet." She unlatched a laser gun and smashed it on the counter. "This has to be kept under the radar."

"Is there a reason why we wouldn't put the entire Union on high alert since they are considered dangerous fugitives?" I inquired.

Head Gardner remained silent until Jade spoke. "She makes a valid point. We don't know who's in their network. We need many eyes and ears on the ground level. Someone will spot them. Bring them to us for a corpulent reward."

"Why is this traitor here?" Head Gardner shuffled her weight from her injured leg to the other.

Jade bore a look of displeasure.

Head Gardner bowed in deference. "Pardon, General Jore?"

"I need you all to get used to my status here. I won't be so lenient if mistakes reoccur." Jade's tone was stern. "Anyway, she's the new Lieutenant Legionnaire. And she's asked you a question that we'd all like to hear the response to."

"I think that conversation is better had among a select few." Her eyes cut to me.

Jade dipped her head. "I see. Well, tell us the plan, then."

"I was tipped off by one of my informants that they are now underground at a fugitive hiding post. We need to send in a tactical team to snuff them out."

Someone from their network had betrayed them. I wondered what they'd gotten in return. Freedom? Wealth? Nothing was worth betraying the cause.

"Are you sure it was even the fugitives?" I pried further. "I mean, you've failed many times before in apprehending them—how is this time any different from the numerous other 'tips' you've received?"

She shook with each word. "I know what I saw."

"Ah, can you tell the cabinet where you spotted them, exactly?" I had to plant doubt. "They couldn't have been underground this entire time; the Union was thoroughly searched."

"Why are you now so interested? Afraid your little honk boy and pet mutt are in danger?"

She was correct. I was more afraid at that moment than I'd ever been, but I wasn't going to jeopardize their livelihoods.

"Head Gardner, I only want what's best for the Union. Father's murder showed me what's most important." I motioned to Jade. "We've decided to start anew, and I'm committed to bringing these rebels to justice just like you."

"Justice, huh?"

I nodded solemnly.

"The justice I'll serve to those scum is a gradual and unhurried death."

Everyone stared in my peripheral vision, waiting for me to break, confess that I was a fraud. Head Gardner's threats were real, imminent, but we still had a fighting chance if I played along.

"Then so be it. They will be an example to the others. Long live the Union of Civilization." I shot my fist in the air with a salute.

"Brava, sister." Jade slapped me on the back. "We will take their severed heads and lift them high above ours in a celebratory parade together."

Blair finally spoke after absorbing everything. "I'll enlist only the best watchmen for the tour."

"Instructor Skylar should be reinstated," I said to Blair. "He's been with Father on many of the tours. He *is* one of the best."

Blair looked at me as if I had just spoken a dialect that was far too advanced. "He's been demoted."

"Yes, but not stripped of his duty as a watchman."

Blair offered me a smug laugh. "Well, he's been relieved from all duties until further notice."

I had no clue that he'd been fully terminated by Jade.

"There's simply something I don't trust about him," Jade offered.

"Well, it's set, suit up, people. We leave at the top of the hour. My first official meeting as the General is adjourned."

Members gathered their readers and shuffled from the chambers to prepare for what was next.

I watched Head Gardner as she struggled to gather her weapon. It seemed to be a lot heavier than it actually was. I wasn't sure who had shattered her, but I hoped it was Saige.

She coughed; blood stained the center of her palm.

"Internal bleeding. Broken ribs, perhaps. It appears as though whoever you fought did a number on you," I told her. "You should head to the physician's ward. It would be understandable if you sat this tour out."

"I'd have to be stiff and icy before I ever miss a chance at watching them die." She pivoted. "You think you're clever, hmm? We know exactly what you're doing."

I stepped in closer, unapologetic, to the woman who'd struck me down from a hovercycle and left me for dead. "I do hope that they are able to sew you back together, Head Gardner. I will see you at the hangar."

❖ ❖ ❖

Soon after, I was suited in full tactical gear like a real watchman. Instructor Skylar pinged me. I found somewhere quiet on the deck and answered.

His face and shoulders filled the display, and he grinned like an honored father.

"Look at you." He gave me a once-over. "Who would've thought, little Avi. I mean, I knew you had it in you. I am proud. Your father would've been too."

I scoffed, looking away; the thought of Father's absence hurt deeply. I wasn't about to go into combat with puffy eyes. "Gratitude," I spoke.

"I heard they were back." His tone switched.

I nodded. "Yes."

I sensed worry.

Behind me, Admiral Butler announced that the team was loading onto the hovercrafts.

"I haven't been completely honest with you, Avi," he started. "About who I am, my father, why I'm here still."

The clock was ticking as he searched my face.

"What is it?" I urged.

"Saige's DNA can prove that my father wasn't her biological parent, and that the Union used him as a scapegoat to hide whatever it was that he was investigating."

"How—" I began.

"All watchmen on deck," the admiral called.

"We will finish this when I return." I started sliding the helmet over my head.

"Protect Saige," he said. "She's vital to bringing this whole network down."

I had so many questions, but my time was up.

"I will," I promised and sprinted to the launchpad.

❖ ❖ ❖

The lone hovercraft landed in one of the farthest worker subdivisions. We stepped out onto the roof of a tall and foreboding edifice. I carefully walked to the edge, afraid to step on a weak spot. The rooftop had seen better days. Colorful graffiti covered the peeling paint of the adjacent buildings. *The Union Is Scum* was repeated in various ways. Overlapping one another to create a mural of animosity in calligraphy.

Thousands of workers lived in the tiny cubes. Yet from our vantage point, no lights or movement were visible through their singular circular windows. I'd forgotten how late it was. How most workers weren't allowed on the streets past their work curfews. How they had to work every day for the Union's gain and had been allotted a certain amount of rest in a twenty-four-hour period.

The hovertram that cut through the Subdivisions and into the grand cityscape hummed in the distance for the groups that labored on overnight shifts.

A modest gust hit me when I removed my helmet to catch a final breeze before we tunneled underground and into the unknown.

Admiral Jemison brushed his shoulder against mine playfully. "Your first sting," he said.

"Hmm," I noised. I picked that up from Saige. Grunting and groaning as responses instead of using appropriate words.

"I just can't believe that it's to apprehend Watchman Wil—I mean, the fugitives," he corrected himself.

"Apprehend?" I replied. "I hardly think solely apprehending them is on their objectives list."

"You're right. I think it's a kill mission." He took a deep breath in. "I mean, she was . . . decent. You know, she saved me in the Cube. She was rough, hardheaded, mean at times, but she was a damn good fighter."

I rotated my head to face him. The wind cut a little deeper with an unexpected chilliness. "You and I both know that being decent doesn't mean anything to the Union."

There was short silence between us as Jemison gathered his judgments. Finally, he said, "Between me and you, something just doesn't feel right. The Union keeping this all hush-hush and—"

"Gather round," Head Gardner bellowed from behind.

The team assembled in one regimented line opposite Jade, Head Gardner, and Physician Odom, an astrophysicist who studied subjects who moved objects, people with telekinesis. He'd given an entire report to Father during my trial last year. He deemed Liyo and anyone like him dangerous, a high-profile threat to the Union.

They equipped us with slim-bodied weaponry with ampoules attached to the bottoms of the barrels filled with a shimmery substance.

"We weren't able to figure out the basis of what genetic mutation caused the psychokinetic abilities of the male subject, but we've created this weapon to disable him with a potent sedative until we can bring him in for further examination," the physician explained.

I wanted to ask a question, but I knew that was something a concerned Avi would pose. I was supposed to play the indifferent watchman. Only present to take orders and act on the Union's impulse. I was a fighter, a body. Nothing more.

Head Gardner stepped in, illustrating the separate triggers. "One's for the laser. The other's for the sedative. Example." She pressed the trigger and struck a nearby watchman in the chest. The pellet attached itself to his armor. On impact, it became a silvery web with prongs, and then it absorbed into the military-grade material, disappearing completely.

The watchman jerked and then collapsed. His limbs continued to spasm until he just stopped, and foam ran down the side of his mouth. Physician Odom attended to him. He scanned his body with the reader and revealed the stats to curious eyes. "Still alive. A weak pulse, but he'll be fine."

Head Gardner paced along the strip of watchmen. "The fugitive Lower Resident is equipped with powers that allow him to manipulate lasers, bodies, and any other object—moving or non." She gestured over to the downed watchman. "That will be you if you hesitate to pull that trigger. Do you understand?"

"Affirmative, Head Gardner," we all said in unison.

"Good." She smirked. "Then we ride."

"Helmets on, watchmen." Jade spoke through the internal channel. "Only use the sedative bullets on the honk boy. We need him for testing. Shoot to kill any and all others."

"Roger that." Voices overlapped through the comm.

Head Gardner led the team through a creaky metal door that took us into the stairwell of the structure.

"We're on the thirtieth level," Admiral Jemison said as he checked the 3D blueprint of the building on his wristcom.

"You four take the evens, and we'll take the odds. Look for anything suspicious." Head Gardner initiated the descent through the corridors. "Eyes and ears open. Barrels up."

I'd missed my chance to join Jade's search squad, and I couldn't object without seeming distrustful. But what if they discovered Saige and Liyo first? It would be hard to intervene when I was on an entirely different floor.

West followed behind Butler, guns drawn.

Jade rapped my helmet with her knuckle. "Wake up, Princess. Your crew is leaving."

"Right, copy." I spun around and hiked to catch up.

The equipment around my neck was becoming much more restrictive than before. I sweated in regions of my body that I hadn't even known could perspire. My mouth was so dry that the tonsils kept getting stuck to the back of my throat. I was delving into the stakeout blind and without reinforcement. I just had to retain hope that I'd find them before Head Gardner and the others did, but even then, how would I be able to keep Jemison, West, and Zuri from shooting to kill?

We dove deeper into the levels.

"You two clear the north wing, and we'll check the south," Watchman West ordered Zuri and me.

The hall was long and dark, with only a singular light fixture flicking in and out. Zuri led, nimble on his feet. He took a pause in front of a door and placed his helmet against the paneling, listening for resonances. I copied his movements.

He came across a utility room and raised his fist, signaling for me to halt. He spoke evenly through the comm. "I think I heard something. Let's check it out."

I nodded once.

I took the left, and he took the right. The space was large with lots of gritty recesses to hide in. Thick pipes lined the ramparts as steam rose from some and others clanked every so often. A generator was situated in the center, supplying the building with power.

"I think I found your noise," I said. "These pipes are antiquated."

"No." He held his hand up. "I know what I heard. It sounded like voices. Keep looking."

I lowered my weapon. Zuri's paranoia caused all types of imaginary sounds in his head. To appease him, I casually checked behind the boilers. I stepped on a lump. It squeaked. I knelt to pick it up. A toy. Just ahead in the shadows, a dirty foot slipped out from behind a cylinder.

I approached the subject with my hand in front of me, holding the ball steady. I discovered not one but two preadolescent girls with straight dark hair, neither over the age of eight, huddled in a crevice. They looked like miniature versions of Pea. Tears made clean streaks on their soiled faces. They must've been using the area as a game room while everyone else slumbered. Both girls were missing shoes.

As I reached in to return their misplaced toy, they trembled in my presence as if I'd brought along a frigid cold. I tapped my helmet to raise the shield.

"Find anything on your end?" Zuri called out.

I put my finger to my lips. The girls comprehended.

"No luck. All clear in this quadrant," I replied.

One of them snatched the ball from my palm, and together they dashed away.

"Hey!" I heard Zuri scrambling through the comm. Then his weapon discharged multiple times. "Stop right there."

I sprinted toward the exit. "What's happening?"

"Two. Subjects." He breathed hard in between each word. "On foot. Heading northeast."

"Coming in. Over," West said.

I caught Zuri at the end of the hall as he kicked in a cube's door. My arms pumped hard as I tore down the path to get to the girls before he could.

"On the ground with your hands up!" Zuri shouted.

When I arrived, the room was dark; only the moon's rays caused a band of light to illuminate the area. Zuri wielded his gun in their faces, his finger too snug on the trigger. They scrambled backward, running into the base of a slumberpod. Inside the cylinder was an alabaster-colored worker resting peacefully with three more hours of inactivity remaining on her timer. I wondered if one of the girls was her offspring. How she'd wake up at dusk to two lifeless bodies.

"Zuri, stand down! They are children!"

"I don't take orders from you." He poked the gun farther at them like he was hunting. "The orders were shoot to kill any targets."

"We are here to bring in the fugitives. Not kill the innocent," I explained.

He tapped on his helmet to retract the screen so I could see his face. "There are no innocents in combat."

From the hall, a male worker appeared in between the entrance with a toy similar to the ball the girls had had. The outer rims of his eyes were pink, distended. His gums rotted. "For the Brotherhood." As he squeezed the detonator, Zuri filled his body with holes. The blood-covered ball blinked rapidly as it rolled across the space, then detonated.

The center of the floor collapsed, swallowing everything in the cube with it. I was able to latch onto something jagged after falling through one or two levels. I tried to hoist myself up, but fragments from the ground above knocked me off. I dropped hard on my back, watching from the bottom as the rubble showered me.

I rolled out of the way as chunks of material smashed into the heap. Uneven lumber planks piled on top of me.

When the wave of wreckage ceased, I began to shove timber pieces to the side. I slunk over the chaos to check for survivors. Zuri was covered neck down in rubble. His helmet was still on, but the part of his face that had been exposed to the blast was blistered. His eyes protruded from the sockets.

The girls? I dug deeper, lifting panels and heaving them away. I found the top of a head. Dark hair covered in sprinkles of residue. No movement. I brushed wood chips from her face. I stumbled back. She was deceased.

I kicked the pile, mucking up more dust in frustration.

There was a moan. A faint one. I followed the sound to the bottom of the base of the debris. It was the youngest girl. Still alive. I slid down and began digging her free. Her entire face, hair, and bodysuit were covered in gray ash. I took my comm offline, then cleaned her eyes with my sleeve as best as I could.

"You've got to get out of here." I sat her up.

She kept collapsing, her lids flickering.

"Hey, hey, what's your name?"

Her light-brown eyes focused a bit more. "Daylia."

"What a beautiful name," I said. "Does it have a meaning?"

Daylia shook her head. "Ma said it was short. Short for daylight."

I carried her to a nearby spot that was off to the side and hidden. "Listen to me, my people will come soon. You need to get somewhere safe."

When I tried to leave, she grabbed my finger. "I have no one. My pa. He's the one who—up there." She pointed. Her father had been willing to sacrifice himself, his daughter to take out a few watchmen. Desperation could make a parent do the unthinkable.

"I know a girl named Saige who watched her mother die too. She was probably around your age. She was hurt and lost for a very long time. But she had to survive. Like you. She had to survive for the others who hadn't. She became a strong woman and a warrior. She's given me the strength too. When I feel like I'm alone and I can't go on, I think about her story, and now I'm giving it to you."

I placed my hand on her shoulder, and her chin dipped to her chest.

I heard the team approach from above. I returned to the mound as if nothing had occurred.

Jade, Head Gardner, and the rest of both teams surrounded the gaping hole.

"Would you look at this." Jade removed her helmet. "She found the Underground compound."

I glanced around. She was correct. It was no ordinary basement but a labyrinth with channels spread about like a centipede's appendages.

Each watchman leaped through the jagged cavity, landing on the dune of rubble. Guns drawn. Jemison referenced the chart again. "This isn't on the blueprint."

"Amazing." Jade twirled, soaking in the mysteries of the cavern. "They live and thrive just like vermin do. This is the true landscape of the Europes. Fascinating yet vile."

I sensed Head Gardner's impatience. "The targets have heard the blast; we don't have the element of surprise anymore. Let's move now before they escape again."

"Everyone into camouflage mode." Jemison's suit had transformed into a matte black color to blend in with the obscure environment.

The inside of the helmet's light source even went dim. We were able to view one another through thermal imaging.

The cavities were extensive. Leading in a multitude of routes. One could get lost and never find their way out. Some paths were tight, fitting only a body in each direction, while others were wide and supported by decaying columns covered in layers of muck. The ceilings were low and concealed by thorny hanging stalactites. A claustrophobe's nightmare.

"Whoever utilizes these tunnels knows the layout better than any of us," I expressed to the group. "And bunched together like this, we are walking targets."

"She's right." Butler formatted a zoomcam. It noiselessly went airborne to cover more ground. "We should split up."

"I'll go with you, General," I offered to Jade.

"You might put a laser in the back of my skull while I'm not looking," she said. "Physician Odom, accompany them, since they are down one man."

"Affirmative, General." The physician stood by.

Before I could contest, Head Gardner's team stalked through the cavities. Leaving me behind once more. Jemison led us in the opposite direction. I had no choice but to follow.

From the rear, Jemison's, Physician Odom's, and West's physiques blazed with red, yellow, purple, and blue hues. Over the comm, all that could be heard was heavy breathing and my own parched gulps. There were too many variables unknown in the sting. If the rebels had provisional explosives, then who knew what other sorts of weaponry they had access to. We weren't at the top of the food chain there. We were idling in their domain.

"How do we know that tip was accurate?" I posed to the group.

The team stopped abruptly without answering.

"This could be a ruse," I continued.

The airways remained silent.

Jemison finally chimed in. "I agree. It could be a plot to lure the General here. We should request backup."

"When did disposable bodies start questioning high-ranking command?" Head Gardner's words were spiked with aversion. "If you two don't shut your traps and obey orders, I'll have you both exiled. Do you understand?"

"Affirmative. Won't happen again, Head Gardner." He looked back and signaled forward. "Let's move."

The zoomcam circled above our heads, scanning the area for movement.

"We got a reading about two hundred and fifty meters this way." Odom pointed toward a splinter of an opening.

The grainy wall scraped at my gear as we crawled through the fissure. I was being consumed by the tight space the farther we trekked into its depths. As the distance between me and them widened, I started to hyperventilate. I became motionless and laid the side of my helmet on my knuckles. My airways began to constrict. I believed that I was going to die there. I choked on nothing. Underneath the earth. I was suffocating.

Someone tapped on my face shield. I must've fallen asleep, or perhaps I was dead. Asphyxiated by my own tongue.

The knocking continued until I finally raised my face. In front of me, Saige was propped on her belly right in the crevice. Her multicolored hair was in a wild and tangled bush, and her eyes were bright. I shot her a toothy smile from underneath the helmet.

"I didn't take you as a nap-on-the-job kinda princess." She smirked.

"H-how do you know it's me?" I inquired.

She whacked the top of the shield again. "I think a real watchman would've tried to apprehend me by now. You know, 'all hail the mighty Union.' Crap like that." She stuck out her tongue and faked a gag.

I chuckled. I missed her humor. "I-I thought I'd never see you again."

"Don't start with the sentimental stuff." She rolled her eyes. "We don't have a lot of time."

I sniffled. She was right: we would have to make time for a proper reunion later. I had to get her and the others away from Jade. "Come with me; we've got to get you somewhere safe."

She started to back away.

"Saige." I clawed at her hand, but she was already out of reach. I began crawling forward to catch up. "Stop. Where are you going?"

She looked at me with sadness in her eyes as she slithered from the opening.

"Come back here," I cried.

Before she went fully absent, she snapped her fingers. "Wake up!"

Trembling, I gasped back into consciousness and heard shots being fired and people yelling over each other in my ear. The tunnel was empty ahead. The exit wasn't too far away, but from my vantage point, lasers flew, crisscrossing over one another.

I wiggled my body centimeter by centimeter until I made it to the jaw of the opening. I looped the weapon's strap around my chest and flew out on defense. I pointed the gun left and then right, and then leaped behind a dilapidated stairwell for concealment.

The shots had ceased. I'd missed all the action. I took inventory of the area. The zoomcam smoked in a heap on the ground, clearly shot from its airspace. There was a pile of dead rebels and a trail of fresh blood leading into another passageway.

Where had everyone gone?

I followed the trail until I stumbled upon Odom, slumped over, dead. Multiple wounds to his body armor and head.

The comms were too quiet. Had everyone been captured? Killed? Was I the sole survivor? Would I be able to convince the rebels not to kill me while I was dressed up like one of the enemies? Until I knew for sure, my finger slept on the trigger.

A light emitted onto the path from an opening a few meters away. The nozzle entered the area first, and then the rest of me followed. It was some sort of provisional examination room. There were soiled towels and a bloody scalpel and gauge in a metal dish on a cart. On top of the counter was a single strand of hair. I examined it in the light. A loose coil.

Saige was there.

"Avi?" Jemison's voice caused me to jump.

"Copy," I replied.

"Where are you?"

"I'm in some sort of examination room."

"You need to rejoin the group." He huffed. "It isn't safe."

"Roger that." I lied, "I'm on my way."

I had to locate Saige first.

I marched on spry feet along the corridor, checking for any signs of Saige. Liyo. I came across another part that facilitated as a connector room to a span of other routes. In the middle, I spun in circles, trying to figure out which route would lead me to them, but there were too many to choose from. It would take me hours to fully explore the cavities. If they found them before I did, it would all be for nothing.

My hesitation on making the wrong decision wasted time that I didn't have. So, I chose a hollow route to the left, in the middle of two other similar-looking ones.

Before I even made it past the threshold, I heard a gun load, and then a slug whizzed past my helmet, missing my head by a fraction of a centimeter and ricocheting from the uneven stone wall, causing a spark.

Jemison asked, "Are you okay, Avi?"

Instinctively, I tossed my body to the side as a barrage of ammunition trailed the first one. I slunk behind a rusted tractor wheel. Bullets pinged off the old metal as I shrank my body to fit the circular armor. By the trajectory and amount of ammo, I calculated three, possibly four shooters. I got to my knees and slowly raised my head to view the position of the rebels, but each time they unloaded in my direction, causing me to hunker down farther.

I crept downward, lying flat with my weapon clutched to my chest. "I need backup," I said to anyone.

There were more echoes of shots pinging through the comm. "We're a little tied up right now," West yelled.

The comm went static.

"Fuck!" I screamed.

My gun flew upward at the sound of a single whistle.

In the grayness was a small muddy foot poking out from an opening.

Daylia.

Her head emerged, revealing only her forehead and eyes to indicate that it was her, and she beckoned for me to follow.

I had to jump into the shooters' path in order to get across. I stroked over my armor, and in one of the bulges was a smokeshell. I clicked it to activate mode and tossed it over the wheel. I wasn't sure of the locations of the gunmen, but it was my only hope at a distraction. Once the area was semifilled with a thick smog, I took the risk. Bullets rang, sailing; one swiped me before I made it to the other side. Daylia pulled me the rest of the way in. I'd been hit in the abdomen, but luckily, it was only a flesh wound.

Daylia began running at full speed. I chased after her.

We wound along the corridors and past connector rooms and up and down flights of misshapen steps. Where was she taking me?

She stopped abruptly, pointed to an opening, and then dashed off.

Above, Jade and Saige orbited one another.

Chapter Eleven
SAIGE

Jade and her cronies had discovered us right before we made it out of the musty underground hole. Then all hell broke loose. We were separated. Foot chases commenced, knife-to-knife combat was in motion, and slugs streamed. Fugitives against watchmen.

Jade and I ended up in an open bunker. Irregular benches sat in the middle, and shelves were stacked high on the rocky walls, filled with dusty tin cans and old silver plates. Above, broken wires hung from wide beams, and melted orange cylinders were in a lopsided stack near one of the exits.

"Do we really need these?" She placed her weapon down, slowly. "I prefer to get a little dirt under my nails."

I placed my weapon down too. She removed her helmet and tossed it to the grime-caked earth.

Her idea to fight without the spoils of technology was a deal that I could oblige.

She took off her gloves and placed them gently on a bench beside her. The General's pair. How could I ever forget them?

When I killed her, I would take them into my possession. They belonged to me anyway.

I gave Jade props. I appreciated her hunger for wanting to get her hands dirty. Respect. We could've had a good old-fashioned shootout and the quickest draw won, but for her, the kill was personal.

Avi was right about us being alike in the wrong ways. She was indeed my little sister. Cocky. Obsessed. Crazed.

She bounced on the balls of her feet and stretched her arms across her chest.

"My first Impure kill as the General." There was a twinkle in her eyes like from a first wet dream.

"You couldn't wait to share that information with me, huh?" I rolled my neck. "For fun: How'd you scam your way up the ladder?"

"Scam?" She posed the question as if it hadn't computed. "You must mistake *scam* for *strategy*."

"If it makes you feel better." I cracked my knuckles.

Her lips split into a fevered grin. "Me—my regime—will go down in history as the one who finally rid the Union of the rotten parts." She widened her stance and crouched low, her palms flat in knife-hand positions.

"Rotten?" I raised my fists. "What are we? Harvest?"

She charged, and instead of coming straight on as I had anticipated, she pushed one foot off the table, whipped back around, and came down with the other leg. I took an entire boot tip to the ear. My head snapped to the opposite side. I stumbled into a ledge, unable to recover from the blow fast enough. She snorted and tossed her head back.

The canal in my ear rang as I tried to shake off the confusion.

"Get up!" she ordered. "Is that all you've got?"

She grabbed fistfuls of my hair, yanking the strands from the follicles, pulling me forward and back into the middle. We tussled, and then she took her knee and rammed my face into it. Cartilage crunched. I tumbled, catching droplets of blood leaking from my nose.

Jade pretended there was an audience in the empty spaces and sprang around in triumph for her invisible fans.

"The north must've weakened you." She huffed; the stray hairs in her bangs flew upward.

She grabbed my leg, and I tried to kick her off. I was dragged, and my nails scraped at the dirt. Jade straddled me and put me in a headlock. Her forearm tightened around my neck. I was starting to drift. Eyes fluttering and everything. I couldn't get her off.

The sound of a whistle rang. Jade let down her guard for a split second. It's all I needed. I threw my head back, hitting her in the face, and then gave her an elbow to the jaw. She let go. I landed on my hands and knees, then leaned over to donkey kick her in the chest. She tore back.

She spat globs out and guffawed, exposing red teeth. "Fucking mutt."

I stomped down, aiming for her face, but she rolled out of the way before my foot could connect.

She staggered to her feet, and at full speed, I rammed into her like a football player, my shoulder in her diaphragm as we both went flying. I slammed her into a tabletop, and she crashed right through the rotten wood. It splintered around her as she moaned from the impact.

I grabbed her by the collar, lifting her from the fragments. She swung wildly, but none of the hits landed where she wanted them to. I lobbed her sideways. Her spine hit the edge of a table corner. She wailed. I tripped forward, wanting to go full force on her, but the adrenaline began to subside.

As she rocked back and forth in agony, I took the chance to kick her in the stomach, then kick her again in the face.

I fell to my knees and took in sips of breath. My abdomen ached something bad. Maybe the sutures had reopened, because blood soaked the area.

I staggered back to a standing position as she strained at a weak attempt of slithering away.

I stomped on her back like the roach she was to slow her down, but she just kept moving. Kept trying. I had to give it to her. She had heart.

I grabbed the back of her neck, and she spun around and struck the area that Head Gardner had pierced. She swiftly put her helmet back on, and she threw something in the air, maybe an EMP, disabling the lights.

The space went dark. I leveled my breaths. I needed to rely on my hearing. She had the upper hand of seeing in the dark. I stayed in one spot. Rotating at the slightest sound, but they seemed to be coming from everywhere, all at once.

The slice of a blade swept across my thigh. Then another paper cut on my biceps. I stumbled into something and tried moving through the web of tables and benches toward an exit, toward a shelter, but I kept bumping into things and tumbling. No matter where I went in the darkness, she slashed and slashed.

I swiped at nothing as she moved swiftly in the shade, keeping me wondering when the next cut would be fatal.

Chapter Twelve
AVI

Jade was a panther playing with its prey. I watched as she danced around Saige, cutting her as if it were a cruel game. I couldn't step in without being discovered. Jade would spot me, and my cover would be blown. I'd been instructed to not break character under any circumstance by Mama Seeya. Even though my body wanted to leap in the middle of the fight, I had to trust the plan. Trust that Saige was strong enough to hold her own against Jade.

I activated a light orb and tossed it into the center.

Chapter Thirteen
SAIGE

A sphere of light flew right at me and hovered overhead like a spirit, illuminating everything around me.

Jade came in for another knifing, but that time I saw her with an arm raised high over her head, the blade dripping with my blood. I thrust my foot forward, knocking her away. She dropped the weapon and tried to catch herself from falling. I spun her around and slammed her head repeatedly on the wall, until the shield she used shattered.

She tried to get away, but there was no escaping. Jade was going to feel every piece of the wrath that she and her family had inflicted on me and mine.

I kicked her in the back once more, and she fell face first into a protruding pile of fragmented wood.

She'd been impaled.

Her body went stiff. Her blood trickled along the stalk.

I yanked both gloves from her dead fingers.

I felt nothing. Not a hint of empathy. It was messed up, kin killing kin, but it's what she'd deserved. Plus, I knew she wouldn't have hesitated if it were me. She'd probably have done worse if our roles were reversed. Her demise was a mercy killing. Jade should count herself as lucky.

Chapter Fourteen
AVI

I removed my helmet and slid down the stone's surface until I became a heap of flesh and bulky gear. I wept like I hadn't been able to since Father's death. The entire time I'd held back the grief, the sadness. Not truly able to mourn his absence because of Jade, her antics, and the fear of what the world was to become under the wrong influence.

Why couldn't she have understood that her method wasn't just? Why couldn't she have stopped being so obstinate and allowed me to rule impartially? Why had she hated my very being so much that she'd killed Father just to prove it?

Mere feet were between us, and there my sister lay . . .

It had all happened so fast. One moment Saige and Jade were dueling, and the next . . .

I hadn't fully imagined what it would be like to have one sister kill the other, but what choice was there? It was slay or be slain. Jade's honor, her pride would've never allowed Saige to leave whole.

I'd attempted to reason with Jade, time and time again. She took those chances and spun them into more intricate plots. How were we of the same DNA but so dissimilar? I yearned to know at what point she'd become corrupt. I racked my brain trying to figure out that very moment she'd morphed. Perhaps I hadn't done enough to peel back the layers and figure out the core of her hatred. Was it ultimately my doing?

There I was again, creating justifications, transferring the blame, because deep down inside, no matter how much I loathed her, I still had tenderness for her. With certainty, Jade was never going to modify her beliefs, and neither was I. No matter how many times she'd had the opportunity to redeem herself. She'd been bent on destroying everything, and I couldn't allow her to proceed.

Saige had cleaned up the mess we'd made. Once more. She shouldn't have been the one to end Jade. In an unflawed reality, it should've been me. I'd allowed Saige to do the dirty work yet again. Add another body to her list of lives she'd been forced to take, weighing heavier on a load that she already had to transport. Saige was more woman than I could've ever been.

I waited for the feeling of sorrow to appear. I wanted to feel anger at Saige for doing what she had done, but neither ever occurred. Jade lying below caused an ease that I hadn't felt in a long time.

Saige stood over the body. I stepped into the light of the drifting orb.

She spun around, on defense when she heard the sound of my soles, but I called out anyway.

"Saige." Her name seemed to hit the air and then trail off like a breeze.

She clenched Father's gloves, and her eyes widened like an animal's caught off guard. Her multitoned hair was in uncombed braids. Near her abdomen was semisoaked with red. The only movement that came from her was a tremor.

I stepped forward farther into the light. My legs felt like they would buckle with each pace. One in front of the other felt like a hundred steps when it was really just a few. Perhaps she thought I was an apparition because she appeared more fearful than anything. Perhaps she wasn't real either. I was in a really good bad dream. I'd dreamed of her before. How was it any different? What was real and what was false in our world? The boundaries seemed to have been muddled.

I knew she was real before I grabbed her hot face with both hands and just studied the lines, the bruises on the surface. The blood and the snot and the dirt streaks told a story. She'd been through hell and back. I gazed deeply into her eyes, the orange specks as vibrant as the first day I'd laid sight on her. As vibrant as they were, they were surrounded by a deep sadness that I wanted to draw from her and carry myself.

"Princess." Her eyes watered, but a tear never fell.

She grabbed me, digging her face into my shoulder. We stood there just holding one another. Taking it all in. I'd found her. She'd found me.

Something pulled at the lower part of my bodysuit.

Daylia had scurried in.

Saige almost jumped back at the sight of her. I held my arm out as if to say she was with us.

"He needs your help." She wiped her nose with her arm.

"Liyo," Saige said.

Daylia had already begun running, her brown hair flapping in the gust she created from her own speed. Saige was right behind her, and I grabbed the helmet and trailed at the rear.

❖ ❖ ❖

The little girl pointed to a cavern and then ran off.

Watchman West wrestled with a sturdy woman with a triangular marking on her forehead.

"Elu!" Saige called out.

West pulled the trigger. The girl she called Elu pried at the web absorbing into her neck, but the sedative was already invading her system. I shot West with the same sedative. Saige caught the girl before she collapsed. She stuttered and then began to jerk.

I laid out a med pack. My fingers scrambled over all the vials, trying to find something that would counteract the poisons in her system. There were beta-blockers and an antihistamine. The last one was a high dose of epinephrin. I filled the syringe to its capacity and injected her with it.

"Let's get her on her feet," I said to Saige. "We have to go. The caverns are overrun with watchmen."

"This way." Saige led as we carried Elu in between us.

A man grunted in the distance. He sounded like he was in great pain.

"Liyo," we said in unison.

I knew his voice.

We searched for the direction of the sound. Not too far away, high on the enclosure, Jemison's arms and legs were spread like a star as Liyo had him locked in place, his palms swirling with the same energy he'd had when he showed me his abilities for the first time. Jemison's shield had been busted. His eyes bulged, and his tongue stuck out of his mouth. Liyo was choking him to death.

"Liyo?" I tapped my helmet, revealing my face.

His head snapped in my direction. The glow in his eyes subsided. Jemison fell to the ground.

Chapter Fifteen
LIYO

My body wanted to plunge. Not because of the power that I had used but because she was there, in the flesh. Her face, her smell, the way her dimples deepened when she grinned were the only thing that got me through being sick in that cave. I didn't know if I wanted to cry or scream or laugh like a madman. She was no longer a vision but something real, and I'd never let her go again. She'd be stuck with me.

I stepped forward and reached for her. I had to get them out safe. Anything else would have to wait.

Avi scooped her shoulder under Elu's arm and looked back at me as if there were a thousand words that she wanted to say.

Saige stopped all of a sudden, leaving Elu propped on Avi. "Where's Miah?" she asked me.

I could barely see her through the fumes of the gas bombs they'd used to smoke us out. "I don't know. We were separated."

"We can't just leave him," she said.

Lasers bounced off the rock. We all ducked.

"He's probably already made it out and waiting for us," I lied.

She wasn't budging like before. We were at a standstill while watchmen were headed our way.

"Elu!" a voice cried out through a fissure.

Saige perked up. "Miah?"

"Saige!" He emerged and grabbed the unconscious Elu.

Saige squeezed his shoulder. "She's going to be okay, but we've got to go. Now!"

He nodded and took the other side of Elu's limp body, alleviating Avi. We pushed forward toward the exit.

"There." Avi pointed to the small opening.

Avi squeezed through first and then pulled Elu through as I pushed. I crawled through next. Saige had poked her head and arm through, when she was suddenly sucked back. There was a tussle between Saige, Miah, and a lone watchman. They were a ball of arms and legs. I couldn't get a clear shot.

Miah managed to get on top of him.

"Saige, go!" He grunted. "I'm right behind you."

I reached my hand out. She took it and clambered through the hole.

When she was safe, I then reached out for Miah. He took my arm. I pulled. His head, then his shoulders and some of his torso made it. He suddenly grimaced, and the pull became harder. He was being tugged back. The watchman wasn't dead. Both Saige and Avi tried to yank him forward too. But he slipped from our grips and was swallowed by the hole.

"Miah!" Saige called out.

The watchman dragged him farther back.

Saige prepared to dive back in, but by that time the whole thing just imploded on itself.

Above were hovercopters and military hovercrafts scanning. They'd have the area swarmed and locked down in minutes. I scooped up Elu, who was sort of waking but still groggy. "They're coming. Let's move."

Saige wasn't moving like before.

"Hey!"

She wouldn't look at me and said simply, "We can't just leave him."

"There's no going back," I shouted. "He's gone."

Saige almost hissed at me and lunged forward.

Avi held out her hand to calm us. "It's not safe here. We won't be much help to him imprisoned or dead. We'll come back for him. Promise."

Saige thought about it for a little too long. There she was, again putting the group at risk for her own selfish needs. We all had to make sacrifices for the greater good. I had. Avi had. Plus, why was she even batting for him so hard? She barely even knew him.

"Saige, please." Avi took her hand in hers. "Let's go."

Saige snapped out of her feelings. I watched her harden again. She lifted Elu and stalked forward as if nothing had happened.

❖ ❖ ❖

Saige walked far ahead of us, holding on to Elu as if it were her life's mission. She hadn't spoken, just hiked. I wasn't sure where we were headed, but I didn't have the nerve to ask. I knew her, and I knew that she wanted to be left alone.

Avi and I kept up. Sometimes bumping into one another as we stalked over the uneven pavement of the Subdivisions. Exchanging pleasant *sorry*s whenever it happened. I wasn't sure how to start the conversation about all the things that had happened in the time we'd been apart, and neither did she. I hadn't expected our first meeting to be as awkward as it was.

Finally, Saige brought us to a hidden run-down spot. She lifted Elu onto a counter and then just left without a word.

It wasn't safe for her to be alone out there. Especially not with the Union having every watchman looking for us, but what could we do?

Avi and I stood in front of one another, listening to Elu snore softly. Finally, we said something, but we spoke at the same time and then offered apologies once more. We giggled uncomfortably to make up for it.

She smiled at me, but behind her smile was a sadness. Moments later, her eyes watered. She wiped the tears away quickly before they could fall.

I drew closer. "What's wrong?"

She frowned in the most beautiful way. "There are no words to describe how sorry I feel."

I had no words either. I could only hold her.

Her face imprinted in my chest. I kissed the top of her head.

"Jade is dead," Avi said.

I breathed a sigh of relief. I couldn't bring myself to offer condolences. Jade didn't deserve that.

She pulled back. "I know that it had to be done."

I nodded.

"The fate of the Union is now in my hands, I suppose." She took a deep breath.

I looked her deeply in the eyes. "Yeah."

I'd had something to say before that, but I couldn't remember anything at that moment. We were the only two things that existed. I became lost when I was around her.

"I was starting to forget how you looked," she whispered.

"What a travesty."

We laughed a little and then stopped. I focused on her lips, and she focused on mine.

Instead of me going in for the kiss, she did instead. Our lips touched, then wrestled hungrily. She pulled at my face, and I wrapped my arms around her waist and lifted her to the tips of her toes. We'd forgotten that we were in a dingy hideaway spot in the middle of nowhere. Our bodies moved as one as we spun around, and I set her on a table, knocking things over. Her warm hands found their way under my shirt, and she urged me forward by grabbing the small of my back. We were out of breath and out of time.

Elu began to whimper.

Everything stopped, and we rushed to her.

"Elu?" She was sweating, so I placed the back of my hand over her forehead to check her temp.

"Miah?" she groaned.

Avi and I met eyes.

"He's not here right now, but you've got to rest. Okay?"

Saige entered with a slimpack and without word, she surveyed the mess that we'd made and then plopped the bag down. From it, she brought water to Elu. It was almost as if we weren't even there.

Chapter Sixteen
SAIGE

The run-down shack smelled even funnier than before I'd left. Avi and Liyo both had wild eyes like they were coming down from a Glitter trip. Maybe they'd shagged while I was gone. Either way, I didn't care. Old me probably would've, but my mind had been on Miah.

I'd left him behind. I didn't want to. I had to. I knew he would've wanted me to get Elu to safety, but I just couldn't get over it. I couldn't stop beating myself up. Going over the ways that I could've done more. What had I missed? I should've stayed. Told the others to go. But the watchmen? They were everywhere. I couldn't . . .

There was a chance that he was still alive. If he was, they'd use him as bait instead of killing him. I knew their tactics. They'd torture him for intel on us. We didn't have a lot of time. I was going to get him back.

I poured water into Elu's mouth like she was a birdling.

Liyo spoke to my back. "It's not safe for you to just go running off."

I grunted.

"I'm serious."

"What were you going to do? Come looking for me?" I turned my neck around like an owl's.

He glanced at Avi.

"Seemed like you two found something to do while I was gone."

Avi crossed her arms over her chest and never made eye contact with Liyo again.

"Anyway, we don't have a lot of time." I emptied out the contents of the bag. Face mold and salvaged tech rolled out. "Let's get this done so I can get back and find Miah."

"Wait, what?" Liyo stepped forward.

"You didn't think I was just going to leave him, did you?" I jeered. "When I get everyone safely to the Underground, I'm going back for Miah."

"Me too." Elu sat up and stretched out her jaw. "I'm not leaving him behind."

"That's a death mission. How do the two of you plan on taking the Union? Finding him, for that matter?"

I began to piece together the old parts of the new face-tech rod. "I'll figure it out as I go."

"Avi?" He said her name, as if anything she said would make me change my mind.

"Let's discuss that milestone when we hit it." She was such a diplomat. "What's the plan now?"

"We find Mama Seeya," he said. "She'll know what to do next."

I sensed a change in Avi's demeanor when Mama Seeya was brought up. Maybe she knew something. A lot had changed since we'd been gone.

"Do you have anything you want to share with the group?" I asked her.

She put on a neutral face. "No."

"Well, if that changes, then you'll let us know." I screwed in a tiny lightbulb to match the other three. They lit bright. The rod worked. "Who's first?"

❖ ❖ ❖

Elu looked like some freak hybrid of a Europe with strange features. I probably didn't look any less freakish. I'd painted and molded our faces to appear as Lower Residents with nude bodysuits to match. I wanted to throw up. At first, Elu scowled when I came at her with a tube of white cream and the tech rod. I told her that we'd been compromised and could no longer move through the Union without a cover until we made it to Drake. She was the only one we could trust. Even Liyo was paranoid about being discovered. He cut his hair until only prickly peach fuzz was left and then added dark contacts that I'd found for good measure.

His disguise was easier than ours. With white skin, it was easier to blend.

"You want to turn me into a Colorless?" She appeared disgusted as she rebraided her hair. "Hide my nature-given skin under dye?"

"We can't leave the Subdivision with you looking like you." I squeezed the cold cream onto my fingertips. I applied it to my cheek to show her what it'd look like. "Or me looking like me. It's not permanent."

"This act is a disgrace to my people, my heritage."

"Yeah, well, your people aren't alive enough to notice, now, are they?"

She shrank into herself. I had such a way with words.

Avi placed her hand on her. "Elu, I understand. I don't know the specifics of your situation, but I'm sure it involves my people doing the unthinkable to yours. I do know what it feels like to lose people." She trailed off before she began again. "We need to keep the larger picture in mind. The Union will not stop hurting your people, hurting the citizens of the region, until we stop them. I know you're uncertain. So are we, but we have to keep moving. This mask's only temporary until we find Mama Seeya."

She nodded.

Avi moved to the side so I could work my magic.

❖ ❖ ❖

We arrived at the Underground Apex without a hitch. The faces had worked. As soon as we hit the end of the tunnel, Elu began peeling at her second skin.

It was much livelier down there than I remembered. New spots and overstocked street trolleys had popped up. More bodies filled the winding pathways. The smell of sour sweat and candy filled the air. Oddly, I felt at home. The same men who'd worked in the mines shot dice off to the side. Men in flamingo-colored headdresses and gem-studded thongs paraded past like a flock of sheep, a pimp always somewhere close behind.

Elu's eyes were filled with either wonder or fear. Maybe a mix of both.

A pair of twin boys with lean bodies and pastel eye makeup grabbed Elu's arms and began kneading her skin like tabbies.

"Fun?" one probed.

"What kind?" Elu barely resisted their advances. She was ignorant to our ways.

"Depends." The other grinned, exposing decorative crystal teeth decals. "What's your desire?"

"Find another customer." I snatched her back.

"Customer?" Elu asked.

"We'll explain later." Liyo pushed through the crowd.

"Let's keep moving," Avi said.

Electronic music and the price haggles of tricks between sex workers and customers droned in the background as my attention went to holoscreens that flickered in the square.

The Dissent

The group followed my gaze.

"This is Sheron Browning with breaking news. Just in. Chaos in Subdivision Six. Sources say that an explosion occurred underground— wait just a moment. I'm getting word that . . ." She concentrated on what was being fed to her through the earpiece. Her eyes widened with excitement. The story was juicy. "Sources are saying that the explosion came from an underground bunker—a rebel hideout."

By that time, the sound of the party had gone down as everyone sat at the edge of their seats figuring out if she was dead or not. I knew the truth already. I just had to wait for the others to catch up.

She listened intently, hanging on to every word and relaying it back to the audience in real time. "The General. General Jore has been located, and she's currently not responsive."

"Would you like to make a bet on if she's dead or alive?" A man in a tall red, white, and blue star-studded hat, perched on a makeshift pedestal, pointed his shiny cane.

People started to line up to bet on Jade's death.

He leaped from the stand, landing in the middle of the public with his arms outstretched like a showgirl. "One bid, two bid, three bid, four, come and make me an offer, and let's see what's in store. Mo' money, mo' money, mo' money, mo' moneeeeey."

A hoard rushed him, holding up crinkled old currency in their fists. "The pot's already a whoppin' and a growin'. And the folks are goin' wild."

I wasn't a gambler, but it was rare that I knew the odds of the bet.

Sheron tapped her earpiece. "Ladies and gentlemen, we have live drone footage of the scene."

Her display became smaller inside a larger screen of the scene.

"Jade." Her name barely left my lips.

There she was. Laid out on a hoverstretcher.

The holocam zoomed. Her chest rose and fell. Or at least I thought it did. Were my eyes playing tricks on me?

Avi touched me, and I almost leaped from my skin.

"I see it," I mumbled.

I'd killed her. I'd seen her impaled. Dead.

But she wasn't dead at all.

She slowly sprang from the hoverstretcher and strutted slow, cautious as if the space were a catwalk.

Sheron gasped. The people who'd lost their earnings groaned. Others rejoiced. Not because the monster was alive but because they'd just tripled their money.

"This can't be," Avi whispered.

Wrapped around Jade's head was a flimsy soiled bandage, partially covering the right side of her face.

A physician trailed her. "General, please allow us to treat you so we can create a replica prosthetic."

She raised her palm, motioning for him to halt.

"No prosthetics. I want my face to stay exactly as is." She slowly began to unwind the dressing. "I want to be reminded of why we fight. Why allowing this so-called race to exist past the deadline was a grave, grave mistake. We've gone soft. Forgotten our roots. Our purpose. This Union is shattered beyond what I'd initially presumed. The Union must rid itself of these parasites. By. Any. Means. Necessary."

Jade revealed a fleshy socket. A jagged gash ran vertically through her brow and ended at the top of her cheekbone.

A titter seeped from her lips as she stalked along the line with her hands glued to the arch of her back.

Head Gardner surged through the entrance with a look of conquest as dozens of shackled rebels trailed behind her like ducklings.

One of them was Miah.

I choked on spit as I shoved bodies out of the way to get a closer look. I clenched both fists as I watched him, beaten to a pulp, stare up into the lens that hovered over his head. He looked confused and grim.

My heart stopped beating. Stopped pumping blood. And my body was cold all over as if I'd just been drained of life.

I should've never left him behind. Why had I listened to them? For the likes of Mama Seeya? To help save a Union that had never done shit for me? Why did I have to sacrifice? Why had it all fallen on me? Why couldn't someone else take the heaviness? And left me out of it. I would never be able to get to him in time, even if I left at that very second.

There was nothing that I could do but watch what they'd do next.

The captives had busted lips and deep gashes in their cheeks, missing teeth. They limped forward as watchmen butted them in their backs with guns. A mixture of colored eyes darted in all directions as they lined up along the ridge, awaiting an inevitable execution.

Head Gardner shot a warning blast into the air, causing Miah and the others to cower.

Children stood among men and women.

"Tell me where the fugitives are headed," Head Gardner demanded. "I know they were here. A traitor among you honks told me so."

Many of them looked at her as if she'd spoken an old language.

"Answer the Head!" Butler panned the weapon in their direction.

"It's judgment day," she announced, marching along the line. "Who's first?"

A badly beaten man whose eyes were swollen shut stepped forward with his chin raised and his chest held high.

Head Gardner scoffed, unleashing a knife from its holster. "This faux heroism that you honks carry never ceases to fascinate me in some sick way."

Before I blinked, she shoved the blade into his artery. Splatters of blood gushed from his neck onto Daylia, and a high-pitched scream escaped her as the tall man plunged to his knees and then toppled over right at her feet.

Head Gardner placed her sole on his head and unstuck the blade, wiping it clean on the back of his collar. She sprang back up and wielded the knife over the others.

The man named Gabriel, the one who'd sewn me up, raised his hands in defense and then stepped out of line. "You promised safe asylum. I-I was the one who gave you the tip. I-I did it."

I knew he was a plant.

Butler chuckled when Head Gardner frowned and wiped mock tears from her face.

"Read the fine print, you snitch. In the event of the 'capture of the fugitives.'" She spun around. "Do you see the fugitives? Anybody? No, I see a bunch of dead slaves standing, but no fucking fugitives!"

They all trembled, moving backward into one another to get out of the way of Head Gardner's sight. Miah tried to hide himself in the center.

"Who's next?" she asked.

No one moved.

"Then I'll choose at—" Head Gardner stopped and dug farther into the group until she yanked out Miah.

No!

"One of these things just doesn't belong," she sang.

Jade took a step. Head Gardner yanked him forward and whispered something in Jade's ear. She gave him a smirk.

"You were with the fugitives." Head Gardner got really close. "Where are they going? Hmm?"

When he wouldn't answer, she grabbed his long hair and yanked it back until his chin nearly touched the sky. I flinched as if I felt it too. She screamed in his ear, spit flying everywhere. "Where. Are. THEY?"

I cupped my hands over my mouth and hyperventilated into my palms. *Please, just tell them what they want to know.*

If he did, then maybe they'd spare him. Keep him as a prisoner. Give me more time to think of something. He didn't have to protect me, us. Why wouldn't he just say something, give them anything? Head Gardner was losing her patience.

She looked at Jade as if to get the okay. Jade nodded so slightly that I barely caught it.

I hadn't known it was possible for my stomach to go any farther than between my knees.

Head Gardner looked into the holocam as if she knew that I was somewhere watching. I didn't even see the blade go in. Miah's mouth turned into a tight O shape as she jammed it in farther and twisted. He grunted. Before she shoved him back into the rebels, she said something to him.

"Miah!" I bellowed at the screen.

He lay on his side in a fetal position. Clutching the wound. With each gasp, more blood pumping onto the concrete.

Tears welled. And I began to pray. I wasn't sure who to, but I knew what for. I just kept saying *please* over and over again with my hands cupped as I begged for a miracle. A sign. Something to intervene. The Union hated religion. They believed in things they could prove. Science. They taught free will. Cause and effect. And that nothing would save or destroy us but the Union. They were the almighty and the keepers of the planet and all the galaxies. Absolutely nothing happened after your borrowed meat vessel returned to the earth. You were nothingness as the universe just recycled you.

Miah took his last breath as I took mine. His dark eyes remained open. Head Gardner nudged him with her boot.

There was no more trying. Like she said, she won. And I lost.

Miah didn't deserve it. He had nothing to do with any of it.

I wasn't sure what I believed anymore, but I knew that I no longer wanted to be around to struggle, watch over my shoulder for Head Gardner. How many more had to die before I got the point? That hope was fake.

"Slaughter them all," she ordered, turning her back.

Cries and pleas overlapped as watchmen began to advance to carry out a massacre.

Someone touched my shoulder, and I almost attacked before I noticed that it was Avi.

"Where's Elu?" Liyo asked.

I checked behind me. She was gone. I darted into the crowd. We all split up.

Mowing through packed groups, I grabbed random people, checking each face, and then tossed them back when they turned out not to be her.

"Elu!" My voice wasn't loud enough to carry over the music of the streets. I couldn't even hear myself think anymore. I spun in confusion. Where the hell was she? Had she seen Miah get killed and run? Taken? Kidnapping for ransom was a big thing down there.

The twins. They'd been so interested in her before. Maybe they knew something. I knew the location of where they stayed. I darted through a group of prostitutes, turned the corner, and jogged along a narrow passageway.

A lookout guarded their doorway. When I tried to get through, his chunky palm shoved me in the chest. "They have a customer. Screw off," he spat.

I let the shove pass even though I wanted to break his fingers.

Not yet, I told myself. "Did you see a girl come through here? She's mine."

He looked me up and down so nastily that it reminded me of the days I used to dance for old currency. "She ain't yours no more." He flexed his chest muscles through a mesh top.

He thought I was joke.

I laughed because it was funny to me, how he thought because of his size that I couldn't play. He became angry, swung first. I ducked. He came forward. I jammed my knee into his nuts. He doubled over and dropped like a bag of bricks. I stomped on the hand he'd touched me with. A whimper escaped his mouth.

I stepped over the hulk of a man and began checking the rooms. In one of them was the back of Elu's head. As I got closer, I saw that her body was tied down. The twins faced her; their eyes swirled as they both played in her unraveled fishtail braids.

I grabbed a decorative wooden mallet from the wall.

"That customer is—"

I hit him in the face before he could finish.

The other twin screamed as I tied his hands together and tossed him into a pile of decorative pillows.

They had her fixed to a contraption, suspended by her arms. She was gagged with a black ball attached to leather straps. I dropped the weapon and unbuckled the mouth binding first.

"Miah," she said as I tried not to look her in the eyes and focus on setting her wrists free. "He was captured with the others . . ."

I felt my eyes begin to burn again.

"Saige!" Her voice shook me.

As I got her last limb free, I said, "He's gone. Okay?"

She waited for me to say something else, but I was out of words, out of faith. Welcome to the Union.

Elu massaged her wrists and made her way over to the boy. "Your age?"

Strung out, the twin answered, "Fourteen."

"Fourteen," she repeated to herself. "They sell their bodies for currency. Illegal substances."

I grunted.

"What *is* this place exactly?" She looked around.

"Come on, let's find the others."

We passed back over the guard still reeling in agony and back onto the main street.

167

She stopped walking. "What were they going to do to me if you hadn't come?"

I sighed and kneaded the stress that had already formed in my neck.

"It's fucked down here. Okay?" I explained, "This is the lot of exploitation. People. Kids. Doesn't matter. The funny thing is that we come down here to get less exploited from the monsters above. Get it now?"

Elu leaned in. "You said *we*, so you also experienced the misuse here?"

I curtsied. "Welcome to my childhood home."

Her gaze lowered. "I'm so sorry."

"Don't be," I said.

She began to cry. I knew the tears were for Miah.

❖   ❖   ❖

Together Liyo, Avi, Elu, and I stopped in the front of the Vixen. I reveled in the memories I'd made at that shoddy strip joint as a juvenile. I was so young when I'd first stepped foot on that stage. It wasn't long after Ma had been executed, and the compound that Liyo and I hid out at was discovered and bombed. He and I got separated and I almost starved to death. I started selling Glitter, hiding the vials in my cornrows to evade capture, just so I could pay off my long-standing debt to Silver. The owner/serpent. The last time we were there was when Silver had tipped off the government. I was wanted for alleged offing of an Elite, and he'd told them exactly where I was for a reward. And after that, life had taken a very violent turn.

Now here we were. A blast from the not-so-far past.

Being here again was full circle. And bittersweet. I was entering not as the property of Silver but as a free-ish being.

"Ready?" Liyo dipped his chin.

"Hmm." I nudged the revolving door forward.

Silver was the first face I saw. His shiny gold teeth appeared when he noticed fresh customers coming to spend mullah, as he called it.

I hadn't had a plan for what I was going to do if I ever saw his stupid face again, but my fists reacted before I could catch them.

They offered him a two-piece special. One to the eye and the other to the jaw. He flew into the dingy velvet pulpit.

Tony B. rushed to the disturbance, but Elu stepped in front, wielding a blade, ready to slice and dice if necessary. The girl was definitely growing on me.

"Who are ya?" Silver cupped his busted eye.

I lingered over him and peeled some of the mask from my cheek and flung it at him.

"Remember me? Your top girl. The one you pimped out at twelve." I put a knife to his nose, ready to rearrange features permanently. "The one you ratted out to the Union the last time I was here."

There was nowhere for him to turn. To hide. His eyes pinged back and forth like laserballs as he tried to mix up more of a story to save his sorry ass.

"I, uh, Lioness. Yeah, yeah, I rememba' tha name very, very well." He swallowed too hard. "Whet a nice su'prize to see ya in da flesh. Alive. Thrivin'. Looks like. Very, very well."

"What did they give you?" I probed, sticking the tip up his nostril.

By that time, dancers, customers, and even the bartender had pooled around the spectacle. Waiting to see what happened next. The fact that no one protested showed that Silver was a trash human who was only tolerated. More of them probably rooted for me to gut him than the ones that objected.

Silver licked his already moisturized lips, trying to lubricate the lie that was about to exit his mouth. The threat of getting his nose slashed wasn't enough. I had to hit him where it'd really matter.

"If you say anything other than the truth . . ." I moved the slant of the knife along his torso and then stuck the point in the fabric over his balls. His body stiffened as I dug farther.

He raised his hand in protest. "Okay. Okay. Okay!"

"What. Did. They. Give. You?"

"Th-they offa'd me anythin' I assed fer." He explained, "They gave me Glittah. The good kind. The stuff them Uppah folks use. We cain't get that down here. And gurls. Lottsa gurls. Young ones wit good bones and nice teeths. I even opened anotha club down the way. See, I am gud. Gud for the economy down here. And you, you ain't shit! I saved ya. I shuda left ya. To die. Rememba that. Ya owe me."

"You used me for currency. I was only a child." I flooded with rage. "You didn't save me because you are good but because you saw me as a break. You're not a saint. You aren't even a man."

"Well, beggars cain't chooze," he snarled.

I stabbed him in the thigh.

The crowd gasped as I removed my knife.

When I stood, everyone scooted back in unison.

Tony B. rushed over to his weeping boss.

"If you get the urge to tip off the Union about my presence again, I'll carve you like a hen on an Upper's dining table next time." I admired the wet blade. "I don't have shit to lose this time around. Understand?"

Silver nodded quickly as he tried to keep the blood from pouring from the wound.

"Nice doing business with ya." I tried to copy his accent and reholstered the knife. "Has anyone seen Drake?"

The bartender began wiping down glasses as if it was another day in the club and gestured to the back.

We cut through the heavy curtains and headed to the private lap rooms. From along the hall emerged Drake with a customer. He slid her money and kissed her on the cheek. She wore a long sheer lilac robe with fur lining.

When she saw us, her eyes almost glowed. She held her robe together and rushed us like a child whose parent had just come home from work. She embraced Liyo and me together for a long time. She grabbed my face and kissed me on the lips tenderly, then did the same to Liyo.

"You can't kill a roach." She chuckled.

"Never." My voice cracked a little.

Drake was the only person who never changed. The only one out of that whole mess who always kept it real.

She searched the area anxiously. "Anyone see you come in?"

Liyo cut his eyes. "Everyone *saw* us come in."

"I stabbed him." I hunched my shoulders. She knew exactly who I was referring to. "But only a little."

"In here." Drake scoffed and ushered us all inside the lap room. Before she closed the door, she gave Avi a look. I wasn't sure what to make of it, but it threw me off.

"Avi," she said.

"Good to see you again, Drake." Avi spoke so formally.

Drake locked the door behind us and then closed the shutters. "Now that you've made your presence known, we don't have much time."

I watched Avi take a step back, almost as if trying to stay out of the way.

Drake finally noticed Elu and looked her up and down. "And you are?"

"Elu from the north."

"Okay." She elongated the word and then slipped the frilly top over her head, exposing her breasts. She then slipped into a bodysuit. "We've got to get to the Outskirts. For the next phase."

"Next phase?" I asked.

Drake began stuffing a slimpack with things she'd need. "We were all waiting on your return, and now it's really time."

I snatched the bag from her so she would pay attention. "Next phase as in waging war with the Union?"

"All your questions will be answered when you see Mama Seeya." She took the bag back.

"What kind of bullshit answer is that?" I said. "All I've been hearing is Mama Seeya this and Mama Seeya that. I didn't sign up to be a part of your civil war."

"*Our* civil war?" She slammed the bag on the counter. "Why do you constantly speak as if you aren't a part of us? What, are you siding with Uppers now? Did being a watchman go to your little head?"

"Drake, do *not* go there," I warned.

She entered my space. Face to face. "I'm going there because I'm sick of your bullshit. Get it the fuck together."

"I kept him alive. My part's done. So, you can go tell Mama Seeya to go fuck herself."

Liyo and Avi pulled us apart. "You two need to quit," he yelled.

"I know what this is about." She motioned to Avi. "It's about her, ain't it?"

"And what if it is?" I said. "I still wouldn't trust Mama Seeya."

She rolled up her sleeves. "Go ahead. Ask her what she wants to do."

Everyone turned to Avi except Drake. She knew something I didn't.

"I-I think we should find Mama Seeya and then figure out what the next phase is." Avi was firm in her decision. I still didn't care. She didn't know them like I did.

"It's not safe there. For an Elite." I explained, "They are used to hunting down people like you."

"It's not safe for me with my own either." She smiled uncomfortably. "I'll take my chances."

I placed my hands on my waist, waiting for Liyo to back me up.

He wouldn't even look at me.

I wouldn't stop staring until he spoke.

Finally, he added, "I think that Avi can make decisions for herself. She's gotten over a year of intel, and she could be useful for the next phase."

They were all holding on to some false hope that Mama Seeya would give us salvation. Dragging Avi into it. I'd already lost Miah. I wasn't going to watch Avi get killed too.

I made my way to the door. "And you call me a coward. You all were so adamant about bringing her into all of this, and now that she's in it . . . you have powers that you can use to help her fight Jade, and you refuse. So, I guess all that whole lovey-dovey shit was a stunt? Oh, you are so damn good, Liyo. A round of applause for the best performer in all of the goddamned south."

A current ran across his eyes. I'd hit a live wire.

"You think the five of us are supposed to walk up to the Citadel and fight an entire army of watchmen to get revenge on behalf of your dead boyfriend? Stop allowing your emotions to get in the way."

Look who was talking. If I'd really allowed my emotions to get in the way, then I would've stayed with Miah instead of choosing them. If they'd gotten in the way, then maybe I would've had the chance to be his girl instead of mourning his death.

I turned the handle. Drake stopped the door from opening with her foot.

"Move." I grabbed her wrist.

"We cannot do this without you."

"I said get out of my way." My grip became tighter.

"You and I both know that if you go anywhere near the Citadel, they will disintegrate you on arrival. A dead Saige isn't as useful as a live one."

"Avi," I said. "Let's go."

She approached me slowly, then took my hand. "Where would we go, Saige?"

Leah Vernon

As I took the time to think about an answer, I was ambushed. My teeth clamped down. It happened quick. Drake placed her hand over my nose and mouth. Something was in her palm. I struggled, but after the second inhale, my eyes got heavy.

At that moment, I couldn't trust Drake anymore. She was like the rest of them. An opportunist.

Chapter Seventeen
SAIGE

I was laid out on my side with my wrists bound behind my back by sturdy twine. Ankles too. There was a coarse mesh sack over my head, tied loosely around my neck. Wherever we were, it was sweltering. Hazy light streaks from the breaks in the transport's sides let me know that it was daytime. I was in some kind of carriage because the wheels churned beneath as I bounced around bumpy terrain.

"Halt." The voice came from the outside.

The transport abruptly stopped.

I tried rotating my wrists inside the restraints to release the grip, but instead I succumbed to the sting of rope burn. Whoever had tied them had made sure they were snug. I started to chew at the sack, thinking that I could remove it that way. Or at least see who I needed to attack. A location. Something. But gnawing at the material only caused my teeth to ache.

A thud emerged from the access flap behind me. The trunk filled with light. I was grabbed by my boots and dragged across the deck.

Fuck.

I wiggled as forcefully as I could, but it didn't cause a break in my arrest.

They brought me to a standing position and ripped the covering off. I squinted, the sun's rays blinding. Once the floating jellies in my eyes subsided, I peeked at Drake surrounded by Impures with face coverings. One had three cuts in her brow, and the other was an albino with white lashes and big lips.

"Nadia. Talon. Show 'em," Drake said.

Electricity crackled over their fingers, and their eyes vibrated. Together they made the sand in the distance whirl like a cyclone.

Where the hell was I?

Behind Drake was an outpost filled with a band of corroded chrome silos and timeworn constructions built into the rock formations. It was a city of abandoned factory clusters. The wind picked up, blowing sand and dust into my nose and mouth.

"What gives?" I kept an eye shut, shielding it from the elements.

Her people ushered a groggy Avi, Liyo, and Elu from the compartment and cut them free.

Another Impure took my fists and sawed through the restraints. Although the lower part of his face was concealed, I couldn't stop staring into his drowsy eyes, surrounded by deep wrinkles. The pupils were of alternate hues, similar to mine. Shades of light browns and specks of oranges and greens. His skin was the same caramel color, but the undertone was pink instead of yellow. He could've been an older sibling.

"I'm Wayal." He finally cut through the rope. "Welcome to Outpost X."

Liyo rubbed his wrist and took the desert all in while Elu turned her back to the sun. She wasn't used to the hot climate. She dropped to her knees and burrowed her palms in the sand and then lifted them, allowing the granules to drizzle through the cracks of her fingers.

She said to herself, "I've read about this grainy earth substance once."

Avi was quiet. Analyzing everything around us like a human computer.

"Follow me." Drake began trekking along the sandy passageway and into the center pit of the complex.

In the exterior, there were antique semitrucks, the ones that they used to transport large loads before highways became strictly airways. Tractor trailers were half-swallowed by time and the elements. Beneath a line of satellite dishes covered in film were older versions of hovercrafts that the Union had tossed and the rebels recycled. Workers wearing metal shields used blowtorches to weld titanium slabs onto the outer body. Seemed like that one was in battle recently. Probably ran into a watchmen hive.

We passed long-standing billboards as we came up on the stained silo. Everything was orange hued, and the air smelled sweet and pungent.

The gate was guarded by two meaty Impure women with laser guns plastered to their chests as if they were natural appendages. I took a wild guess at them also having abilities like Liyo. The one with the fake leg looked at Elu from the top of her head to the soles of her shoes while the one with wide shoulders and the biggest tits I'd ever seen hocked a loogie into the sand.

"Those two are Aura and Dice." Wayal waved two fingers, and both women split, retreating to the edges of the gate and allowing us entry. "If I were you, I'd stay on their good side."

The inside of the plant was a long tubular storage tower that spanned at least five hundred meters high. Although the middle was hollow, levels surrounded it, each occupied as far as I could see. A housing complex for rebels. Hundreds of metal steps led to the very top, and on the other side one could use the ladders attached to the walls to reach the top as well.

A hoverlift transported slabs of steel to workers down below. While others at the base worked on spherical-bodied hovercrafts. Misshapen earlier-version androids carried trays of tools to greasy mechanics under the hoods.

177

It reeked of oxidized metals, but it was their home.

Wayal led us to a row of shipping containers. He waved us into one, halting at the entrance. Liyo led. Avi. Then Elu. Drake. I was last. There she was. In the flesh. Mama Seeya was light skinned but could still pass as an Upper. Her Bantu knots were fresh and covered in gray stripes. One of her eyes was lower than the other.

She gasped as if someone had sucked the air from her lungs. She was never the lovey-dovey type, but her disbelief seemed genuine.

"My children have returned." She took the back of Liyo's head and brought his forehead to hers. "I have waited for this moment for a very, very long time."

"Us too." Liyo got emotional. "Eve? Where's she?"

"She is safe at another compound."

Liyo let out a breath of relief.

For some reason, the reunion didn't feel as sentimental as I'd thought it would. I'd dreamed of the day when I'd be reunited with her since I was a kid. The last time I'd seen her, I was a little waif that had nowhere else to go after Ma was executed. She became a caretaker, a second mother. She'd taught me how to fight, how to strategize and read. How to survive. I owed so much more than I was willing to give at that moment.

Circumstances had changed. I had changed. I wasn't the same orphan anymore. I was a full-fledged damaged adult.

"You two have grown."

Liyo took her hand and kissed the back of it.

She eyed me as I remained at a safe distance, sensing the strain.

"And who might you be?" She turned her focus to Elu.

"Elu." She stuck out a hand. "From the north."

Mama Seeya embraced it. "Welcome to the south, Elu."

"I wish I could say it was my pleasure . . ."

Mama Seeya became thoughtful. "You've been through some horrific things to get here. I already know, but I'm hoping to get to know you more. How we can help one another. You are a guest here. And you are safe. That I can guarantee."

Elu dipped her head.

Mama Seeya squeezed Drake's shoulder. "We offer much gratitude for making the trek and bringing them home."

Drake's shoulders rose with a pride that I'd never seen before.

"Why didn't you come for us?" I thought it was way past the time to disrupt the happy reunion. "You saw what was happening, and you stayed hidden. Like a toad in mud."

Liyo's face dropped. I waited for him to zap me from where he stood.

"Saige, you—" he started.

"Stop," Mama Seeya interjected. "Her question is a valid one."

She leaned on the counter with her arms crossed over her busty chest. She laughed to herself as she inspected the ground for nothing.

"Leading this rebellion for all of this time, I've lost so, so many." She looked sleepier all of a sudden. The memories of ghosts always took their toll. "I was created in a petri dish by the disposable-gloved hands of Union physicians."

I hadn't known where she'd come from. She'd never shared that information, and I was too young to have thought to even ask.

"My first memory was standing in line with other Impure specimens— that's what they called us, specimens—in oversize bleached bodysuits. They made us watch each child be secured to a high steel chair and injected with who knew what." She moaned. "It was all psychological reconditioning. They wanted us to know early on that we didn't matter. That we had no choice. That our bodies were the sole property of the Union.

"It happened over and over and over again. Some of us didn't make it out. Some committed suicide. Jumped right from the windows in the mess hall. Whatever high place they could find in the hospital, really. The desperation was great.

"One day, I was able to wiggle free from the restraints and slapped the needle from one of the physician's grips. It ended up piercing their skin. They began to convulse; they foamed at the mouth. I was hit in the face with the butt of a gun and tossed into solitary confinement with a few other troublemakers. They left us there for who knew how long. During that time, we trained. Shared stories of what we imagined the outside was like. Came up with an escape plan. I was twelve when I led my first rebellion.

"One of the watchmen who brought us evening nourishment always had his guard down. He hadn't expected a group of children to fight. We overtook him. Killed him, perhaps. I don't know because I didn't look back. None of us did. Only forward movement, we repeated to ourselves, because there was no turning back after that.

"We became the violent organisms that they'd created, told us we were. I don't think they expected us to ravage the place like we did. It had never happened before. So why would they think otherwise? We took his gun, then cut down another, then took theirs. Every physician that we came across, we slew. Even the so-called nicer ones. To us, they were all the same."

She paused, meeting the eyes of each person. "It was not easy for me to stand down, Saige. You are my children. When I saw you on the broadcast beaten, barely alive, I wept like I'd never wept before. I suited up, ready to bring on them a storm of all our resources to get you back, but . . ."

"But what?" I needed to know.

She chewed her top lip. "We had to put our emotions aside and put the whole first. We couldn't attack on impulse."

"Makes perfect sense." My reply was spiked in sarcasm.

"I knew that if this played out and that if you were able to survive, come back to me, then we'd truly be ready."

"Ready for what?"

She stood taller. "I've seen the Union plot and cover up and scheme for all of my life, but now I see the cracks in their foundation. It's been confirmed. You, Liyo, Avi, the rebels have shaken the berries from the highest stem of the bush."

"What are you saying?" I leaned in.

"My dear Saige, it's time to bring the storm upon them."

She wanted war.

Wayal stepped in. "This all ends after the duel takes place."

"Duel?"

"That's where Avi comes in."

It was as if no one else existed in the room.

I got in front of her. "Avi, what is she talking about?"

Before Avi could answer, Mama Seeya did. "She must return to the Citadel and challenge Jade to a duel."

"She has nothing to do with this."

"She has *everything* to do with this." She pounded her chest.

"Saige." Avi said my name softly, but it wasn't enough to stop me.

"Was that your plan for Avi all along? Use her as a scapegoat for some bigger scheme?"

"Her people would've ended her if it wasn't for me," Mama Seeya explained.

"Would you like a medal for your service?" I retorted.

"Saige!" Avi said again.

"What?"

She looked at me funny.

Mama Seeya sucked her teeth. "You always thought you knew everything, had all the answers. I would've thought that life's circumstances would've humbled you by now."

I wanted to laugh as much as I wanted to cry. She circled closely as the tension sprouted among us like overgrown weeds.

"Avi, I'm asking you to join the cause." She stepped forward. "Your people have done the unthinkable to not only us, to the north, but to

181

you. The only way we have a fighting chance is if you take back what's yours. You must challenge Jade. There's no other way."

I stared at her real hard as she calculated everything in her little big brain. Avi the thoughtful. Avi the liberator. She was always trying to save someone. Do the right thing. I admired her for it as much as I hated it. Why couldn't she just be selfish for once? She'd already done enough and done her part. It was never enough with these people. They wouldn't stop until they had it all at her expense. It all just felt . . . wrong.

"I agree." She was hyperfocused on Mama Seeya. "I agree to do whatever it takes to secure my position as the next General. I will work in tandem with the rebels to ensure that the future of the Union is an equal and just one."

I was so worked up after hearing her profess allegiance that I threw a stool into a table and raged out. I didn't have a direction, but I just needed to get out. Get away from it all. How could she do that without talking to me first? Asking what I thought or felt? She didn't know them like I did. It wasn't going to be as easy as just parading in and asking for a duel. She'd have to actually win it. Plus, who said Jade would play fair? Who'd be there for Avi? Mama Seeya? The one who hadn't even been there for her own?

"Saige?" Avi's voice echoed along the containers.

I was lost, but still, I didn't answer.

She cut through and somehow sprang in front of me.

"I thought you'd be gone by now." I faked her out and slid behind her and continued trying to figure out where the hell the exit was in the stupid maze. "Don't you have some political duel to partake in?"

"Saige, I—"

"You what?" I stopped. "What?"

"Do you think I'd be doing this if there was any other possible way?" she almost pleaded. "While you and Liyo were gone, I analyzed all the methods in which we could come together. Things changed when Jade was elected. When Father was murdered."

I stiffened at the mention of him.

She continued, "When she gained power, things shifted. I thought that I'd have the Union behind me, that custom would rule, but that's not the way it happened. Now, we are here making decisions that no one wants to make, but they have to be made. People's lives are on the line."

"What about my life? Your life?"

She looked at me odd as if she'd never thought about it. "What's my life if it is overcast with the oppression of others, of you?"

"You don't ever have to worry about me."

She chuckled. "And you don't have to worry about me."

The girl was getting under my skin. "That's not how this works."

"Then how does it work?"

"I don't need saving. I'm used to this. The fighting. The struggling." I poked my chest. "And you—you're—"

"I'm what?"

I was suddenly nervous, tongue tied. "Well, you are—"

"A feeble Elite from the Citadel who's never tasted inequity in her life. Some spoiled brat that doesn't like to chip her freshly manicured nails. A weakling who expects everyone else to put in the work while others sacrifice."

"No," I stuttered. "That's not what I meant."

She took a deep breath, trying to compose herself. "Then what is it?"

"You could die if you go back." I frowned.

"A risk I'm willing to take for the greater good."

"You never asked me how I felt about any of it."

"I don't have to."

"You can't just leave."

"I can and I will." She was stone. "You are *not* the boss of me."

"You sound like a child."

"And you, a mother."

My nostrils flared with irritation. "Then I'm going with you."

"You will stay here and carry out the plans that Mama Seeya has for you. You will not accompany me, and you will not follow me back."

"You're kidding, right?"

She offered me nothing.

My smile faded. "Avi, don't do this."

"I'm going," she said with surety.

"If you leave"—I shook—"I will never speak to you again."

I meant it, and she knew it.

But the threat wasn't enough.

She backed away a few paces, wiping the tears before they could run along her cheeks, and then she disappeared.

I pulled my arm back and then slammed my fist into whatever was nearest, busting the skin on my knuckles.

Mama Seeya had started all of it. With her crazy schemes. She'd pumped into Avi's head crazy ideas like she had with Liyo. Now, I looked like the bad guy when I only wanted to protect my sister. I sat there wondering if I had told her the truth, it would've made a difference, changed her mind.

Either way, I had to convince Mama Seeya to stop her. It was my last chance.

I returned to Mama Seeya's container. She made everyone leave.

"You are upset," she said.

No shit.

"I understand that you became rather close with Avi during your time at the Citadel."

I wondered where she'd heard that from. Drake maybe.

She bowed her head. "From my understanding, Avi has chosen to become one of us. To join the cause without prejudice and of her own free will."

I rolled my eyes. "And what exactly did you tell her to get her to become your soldier?"

The Dissent

Mama Seeya studied my face for a long time before responding. "What does it matter now?"

"It matters because she's going to get herself killed trying to carry the entire rebellion. She doesn't deserve that. No one deserves to carry it all." My voice broke through the last few words.

She laid her warm palm on my cheek. I leaned into it against my own will. "No one would choose to be a martyr, but it is duty."

She'd sent Avi into the den knowing that she'd never make it out alive. None of it was fair. Avi was so stupid, trying to be so brave. Trying to rectify her father's wrongdoings. She hadn't had a choice what family she was born into. Neither had I. We all just got dealt the cards and had to play our hand however we saw fit, but none of that lessened the ache in my chest when I thought about losing her. Again. She was annoying and hardheaded and full of heart. She was curious and nosy and overly helpful. She was selfless, and she was the only family I had left.

I removed Mama Seeya's hand from my face and retreated through the exit before I exposed myself any further. I didn't want her to ask why I was crying, why I even cared about Avi in the first place. I couldn't tell her that we were related. I wasn't going to be a pawn in Mama Seeya's game with the Union. Who knew what they'd do if they found out.

No one would benefit from knowing that I was of their blood. I wasn't even sure what it meant exactly. But I didn't want to find out.

❖ ❖ ❖

Drake came out of nowhere and took a bite of a pear. "So you're really not gonna say goodbye."

I didn't have to explain anything to her.

Another juicy crunch. "Man, you're one stubborn bull."

I gave her a dirty look. She was the one who believed in Mama Seeya's ridiculousness so much so that she'd brought us out there. It felt like a setup to me.

185

"Trust me. It'll all work out." She popped the entire core in her mouth. Nothing went to waste.

"Do you know something that I don't?" I watched her like a hawk. She swallowed the last bite and grinned. "When are you going to learn to trust?"

Drake already knew the answer to that question. Never.

"If she gets hurt, in any way, I'm going to hurt you too," I threatened.

We watched each other. Waiting for a move. Sized the other up for what seemed like a long time.

"Go say goodbye," Drake said and left me.

I followed her steps from afar. We went outside where we'd initially come in. Deep oranges and burnt yellows lined the horizon. The only sound came from the whistles of the broken wind. In the distance was a pieced-together hovercraft climbing.

Avi flew away. Back into a trap. I had gambled and lost. I believed that she would have second thoughts and stay. Give us some time to figure something else out, but I knew her better than that. She would never have chosen to hide when there was an inkling that she could make a difference. Her pride would get her killed, and there was nothing that I could've done.

Just like with Miah. I was proving to be more useless with each passing day.

But maybe I didn't have to be.

Forget what Avi said. She didn't know any better.

I strolled through the network of containers to clear my head. Come up with something other than feeling sorry for myself, for Avi. How could I help her from an outpost deep in the remote desert?

The only idea that came to mind was that I couldn't allow her to fight Jade alone. The entire Union would be preparing for the show, so I could conceal my identity, turn myself into a Lower Resident again. I'd get close enough to a watchman. Disarm him, steal his gear, and sneak into the arena somehow.

When I got close enough to the stadium, I'd end Jade once and for all. By default, Avi would win. They'd tackle the rogue watchman and discover that it was the fugitive Impure.

It was a death mission, but what else did I have to live for?

My mind was made up. I was going back to the Square.

Chapter Eighteen
AVI

I left Saige without bidding her a proper farewell. I had to respect her wishes because Saige meant every word she spoke. She wasn't the type to backtrack. I understood completely, but it still killed me to depart on that note. Not knowing if that moment would be the last time that I ever saw her. I hoped she knew that I never meant to hurt her by defying her wishes or by acting like I knew more. On the contrary, she was right; I was going off pure faith and very little direction.

It was my own test to trust the people that I had been told never to trust, never to ally with. If I couldn't do it, then how could I ask it of the Union?

Saige would have to do the same: build trust with the rebels and place herself on the back burner until the goal was met. I wished that we could've battled these tests together, side by side, but in life, I've learned that the hardest battles must be faced alone.

Somehow knowing that fact hadn't made the decision any easier.

I was still dressed in the same bodysuit and gear that I'd had on during the coup in the caverns. I'd made one of the rebels bang me up a bit to make the story believable. I had technically only been gone for a few hours. It was a good cover, but Jade was unpredictable. She could've put a hit on me for deserting or just been pleased that I was gone and out of her hair. The exact response to my return was muddy.

I took a deep breath before entering the Citadel and steadied the shakes in my hand. No one had shot at me. I stepped over the threshold without opposition. None of the watchmen or droids paid me attention once I was inside.

I needed to see Jade.

Before I even got close to the entrance of the viewpoint, both doors slid apart.

She knew I had arrived.

The high-level quarters of the Citadel were all white, and the interior was designed with sharp edges. From the walls to the seating to the decor. It was a dangerous place to play as children, but Jade and I would still sneak up there because it was the only place where we could see the entire region. We called it the Tip. Almost like an observatory where one could see even as far as the Square.

Inside a huge, clear cage in the center of the space, Jade wore digigoggles as she observed sector maps. There was another opaque box sitting in the corner.

She no longer had on the matching tactical gear but had been cleansed of the grime of battle and cloaked in a dark chocolate bodysuit with a high neck and leather panels on the abs, arms, and thighs. Her platform boots *clip-clopped* around the center mass until the cage's walls turned opaque like the smaller box's. Moments later, she stepped out.

She slunk about catlike, until she stood about two arm's lengths away from me.

Her left eye was cloudy and gray, and a gash the length of a pointer finger cut across the socket.

"Has anyone ever told you that it's rude to stare?"

I swallowed.

She turned around and poured water from a crystal jug into a glass. "Physicians reconstructed it, but it's not functional."

I played into her game. "We possess advanced tech that would allow you to have functional optics even after detachment."

"My first battle scar." She poured another glass and brought them over. "I shall wear it with the same pride Father would've."

I remained stationary as she tried to offer it to me.

A small chortle escaped her as she pulled the offering back.

She motioned toward the white couches.

"I prefer to stand." What I was going to say wasn't going to take long.

"After the explosion, I had a team search for your remains." She began to examine my face, my body for changes with her operative eye. "The next question is an obvious one."

"I was pursuing rebels in hopes that they would lead me to the fugitives." I pretended to try to remember the fake story. "I was discovered, but they trusted me because of the broadcast."

Her face turned sour, recollecting the time when I'd told the Lower Residents to hold strong and unify against the powers that be. Us.

"Shortly after, there was an explosion. I was hit in the head by falling debris." I shifted my weight from one side to the other. "When I woke up, everyone was gone."

Jade took a gulp and clutched the glass so hard I thought it would burst.

"Hmm," she noised. "Lucky you."

I was shocked that she didn't dig deeper into the story. Something wasn't right.

It was the perfect time to request the duel. Fulfill the plan that Mama Seeya had sent me back for, but I paused for too long. Each time I thought of a way to relay it, nothing surfaced. Words wouldn't come. Sentences didn't make sense.

Then I came to a swift conclusion: I wasn't the right person to duel with Jade. I'd never beat her. I kept hearing Saige's voice urging me not to. Fear crept up like a winding vine. I was afraid of Jade. Afraid of losing. Dying. I didn't possess the self-confidence that I'd thought I had to go through with it.

She sensed the apprehension like I had it plastered on my chest.

"Would you believe me if I told you that I found your mutt and honk?" My eyes darted back and forth.

"Now that we know they are back in the region, it's only a matter of time before we get them." Jade slithered and constricted. "Can you imagine?"

I imagined it very well, too clear. She'd torture them first as I sat behind her, watching it all unfold because I didn't have the guts to challenge her.

"What a triumph it would be to catch the people"—she had got very close and tried to touch my face—"who had a hand in murdering Father."

I caught her hand before it could land on my skin. She tried to pull away, but I wouldn't let go.

"They didn't murder Father," I said slowly. "*You* did."

She snatched herself away and placed her hands behind her back. "You've been talking to someone."

I stepped forward into her space. "Confess what you've done."

Her eye was ablaze, but her expression remained stoic. "I knew you couldn't be loyal to the Union."

"If this is about loyalty, then you've failed," I sneered. "How does it feel to win the seat through deceit?"

"I took the seat fair and square." Her body shook with each word.

I laughed at her. She'd hated that even when she was little. "You would never be standing here if he wasn't dead. In no multiverse known to man would he have *ever* chosen you—even if you were the firstborn."

"Liar!" She charged me but stopped midway. "He put everything into you. For what? You were never the right choice. How could he not have seen that? It was like you had him blinded with your nobility. He was choosing the one who would make what we built crumble.

The Union never needed someone noble. It needs someone like me. Someone who would do what it takes to keep us afloat. You are nothing but a weakling. You are worthless."

"Yet I was still selected over you." I looked down on her.

Her cheeks ballooned, and she held on to her stomach. She blew out hard and then smoothed her hair to the back.

Jade was that same insecure girl on the interior. If I wanted to win, I'd have to exploit that.

Before I could get another word out, she tapped her wristcom, and the walls to the cage turned translucent once more.

Inside was Daylia. Shivering. When she noticed I was in the room, she immediately pounded on the partitions. I couldn't hear her weeping or the echoes of the bangs because it was soundproof.

"We are always a move ahead." She dragged her finger along the surface of the plexiglass. She studied Daylia. "They are even more abominable up close. The limp hair. The blue eye transmutations. The stench of a wet mongrel."

She flinched at the girl, and Daylia flew back into the center of the box and hugged her knees.

"A child, Jade?"

"General Jore." She punched the barrier.

I couldn't have done or said anything that would've upset Jade any more. "Yes, General."

"Better." When she tapped her wristcom, the door unlocked and slid open.

"What are you going to do?" I lurched closer.

"You think you are *so* smart, so cunning." Jade yanked Daylia hard by the shoulder until she was upright. "But no matter what Father, Mother saw in you, I was always the better selection. The better daughter."

The child was being jerked about. I held my hands out to calm the situation down. "Listen to—"

"No!" she screeched. "You listen to me—"

Jade had made the mistake of grabbing Daylia's mouth, and she bit down. Jade threw the girl aside. I grabbed her as Jade reeled from the pain. Blood stained Daylia's teeth.

It was now or never. I took the girl, and we ran. Jade's shrieks resounded along the halls. I held on to Daylia's hand, and together we climbed higher and higher because going down we'd be met with every watchman. I had no plan, but once we got far enough, I'd come up with something. She was depending on me to save her. I hadn't been able to the first time, but my second chance had come. We were out of breath as we screeched round corners and burst through droids working in the landscaping. They watched with apathetic expressions as the Elite ran hand in hand with a Europe girl. I was surprised that Jade hadn't programmed them to attack workers on the premises yet. I was sure after that she would.

We came to the highest tier of the Tip. The only sound came from the chirps of birds and the whistle of intermittent winds.

Daylia was hunched over. "Where do we go now?"

I caught my breath and kept spinning in circles, looking for a way out. There was nothing but sky surrounding us.

"I-I don't know," I replied.

"You told me to be brave like Saige." Daylia took my hand again. "I don't want to die."

I hugged her and wiped her tears. "I promise that I won't let anything bad happen to you."

She sniffled, nodding.

"Over there." I pointed to a steel bar that was fastened to the side of the ridge.

It was barely a ladder. It led to the same floor we'd just left, but not too far away was a thinner ridge that we could jump and latch onto and use to shimmy the rest of the way down.

"I'm afraid of heights." She pouted.

"This is our only way down," I told her. "Do you trust me?"

She nodded again.

"I will go down first and make sure it will hold our weight." I handed her a small laser gun. "Point and aim."

Daylia held it with confidence. "Be careful."

I put my foot on the first bar. It was wobbly, but it held as I put the rest of my mass on it. I glanced up. Daylia's face peered over the ledge.

"Okay, you can come now." I reached out. "Give me your hand."

I looked down to see how high we were. I clutched the bar and got my bearings. One small slip and I was pulp.

A laser shot went off.

"Daylia!" I screamed and began climbing.

"Let go of me." She kicked and fought, but a watchman that she'd wounded had already swept her up and delivered her to Jade.

I threw myself over. "Don't do this."

Daylia gasped as Jade snatched her like a doll and dangled her over the edge. Her legs swayed and her hair thrashed. Jade held her by the bodysuit's neckline.

Watchmen aimed at me, daring for me to make a move on their General.

"Jade!" My voice deepened as I stepped forward. "Release her."

Watchmen were anxious for a reason to fill my body with holes. I kept my hands visible.

Jade observed me over her shoulder. "You are such a bad performer, Princess. I knew your loyalty to me was all a stunt."

I retorted, "You are not good for the Union."

"And you are?" Her arm trembled, lowering the girl farther. Daylia scraped at Jade's wrist.

"She has nothing to do with this." I held my arm out. Watchmen moved in closer. "There's still time to do the right thing. I swear it, Jade."

Her remaining eye was glazed. Perhaps with doubt, I thought. I'd hoped that I had gotten to her, that I'd touched the humane part that was buried far below the surface.

"Sister, please." I cupped my hands. "I am begging you. You do not have to do this."

"But I do."

She opened her hand, releasing Daylia back to the ground. My relief was short lived.

"You won't be running from me again," Jade said as she stomped on Daylia's shin, cracking the bone. It protruded from beneath the skin as Daylia let out a shrill scream.

My fingers curled into claws on the concrete. Red dots blinded my vision. No one else existed up there. Just Jade and me. A fire welled inside that couldn't be quenched unless I inflicted the same pain on her as she had on others. That was what she truly wanted. For me to be ruthless like her.

I charged, snarling like a diseased creature. Watchmen intercepted, preventing me from even getting near. I slipped from one's grip and palm-thrusted another. I cut two more down on the path of wrapping my hands around her neck. The more I fought, the more watchmen appeared. Finally, I was subdued. Jade never even moved a muscle.

She wore a smirk that I wanted to shred from her face. I'd wished that she was never born. That her fetus had perished in Mother's womb before she even took a breath. Jade was everything that I detested. I despised her.

She began to walk away as her men hauled an unconscious Daylia.

"Jade!" I tried to wrestle the watchmen that pinned my arms and shoulders to the ground.

She whirled around. "Yes?"

"According to the law, I can challenge you to a duel."

Jade angled her head in amusement.

"You know exactly what I'm talking about," I sneered. "I challenge you under the law to a duel to the death."

She bit her lip. "I thought you'd never ask."

When she'd gone out of sight, the watchmen stripped me of all gear. After that, they began to beat me. Four to one. I was punched in the face, slammed into the concrete, kicked in the back and abdomen. Stomped more times than I could count. At some point, I knew that I would never have a chance to duel her because they'd beat the life from me.

I curled into a fetal position and waited for the end.

As I lay crushed on the cement, I counted ragged inhalations to make sure that I was still alive. One. Two. Three. Four . . .

Both eardrums had been ruptured, so I couldn't really hear anything.

I waited some more. That was all I could do. Detailing Daylia's simple features and locking them into memory. To remember that moment. Remember that I needed to get her back. To look back on it when I hesitated to jam a dagger into Jade's heart and watch her eyes fill with that same fear as she bled out in the arena.

Jade was already dead to me anyway.

My face rested in a puddle of my own sweat, tears, and congealed blood. I was unable to move any part of my being, my body. So, I rested my eyes and hoped that the crows hadn't begun circling and picking away.

"Avi!" A small voice startled me back to consciousness.

I'd lost mobility in my jaw to even attempt to respond.

I was turned over to my back. My body was on fire. I let out a closed-mouth moan.

Admiral Jemison stuck me in the thigh with medicines as a medbot coasted above, examining the many bone breaks and contusions I'd suffered.

His lips moved, but I couldn't make out any of the words. His eyes scanned the report, his fingers bowed over the reader as if he wanted to break it in half. I took that as the results showed that they really had done a number on me.

His eyes watered as he stroked my cheek. *What did they do to you?* I could read his lips that time.

I failed was what I willed my lips to utter, but nothing emerged but a wheeze.

He scooped his arms underneath my wilted form and hoisted me up to his chest. The medbot shadowed us for a while. I passed out.

The next thing I knew, I was on a craft. He carefully laid me inside a whitish tube and secured the lid. The machine started to repair the damaged parts, but because I was so battered, it'd take time. He pressed his palm to the outer layer of the glass case and smiled a weary one. I opened my eyes wide and then closed them tight, showing my gratitude the only way I knew possible.

He nodded, receiving the message.

He tapped the reader, and from tiny hoses emitted hazy mists, filling the tube in its entirety.

After a few seconds, my lids became heavy, and I drifted into a deep, deep slumber.

❖ ❖ ❖

I gasped, returning to consciousness and into a seated position. I was in a slumberpod dressed in a simple bodysuit. Where were my weapons? Jade? Was she around the way, waiting to strike? I tried to slide from the tube but ended up falling into a metal pushcart. All its contents crashed to the floor with me.

Instructor Skylar rounded the corner in haste and assisted me to a stall.

"Thirsty." A fine grit was stuck at the base of my tonsils.

He fetched an H_2O pack. I drank greedily. It spilled along the corners of my mouth as I choked but continued to drain the contents.

When the pack was compressed, I inhaled deeply and cleared my throat with relief.

"How are you feeling?" he asked, pushing coiled hairs from my face.

"How long have I been . . . ?" I tried standing on my own again. My bearing was unsteady, but strength was returning.

He grabbed the reader and revealed the stats. "Fifty-six hours. Thirteen minutes. Twenty seconds."

"Jade?" My pulse was starting to climb. I felt the thumps against my chest beating harder at the mere sound of her name. "Where's she?"

"At the Citadel, I'm assuming."

I began searching the room for my gear. "Why didn't you wake me earlier? You could've used adrenaline injections."

"Avi, if Admiral Jemison hadn't found you, you'd be dead. I had to place you into a medically induced coma." His posture was weary. "Your body needed rest to heal. You had lacerations and breaks and tears all over the place."

"Where're all of my things?" I ignored the data.

"Avi?"

I began opening doors and rummaging through drawers. I had to find my things; I had to get to Jade. There was no more postponing.

"At ease, Watchman Jore!"

I paused. Then faced him. I remembered that tone that he often utilized during trainings.

He spoke through his teeth. "I know that you challenged Jade, and I know that you're in a hurry to finish this, but if this is going to work, then it cannot be rushed."

He was right. I had to calm down for a moment. I needed a well-thought-out plan.

"Have a seat." He interlaced his fingers behind his neck.

I returned to the stall and placed my palms gently at my sides.

He leaned against the cabinet and strummed through the end of his beard.

"I've never fully agreed with the Union's legislations, you know. I have played the part for decades, well, I may add. I have excelled, risen through the ranks, remained loyal—to an extent—to the Union. I've also done things to make these people, your father, trust me after our name was tarnished by my own father. I had to prove myself. And I did just that." He winced, silently recalling all he'd done. I could only imagine what my father had asked of him over the years.

"After my father was framed and executed for a crime he didn't commit—by his own squadron, for galaxy's sake—I have been waiting for the moment to relieve myself of this . . . this anguish. But I wasn't sure how until I saw you creating a bond with the Lower Residents. No one has ever tried before. You were the only one who stood up against the naysayers. No matter how many times you were ridiculed, you stuck with it."

My lips trembled as I tried to hold it all in. The emotions burst at the seams. I'd never felt so seen. I was always the only one, the outsider, when it came to my ideologies. The road I traveled was a lonely one.

"You, Avi Jore, are the most gallant person that I've ever come in contact with." His smile grew. "And I've trained thousands upon thousands of watchmen over the course of my occupation."

I fumbled with my thumbs coyly. I hadn't felt that way about myself at all, but coming from the instructor, it meant something more.

"The plan was to take down the Union from the inside," he confessed, "but now that's all changed. I believe that you're the future of the Southern Region. I believe that we don't have to eradicate them or them eradicate us. I know it sounds foolish, stupid even, but we *can* change. But I know that we can't move forward with Jade and her regime in the way."

It seemed as if Jade was the spike wedged in everyone's side and not just mine.

"I watched her grow. She used to be such a stubby little thing."
His eyes became glassy as he covered his mouth in recollection of her
memory. "Now we have to—to kill her."

"I would never ask that of you." I rose from the chair. "She is my
responsibility, and I will carry that burden."

He sighed. "I want you to know that you have allies, Avi. They're
just so afraid of challenging the government, the system. They just need
to see that you've got this before they publicly pledge allegiance."

"I understand." I thought back to the last conversation we'd had.
"I saw Saige. In the mines."

"Then she's alive?"

"Hmm," I said. "What did you mean when you said that Saige was
the key? And your father. Who was he?"

He delayed only slightly before speaking. "He was a good person.
Like you, he wanted to see change. Our entire family was exiled after
they accused him of breaking the purity law with Saige's mother and
then gunned him down like an animal to cover the true paternity. I
had to grow up without him. They stole that sense of stability from my
mother and me. He didn't deserve that. He'd been loyal to the Union,
to your father. And they just got rid of him like it was nothing."

The topic was troubling for him, and I knew why, but the truth was
always revealed in due time. I wasn't in a position just yet to divulge
anything that I knew because I wasn't sure I could fully trust him with
everything that Mama Seeya had told me.

I embraced him for a long while. That was all that I could offer.

A nationwide emergency broadcast materialized on a holoscreen.

Profile photos of Jade and me with a waving "versus" sign planted
in between us.

"This is Sheron Browning with breaking news. This morning it
was officially announced that recently elected General Jore and Avi
Jore will be partaking in a live-streamed duel to the death." The tele-
caster switched positions for another camera angle. "We are live with

our political strategist Javeri Mazai, who has much to say about this recent update. Javeri, what say you of this governmental-level sibling squabble?"

Javeri adjusted the mic and cleared his throat. "Well, it is fundamental chaos, to say the least. Avi Jore has dug up a primordial law that was made when our founding members first created the Union after the United States was reborn. In my opinion, it was a last-ditch effort of dethroning the recent General, which I believe was well played."

"Well played indeed, but what about what the people want, Javeri? I mean, she lost the Union's vote by a record landslide. The people don't want her as their General. Care to add to that?" Sheron pouted.

He pushed his glasses up the bridge of his nose before he answered. "This is a fact, but my job as an analyst is not to persuade. I can only be objective and state the facts. Either way, the Union has been through a lot since the former General's assassination. I'm not sure what's in store for the Union if either side wins, but it's a consensus that the people want to get back to normal."

"Hear, hear." Her lips pursed, and then she tapped on her earpiece. "We just got confirmation that the General has an urgent announcement to make."

Jade wore a slim patch that shielded the damaged eye but showcased the new slash. The covering was made of black scales that matched her body armor. Her hair was neat and slick.

"This will be the third and last announcement," she declared to the region. "Avi Jore has until sundown to arrive at the arena to finish, once and for all, the deciding duel. If she fails to arrive, then she is considered even more of a defector from the Union and will be executed for her crimes on sight."

The recording ended.

Chapter Nineteen
AVI

Every single insignificant move I made up until that point, I wondered if it'd be my last. My last sip of cool liquid, my last time twiddling my thumbs, or my last time riding in a hovercraft. Small gestures that I'd taken for granted I hyperfocused on. I savored every inhale and every exhale. Perhaps it wasn't the best strategy to enter into combat with the mentality that I'd be the one to lose, but it'd be stupid of me to go in too brash and miss out on all the little spoils of life. Each moment was worth so much more now.

The armored hovercraft skated through the airspace. It was similar to the one Jade and I used to ride every morning to the Academy during our formative years. The leather seats were soft, molding to the curvature and weight of my form. Instructor Skylar sat beside me while Jemison rested across from us. I was glad to have some backing. I wasn't sure what it meant for them if Jade won, but their show of support would surely not go unnoticed.

I huffed on the thick-paneled display and used my sleeve to clear away the condensation. I'd made them increase the temperature. My nerves caused me to be much colder while perspiring simultaneously.

The airways were congested as, along with other crafts, we headed in the same direction to the main and final event. The tickets for the duel had sold out in seconds. Whoever marketed the affair had made a fortune.

The Square brought back many recollections. It wasn't that long ago that Saige and I were there for a concert and failed courting with Phoenix, creating havoc. Although I'd been afraid for my life similar to right now, I couldn't deny that it was the most excitement I'd experienced in my existence. It was the first time that I'd had an actual purpose.

I remembered Saige being so annoyed with me the entire duration. The thought of her frowning or tossing insults caused a warmth.

The Square used to be a source of pleasure for me, for all Elites really. During the day, families would ride the trolleys with their off-spring, and runners would course laps through the picturesque paths with their spliced pets not far behind.

A paradise for the Upper echelon.

But I knew what crept underneath the fabricated surface. It was the same sludge that Saige had tried to forewarn me about. It took me too long to believe her. Perhaps things wouldn't have gotten so chaotic if I had only acted earlier, instead of trying to anticipate the best. That part had never arrived. What I had was what I was always going to have.

I should've put Jade out of her misery a long time ago. Before she killed Father. Before she tried to kill me. I'd made mistakes, and I had to rectify them no matter the outcome. It wasn't solely about me anymore. I was doing it for the people. For humanity. The system that the Europes built, that we sustained was not moral. It never had been. When had we occupied the exact level of our oppressors? When had we lost sight of our principles?

It didn't matter which side won. No side was better than the other, more righteous than the other. The Union prided itself on longevity at the expense, the labor of others. I couldn't do it anymore. It stopped there, and if it took my mortality to demonstrate that what we were doing wasn't right, then so be it.

Someone had to rise. I truly believed that one person could spark a revolution. Just a single entity was needed to tip the scale. So even if I didn't leave that arena victorious, then my task was still completed. Complacency was conformity, and I'd rather die than live another day contributing to the suffering.

At dusk, the Square transformed into an adult wonderland, a fluorescent city. Towering light pillars guided the hovertram over a bridge and into the city's center. The buildings were excessive with pointed peaks at the tops poking through the clouds. They weren't menacing like the ones in the worker Subdivisions but attractive and busy. As we lowered in altitude, the towers consumed us invitingly. Vertical neon banners buzzed to life on the face and corner of every construction.

As traffic slowed to a crawl, I got to see the fashionably arrayed crowd beneath. It didn't matter what type of gore would occur; Upper Residents twisted any event into a full-blown gala.

Holocams and paparazzi swarmed only the chicest of spectators. A group of plus models emerged from a luxury craft. Their guards trying their best to keep the frenzied crowd at bay, but everyone encircled them, lights flashing in a flurry, devouring them with every comm device on the market.

The abundant trio didn't seem to mind as they stood in a tight V formation and posed for their devotees. One wore a pastel vinyl short-set bodysuit with a deep neckline, exposing her full breasts. Matching butterflies fluttered around her. I wasn't sure if they were real or simulated. The next sported a high synthetic ponytail that dragged on the ground and a shiny and stiff metal trench with thigh-high armored boots with tips sharp enough to penetrate the skin. The last had on shades that resembled robobee eyes and a completely transparent bodysuit made from a plastic material. She left nothing to the imagination.

Other patrons wore bright-colored Afros, thin live snakes as chokers, and long acrylic nails with chains and crystals hanging from them. Tattoos covered shiny bald heads while others donned excessive feathered headpieces. It was remarkable and wretched at the same time. Were those the people who coveted real change? Could I influence them to do better, be better if this was what the norm was?

The holoscreen illuminated in the center console. It was a call. Reba was the last person that I had expected. After the whole Marco Grant concert debacle, her parents had forbidden her to ever have contact with me again.

"A pleasant surprise." I put on a friendly face despite rising anxieties.

She also wore a pleasant face, but there was clear discomfort underneath.

"Avi," she said simply, struggling to find the right words. Any words.

We both tried to speak but ended up overlapping each other with streams of stammers, then tittered in unease.

Like me, she was in the back seat of a hovervehicle heading to the arena, but she was getting her hair plaited by a droid.

"Machines are definitely not as good at braiding as workers." She laughed at her own joke. "Surprise. You were right, the droids not being the greatest idea."

We shared an amiable smile.

She cleared her throat, then began vomiting words. "Avi, I'm so sorry that I wasn't there for you when you needed me the most. My parents—they—well, it was complicated. But I had no right as a friend to just abandon you like that. It's fucked up. I just—"

"Reba, you don't—"

"No, I do. I do have to." She blew stray hairs from her face as the droid tried to trace even parts in her scalp. "I promise that from now on I will back you. I don't care what my parents say or my friends. This isn't right. None of it is. I was just too afraid to say anything. But you—you have always been true. Brave. We don't deserve you. I don't deserve you. Please accept my deepest regrets."

My sockets burned as I fought the urge to weep for the hundredth time. "Gratitude." I sighed.

"We owe you gratitude." She wiped her eyes. "Anyways, umm, I never liked Jade anyway. She's always been a real bitch. So, I will see you on the other side, my friend, so we can catch another Marco Grant concert. Yeah?"

I nodded. "Yes, yes. Of course."

"Ouch!" She cringed at the droid, who dug too deep into her scalp with the parting comb. "Gotta go, love."

The call ended.

I turned to Instructor Skylar, hopeful. "Were you able to get Mother on a call?"

He shot Jemison a look, but he remained motionless.

"We tried." Instructor Skylar loosened his collar. "But I think with your father's death and now this, it's too much for her to bear."

"I see." Optimism for final contact dissolved. For a mother to lose half her family in such a short period . . . I wasn't sure she'd survive another blow, but one of her children wouldn't depart that ring alive. I wished it were different. I hoped she knew that I'd tried and exhausted every alternative.

I expanded the holoscreen, then raised the volume on the broadcast that Jemison was so intently monitoring.

"Avi, I don't think—" Instructor Skylar began.

"I want to hear it."

The broadcast showed people wagering to see who'd win the duel. Of course, Jade was ahead. The journalist interviewed spectators waiting in the long lines for access.

Sheron Browning placed a mic in a teen boy's face. "Who do you have currency on?"

The boy stroked his smooth squared jaw with a sparkly glove. "Well, I like to mix it up, you know? I always gamble on the underdog, always. It makes things more interesting; you feel me?"

She jerked the mic back to her mouth, while adjusting her earpiece. "Oh, I 'feel you' indeed, young man. Let's go to the next."

The holocam glided through figures, following the woman as she scoured the queue for the next interviewee.

"Look at this little darling," Sheron gushed into the lens, then lowered herself parallel to a girl. "And what sign are you holding?"

She couldn't have been older than Daylia. She had little knots in her hair, and her edges were squiggly and greased down at the sides. One of her front baby teeth was missing, and her skin was a vibrant umber color. In her hands was a digital drawing of me.

I leaned forward to get a closer look.

"I want Avi to win because the Union took my worker away. I liked her. She was my best friend. We played tea party." She spoke with the softest voice. "I-I drew a picture of Avi because she had a worker friend too."

"How dare the Union take this little girl's tea party guest away?" The interviewer puckered into the holocam, then focused on the mother. "And what say you about your daughter's far-left decision?"

The woman seized the mic from Sheron's grip. "I believe that as a parent we should support our children. No matter what. I support free speech. Maybe if the General had supported Jade, then we wouldn't even be in this mess. How sad is it that two siblings must kill the other to reign? I couldn't imagine offing my kin like that."

The journalist's eyes widened as she snatched the mic back. "Well, look at that; we have some people stirring the pot today! We will see you on the inside for more live coverage of the Union Duel 3010. Back to you in the studio."

I leaned back, satisfied. That young girl reminded me so much of myself. She didn't quite know what she was feeling, but at the core, she knew that the world she thrived in was unequal. I hoped that on that day, I could show her that the fight was worth fighting. Perhaps it was over for the rest of us, but for her generation, there was still a chance to resume with an unpolluted slate.

We climbed to a steady speed, gliding past a transparent globe that had purple luminescent webbed beams attached to the exterior. It was where the final battle would begin. An energetic projection of a massive Marco Grant flashed through the ceiling of the dome. She wore a bubble gum–pink wet-looking wig, and her dress resembled a candy wrapper.

"Greetings, Marconites, and welcome to the Globe Gamba." Her projection signaled to the audience. "Before the duel is set to begin, I'll be bringing in the tunes and performing my latest EP: *Legionnaire*."

Was it a coincidence, or had Jade heard the song and named my position as some tasteless pun?

"After the performance, we'll shoot you a QR encryption so you can access *Legionnaire* on all streaming platforms." She placed a peace sign over her forehead. "And may the best woman win."

When the hovercraft landed, I didn't feel it. Instead, I was jolted by the horde pounding on the shell and the windows so much that we all began to sway. They were everywhere. Like a colony of termites trying to get a glimpse of the queen. But I was no queen; I felt more like the jester.

Instructor Skylar took my hand and, with the other, guided my sight to match his.

He sensed my immediate panic.

"Listen to me." He explained, "I will not let anyone hurt you."

I took a deep inhale.

He motioned to Jemison to raise the door.

"Here we go." Jemison stepped into the horde first.

"Keep your head down and stay tight." Instructor Skylar scooted across the seat, pulling me along.

The throng was tense as Jemison yelled for people to clear a path. He bulldozed through while using the other arm to shield me from side attacks. We bumped back and forth like laserballs as we edged to the entrance. Lights ignited and feet scuffled, and hands attempted to grab at any part of my body. I slapped unwanted feels, and Instructor Skylar rammed and elbowed the overzealous advances. I couldn't hear a thing but yelling and screaming and snarling.

Keep your head down and stay tight, I repeated.

A metaphor for life in and of itself. Eventually one would get to their destination despite the impacts and despite the slowness of the journey. I would get there. I just had to push forward.

Jal shouted my name. Then he and the style team beat back the crowd from entering the access. They yanked me inside. Jemison and Instructor Skylar shoved the remaining heads and flailing arms through the cracks and finally slammed the doors shut.

Jal, Onyx, and Parade interlocked their arms around me, laying their heads on top of mine. I'd missed them dearly and hadn't seen them since my crowning ceremony, when they'd turned me into an enhanced version of myself. It was back when Father was alive and all my problems were small and manageable.

"There's our stunner." Jal gleamed. He was much shorter than me, with a black bob with hot-pink layered bangs, and he wore a signature peacock-feather shawl around his shoulders.

Parade took my hands and kissed them both. "Come see what we have laid out for you, General Jore." He was a slender mahogany man wearing all black with a stiff turtleneck that covered his mouth. His eyes were lined thickly with kohl.

Onyx was a bald woman with skin so smooth and dark it was almost purple. She draped her apple-shaped figure in a zebra-skin tunic. She snapped her fingers. "And the only General we will ever acknowledge, okay?"

Unlike the last time we worked together, I was so delighted to see them. It was starting to feel like I wasn't alone in the fight, and now I had an entire squad.

Jal skipped ahead while Parade took me by the waist and guided us into the dressing chamber. I was expecting them to have gone all out, with mannequins on top of mannequins draped in trendy bodysuits and glitzy form plates and elbow and kneepads with spikes on them.

Instead, there was a solo bodysuit positioned on a shimmering platform.

The armor was iridescent. I reached out, allowing my fingertips to skate over the intricate weaving. Although it was black in color, a deep purple shone whenever the light hit it a certain way, almost like a mood ring. In the mannequin's hand was a polished staff with a sharp spearhead at the end of it that had minute engravings. *Adesina* appeared repeatedly.

"*Adesina* means 'she opens the way,'" Jal explained.

"We thought it would be fitting for the occasion," Onyx added, covering his eyes.

"She opens the way," I repeated, allowing the words to absorb.

"Do you like it?" Parade took my shoulders from behind, offering an encouraging squeeze.

A heavy tear fell. "'Like' would be such a sore understatement."

Onyx and Jal embraced each other, one lifting the other off his feet.

Parade planted a soft kiss on my temple. "Let's give the Union something to talk about, shall we?"

Every crevice of my being was scrubbed spotless, my nails were polished, and bruises were covered with their cosmetic magic. They turned me away from all the mirrors as they collectively worked their styling enchantments. I told them that it wasn't necessary, but they all treasured a reveal, so I obliged.

I wished that time would slow to a creep, but it seemed to pass at warp speed. By the time we began, we had already finished, and the occasion had arrived.

"You ready?" Onyx leaped up and down, clapping.

"As I'll ever be," I said.

Parade covered my eyes while Jal led me to a podium.

"No peeking," Onyx cooed.

Someone placed the spear in my hand. I latched on.

"Voilà." She uncovered my vision.

There was no more formal braided halo that I had worn since I could recollect. That Avi, that girl, had vanished. My hair was in a poufy Afro with two cornrows braided along the sides. The makeup was light, natural. Fitting.

I was a watchman, a warrior. A leader. The next succeeding General.

And I was equipped for battle.

"She loves it," Onyx whispered in Jal's ear.

"Oh, honey, I can tell," he replied, elbowing her playfully in the side.

I stepped from the podium as my crew encircled me, waiting for a word. "Gratitude. To all of you. I couldn't have done this alone."

There was more that I wanted to say, but Instructor Skylar summoned me. The occasion had ended.

I sauntered toward the exit, leaving the band behind. Jal began to sob, holding Parade for support.

"Adesina," they called out in unison as I stepped over the threshold. *Adesina.*

❖ ❖ ❖

We were on the highest level of a premier building in the Square inside of a massive sphere. The top had been unsealed. Moist air circulated through the stands. I tasted humidity. Rainfall was nigh.

There were thousands of spectators, packed in like sardines in a tin. They hung suspended from the banisters on exclusive decks and crowded the mezzanines. I felt claustrophobic as they enclosed on me, appearing as if they would topple over like building blocks on an unsteady base. At the midpoint was a hexagon-shaped ring. The outer edges and laser rails glowed a phosphorescent green. Below that, bodies filled the pits. The best view from which to witness the carnage. So close that blood spatter would certainly fall upon them. Above, transparent circular holoscreens with my opponent's face as well as mine had our names and stats displayed.

A banner remained constant and read in bold, scorching letters: *Union Duel 3010.*

The arena blackened. The crowd became silent. For a moment, I thought that Mama Seeya had brought in the brigade, and they were finally going to put a stop to this nonsense, but I should have known better. The place was crawling with every watchman in the province, and she wasn't going to risk her people. Nor would I have asked her to. They'd made more than enough sacrifices.

It was my turn.

A solo spotlight hit Marco Grant. She posed like a damsel in anguish with her head leaned back and her forearm resting over her eyes. The other hand brought the gold-leafed microphone to her glossy lips. She snapped into another pose; fireworks exploded around her like a fiery typhoon. She sashayed and began the lyrics to her song.

Dancers dressed in erotic watchmen gear paraded around her. Male dancers in the center lifted her body and spun her in a circle as she hit a higher octave.

Former Avi would've sprung to life and swayed and sang the already-memorized verses, but after the concert ended, I had to face Jade. If that wasn't a buzzkill, then I didn't know what was.

The music, the pyrotechnics, the sounds started to fade into one descant. The dome began to move underneath me, caving in like a mudslide. The colors swirled like heated magma and merged into one harsh reality. I swayed, struggling to keep myself upright, present. The holocams hovered and zoomed in as expected. Watching every insignificant move and probably overlaid with snarky commentary on the live broadcast.

Instructor Skylar gripped me before I collapsed and leaned in as if he were an affectionate coach and not a human crutch. I played the part and rested my head in the nook of his shoulder. He smiled to seal the deal.

"Mind games." He kept his attention on the performance; his lips moved deliberately. "This whole ruse is to get you away from your center."

"She's succeeded."

"No." His forcefulness jarred me. "She has not. Until your last breath, you play the game to win."

He'd given me the same advice before I entered the Cube for the final test for watchmen training. Many died, but I made it out, crushed but alive. That meant something. It meant everything. That I was stronger than I gave myself credit for, and that it was okay to be frightened. Fear was in all of us. It made us human. It was necessary.

I was more terrified of a future with Jade in it than of Jade herself.

The performance ended. I stood higher than before with a straight spine and clapped as the crowd did.

Marco Grant exited the stage.

"For the grand moment that we have all been anxiously waiting for . . . ," the presenter announced. "The duel of the century. We have challenger Avi Jore." Jeers were mixed with applause as I followed Instructor Skylar to the base of the ring. He led me to the stairs at one apex of the hexagon and handed me the spear.

"May the universe shield you." His chin met his chest.

I dipped underneath the blue laser cable and stationed myself next to the presenter.

"We have defender General Jade Jore." He elongated *Jore* for effect.

The people erupted in cheers and ovation, squeals and fists shooting into the air.

She strolled through the pit with a long cape fluttering behind her. She high-fived fans and blew kisses, soaking up all the devotion, the admiration. Head Gardner stayed cemented to her side; her eyes locked on me. I jerked my chin in an upward motion, signaling that I wasn't afraid.

Head Gardner sneered.

Jade jogged along the steps and hopped over the highest rope, flexing her acrobatic dexterity.

She tore off the cape, exposing a silver holographic bodysuit with shoulder plates and breastplates made of chrome. The eyepatch harmonized too. Head Gardner tossed her spear high into the air, and Jade caught it without even looking.

Spectators nearly fainted at the trick.

I expected to cower at the proximity of Jade after the carnage she'd allowed to be inflicted upon me. She'd left me for dead too many times to count. She'd taken Father away from me, from Mother.

And she was mine now.

"The stakes are high," the presenter explained.

Jade couldn't keep her sights away from the doting crowd, and I couldn't keep mine from her. My grip tightened around the hilt of the spear as I fantasized about how it'd feel to jam the weapon into her.

"The reward of this duel is the position of reigning General." The presenter cleared his throat then allowed the r to roll from his tongue: "Rules are as follows . . ."

She finally allowed her vision to rest on me, matching the intensity. Jade could finally do what she'd always wanted—battle me with no constraints.

"Fight to the death." He slid back, leaving Jade and me.

The ropes converted into a vivid red. There was no way in. No way out.

I stepped forward on my dominant leg, bent my knees, and set my body low, clenching the stick across the central part of my chest.

Jade mimicked the stance but pointed her weapon at me. The spear's head wasn't pointed like mine but curved, sharp, equipped to tear into armor and rend flesh from the bone.

"Let the countdown begin," he roared.

The crowd joined in: "Five. Four. Three. Two. One."

Digital confetti banners burst.

Fight!

Jade didn't waste a millisecond, and neither did I. We both darted forward and clashed titanium rod to titanium rod in the midpoint.

I didn't have time to ponder a specific strategy. Jade didn't have many combative weaknesses that I was aware of. She was an offensive fighter. She was strong and agile when we used to spar. Deliberate. Articulate in her movements.

Although I may not have been at a physical advantage, my ingenuity was higher. Jade cared much about how she appeared. I'd use that. I reminded myself that it wasn't a sprint but a test of endurance. I would strike her armor as needed in order to weaken her defense system and then deliver the killing blow once her defense was at critical levels.

I just had to dance around and aggravate her.

She thrust her weapon forward at a whirlwind speed. I blocked all her blows and then backflipped high in the air and landed on my thrustboots.

"Is that all you've got, Princess?" she said.

I jetted higher, floating above the arena.

Her upper lip twitched as she twirled the spear above her head and then thrust upward to meet me. I spun around, making it seem as though I'd use the stick to strike her, but instead I brought my heel up and lunged my boot into her chest with a side kick. The mob went crazy, forgetting who they were even cheering for at the fake-out, desensitized to the butchery.

Her body curled inward as she tore through the space and slammed into the ground. She was disoriented, so I dove, spear headfirst.

I wasn't fast enough because she rolled out of target just in time. The metal sparked on impact where her head should've been. She swiped the staff, trying to use it to flip me, but I saw it coming and flipped backward, landing on one hand and a knee. She hopped up and stretched her neck from side to side.

"You've got some good tricks." She clapped. "But how long can you really keep this facade up? We both know that you could never beat me. Not when we sparred as adolescents and certainly not now."

I rammed her with my shoulder into the top laser rope.

I drove the hilt into her face with a downward diagonal strike. She palm-thrusted me in the sternum and then came down on me with her weapon. When I tried to block, the hook sliced right through the metal, turning my staff into halves.

She poked and prodded and swiped like a madwoman. The last assault advanced in what seemed like slow motion. I bent my back at a ninety-degree angle, and the sharpness nearly missed my face, nicking the skin as it sliced the empty space.

The crowd gasped when I popped back up, only sustaining a surface wound. It seemed like as the match progressed, they were questioning who they rooted for. Perhaps they needed to witness that I was a serious warrior and not the meek Avi they'd watched growing up in the Citadel.

I motioned to the little girl with the sign she'd drawn of me.

Jade spat blood and ground her teeth.

"Not everyone is on your side." I toyed with her ego. "They only voted for you because they pity you. Must be a sad existence to live in the shadows of an older heir. A shame that you had to stoop to such levels in order to secure a position that was never meant for you."

Her voice was raspy as I circled. "Fuck you."

"I was all our parents ever needed, Jade. The firstborn. Even given the mediocrity that you accuse me of, you still aren't number one, and that's where all of this animosity stems from." I wrapped up the deal. "Mother should've terminated you when she had the chance."

Jade lifted her face to the sky. A few drops fell onto her head from the rumbling clouds above. She returned her sights to me as if I had tortured a longtime lover, and she was out for nothing short of revenge. "You're already dead."

She charged, bringing the full weight of the hook down, attempting to split me in half, starting at the crown of my head. I kept the slice at bay by cross-blocking the spear with the two pieces. She pried farther, specks of spittle flying from her mouth as she grunted.

I headbutted her, she relaxed, and then I delivered an axe kick to her skull. She stumbled but still remained upright. I continued to strike her with the sticks, landing most of the blows as I forced her into the corner of the ring.

I leaped high and then came down with the final strike, but I had overestimated her fatigue. She coasted up, meeting me in the middle with an uppercut to the jaw. I twisted sideways through the air and then smacked right on the ring's surface, losing both weapons.

I lifted my head, searching for a sign of my weapons, but was met with Jade hovering over my torso and hacking away. Instinctively, I blocked the hook with my hand. I expected all my fingers to be hacked off at the joints, but the armor morphed immediately into a titanium claw, encasing my hand with reinforcement.

I caught the blade and gripped, crushing it with ease. Her eyes widened as I created a fist with the other hand and punched her in the chest. She flew back but stopped herself from slamming into the ropes as sharp platinum wings sprouted from her bodysuit. She flew higher and higher, and I thrust upward in pursuit.

We coasted around the arena, exchanging blows as all the heads were now turned upward at the display. My claws were pitted against the sharp blades of her wings as we swapped strike for strike. She shoved me; there was screaming and spectators scrambling to get out of the way. I flew right into a railing, crashing into a gallery full of VIPs.

Jade landed in the fragments as I slunk away.

The blades of her wings stabbed at me as I lay on the ground. I rotated to and fro, trying to dodge each shot.

I rolled backward and flipped onto my soles, then jetted right at her, clawing her breastplate at full capacity. The damage was done. Her body armor started to malfunction at critical levels. She gasped as if the wind had been completely extracted from her. With two huge steps back, she dove from the balcony.

I crawled forward to peer over the ledge and saw her facedown in the epicenter of the ring. The wings had retracted.

Upon descending from the desecrated balcony, I landed delicately. She was very much still alive; her back rose and collapsed slowly.

My nemesis had given up. I'd won. But why didn't it feel that way? She had done so many corrupt things, but I couldn't help but feel bad for her despite all of it.

I activated one claw. I'd ensure it was a quick and merciful death.

I turned her around, and as I went to cut her throat, she jammed my own spear into my abdomen.

I coughed, slobbered as she stood, holding the other end, and twisted it deeper. I wheezed, backing up. She followed with a fevered expression and, for good measure, crammed it in once more.

The once-silent crowd gasped when I collapsed on the base, slick with rainwater. Blood trickled from my mouth, from the abysmal wound. I caught a glimpse of Instructor Skylar trying to enter the ring, fighting watchmen who attempted to prevent him. In reality, what could he do?

I was dying.

After one last painful twist, Jade finally released the stick. A pleased smirk was permanently etched on her face as the life drained from the wound. I was half sitting and half sprawled out as liquid crimson collected around me like spilled ink.

That was it. I'd lost. In front of the entire Union. I'd sacrificed my life for the greater good.

Our plan was completed.

Jade sat on her knees, patiently observing the hemorrhaging, waiting to witness which labored breath would be the last.

I started to snigger, which made the bleeding even worse.

Jade wasn't pleased anymore. It was hard to knock her from her square, which made me laugh, choking on my own gore even harder. My vision became blurred, and my heartbeat decelerated.

"What's so funny?" she sneered.

I felt a calmness I'd never experienced overtake me, willing me to come, to join it. So, I just stopped fighting.

My eyes lowered as I took one last exhale. "That you think that you are now the sole heir."

Chapter Twenty
SAIGE

An intense sound, a wail, escaped me before I could even stop it as I clenched my stomach as if Jade had nailed me instead. When the spear pierced Avi, it pierced me too.

Everyone stared, but I didn't care about any of it. I didn't care about their speculations about my loyalty or why I cried out for an oppressor. I didn't care about their stupid war. The war that kept taking and taking and fucking taking. Rampant pillaging and loss of lives. In the name of what? So someone who's clever enough, heartless enough, inhumane enough could claim it as their own? Leaving the rest to scavenge through the piles of garbage?

I staggered closer to the screen. So close that I could almost touch her. Comfort her.

She shouldn't have had to die alone. Mama Seeya should've never sent her back. I told her not to send her back.

But it was ultimately my fault. I should've checked to see if Jade was dead for real in the caves. I should've stabbed her again and again for good measure. The bitch just wouldn't die.

I should've knocked Avi out, tied her down, and forced her to stay. Or followed her even when she told me not to and kept an eye on her.

She'd have been mad at me, but I could've lived with that as long as she was alive. I should've feared less about everything else and should've died at least trying.

I should've never, ever listened to Liyo, Drake, Mama Seeya, who'd do anything to see the current powers fall. At any cost. At the cost of Avi.

Where had we drawn the line? Because the fine mark between us and them had already merged.

Avi began to chuckle as she transitioned to another place. A dark place. Had she seen the humor in dying at the hands of a sibling that she so badly wanted to rehabilitate? Wanted to believe in? Was there humor in dying so young for a cause that hadn't cared about her in return? Maybe it wasn't something so deep at all, but she'd remembered some ridiculous fact about Marco Grant or whatever silly shit she used to enjoy when her life was simple.

I thought so until I heard what she said.

You think that you are now the sole heir.

The phrase repeated, ping-ponging between my ears, inside my skull.

She knew.

Mama Seeya had told her. Of course she had.

Avi's chest stopped moving. And she let go on camera.

The holocam whooshed in on Jade as she staggered to her feet; the same phrase that troubled me troubled her. The game face that she'd crafted so well had thawed, and she couldn't hide it. The crowd murmured in confusion.

"What in the . . . ," the announcer said over the live stream.

In the next instant, the entire arena blacked out. There was a muteness. Then there were crashing sounds followed by thousands of loud spectators.

The broadcast ended. Static.

I concentrated on Mama Seeya. She was a dead woman walking, if I had anything to do with it.

I didn't recall meandering through the passages and reaching the container, but when I appeared in the doorway, I could tell that they all already knew. Liyo's eyes were veined, glassy. Drake's nose was red. Mama Seeya wasn't sad enough for me, so I attacked on impulse. I was so close to getting my fingers around her neck, but Wayal intercepted. I fought him. He was good too. But it didn't matter; someone was going to lose the fight. I didn't care if it was me. Someone had to pay right then.

"Enough!" Mama Seeya roared.

Wayal shoved me off and wiped the blood coming from his nose with his thumb.

"If you attack anyone else on this compound like that again, I will string you up." Her lips were taut. "I'm your mother, and you *will* respect me."

"Mother?" I scoffed. "Ma was nothing like you. She was good. You are a deceiving bi—"

"I said"—she stepped forward—"to watch it, girl."

"You told her that we were blood." I scanned the room, gauging reactions. "Drake, did you know?"

Drake just stared at me. I glared. How could she?

"You knew all along." I pointed to Mama Seeya. "That's how you got her to agree to your half-baked plan, wasn't it? You knew that blood meant everything to her, and you preyed on it."

Mama Seeya tried to reach out, but I stepped back, repulsed by the thought of her touch. "Saige, you're vital to taking this whole institution down. Once and for all. Does that mean anything to you?"

"Don't play your mind games with me. I'm not that orphan girl anymore."

"Then stop acting like one," she retorted. "This is much bigger than one Elite death. The whole rebellion rests on what we do next, and I don't plan to squander it. The Union must fall. With or without you."

"Fuck you," I said and slipped away.

Drake caught up near the exit as I passed the gates and trekked through the sand.

"Saige." She took my shoulder. "Stop."

I shrugged her hand away. "Touch me again and I'll make sure those fingers can never pleasure another dirty client."

She got in front of me and flapped her arms. I paused.

"Why are you doing this?" Drake asked.

I tried skidding to the left, but she intercepted.

"Are we not of your blood?"

"Move!"

"Why do you treat us like how the Uppers do?" She stooped to a low level. "You owe me that."

"I don't owe you or the rest of your little rebel group fuckin' squat."

I finally got past her, but she kept following. "You hate yourself so much that you'd do anything to align yourself with them, but they'll never accept you. You aren't one of them, Saige."

That was it. She'd clipped an active cord. I butted her. Drake fell hard, and I just started punching, anywhere that she couldn't block. Drake was a fighter. But she never tried to hit back. I got tired of striking her after a while. She finally uncovered her face. I had busted her lip and a brow. But it still wasn't enough, so I started to choke her.

"Fight back." I shook her; her head flopped back and forth. "Why won't you fight back?"

Maybe, like me, she wanted to be put out of this life, the misery that we'd all lived.

I loosened my hold and then drove my fist into the sand beside her ear.

She took my fist, opened it, and interlaced her fingers with mine. She pulled me down into a hug, and I collapsed into her. I sobbed so hard, and I couldn't stop it from coming. I'd lost control, and there was no bouncing back that time.

My face was covered in granules of sand and snot. I lifted my swollen eyes. Drake and I were nose to nose. I could smell the sweetness of her breath.

"Take me back."

"Saige, I—"

"Drake, please," I whispered. "I've got to go back."

Drake looked as though she'd lost a best friend. "Okay."

Instead of using the chemicals as before to knock me out during the passage, she struck me as hard as she could in the face.

I deserved that.

❖ ❖ ❖

Huge cacti and pebbly formations were replaced by men aggressively making out in an alleyway and Glitter being ingested from a prostitute's belly button.

I woke up back in the Underground Apex.

The low-level home that I just couldn't seem to escape. It was sad that the dump was my go-to when shit hit the fan aboveground or in the Northern Region or, recently, the rebels' lair. I kept getting sucked back into the debauchery. Maybe that said something about me. Maybe I was more of a Europe than I thought.

I sat up, extending my jaw. It still ached from Drake's punch. The girl had a mean left hook. All that mattered was that she'd made good on her promise. I knew that she'd be reprimanded for letting me go, but that was on her. Mama Seeya had given me an ultimatum. With or without me.

I chose without.

A random flask near the two lovebirds filled with who knew what taunted me. I staggered to my feet and swiped it before joining the always-rowdy crowd on the row. I twisted the top off and sniffed the contents. The odor singed the fine hairs in my nostrils. Fire. My drink of choice. Whoever was pulling the strings out in the far universe was looking out. I threw my head back and allowed the cinnamon liquor to run its course. I was feeling better already.

The grand plan was to drink as much Fire as I weighed. And that was all. Nothing more, nothing less. I wasn't attached to anyone any longer. No Miah. No Avi. No Union and no rebels. I was me again. Solo. That was the cold freedom that I'd earned.

I staggered through the lines of people, swaying and swiping more bottles of Fire as I finished the last. I didn't even know what number I was on after a while. I'd lost count hours ago.

I hiccuped and stumbled into the center where the big holoscreens were. The man who took wagers was now paying out the long line of gamblers who'd predicted Avi's defeat. My hold tightened around the stem of the bottle as they replayed Avi's death, proving to the gamblers that they'd either lost or won. They even animated the spear entering her abdomen. They were all sick. Every single one of them.

These were the people that Drake had tried to force on me. My people, they said.

I chuckled, and then that chuckle turned into a sob. I took another swig to drench the pain, the ache that swelled inside of me, but after a while even Fire wasn't enough. I needed something stronger before something really bad happened. I felt myself spiraling, swinging in the repeats of their deaths. Ma. Avi. Miah.

I bumped into a man enjoying a triple-decker cream cone. It smashed into his face and all over his hands. He was covered in it.

"Hey!" He threw the cone; his brows knitted in the center. "What gives?"

I swiped the cream from his cheek and tasted it. Pistachio.

He shoved me. "Get away, you mutt."

"Music to my ears," I sang.

When he was out of sight, I counted the currency that I'd nicked from his wallet.

I finished the drink and tossed the empty bottle into the counterfeit grass.

"Hey!" I waved down a trader that I knew. "Yellow!"

He'd had jaundice for as long as I could remember. The nickname was fitting. From the other side of the street party, he caught me screaming, then began to sprint. I chased. He ran into people, tossed them in my way, and wove through trolleys. I leaped over downed bystanders and zigzagged to the other side of an alley that intersected with the one he took. I knew the layout of the Underground better than anyone.

I cut him off at the next turn, tackling him from the side into an abandoned barrow.

Yellow grunted, twisting in agony under my weight.

"Don't be so dramatic." I burped. It tasted acidic.

"Wh-what do you want?" He shielded his face, ready for me to strike.

Instead, I held my hand out. He looked at it as if it were a fiery handle.

"I'm not here to fight you, okay," I said, pulling him upright. "I just need something."

He smoothed out his dingy peacoat and straightened the neckline. He ushered me into a discreet area. His eyes shifted back and forth. "What ya need?"

I poured the contents of the wallet into his palm and hiccuped. "The best Glitter you got."

"Wait a minute." He tapped his temple. "I remember you running me clean out of the Vixen for Glitter and now, *now* you want it?"

I shoved him hard into the brick barrier until dust mushroomed around his form. "Please don't make me hurt you."

With a shaking hand, he dug into an inner pocket and pulled out a vial. I snatched it and stalked away.

❖ ❖ ❖

From that high up, I viewed the whole Underground Apex in all its grayish splendor. I'd forgotten all about the deserted spot on the bridge that overlooked the Southern Region's ugly cousin. It was laid out similar to the above. I wondered if that was on purpose. Or maybe the Union had built it originally as a base model of what they wanted and then built the 2.0 version up top, leaving us the scraps as usual.

When Silver first brought me to the Underground when I was little, I'd hated it. I'd yearned for the outdoors. Space. Air. I'd lived some of my life stuck in a tiny cube with Ma because she knew that they'd toss me from a window if they ever found out about my conception. After she was executed, I was spoiled by living in the Outskirts with Mama Seeya. How lucky I was to experience that when many others had remained underground and in the dark.

When I wasn't scrubbing questionable bodily fluids from stall tiles at the club or hand drying mugs behind the bar, I'd take the meager earnings and get a flask of Fire and a bag of lollipops. A working alcoholic by my early teens. But it was my only form of escape. I wasn't much into big crowds or loud noises, so I ventured away and up. Most people didn't come to the Underground to be alone. They came to connect, let loose, have some version of liberty that the Union would never provide.

The farther I traveled up, the fewer people were around. There was a rickety bridge, an eyesore located right over the Apex. I found a way to get to the top and discovered emptiness and solitude.

I kicked the empty Glitter vials left by past junkies who wanted the same serenity in the chaos as I did and plopped down in the middle. My feet dangled from the edge as I took a whiff of poorly ventilated, stale air.

The vault of the Apex looked like a floating mountain base with strategically positioned stony pillars as huge as the Transmega keeping it from caving in. Block-shaped structures with honeycomb-framed windows were closely crammed together. Fake trees and fake grass filled the makeshift parks, adding texture, pigment to the dullness. Knots of colors were woven throughout, attempting to brighten the mood, the atmosphere of the sooty city. Day was night and night was day. Time merged into one long bout of never-ending repetition.

A hell loop on earth.

The vial rolled back and forth in the pit of my palm, the contents swirling inside. Inviting me to try, even just a little bit. I was disgusted with myself for even holding it, considering it. I'd always looked down on people who snorted it, stuck it in their orifices. I'd once pegged them as weak, but now I got it. It was too much to live sober. Hell, it was too much to live at all.

And I didn't want to live anymore.

Tears. I wiped my face quickly before they could fall. Embarrassed that I even cared. Angry that I couldn't control anything, including my emotions. I'd been wounded because I'd broken the cardinal rule: never care about anyone.

I deserved it all, though. Everything I was feeling. I never should've crossed that boundary. I should've learned my lesson after they took Ma from me. That feeling, grief, was too much to bear. The heaviness on my shoulders, on my chest. The dark cloud that continued to pelt me with hail. I couldn't move forward. I was content with being the hard-ass. It was lonely, but that was at least safe.

I'd allowed myself to open up, and look where it landed me. Still isolated, but now more broken than ever before, sitting above the city about to down a whole vial and end it all.

The Union didn't believe in religion, the afterlife; God was a guise created by Europes to keep them in their place with the promise of a better life after death, they said. It gave slaves something to look forward to. To ease the pain of being chattel. So, when they took over, they disbanded religion and rooted themselves in science, only things they could prove. The here, the now.

We had something in common. I believed that when we died, there was nothingness.

On the other end, Lower Residents trusted that when we died, we'd reunite with our loved ones. But the bad ones were destined for eternal torment.

In this world, I wasn't sure who was good and who was bad. We all seemed neck and neck from where I stood.

Either way it went, I wouldn't know until I left the realm of the living. I kind of hoped that there was nothingness because I was a bad person who'd done a lot of bad things. Some of them I didn't regret, though, but if the Lower Residents were right, then I was surely headed for damnation.

What torture could be worse than the underworld I was living in currently?

I'd take my chances.

There were several hits in a vial of Glitter. The body would build an immunity the longer you took it. I didn't have the time or patience for that. I poured the entire thing into my palm and sniffed it all until only fragments were left and Glitter dripped from my nostrils. The cavities in my nose and inside my brain began to tingle. I lay back in slow motion, falling onto the bridge floor, into a puddle of water, and into another realm completely.

Was I dead? Because I couldn't feel my body. I got to my feet, I thought. I wasn't sure exactly, but I was standing. I was on the same bridge overlooking the Apex, but it was a different Apex. It was beautiful. The roof was smooth and white, and the buildings were silver and glowing. The vegetation was the greenest color that I'd ever seen, and even a stream ran through the epicenter. A butterfly landed on the tip of my nose. I couldn't feel it, but that was okay.

"Sister!" It was Avi down below waving her arms overhead, standing in a patch of grass. Real grass. "What are you doing up there? Come down. Come join the others."

"I-I'll be right there," I replied.

I was definitely dead.

I couldn't remember how I got down, but I must have because I was standing across from Avi. There seemed to be fragments of time, gaps that I couldn't account for.

Avi threw herself into me, but I was numb still.

"I've missed you." She looked up at me with those cheerful eyes. "Where were you?"

"Does it matter?" I grinned. "I'm here now."

"You're absolutely right. It doesn't matter. You *are* here now." She pulled back. "Follow me."

We strode along the path, but then we transported to the outside of the Vixen, but it wasn't really the strip club anymore but more like a greenhouse.

"What is this place?" I asked.

"What's gotten into you?" She spun around with squinted eyes. "You are acting weird."

"Avi, you died yesterday."

"Died?" She placed my hand over her heart. I couldn't feel the pulse. It was odd. "I'm very much so alive. Now stop playing games, Miah is worried sick."

We hadn't walked through the revolving doors, but we were now inside Silver's old office. It was covered in thick vines concealed in an array of pastel blooms and vases of blossoms.

Miah was behind the desk too busy pruning roots to notice us.

"Miah." His name barely left my lips.

He dropped the clippers. "My love! Where have you been? We've been worried."

I began to cry. "Why can't I feel you?"

He squeezed my shoulders. "What are you talking about? I can feel you. You're as real as the summer day is long."

I nodded, painfully.

He kissed me. I waited to feel his long lashes sweep across my lids or the warmth of his lips, but there was nothing.

"Your mother, she's been waiting for you."

"Ma?"

Miah bowed his head.

We were then in the heart of the city. Big holoscreens played clips of Ma and me during the earlier years. The songs we'd sung and the games we'd played. The memories that I had thought I'd lost. She'd been gone for so long. I was starting to forget even the sound of her voice.

She was picking yellow flowers and using them to weave a headband.

"Ma?" I gasped.

"Saige?" She turned around and dusted loose straw from the knees of a nude-colored bodysuit.

She placed the crown over my head; then she took my numb hands and placed her forehead on mine. "My baby has gotten so big, so stunning. How could I have missed this?"

"It's okay, Ma. It's okay."

She sat me down in a spot of the meadow. "Where have you been this entire time? We've all been looking for you."

"I was alive. In another world. I think." I watched more butterflies flutter, wrestle with one another.

"You always loved a good story." She grinned and started weaving more flowers onto twine. "It's beautiful here, isn't it?"

Tiny blue birds dove past, and the wind gently blew through the field. "Hmm."

She turned her body to face me. "There's nothing in this life that I want more than for you to stay here with me. With the others. You know that, right?"

I grimaced. "What?"

"You can't stay here." Her blue eyes started to glaze. "You've got to go. Go back."

"Ma, no. I'm not leaving you again. I won't do it."

"Saige." She lowered her eyes. "Go back."

"Ma? No!"

"Go back." Her voice echoed.

Then there was nothingness.

I awoke in the middle of the row, Yellow and Pea turning my body to the side as foam and lumps of puke spewed from my mouth. I was seizing. Pimps and dealers surrounded us, while others pulled out devices and live streamed. Then flashing lights overtook my vision as all control left, and I jerked violently.

❖ ❖ ❖

"I know you're awake." I sensed Pea hovering.

I unpeeled an eye. I was in a tiny chamber decorated with the bare minimum. A sliver of a bed. A tiny stove with an old pot on the burner. A bucket in the corner to piss in. A rectangular window facing another building. Low light.

"It's all I could afford down here without turning tricks, but it feels good to have something of your own." She poured room-temperature water from a pitcher into two wooden cups. "I will say that even though it's a bit grim here, I don't miss the Citadel."

With the good arm, she placed the drink next to me. "I always thought I would, you know."

The other was missing and bandaged at the elbow.

"Oh, this." She noticed and lifted the nub to face level. "We can thank our newest General."

Pea laughed uncomfortably before taking a sip and staring out the window at more brick.

"Never thought I'd see you again." She gulped more liquid that time. "I thought I was a dead girl after stealing that access card for you—for us. I guessed it was too much going on for them to pinpoint who the culprit was. I was—well, am—lucky to even be alive."

She took a seat on a wobbly stool, rested the cup in between her thighs, and focused on me.

After a few beats, she rose. Pea could never just sit still. "Come on. I want to show you something."

I wasn't in the mood for movement. Breathing. Anything really. But I knew that she would get more annoying and persistent if I didn't. Pea wasn't the type to take no for an answer. I hoped she didn't think that we were friends or that we'd trauma bond over how bad the Union had treated us.

I slid from the bed and trailed behind her.

She led me to an underpass with subway tracks almost buried by rock and dirt and time. Split towropes as thick as my arm meandered from the top and along the walls in sets.

"It's up ahead." She stalked over piles of cables, spry on her feet like a garden mouse.

She pointed to a mural at the end of the tunnel. "There."

It spanned several meters each way on a concrete barricade. Avi's face was spray-painted in all the most vivid colors of the earth. Stars and asteroid belts were suspended while her hair was in two puffy balls that resembled planets in orbit. She was surrounded by the entire solar system. From her palm, the sun illuminated bright as she smiled gingerly. Hope etched in her eyes.

I trembled as if I'd been planted back in the Northern Region with no furs to shield me from the climate.

"These have been popping up everywhere. Above and below." Pea laughed through tears. "She's given them courage. She's started a revolution. Through goodness. And kindness. I-I never thought it was possible."

"Why are you showing me this?" I snarled.

Pea remained relaxed in her stance. "I can't believe you still have to ask."

She was right. I had forgotten that everyone knew that she was blood.

It was time to go. I'd seen enough.

As I turned my back, Pea called out, "Avi never stopped waiting for you."

I hesitated.

"She looked up to you. Mimicked your ways. I wasn't sure why at first, but I noticed how much braver she became after you'd met," Pea said. "I wish you could've seen the look on her face, the disappointment, when there was no word from you. Somehow, she knew you were alive and that you'd return. She once told me that she always believed that you'd do the right thing."

"And the right thing is fighting beside rebels who can't even bear to look at me? Call me mutt this and mutt that every chance they get. Used as a nameless and faceless pawn for someone else's battle over power and territory? Is that the *right* thing?"

"I don't have the answers, Saige. I can't bring people back from the dead. I couldn't even manage to keep both arms." She offered a sad chortle. "But I do know that we need to finish what Avi started. In our own way. We don't have to be this or be that. We need to be true. Whatever way that looks."

"Oh yeah?" I sniggered. "And what's that to you?"

"Kinda looks like the shit we just pumped from your stomach." Pea kicked at some cables near her foot. "A mess."

I let out a howl.

"A lot has changed since Avi's . . ." She looked away; her childlike expression hardened. "I don't know which side I'm on anymore—the rebels, the ordinary worker—but we have to destroy the Union. Avenge Avi. Then we figure out the rest from there."

Like her, I wasn't sure, either, but I was down for payback. The ultimate takedown. And if I had to use Mama Seeya and her cronies to do that, then so be it.

"I guess we don't have shit else to lose." I shrugged. "If you're down for one last suicide mission, then I'm all in."

Chapter Twenty-One
LIYO

Saige had stormed in like a banshee. Attacked Mama Seeya. Her hair, her eyes as harsh as an uncontrolled blaze. Fists flew in a haze. As for me? I was stuck. An onlooker, witnessing it all unfold. How was it possible that I had all the power, yet none at all?

Life happened to me, not the other way around.

Thick and skinny currents popped around my fingers, and I even felt them bouncing around the backs of my eyeballs, hitting the cavities, and then reflecting back to the other side. They also cracked in my skull and inside my chest. Even my toenails sizzled. It felt like I would self-detonate soon, taking the whole region out with me.

You need to calm down.

Calm down, Liyo.

Now.

I curled my fingers into claws then into clenched fists.

Wayal rushed back into the container and notified Mama Seeya that Drake was missing, too, and that there was no sign of Saige.

The underside of my tongue went dry at the news.

Mama Seeya nodded once and then turned to me. She placed her hand upon my shoulder. "Go with Wayal," she said. "We have much to discuss. Tomorrow."

Elu was led to one place and I to another.

She said something to me before disappearing into her quarters, but my ears only replayed Wayal's voice telling Mama Seeya that Saige was gone.

A mirror was perched over a copper sink. I caught a glance of myself. Or at least who I thought I was. I had forgotten how I looked. It'd been days. Maybe longer. The purplish bags under my eyes and the uneven buzz cut I'd given myself to camouflage myself from the Union and the cracked lips from the moisture suck of the desert. I shrieked from the depths of my soul, and electricity sparked from every surface of my skin. A human light orb. The glass splintered. The basin ripped from its station. The wooden base of the bed split into lopsided parts. After I was done, the area looked like a hurricane had torn through it.

I snatched the lumpy cot from the broken rail, tossed it on the ground, collapsed into it, and stared vacantly at the rusty ceiling.

When I began to weep for all the people lost, I closed my eyes tight. This couldn't be all there was to living. Existing. What if Saige was right? Was I on the true side? Avi, an innocent, had died for the cause. Mama Seeya's cause. Had she planned that? Had she known that by telling Avi that information, it would drive her to go all in?

I was flailing, making one desperate decision after another and losing sight of the actual purpose. I'd been so set on getting to Mama Seeya to get answers. Clarity. And I was just as confused as I had been living in the caves.

What were we fucking doing?

Avi. The blow that had taken her life . . . I couldn't unsee it. I couldn't unlive it. Couldn't shake that image from my memory. I tried to replace that copy with the passionate one we'd briefly shared. Anything else. But it always returned to Jade's spear jammed into Avi's body. The slickness on Avi's forehead. The look of betrayal on her face as her own sister drove it farther and farther.

The pain in my chest grew. It was unbearable. I couldn't breathe lying on my back anymore, so I turned to my side to alleviate the pressure. But it was still heavy.

❖ ❖ ❖

I was nudged awake. I'd forgotten where I was after a load of nightmares of the Union caging me like a hound, so I vaulted from the ground with a knife in hand. Ready.

Wayal put his arms up in surrender. I let go of his collar and scratched the back of my head. "My apologies."

"I would ask how you're doing, but I can see not very well." He pressed out the wrinkles.

I sheathed the blade, grunting.

"Mama Seeya wanted to come, but she's preoccupied, getting ready for today's brief on—well, you know." He gestured. "So, she sent me to take you to breakfast."

My stomach grumbled at the thought; I'd forgotten that I was starving. I couldn't remember the last time I'd eaten. "Lead the way."

We bumped into Elu. "How'd you sleep?" she asked.

I shrugged.

She offered me a warm smile.

"This way," Wayal said to both of us.

We followed him through the shafts as rebels filed into the larger eating space. They had preallotted H_2O packs, protein jerky, and a block of bread. Reminded me of living back in the cubes.

Wayal must've sensed something. "We ration food and water here just until we can return to the land—our land."

"You've been here for many years." Elu broke her dried meat into smaller, more manageable bites.

"Too many." Wayal took a morsel of bread and chewed hard, crumbs dotting his beard. "One day soon, we can have a proper meal. Until then we consume food that wears down the molars." He gave a hearty laugh.

Elu chirped.

I didn't crack a smirk.

"How have you been able to keep the Union from finding this place?" I asked.

He looked as if I'd just spat in his eye. "We never get comfortable in one place."

Wayal sucked his pack dry, trying to get every drop on his tongue.

"We've been preparing for the occupation. Outposts like this one are all over the desert. In the mountains. Underground even. We've created a whole network of rebels. Fighters. Workers that are sick and tired of this shit every day." He juggled the last bite of jerky in the air. "And all of them are ready to jump when Mama Seeya commands it."

He popped the last piece in his mouth and ground away as he pointed to a table of the Impures we'd met when we'd arrived.

"Let me show you how bad they are." Wayal projected a 3D display on his wristcom. On the transparent screen the four Impures took down a watchmen hive in seconds. "Nadia is the baddest of 'em all. She might even give you a run for your money."

Elu and I just listened.

"We were able to get our hands on some of the tech that Union scientists produced to make humans with abilities." He was proud.

I was disgusted. "That tech killed thousands of people just to produce a few."

He tapped the screen, and the footage withdrew. "Those people weren't willing subjects. The Union tested on people by force. We gave each of them a choice."

"So that makes it better?" I countered.

"They have Transmegas, and who knows what else the Union has up their manicured sleeves." Wayal sat back, his irritation visible, rising with each word. "I would've volunteered in the trials if Mama Seeya had let me, if it meant we were even a little bit closer to a better chance at freeing ourselves from the Union's chokehold. There's no success without sacrifice. Maybe you've been living in the hollows for too long and forgot what it's like to be here. In the same shit. Every fuckin' day."

Electricity cracked. Nadia and the others began to stir. Elu placed her hand on top of my fist.

Wayal rose from the bench and bowed partially. "Enjoy your meal, Savior."

I watched as he wove through lines of hungry workers. I felt an urge to toss him over the crowd into that vat of muck they were preparing for supper.

Elu's grasp stiffened, pulling my attention back.

She scooted closer. "You have reservations."

"No, I-I just, uh." There was too much going on inside my head. The thoughts, the fears toppled over one another, creating an avalanche.

"It seems as though you people love to speak in riddles. Withholding pertinent information from one another." She asked, "How's that been working for your society so far?"

I hadn't expected the bluntness. She was onto something. There was no longer a place for our old toxic ways.

"Saige." Mentioning her name out loud caused throbs of guilt. "Maybe she was right about all of this, and because I didn't believe her—she must feel . . . abandoned. I'm starting to question what we're doing here—why I came back."

Elu took a look around, absorbing the bustle of my people.

I'd been selfish. I hadn't taken the time to ask her how she was coping after Miah's death, too buried in my own issues.

"What do you want, Elu?"

She focused on a mother feeding an infant. "I'd like to live in a world where amity is the core and not division. One where that child and that mother could move from space to space, region to region without barriers. We've spent our entire lives and the lives before that and the lives before that alienated from one another. When does it end? When do we figure out that we're chasing dominance over the other because we fear the things that we do not understand? No one is innocent in this sphere. Not even the so-called noble ones. We've conformed to this way of life too easily. Fighting a fight that our forefathers started and died trying to maintain. Perchance we don't have to follow in their shadows."

The mother nuzzled the baby with the tip of her nose, then wrapped the child in a long cloth and propped them onto her back, tightening the loose ends around her waist. She had work to complete.

"You and me, we can do better, you know? It won't be easy." Elu took a long exhale. "But living never is."

She was right. We had choices, even if it didn't always seem like it.

"Just like Avi, who laid down her life for change. Like my people, like Miah." She looked at me straight. "We can too. What else is there?"

❖ ❖ ❖

The command room had the same coppery layout as the rest of the outpost. In the farthest reach were massive waterwheels, slowly churning on posts. Cloudy-faced pressure gauges with steady pointers lined the stockades. They were attached to heavy oxidized valves that ran along the bottom. A giant square slab of concrete was stationed in the middle. High-ranking rebels positioned themselves at the edges with their arms crisscrossed tight over their chests or looped behind the smalls of their backs, waiting for Mama Seeya.

"I appreciate you all for coming." Mama Seeya widened her arms as if she wanted to embrace each person. "This is an occasion. One that we've all been waiting for—working toward—some of us for decades, some of us only recently."

She picked up a reader and tapped the screen. From the center of the stony block materialized a holographic inverted cone.

Avi taking her last breath replayed. Then it transitioned to a triumphant Jade being inaugurated as official General.

"Let the members recognize that Avi was indeed working with us and has unfortunately lost the battle." Mama Seeya bowed her head in tribute. Other rebels held expressions of triumph, gratification even. To them she was just another Upper.

I expected Mama Seeya to say more about Avi's plight, how she'd secretly helped progress the rebels' cause, but she just went on, business as usual.

"Jade's young, but she's abysmal. Ruthless." The 3D hologram of the newest General rotated. "She must be exterminated along with Head Gardner and the rest of their appointed members."

A man with circular frames and a crooked jaw spoke. "So, we strike the Citadel first?"

Mama Seeya typed on the reader, and a landscape map of the Southern Region emerged and then zoomed to the Citadel's massive estate. "That would be ideal, but that fortress is ironclad. We need to draw them out."

"And what would they want so bad that they'd leave their fortification?" a young woman with a metal leg asked.

"Me." There was a gleam in her eye as she shot the woman a lopsided grin.

The rebels were up in arms, mumbling objections and breaking into side arguments.

The display had swapped from the Citadel to the original terrain map. Strategically placed red, pulsating orbs covered the plot. She selected one, and it showed Dice creating carnage. She was a human explosive. Mama Seeya called the team Tele-Impures.

"Head Gardner currently has a mole named Gabriel in custody. She thinks he's on their side. He's already planted the next phase in her mind. She knows exactly where I'll be next. She and the General will arrive, expecting to leave with my head. We will have the Tele-Impures ready to create chaos in their assigned quadrants."

The next clip was of hundreds of thousands of rebel fleets ready in each sector.

"We clip the head of the serpent, and the rest will collapse."

"What about the Transmegas?" the man from before added. "We don't know exactly how many they even have. And the new droids. I hardly think this is as easy as you've laid it out."

Wayal grabbed his blade, ready to pounce on behalf of his monarch. Mama Seeya shot him a look. He backed down at once.

"Dag, no plan is ever clear cut. No war is ever easily won. There will be casualties. Thousands, if not millions of them." Her eyes were much wider as she made her way over. "I'm willing to sacrifice it all in order to retrieve what was stolen. Are you willing to sacrifice for us, yourself, Dag?"

He lowered his head in humiliation. "I am. I'm with you. For the cause and to the end."

She stroked his face tenderly.

"We do have the upper hand." She then turned her attention to Elu. "The creator has placed something rich into our hands, and I don't believe in coincidences."

What did Elu have to do with any of it?

"Elu has journeyed all the way from the Northern Region and has aided in bringing Liyo back to us. For that we owe her our deepest gratitude." She made a steeple with her hands. "Elu's colony was massacred by the Union. She's like many of us, forever stained by the Union's treachery. They will not stop, unless we stop them."

The people hung on to her every word as if God himself had graced them. I watched as even Elu was drawn in by her gift of gab.

"Can you tell us anything about the blue flame that would aid in the upcoming battle?"

Elu leaned forward in her chair. "The blue flame is a mixture of hot gases. Flames are the result of a chemical reaction, primarily between oxygen in the air and a fuel. This particular gas is mined in small amounts underground. We use it for weapons, energy. But when it is volatile, it can destroy. One cannot come back from the burns of the blue flame, and they used it on us."

Mama Seeya bore a sympathetic look. "Are there more colonies, perhaps deeper into the north, that have access to any other reserves?"

I interjected. "You always said that the rebels had ties with the colonies."

"We have loose connections, yes."

"Then why haven't you used those connections to create a merger?"

"The colony that we made contact with wasn't interested in joining our cause but wanted to keep the channels open."

"Maybe they're playing it safe because they've been taken advantage of and stripped of their resources before. It wouldn't be to their benefit to just give away their numbers, their reserves like that."

Mama Seeya and I had a stare-off. The room went cold. The only sound came from the clunky churning of the waterwheels.

"If there are more colonies, then they're surely in danger. I'm sure after seeing the desecration that the Union inflicted on their peaceful settlement, they will want justice too." Mama Seeya placed her sights back on Elu. "And the Union will never stop hunting them for their resources. Your township was the first, but it will certainly not be the last. We don't have the luxury of remaining under the radar, being complacent. You die, or you die fighting. It's that simple."

Elu's face was void of color as she began to realize the truth in Mama Seeya's words.

"I want you to return to the north and tell them that they need to join ranks. I want you to be the liaison. With your own eyes, you've seen what they're capable of. Make them see that this is the only way to survival. Together, and only together, we can end this."

Elu leaned back, weighing the options. She'd witnessed the carnage by the Union not only on her territory but on ours. I didn't blame her for what she agreed to next.

She finally nodded. She was on board.

I felt like a ghost. Light and see through.

"I'll have my best accompany you to the other side," Mama Seeya assured her.

What would her "best" do if the Union decided to bomb their transport on the journey back? She couldn't guarantee safety. Hell, Saige and I had barely gotten out alive. I wondered if she'd promised something similar to my parents before they were executed as she managed to get away scot-free.

Mama Seeya's voice droned in the background as I tried to regain control of my theories, my emotions. Something was off. That wasn't the same Mama Seeya on the Outskirts that I'd remembered. The new version was different. More fixed. Cutthroat even. Was it that we had all just evolved? Had circumstance, the Union's savagery created fresh monsters, or had we always had it in us? The longer she spoke, the longer I stayed there, I felt like the further and further away I got from whatever the real goal was.

"After the Union heads fall, what will happen to the Upper Residents?" I asked.

"I thought it was obvious, Liyo." Her face settled into a stoic glare. "They'll all burn."

The chamber erupted in cheers and howls.

❖ ❖ ❖

I followed Mama Seeya and her confidants away from the command room and through the vessels and along the pathways where workers labored in units until they finally stopped near the exit. They separated, and she continued into the calm desert, solo. In the distance was an old gazebo, from the looks of it, on its last leg. It was enclosed by an array of misshapen cacti. An unpolished garden to blend in with the ugliness of the landscape.

"If you wanted my company, you could've said so," she said without looking back.

I joined her side, and together we made our way to the bronzed eyesore.

"You have something on your mind." It was more of a demand than a statement from her. "Speak."

"Why can't the rebels get rid of the Union's government and then give the residents the choice to—"

"To what?" Her head snapped in my direction. "To work beside us and live happily ever after? Do you really think that after we destroy their way of life, their privilege, their power that they wouldn't want to retaliate?"

"The only reason I'm alive right now is because Instructor Skylar helped us get to the other side," I explained. "Does that not count for anything? Does that not say that people can make amends?"

"Hmm, Instructor Skylar. I made him an offer long ago." She appeared winded. "He's not with them, but he's also not with us either. That means he's the enemy. We don't have space for second-guessers."

"Then we're no different from them."

If her vision were blades, then I'd be chock full of cuts. "You've got a lot of nerve coming into my base and tossing around self-righteous discourse. Need I remind you how they had your mother, your father down on all fours like cattle waiting for slaughter. Blew their brains out right in front of you. Ah, how forgiving you are."

"I have never, *ever* forgotten that day," I hissed. "And I have *not* forgiven."

"Then what?" she asked. "Have you truly taken a liking for an Upper, fallen in love with her romanticized views of a false world?"

"Don't bring her—"

She grinned and continued trekking through the grains.

"Is it so bad that I want to change? That I want us to change? That just maybe Avi was showing us something that we haven't considered before? Don't we have a duty to give it a chance?" I asked.

"You speak of duty as if my entire life hasn't been devastated by duty." She spat in the dirt.

"Mama Seeya, I'm begging for you to hear me out. They—the Uppers—are a people of custom. That's everything to them. They'll listen to blood."

"And they will indeed listen to the blood of their own sloshing through their picturesque streets."

"Saige *is* the rightful heir."

She whipped around and pinned me against the gazebo's fence. "Saige, Saige? Where's she now? Gone. Selfish as usual. Unfit to rule even herself."

Saige was gone, but not for good. She was like a wild feline. She always came back.

"But what about democracy?" I countered.

She released me, sucking her teeth. "Democracy. Mankind's biggest myth. Higher-ups use it to control the masses. Democracy is false freedoms."

"I know that Saige can do it. With the right band. You by her side. She could even enlist a liaison from each nation."

"When in the history of humankind has that ever truly worked?"

I shook my head. "Only the now matters. Avi thought it was possible, and so do I. We can be the change. We don't have to rule in blood and tyranny like them."

"My dear boy, lives are on the line. One mistake could lead to a catastrophe worse than the ones we've ever faced. We've got one shot—one damn shot at this. I truly want to believe in mankind, that they can change. For the better." She continued, "To prove your theory would take time that we do not have. I'm sorry. I truly am. But all they know is carnage, and they will never break, and so we will never break. I will break them or perish trying."

I wiped the drippings from my nose. "Then I can't be a part of this any longer."

"You will be a part of this, Liyo. You will see it to the end as planned, just like the rest of us. And you will do it for your family, you will do it for your dead parents, and you will do it for Eve."

Chapter Twenty-Two
JADE

The Caucasoids, the modern-day Europes, have bankrupted everything decent on the planet, historically speaking. Whether they derived from Neanderthals, the Caucasus Mountains, or an alien vessel, they are mankind's fastest and most lethal spreading virus. The elders knew it when they orchestrated the Revolt a thousand years ago, and I knew it currently. How they themselves did not understand that fact was beyond me.

The answers to their destruction of today and yesterday were recorded in great detail. The Union hadn't allowed them to read, but we were all taught why they'd had to fall. We drilled into them why they could never, ever lead again. Scientists had proven that something in their frontal lobe would never be fully developed. Perhaps it was evolution. Certain species had different functions. Possessing power wasn't one of theirs.

We were the first on this planet to rule. To exist. They came from us. After us. Somehow our weakness and their cunning created a saga of thousands of years of inequity.

I would not repeat the blunders of the ones who came before me. I was a different breed.

I did not blame the Europes for taking advantage of our greed, our inability to assemble tribes, our trusting of foreigners. Settlers saw an opportunity and snatched it before any of us could blink. The ancient Europes were convicts, cast away from their own lands and seeking new ones. The new worlds they stepped foot on were already occupied, but what did that mean for an invader with a record of violence, butchery? Instead of peacefully entering a new society, they wanted it all minus the original peoples. They brought weapons to tribes who'd never laid eyes on guns before. They brought plagues. Raped. They connived their way to the highest positions. On all continents. Even fighting one another for rights and access to stolen land, and they seized kingdom after kingdom. Spreading the lies of religion. Breeding humans for stock like mere heifers.

There were churches preaching the love of God above enslaved people's dungeons where human feces would rise to the calves of the ancestors. My blood. The same lineage that courses through me now.

Slaves, obey your earthly masters with respect and fear and sincerity of heart, just as you would obey Christ. Ephesians 6:5.

I applauded them for keeping power by any means necessary, but we studied them. I studied them.

Now it was our turn. Our duty to complete the cycle. I was doing creation a favor by introducing a purer, untouched race.

The people would discover my treachery at some point, that I knew, but they'd be too busy thanking me to even care for longer than an evening at the symphony. I was willing to take the fall, the hate in order to better society, propel it forward from the rut that Father had gotten us into. We all had to make sacrifices for the greater good. He'd taught me that. Even my dead sister.

A droid entered my quarters with a shiny engraved tray of fresh berries, cubed mangoes, pastries, and steamy mint tea. She set it beside the chair facing the large picture window overlooking the Citadel's grounds. She scooped a spoonful of honey into the cup and stirred. The metal clinking on the inside of the porcelain. She handed me the fine china, and I took the delicate handle, then waved her away.

The day was picture perfect. Vivid. I just wanted to dive right in. Altocumulus clouds dotted sunny skies. They sailed ever so gently across the plains. Hundred-year-old lush trees and foliage went on for hundreds of kilometers each way. The Citadel itself was a fortress with many smaller castles attached, creating our own utopia. An architectural anthill was what the original maker had described it as.

My home.

Father would've been so pleased to witness it thriving. I knew that he'd be proud of me. That I had done what was required to ensure our survival for another thousand years and beyond.

Head Gardner had propositioned an agreement that I couldn't oppose. Removing Father from his pillar. I knew that he was much too proud and that he wouldn't have budged any other way but by force. Even with reason, I witnessed him shoot down Head Gardner's concepts. I always believed that her ideas were extreme, but they were suitable for the current climate. Impures and rebels were running rampant.

I'd gone to Father personally, giving him one last chance to redeem himself. To show us that he was fit to lead us into the future, but he refused.

That was a sad day, indeed.

But he'd had a choice in the matter. We all did. He made an oath to protect and advance the Union even if that meant his own demise. It's the very oath I took, and the one Generals before him took. He hadn't delivered on that pledge in life, but I made sure that he did in the end.

Head Gardner revealed that Father was concealing more than he shared with the Union, the cabinet. We had entered a regression. Crop shortages, water reservoirs dehydrating, declining currency. He was losing control. Head Gardner suggested that they expand the territory into the north, where there were better resources, but he declined, not wanting to interrupt the treaty. She told him that they could utilize the Transmegas and watchmen reserves to level them off quickly. He cautioned her to never speak of it again.

Head Gardner, a true patriot, made a pact with some lowly workers and began distributing Glitter in order to keep the Union afloat without Father's consent.

He discovered her involvement with the operation shortly after the last battle in the Outskirts and planned on stripping her of her rank after Avi's matrimonial ceremony.

She couldn't allow that demotion, and neither could I.

The plot was modest, straightforward.

We'd spread the illness in the north. Give them the antidote. Mine the blue flame. Supply it to the workers. Pin the blame on the rebels. It'd rile the people up. Create doubt, fear. Frightened people were agreeable people.

It all worked in our favor.

Father was weak, and so was his cabinet. He had to go.

It was my first day as the official General—for the second time—and the next phase was nigh. Enact the latest regulations on workers. Use the fury of the people to flush out Mama Seeya. The head of the rebel syndicate. Once the heart was void of lifeblood, their whole structure would weaken. We'd fearmonger and give every Upper Resident the right to hunt the remaining Europes down. It had to be a united effort. They had to believe that it was truly them—their own will—that had come up with the idea to eradicate the disease for good. The people had to make that decision for themselves. I was just helping them along. Speeding up the inevitable.

Afterward, we'd share with the Union that our land no longer had longevity and that the only viable option was waging war with the colonies in the north. Starting a newer, purer world.

An alert from my wristcom sounded.

A broadcast displayed on the small screen.

Head Gardner made the announcement on my behalf.

She sported a deep-red bodysuit with leather plates for shoulder armor. Her hair was freshly braided in thick cornrows cascading down and ending at her lower back.

Behind a podium in front of a group of journalists packed into a conference chamber, she introduced herself. Holocams rushed in, in unison. Too many lights flashed for her comfort. "On behalf of the newly appointed General Jore, we will be enacting a new regulation effective immediately."

The holocam zoomed in on only her profile.

"To further the efforts of population control for not only the people of the Union but the environment itself, it has come down that all workers must report to the clinics for immediate sterilization."

The room exploded with hands jetting in the air and side conversations and triple the number of flashes.

"What are General Jore's thoughts on Avi's departing statement? And I quote: 'You think that you are now the sole heir.' End quote. What did she mean by that? Did the former General have an illegitimate child that the Union doesn't know about?"

Head Gardner wasn't prepared. I scrolled through the wristcom, trying to contact her and tell her to end the press conference, but before I was able, there was a strained voice approaching from behind me that I didn't recognize.

"The body." A long wheeze. "Where's her body?"

I tapped out of the announcement and rose from the comfort of my seat.

"Mother," I said softly. I'd forgotten she existed. After Father's death, she'd been moping about and refused to leave the confinements of her quarters.

I opened my arms to embrace her, but before I could even touch her, she struck me. My cheek stung like tiny needles pricked underneath the skin. Still in shock, I grasped the area with both hands. What had I expected? A warm greeting? I'd just killed her firstborn. Her favorite.

I was nothing to my mother. She'd made that clear. Without words. I couldn't remember the last time she'd hugged me, told me that she was proud of me. As far as she was concerned, we were associates.

"Where. Is. My. Daughter's. Body?" She raised an open palm to strike me again.

I cowered. "I-I don't know. Someone disabled the circuit boards, and then when the power was restored, she was gone. I had watchmen search the dome in its entirety."

"Why didn't you look for her personally?" Her nostrils spread as she lowered her arm slowly.

"I tried—"

My voice had the decibels of a tiny mouse. Nothing I said mattered. She stormed over to the tray, grabbed the teacup, and hurled it into the wall. It busted. "While you sip on hot drinks and fill yourself with desserts." She took the whole plate and launched it at me.

I ducked; it missed me completely before it also shattered.

"That's the least you could've done was locate her. The least!"

"Mother, I—"

"Don't." I knew that look in her eyes. Pain. Vengeance. She wanted Avi to be standing in front of her instead of me. I wondered if she would've put on the same show if Avi was in my shoes. Would she have even shed tears? For the holocams, perhaps, but inside she'd rejoice that her first heir had been triumphant.

Without words, her posture, her expression wanted to end me, cause me to join Avi and Father.

She turned her back, and before exiting, she said, "I will never, *ever* absolve you of this."

The partition slid and then sealed behind her.

Tea and honey dripped from the walls, and fruit and pastries and chunks of bread and crumbs littered the floor.

I darted to the bureau and, in a rush, pushed every article to the ground. What remained, I grabbed and smashed, including Father's glove case. I drove my fist into the smooth surface until the skin on my fists peeled. Even in death, she caused me anguish. Mother must've forgotten the fact that her beloved had challenged me. Attempted to kill me. Did that even matter?

She could do no wrong in their eyes. She was a worthless child. An even more worthless adult. I was better than her in every way. Academics. Combat. I'd even outsmarted her during the duel. I'd proven time and time again that I was the better choice. The better adolescent. But my parents never took heed. Their loss, really. What more could I have become if I had experienced the same nurturing that she had? Pipe dreams. In the end, I became exactly what I was destined. I made that happen. Not one other soul could take credit for my blooming.

If Mother wanted to blame anyone for how things turned out, then she should blame herself. She was as much at fault as I. She wasn't going to enter my quarters and strike me like some commoner. I was the General. I made the rules.

A dreadful thought crossed my mind. Disposing of her too. She didn't play an integral role in anything anymore. She was only a wife, a trophy to Father when he was alive. She probably wouldn't be missed either way, and if she would, then it certainly wouldn't be by me.

That day was supposed to have been a victorious one. Mother had ruined it, just like Avi had. Spewing lies about another heir. Head Gardner and I would have to do much damage control because of her departing statement. She'd known what she was doing: planting suspicion within the region about the legitimacy of my position.

Nonetheless, a clever attempt.

I glanced over at the vacant glove case in the pile of my rage. I'd had it specially created to preserve Father's original combat gloves. They were his favorite pair to wear in battle. I planned on wearing them during the inauguration ceremony. Keeping a piece of him with me.

The last time I had worn them was when we stormed the rebels' Underground. Avi must've taken them when I wasn't looking. I remember someone nicking something from my hands. Avi and I had been separated during the rebel attack. I remembered having them on during the altercation with Saige. Saige and I had gone at it. Then I'd fallen headfirst into that stake.

After that I hadn't had them anymore.

Her.

Saige.

My legs folded beneath me like dough. Why would she have a reason to steal the General's gloves?

I clawed at my face, screaming bloody murder when I came to the conclusion.

Avi wasn't dishonest. Saige was an heir. The heir. Another secret that Father had managed to keep hidden.

"FUCK!" I yelped. "Fuck."

Head Gardner strolled in, slicing an apple with a reflective razor blade. She crunched on the slice, disregarding my apparent breakdown.

"I bring good news." She chewed.

I clambered toward her, sliding across the tile. "W-we must kill Saige."

Her head dropped backward in joy. "Yes, yes, rid ourselves of Saige. The ongoing plan. I know."

"No, no, no," I mumbled and motioned to the case. "She took the gloves. Father's gloves. During the fight. Avi said that there was another rightful heir. Do you see now?"

Head Gardner looked more confused than I'd ever seen her before.

"The firstborn," I explained. "Father's mongrel offspring."

Head Gardner popped another juicy wedge into her mouth and shrugged. "Your father had many secrets. None surprise me at this point in the game."

I gave a deep, deep exhale.

"But I have something for you that will make this seem like child's play." She grinned ear to ear.

"I'm listening."

"Remember that mole that was feeding me information about the whereabouts of the fugitives—well, your sister?"

My eyes narrowed.

"Too soon." She tossed the core aside. "After a series of waterboarding and a few choice cuts, he finally broke. He said that Mama Seeya planted him and that she wanted us to know her exact location so that they could strike with some magic-wielding roaches."

"Get to the point!"

She whistled. "Bring her in."

Watchmen carried in a girl, struggling against the restraints and with a sack over her head. She was tossed in a heap at my feet.

Head Gardner removed the sack, revealing a white-haired girl with fierce, arctic-blue eyes. Weak voltage swirled in her irises.

Head Gardner took a handful of the girl's hair and pulled her head back. She hissed like a feral animal that had just been trapped. "Liyo will come for her, Saige will accompany him. The bait will draw them out. Guaranteed."

Chapter Twenty-Three
SAIGE

Pea told me that she'd heard that the rebels would be posted in Subdivision Eleven. Eagerly awaiting Mama Seeya's arrival. Aboveground. No more bottom feeding. No more hiding.

Before leaving the Underground Apex, we heard the debut of the new regulation. Castration of all non-Uppers. Nothing surprised me about their lengths of cruelty, but I wondered why she hadn't just waged war already. Ordered the execution of us all. The droids were ready. Most of the workers were no longer needed in the region. What was she waiting for?

The unknown was what worried me.

We traveled through the tunnel and back through the secret hole in the cube. Pea knocked on the wooden flap and waited. No one came. She knocked again. We both listened for movement, footsteps, anything on the floorboard above. Again, nothing.

She shot a concerned glare. When she tried to knock again, I shoved her to the side. I pushed, but it wouldn't budge. I used my shoulder to force it open. Pea joined the other side, and together we shoved upward. Something heavy fell over as the dim light glowed through the crevice.

We lifted our heads from the hole. No signs of the man who always operated the passage. The cube was disheveled. Stools tipped over, jars strewed about, and glass everywhere, like someone had come and dragged him out.

Pea stepped up, brushing paint chips from her knees. "What happened here?"

Faint noises came from outside the complex.

From the top of the stoop, madness. Watchmen chased workers along the sidewalks and into passages. Trash swirled in mini tornadoes as pale bodies zipped and dodged. People tumbled over legs and fallen forms. One even tripped a young man, using him as watchman bait, in order to get away. Live another measly day. The man was restrained on the concrete by several watchmen. One even placed his knee in the back of the squirming worker's neck and pulled out a compact silver-looking gun. He placed the tip of the long nozzle on the upper arm area of the man and pulled the trigger. I expected a laser to emerge, but instead it left a raised scar. The watchmen released him at once and then proceeded to trap another subject.

Pea cut through the crowd before I could grab hold of her. She knelt and checked the man's pulse. Still alive. She grazed the mark on the side of his biceps. It was a thick circle with an X in the center.

"They're sterilizing them." She looked up at me, stress lines forming around her mouth.

"We've got to get out of here," I said. "We can't help any of them right now."

Pea witnessed watchmen pin a sobbing mother face first into the ground. Through swollen eyes, she watched her child be poked with the same sterilizer. The baby shrieked at the prick.

Pea approached.

"Hey!"

My voice stopped her for a second, but then she kept moving as if I was only a hiccup.

I stepped in front of her. Her eyes full of pain.

"I know." It was all that came out.

She shoved me, but she wasn't strong enough to move me. She tried again and failed. The last time, she stepped back, brandished a knife.

"Move." She lunged forward.

My palms faced her. "You cannot fight an entire horde."

She swiped the blade. I skipped back.

"I said move."

"Listen to me. Remember in the Citadel, when we first met. In the washing chambers, and I was trying to escape. I was going to fight every damned watchman that got in my way. Do you remember what you told me?"

The knife remained at face level.

"We cannot do this without backup. You'll get yourself killed right now," I explained. "We can die tomorrow."

Using the back of her hand, still holding the weapon, to stop the tears from flowing too far along her cheeks. She scoffed.

"Let's go." I lowered the knife to her side.

She nodded, but before heading in the other direction, she asked, "Who said getting yourself killed was the worst thing that can happen right about now?"

❖ ❖ ❖

Drake, Wayal, Liyo, Elu, and every rebel head in the region faced Mama Seeya in an expansive deserted cellar in a rickety construction in Subdivision Eleven. Watchmen hadn't ventured too far out into the Subdivisions, but since Jade was switching it up on us, it'd only be a matter of time before she ventured that way too.

Before Pea and I busted into the meeting while Mama Seeya was midsentence, a guard tried to stop us. I took his legs out from beneath him, and he fell flat on his back, causing a ruckus.

"I'm back," I announced to all the folks that turned their heads.

Pea scurried to my side, her bob flapping with each step.

"Oh, team, this is Pea. Pea, team." I waved.

"A pleasure to meet you all." She bowed quickly, and then she laid eyes on Liyo. She shot him a toothy grin.

Mama Seeya examined me carefully as I squeezed between Liyo and Elu.

"And to what do we owe this pleasure?" she asked.

I glanced over one shoulder and then the other. "Ah, you mean me."

Wayal looked like he wanted to cut me in half.

"I had a change of heart." I leaned back in my seat. "I'm ready to become a full-fledged rebel. Just like you wanted."

Mama Seeya cupped her hands behind her back and paced the length of the counter. "So, you're here to claim your sovereignty?"

It was as if a string stemming from the top of my skull had pulled me upright. "What? No. Why would I—?"

"Don't tell me that you've never thought about it," she almost teased. "What being half Jore, part Elite, meant."

Irritation rose, but I couldn't allow her to sway me. Especially not in front of her people. "I came back so we could expose the Union. Isn't that what you wanted?"

"Hmm," she sighed. "Saige, you're still that opportunistic girl. The one always trying to one-up the others. Get the most for the least. Tell me: Why are you *really* here?"

I wasn't the best speaker like she was. I couldn't command rooms or lull the masses. She thought if she put me on the spot, I'd stumble. Run away again. But this time, I knew exactly what I wanted.

"I'm here to get revenge. Against Jade. Head Gardner. To make sure that Avi's death was not for nothing. I owe that to her, to her memory. A lot of us in this room owe that to her. Whether we want to admit it or not." I continued, "The Southern Region has been my nightmare since I can remember. You—the rest of you—can have this miserable place.

In exchange for my assistance, and when all of this is over and done, all I ask is that you send me back to the north. That you honor the treaty in place. And never, ever step foot there again."

Mama Seeya studied me for a long time. It was nothing for her to just leave the north be. Leave me be. If power was what she wanted, then I'd gladly step aside.

"Agreed," she said simply, and the meeting continued as if it was never disturbed in the first place.

❖ ❖ ❖

While I was gone, they had made an agreement to send Elu back to the north to rally the colonies to join an inevitable war. I'd wished I had known that before I started making demands at the top of the meeting. I would've negotiated for her too. Maybe I shouldn't have left.

Elu swapped out her bodysuit for her tattered parka that she'd worn in the north. She tossed a slimpack to a rebel that was loading the hovercraft. She placed her forehead to Liyo's. They lingered.

"We shall meet again."

"Take care of yourself," he told her.

Elu turned to me, but I couldn't meet her gaze. I counted the divots in her boots.

"I'm glad you came back so that we could share a proper farewell. I thought for a moment that that would be the last time I saw your face. I know that Miah would be proud."

I might've blushed a little bit. "Yeah, well, you can't kill a roach, right?"

"What's wrong?" She forced me to meet her eyes. They were dark and clear. Like Miah's. They looked so much alike.

"This isn't right." I shook with anger. "The colonies shouldn't be getting involved in this. It's not their war to carry."

"Oh, Saige." She shrugged. "This war *is* everyone's war now."

"You sound like her."

"No, I sound like me. A warrior. Someone who knows that some people will never stop until they have it all."

"But what if she's wrong?" I couldn't stay still.

"And what if she's right?" Her smile faded. All the warmth left when she let go of my fingers, one by one. "This isn't really a farewell."

Liyo and I watched as she stepped inside the hovercraft. The hatch closed itself. The engines accelerated to full speed, creating drafts of residue in the air. It elevated higher and higher, until the craft vanished into the fog.

Was that it? Just people leaving suddenly. Was that the arc of life? Becoming attached to another so that in their absence you couldn't survive, couldn't breathe. The weight of living without them crashing into you like a flood of grief back to back. What a cruel maker. Whoever, whatever it was.

Elu was the last link that I'd had to Miah, and now that was gone. I had no pictures of him, no keepsakes. No lock of his long, silky hair to keep in my pouch or a piece of his pelt to sniff when I got lonely. All that remained were passing memories, and even those wouldn't last forever. Time would chip away at it, sweep away the pieces the older the memory got. It had happened to Ma, and it'd happen to him too.

I closed my eyes for a long while, wishing that if they stayed closed long enough, then maybe, just maybe I'd wake up back in that world where my loved ones resided. Maybe that was reality, and where I was standing was a nightmare. Please let it be a nightmare . . .

A hand fell on my shoulder, jerking me back. For a moment, I thought it was Miah, but it was just Liyo.

He looked as though he hadn't slept in ages.

"I'm sorry for leaving," I blurted. The last word barely left and trailed off somewhere into the dirty atmosphere.

"You never have to—" His head dropped like a resting puppet.

"I do."

"I know."

We stood arm in arm. His blue eyes carried worry as they darted up into the sky in the exact spot that the craft had vanished.

"You should be guiding the Union," he said. "You're the true savior, not me. Not her."

I nudged him in the ribs with my elbow. There he went again. Now he wanted to come to these realizations after he'd dragged us all back into her lair.

"Mama Seeya . . ." He hesitated. "She's not the same."

"This is the part when you say 'kidding'?"

"I'm not kidding, Saige."

"Stop." I yanked his chin in my direction. "The people would never go for that. And I would never claim Elite."

"Why?"

I shoved him. "Why what?"

"Are you afraid of Mama Seeya?"

"Have you lost your shit?"

"I haven't lost my shit. Things have become clearer," he said. "I think that you'll never see what I see in you. What I've always seen in you. When we were kids, I used to always follow your lead because even then I knew you were destined for greatness. Galaxies, I wish you could see you through my eyes."

The inside of my nose burned. "Stop. Talking."

"You're the first and rightful heir of the Jore line. I don't care what anyone says. You were never Impure. You're the purest, and you will be the one to unite us."

Before I could react, respond, Drake rushed out, breaking the little heart-to-heart.

"You two. Come." She was out of breath. "Quick."

We returned to the basement to the backs of everyone's heads and sights glued to the holomonitor. Mama Seeya's eyes were moist.

Eve was in the center of a grainy display. Tousled white hair and pink eyes. Her nude bodysuit stained. Hands and feet bound. She sat in a metal chair. She kept glancing at the upper-right corner of the lens. Someone was drilling her.

"Th-this is a private transmission . . ." She looked into the holocam, then back at the demon waiting in the shadows. "F-for Liyo, Saige."

She began sobbing, but then she saw something that caused her to stop immediately. What were they showing that child?

"Y-you have until midnight to make a trade. M-my life f-for yours."

Eve adjusted her wrists against the restraints.

The broadcast cut.

A gust of energy glided past me; I heard the crackles of the surge. Liyo was fully aglow and destroyed the entire pillar that the holoscreen was projected on. Half the vault caved as rebels leaped out of the way of deteriorating rubble.

"Enough!" Mama Seeya commanded.

Liyo's eyes never went back to normal. Currents surged around his finger as he pointed it at her face. "You were supposed to protect her!"

Mama Seeya seemed to be unaffected by the hostility. "I did. Someone must've tipped them off on her whereabouts. Not all skin folk are kinfolk."

"We're all going to retrieve her. Now." He calmed down, but only a little. "Tell your people to suit up and prepare for battle."

No one moved a muscle. Not even a twitch.

"What're you all waiting for?" The bass in his voice deepened. "Huh?"

"We can't do that." Mama Seeya met his glare.

"Don't"—Liyo stepped away from her as if she were the plague in human form—"do this."

"We don't have all of the people in place right now."

"When will your perfect plan be in place?!"

"Soon," she offered, meekly.

"Soon isn't good enough," he said. "I'm going to get her with or without you. Any of you."

"I want to save Eve and tear them down just as much as you." She scowled, tearing through the empty space between them. "But they're using her, using you to derail the larger purpose. It's all in their plan to use our emotions against us so that we will attack wildly, blindly negating decades of effort, of prep."

"You'll allow them to kill her?" Liyo whispered.

"Will you allow them to kill us?" she countered. "I cannot allow you or anyone else for that matter to ruin our only chance at salvation."

"Your chance?" It looked like Liyo had been gored. "At the expense of a child?"

Mama Seeya shot him a grave look before answering. "Even at the expense of a child. There are millions more children that deserve a chance at life that I simply cannot ignore, cannot wager for just one."

Before Liyo could attack, rebut, run away, Wayal shot a tiny dart in his neck. It was filled with sedatives. Liyo staggered, dropped to his palms and knees, and tried to shake off the tranquilizers, but seconds later he was laid out flat. I wondered if they'd known that would all go down as it had and had that dart ready for his transgression.

"No one's to leave the premises without authorization." She remained in the same spot, motionless, watching his unmoving form. "I apologize that you all had to witness this. He would've ruined years of work. Countless deaths would've been for nothing. I'm in charge because I can discern the hard decisions that need to be made. I'm not a tyrant, I'm not a bad person, but none of us can allow what's about to happen to fail, or it will truly be the death of us all. No one's safe until the Union and its predecessors are completely abolished."

"This would be the only time I agree with you." I moseyed over and used my foot to make sure he was out. "It definitely screams 'trap.'"

I watched Wayal and his men drag Liyo away. They placed him in a cor-roded cell. It wouldn't hold him for long if he woke up, but I knew that Wayal was smarter than that. He'd probably given him an extra dose to keep him knocked out for a while. I guessed they planned on having him sleep through the execution and would deal with the repercussions of drugging him later. Bad idea.

A pale man with a receding hairline and low-set ears and a woman with beady eyes guarded the entrance. They were armed, and we didn't have much time before the sadistic Union offed Eve. I told Pea to smug-gle some adrenaline from wherever she could find it—lots of it—and meet me back at lockup. The girl was fast, even with one arm. She patted her pocket where the goods were and nodded. The plan was a go.

She stepped into full view of the guards.

"Whaddaya want?" The woman gnawed on tobacco and spat dark juice to the side.

"I just came to check up on my friend. See if he's okay," Pea said.

The man exposed brownish teeth that looked like small pond peb-bles. "Oh, he fine. Boy is pumped wit so much tranq. He prolly gone be out till the war's over."

The woman's belly jiggled with every chuckle. "This ain't no place for a liddle birdie like you."

"Dassit, scram." The man laughed so hard that he began a fit of rasping coughs.

"I'm not going anywhere," Pea said. "And as a matter of fact, you will unlock that door."

Their titters ceased as they gripped their guns.

"Liddle birdie best get goin' nah, or she gone get her liddle head blown to bits," the woman said as the man moved in.

While she had their attention, I crept from behind and knocked out the woman. She pulled the trigger, and lasers flew all around, ric-ocheting off the concrete. The man paid no attention to Pea but tried to attack once he saw what I'd done to his partner, but before he could lunge, Pea stuck him in the fatty part of his calf with a needle. He pulled the syringe out and surveyed the vial.

"You liddle—" He twirled in a circle, confused, and stumbled into the crusted bars.

He slid down slowly as I yanked the keys from his belt.

Pea and I watched over him as he tried to fight the heaviness of his eyes, the fog that Liyo had felt not long ago.

"This boy is pumped with so much tranquilizer. He's probably going to be out until the war is over," Pea mocked. "Sweet dreams."

I hadn't known she had it in her.

Inside the cell, Pea lifted one of Liyo's lids. His eye was rolled into the back of his head. He was *out* out.

"How much should we give him?" She weighed the vials in her hand like a scale.

"Not sure." I eyed the milligrams.

She popped off the top and stuck him with one. Then another. And as she went in for the third prick, he popped up like the undead.

"Guess it was two then," I said.

Liyo trembled as if he'd been doused in freezing water and gasped.

"It'll all stop once you get moving," Pea told him.

"You!" Liyo went from trembling to angry in the matter of seconds. "I heard what you said."

"And I stick by it. It *is* a trap."

He slowly scrambled from the cot and stepped over the downed guards. "I'm going to get Eve. Don't try and stop me."

"Stop you? We're trying to help you get her back. Why do you think we did all of this?" I raised the empty syringe and wiggled it for proof.

"Good. Then let's move."

"Is there a plan?" Pea asked.

Liyo spun around. He looked over at me. I hunched my shoulders. I had nothing.

Pea raised her hand. "That's what I thought."

"If you have something to share, then let's hear it." Liyo was losing patience.

"Neither one of you is going to like it."

"Spit it out," I urged.

She grabbed her elbow, right above the nub, and switched her weight from one foot to the other. "Instructor Skylar."

Chapter Twenty-Four
SAIGE

We wore heavy hoods and masks and kept our heads low as we made our way onto Subdivision Eleven's potholed streets. Luckily others were bundled up as well, so we didn't look too suspicious. It was a chilly night. Evening workers shuffled wearily to the hovertrams by way of one thin, long escalator, all in a disciplined assembly line, going up and up, funneling onto the raised platform like ants. I supposed that there were still jobs that the droids couldn't do yet. The Union would milk workers until their last inhalations. I was surprised that Lower Residents still scurried to their assignments after the whole sterilization announcement. They should've been in an uproar, not going to clock in. Maybe the rebels were overzealous about how on board everyone would be with their plan. Maybe the rest were so brainwashed that they couldn't see the Union for what they really were. They were lost. We couldn't count on those people to fight back, even if the choice was clear.

Pea led us to the moving stairway and tried to hop on.

"No." I grabbed her flat biceps, stopping her from boarding. "It'll be crawling with watchmen."

"I know," she said. "This *is* how we get to him."

I released her. "Pea, this isn't the time for bullshit."

"No bullshit." She got on the escalator. "This is how he told me to get in contact with him."

Liyo nodded, taking her lead. He was willing to do anything to get Eve back. Desperation made us do crazy things.

I waited until they were almost to the top to get on. "Fuck," I grumbled. Watchmen were stationed at the edge of the platform. Armed. I immediately went stiff like a hard-on.

"This way." Pea slipped between the sliding doors as soon as they stripped open. She moved through the crowd of workers like an inconspicuous mouse.

It was hard to keep up. When I finally found her again, she was comfortably positioned next to a group of elderly workers with her only hand pressed against the window. The bullet-shaped section began to move, smoothly thrusting us forward, toward the city's Square. She stared onward. Liyo faced the window, too, blankly watching as the neon beams—one after the other—zoomed by, signifying each kilometer traveled.

The hovertram's alert system dinged, and then it came to a complete stop. The sliding doors split down the middle, allowing workers to hurry out and others to rush in. *Ding.* Doors closed. Dim lights emitted from worker cubes whizzed by as the thrusters *swooshed* quietly. *Ding.* Doors. A sole watchman entered. Boots heavy and stature even heavier. A bulky build like a bull. The hovertram began its ascent over the bridge.

Pea took a deep breath, then visibly gulped the rock that was in her throat. She walked toward him. I whispered her name, but she just kept going. Liyo finally broke from his trance. We locked eyes, both of us going over possible escape routes in our heads. There was only one of him and three of us. If need be, we could take him, but there were holocams perched in the corners of each bullet. If we made a ruckus, they would surely alert the brigade and have us detained before we could even blink.

What was Pea doing? The girl couldn't be that stupid.

Liyo leaned into me. "We get off at the next stop."

I nodded once. She was on her own.

Ding.

Liyo and I blended in with the pack and skated through the exit.

"Halt," a voice said. We had almost made it to the top of the escalator.

Liyo and I turned around. Little Pea stood next to the watchman, who had his gun drawn.

Traitor.

"Walk," he said, ushering us forward.

No one around us batted an eye at the stickup. Workers were trained to mind their business, if it didn't mind them.

He guided us to a dirty underpass beneath the platform where Disposables resided in rickety camps.

"Remove your face coverings." He waved the weapon at us.

I was going to kill her.

I slowly slid the cloth down to my chin. Liyo did the same.

"Keep your hands where I can see them."

He palmed us down for weapons. Then stepped back. "All clear."

Liyo's eyes began to create static.

The man lowered his weapon and then stood at ease.

I glanced at Pea. She couldn't hold it in any longer and burst into a fit of laughter.

"What's going on?" My eyes bulged.

"The look on your"—she couldn't even get the last word out—"faces."

The watchman didn't chuckle but looked straight ahead with a blankness that I'd seen before.

Liyo and I stayed still.

"It's a droid." Pea stopped laughing and cleared her throat. "It's going to take us to Instructor Skylar."

"I almost killed you," I said.

She looked offended. I kept forgetting that even though she'd lived a long, hard life, she was still only a kid.

Liyo knocked on the droid to test the hollowness and then put his ear to its chest. "She's right. No heartbeat."

"Although stupid . . . ," I began, "I'm not going to say it isn't a good plan."

She smiled with all her teeth.

"What's next?"

"Droid 276, cuff us and take us to your hovercraft," she commanded.

The droid landed the armored hovercraft on a patch of grass in the lush Elite Subdivision One located at the outer edge of the Square. After it shut down the system, it released our shackles before allowing us to exit the craft. There was Instructor Skylar, leaning on the side of a huge lotus-shaped dwelling partially covered in bushy moss and trophy-colored shafts. It was as if he were waiting on a friend that he hadn't laid eyes on in ages.

He still had that overpowering smile.

I had to fight myself not to match it.

The instructor stuck out a hand. I took it. He tugged me forward, shaking steadily. "Wilde."

"Instructor Skylar."

"My best student." He released my arm.

"My only instructor," I replied.

He took Liyo's hand. "Welcome."

Pea burst through both of us and leaped into his arms. He twirled her around like a child. Her stringy hair in his mouth as he tried to spit it out.

He set her down and glanced at her arm. "I'm so sorry."

She lifted the nub to eye level. "This is nothing compared to what's coming for them."

Pea and Instructor Skylar led us inside.

The entrance looked like a wide metal fish mouth. The interior was dim; the only real light came from the moon outside shining in through the gold-rimmed frames. We traveled deeper and deeper until we came across a door leading below. The hallway was long, made of stone. Triangular fluorescent beams created a 3D illusion of a never-ending path.

My ears popped as we took a hoverlift down more flights.

"I was expecting you," he said, watching each floor pass, blending into the next. "I knew you'd make it back."

"Can't kill a roach," I crowed.

"Indeed."

We made it to the bottom floor. He flicked the lights on, revealing rows upon rows of droid models. The original N17s and a few of the newer ones were mixed together. Some were missing robotic limbs, while others were only half-covered with skins. There were fat ones and short ones. Rusted ones and shinier ones.

"I know you're here for Eve," he began. "This is how we'll get her back."

Pea began to run along the aisles, checking out the stolen collection. "Whoa."

"So you've been randomly sitting on an army of malfunctioning droids this entire time?" I asked.

"They're all functional." He tapped on a reader, waking each simultaneously. Red bulbs for eyes began to glow.

"I've rehabbed the droids that the Union pitched," he said proudly. "I knew there was a day that would come when we'd need them."

"We?" Liyo asked exactly what I was thinking.

"Have we not been over this before when I helped you two escape the first time?" The instructor was insulted. "I'm not the enemy here." "Yes, yes, you want to avenge your father and expose the Union, blah, blah," I mocked.

He powered them off with a single button and glared.

Liyo said, "We're sorry. We just—this is all—just tell us what we need to do to get Eve back."

"Now that's more like it. Teamwork. You should teach Wilde that concept every once in a while." Instructor Skylar grinned and pointed to another area. "Come with me."

He led us into a separate office, a war room by the look of it. An illustration of the location of the Outskirts where they had Eve captive. It was the same place that I'd killed that man in front of the General, in front of my father, to get him to trust me. Instinctively, I patted the bulge of gloves that I had packed inside of a thigh pocket.

I shuddered at the thought of returning. Jade knew exactly what she was doing when she chose the wretched place. She was taunting me.

"Before I tell you the proposal, I need something from you." Instructor Skylar paused.

"Like?" Liyo leaned forward.

"What does Mama Seeya plan on doing?"

Pea was going to speak up, but Liyo shot her a look. A silent *shut your damned mouth.*

"I know you're still wary of me." He opened his arms. "I would be too. Historically people who've looked like me haven't been the most trustworthy, but I could say the same for yours. We've both done horrific things to one another over the millennia, and those horrific things will keep happening if we don't come to an agreement. Trust. You have much to lose, as do I. I don't know what Mama Seeya told you about me, but I don't work for either side. I'm on the side that wants equality across the board, but I won't cater to any power that wants complete control."

"Was that why you turned her offer down?" Liyo asked.

"I've not come this far to be shoved backward with the same regime with a different hue."

He didn't trust her. And neither did I. We had something in common.

"She's gotten hold of data that has allowed her to create more soldiers with powers. She planned on giving herself up as a ruse, and then when the Union surfaced, rebels would create chaos in strategic parts of the city," Liyo explained. "Then a full-on war. She wants you all gone."

"Hmm." Instructor Skylar was in deep contemplation for a moment and then said, "My sources have also shared similar information on the Union's part. But they have Impures. They've been bred in incubators, have never known love or empathy. They're produced to obey. To eradicate."

Pea twirled the ends of her hair around her pointer finger and thumb. "They have Transmegas, droids, watchmen, and now killer Impures? For galaxy's sake."

"If Mama Seeya comes anywhere near them, they'll blast them all, and they know about that plan of hers too. That's why they took Eve." The instructor stretched his neck from side to side, the stress already forming knots.

"Who told you this?" Liyo asked.

"I can't give my sources up yet. They need to see that the rebels are at an advantage before they step in, reveal themselves. Trust me when I tell you that there are others like me, but they have to play their cards right. They don't want to move prematurely. Jade is unhinged."

"Go figure," I added.

"I can help, but my authority is limited since Jade stripped me of rank. We can use the droid army to shield us as we make our way through the Outskirts. They'll fight on our behalf." He pulled up a 3D rendition of the plan of attack. "Time's running out. We suit up and leave."

❖ ❖ ❖

The ride over was too quick. My stomach was queasy, and if I had eaten, then I surely would've thrown it up. I couldn't even look out the window because my brain was spinning. Vertigo for the first time. Maybe. My head hung low as I tried to keep the memories of the atrocities of that last visit at bay.

It wasn't a good time to develop anxiety, but I couldn't stop it.

How was I supposed to be of any help if I couldn't get my shit collected? The fear, anxiety, whatever the fuck it was, was going to get me killed, others killed if I didn't pull it together.

I jumped when the instructor laid his hand on me.

He pulled back quickly. "My apologies."

I rested my head back and rubbed my eyes. "What?"

"We've arrived."

The craft stopped, suspended in the air. Dozens of crafts floated meters away from one another. The one that Liyo and Pea were in wasn't too far away. Their forms already rappelling down the silver lines. Instructor Skylar had said that it was best if we split up. There was a chance that we'd be met with force that we couldn't handle, and we couldn't afford to all be caught at the same time.

Someone had to make it out. Continue the fight. I wasn't sure I had much left in me, if I was being honest, but none of that mattered. It was go time.

Droids leaped from the hole in the craft's floor. Landing in the tall grasslands with heavy thumps from their dense titanium masses. I strapped the weapon on my back and began to slip my thighs into the harness.

Instructor Skylar did the same.

"Hey." He stood on the opposite side as I stared through the hatch. "Look at me."

My head stayed facing the hole, but my eyes followed his voice.

"You are *not* alone in this." He tossed me the cord. "I'm here."

I attached it to the harness and jumped into the madness that was the Outskirts.

It'd been almost a year since I'd witnessed bloated body parts floating in murky waters during the rebel war, the fiery flames that watchmen bathed the inured in, the life that I'd taken. I could still feel the bones of innocent workers who thought the Union, someone would save them crunch beneath my soles.

I didn't want to be there. So, I counted down the seconds until we found Eve and got the hell out. The place was eerie. Vile. It would turn me into something that I had never wanted to go back to if I overstayed my welcome.

The air was thick. I could taste death, and the dust caused my tongue to stick to the roof of my mouth and dried my lips out like rawhide. Working light markers were staggered, some buzzing in and out while others had toppled over. Buildings had huge pits blown through them, like a giant had taken a chunk out of the sides. Brick dwellings leaned over to the side, the foundations crumbled by detonators.

Laser fights and explosions happened on the horizon. Coming from several directions. Instructor Skylar's droids versus the watchmen and who knew what else.

The Union knew we'd arrived.

"Let's move." Instructor Skylar picked up the pace, his droids covering us from all sides.

Watchmen tried to attack, but the droids would quickly push them back, into the woodlands. A handful got lost in the shuffle or injured beyond repair. We surged forward, getting closer because the watchmen hives were becoming thicker. Protecting whatever lay ahead.

We reached the edge of the trees, and before us was a group of cathedrals in the middle of a huge plot of land. Eve was in between Jade and Head Gardner. And below were watchmen swarming into position like robobees, suited and ready to defend their so-called General.

Not too far, located right in front, were Liyo and Pea, behind them an army of droids who were fixed at ease.

"No," I said and prepared to make a run for it, alert them, something. They were past exposed, and the watchmen were going to enclose them.

Instructor Skylar grabbed the back of my collar and towed me into the brush.

"Let's go." I tussled with him.

"We can't let them know we're here just yet. Allow Liyo to speak first. If we attack now, you'll get everyone killed."

For some reason, I knew that this had been Liyo's plan from the start, and he hadn't let me in on it. I stayed vigilant, hidden, but if anything was to pop off . . .

"Let her go!" Liyo's voice boomed through the clearing.

"Where is my beloved sister?" Jade called out.

Liyo didn't dignify her with an answer.

"Hmm, I would've thought that she'd want in on some of the action. She put up a much better fight than Avi ever did."

Head Gardner chuckled.

I seethed at the sound of her voice. She didn't deserve to laugh, to even exist after all that she'd taken from me. Her entire existence had been to cause as much pain for me as possible. She'd stabbed Miah to death knowing that I was somewhere watching, and I'd make sure I gave her the same death, if not worse. I'd gone over what I'd do to her a million times. I fell asleep with the image and woke up with it. Her bloodied and battered. Begging for me to just end her. But each time, I'd say no and ramp up the pain until I was satisfied.

I had to get her. She was mine and mine alone for the punishing. It wouldn't bring Miah back or Ma, but it would make me feel so damn good to cut her tongue out of her mouth and make her swallow it.

The instructor put his arm out in front of me, reminding me of the plan. Stay put.

"The deal was that you and Saige turn yourselves in, in exchange for the girl." Jade made a bridge with her fingers. "You have not upheld your end of the deal. So that means the honk dies. And so do you and your pile of reject metal parts."

As she turned away, Liyo lifted himself to higher ground. "There'll be no lives taken today."

She spun around in fake shock. "And why is that?"

"Return Eve to me. She's a child," he said. "Let us fight it out on the battlefield like soldiers. With honor."

Jade's face dropped, aging her beyond her years. "Honor? Honor! There is no honor when you deal with honks. You will comply, or you will die." She took out a blade and sliced Eve's face.

The ground around us quaked. Rocks, trees, bushes began to uproot as Liyo began to ascend. His palm faced her. He took the weapon from Jade's grip and, with the flick of a finger, flung it over her head. With one hand, he choked her, lifting her to the tips of her toes as she struggled to fight off the invisible force crushing her airway. When Head Gardner tried to intervene, Liyo used the other hand to hurl her into the pillar of the third archway.

Watchmen snapped into action and began shooting into the air, a barrage of lasers headed for Liyo. As they unloaded, he created a barrier of voltage around himself. Lasers pinged off the barricade like pebbles against plexiglass.

The droid army followed his lead and began attacking watchmen on the ground level. Pea began the descent, making her way to Eve.

Instructor Skylar's attention was occupied as if I were no longer crouched next to him. At first, I didn't see anything, but then I saw something faint heading in Liyo's direction. The instructor and I raised ourselves to get a better look.

It happened so fast that I couldn't remember sprinting toward the chaos.

Instructor Skylar bellowed. "Attack!"

Our droids came to life and began shooting, running at triple the speed of a human.

An assembly of young Impures in nude bodysuits with electricity swirling in their eyes and sizzling at the tips of their fingers stood in a square formation and aimed at Liyo. They all dressed uniformly. Same buzz cuts. Even the women. Jade had created herself a little army of me and Liyo combined into one.

Jade's legs dangled meters from the ground as he continued to squeeze the life force from her. He hadn't even noticed the killer crew forming beneath him. Three of them removed Liyo's barrier. He broke from his trance, yet he still kept Jade up with one hand and lifted a huge piece of concrete with the other. It tossed itself at one of the Impure girls. She moved out of the way seamlessly. The other two uprooted the weighty arch and chucked it at Liyo. He had no choice but to let Jade go.

Jade fell from the sky, and one of the male Impures caught her in an invisible net and guided her gently to the dirt.

It hurt to see them treating an oppressor like a priceless urn. They were bred to be her protectors. It was sick to watch.

I clashed with a few watchmen below as the battle above with Liyo raged on. I wanted to assist Liyo. He wouldn't be able to fight four people like him. But I knew that he'd want me to get Eve, so I blasted watchmen who dared get in my path while droids on the ground continued to fight.

Pea had finally gotten to Eve but was met with Jade. My legs pumped harder as I dodged explosions and leaped over downed watchmen and dodged lasers whizzing past my temples. One of them sliced across my hand. I paused to survey the damage.

It had burned the top layer of skin.

I started feeling around my armor, my pockets for anything to cover the wound.

Father's gloves.

I slipped my trembling hand inside of the fingers. It'd have to do.

Just before I made it to the first row of arches, Head Gardner emerged from twisting the head off a droid like a pop-top soda.

I couldn't go any farther.

I began shooting, and she leaped out of the way before I could blow her face in. The laser ended up hitting one of the watchmen tussling with an N17 instead. We both exchanged lasers, dipping in between concrete pillars and unsuspecting soldiers, using them as shields to not be eviscerated by a stray shot. We weaved in and out of columns and bodies as I glided closer to where Pea and Jade were. Head Gardner was in hot pursuit.

Droid frames became more scattered as she discharged shot after shot. I had to take cover behind a disintegrated block that barely covered my body. I couldn't move any farther without her gunning me down. Every so often, I'd shoot back just so she wouldn't get confident and try to slink up from the side.

"Come out, mutt," she almost purred. "Meet your inevitable fate."

Another laser bombardment from her gun showered the exterior of the rock, taking off chunks like carved ice.

I heard a single laser discharge and then Head Gardner moan.

"Go get Eve!"

It was Instructor Skylar. He'd finally caught up and waved for me to go.

I jolted back and sprinted toward the platform of the arch.

Briefly, I looked up and behind me. Liyo was losing the battle. Forward movement only, I repeated as my arms propelled me and my heartbeat pounded outside of my chest.

Pea threw herself in front of the trembling Eve, whose legs were shackled with laser restraints. Jade backhanded Pea. She fell to the ground hard. Jade began stomping on her back as she tried to get to her knees.

"Why don't you vermin just die!" She drove her boot into Pea's ear.

I pointed the gun. She heard the whirring of the laser preparing to eject.

Jade ceased the assault and raised her hands.

"There's my kin." She became fixated on the gloves that I'd pinched. "How quaint."

I tapped my finger on the trigger.

"You should really give those back. They don't belong to a mangy crossbreed."

I lit her up. But she was agile and leaped, rolling to the side and grabbing Eve in the process. She used her body as a shield. I had no clear shot. Pea watched in horror from below, unable to move.

The blade pierced Eve's neck. Jade kept her face buried in the girl's white hair.

"Is this what you want?" Jade hissed, tugging the girl backward. "Look around you."

Liyo had been subdued by the robot-like Impures. Pinned to the ground by his own abilities. Watchmen were lighting up the makeshift droids with blue flames. And Instructor Skylar was missing in action.

"See." She yanked Eve back and forth. "You may have Elite blood in you, but you could never be us."

Drake had asked me why I hated myself so much back on the compound. It bothered me because she was right. I did hate myself. I just never wanted to admit it. Not out loud. Not to her, and not to myself. I hated the fact that I was of both bloods but of neither. How none of it was my choice, but somehow, I had been roped into this mess. How was that fair that I had no choice?

In a perfect world, I wouldn't have ever even existed. Just like what the Union wanted. If I had to choose, I would've never chosen to exist. Not like this. Not under the circumstances.

I felt like I was fighting a marathon war that would never, ever end.

How I'd come to be was always in the back of my mind. Gnawing away like termites on moist wood. Was I a product of assault? Had he used Ma's body for a release and then tossed her back into the pile of workers once he was done? Had he loved her, but that was forbidden, so he'd had to leave us behind?

Either way, I was his mistake. Her mistake. Whether Ma wanted to admit it or not. And I hated them both for it.

And I was of both of them. The good. The bad. The beautiful. The cruel.

How could I stop hating when that was all I knew? I stewed in that resentment. I was trapped by it, in it, and there was no exit.

Who was I? What was I?

I still had no answer.

Jade enjoyed the banter. Got off on it. She waited eagerly for me to reply about his gloves. Tell her that I would never be an Elite, but that I was proud of who I was despite it all. A rebel in the flesh. But zero words surfaced. The reality was that nothing I said would lessen the gravity of what was happening.

She had Eve. The droids were losing. We were at her mercy. Again.

"That's what I thought." She pulled Eve's head farther to the side and dug the blade in.

She was going to kill her. I couldn't let that happen. I lowered my weapon slowly to my feet. Jade watched my every move.

"You can have me." I raised with my hands, outstretched. "For her."

"Who said that I was inclined to bargain?" Jade scoffed. "When I can have it all."

"I'm offering you myself, no fight, no gimmicks. I'll be your slave, if that's what you want. Whatever you want, but just let her go."

I could see it in her eyes, her expression, that she analyzed the proposal with a fine-tooth comb. She'd always wanted me to bow down. The ultimate flex that she'd never get otherwise.

I inched closer. "What better way to show the Union your power by taking down the biggest fugitive next to Mama Seeya and making her your bitch. The others would lose hope. I'm their hope."

"Hope. Such a facetious concept for your kind. Our goal since the beginning has been to annihilate it. Yours, theirs, the ones before, and the ones after you." She glanced off to the side.

"Like right now, you still believe that you are in control, that you somehow have the upper hand. You *hope* that this honk will make it out. Live to see another day."

"Jade . . ." I sighed. Everything burned inside of me.

Eve shut her eyes firm, preparing.

Jade noticed that Mama Seeya's calvary swarmed the skies. The grounds. They outnumbered Jade's remaining legion. Hovercrafts sprayed watchmen with firepower that I'd never seen before as Jade watched her military overwhelmed.

"It's General to you." Jade brought the blade across Eve's neck, creating a grin-shaped gash spanning ear to ear.

Warm blood spurted from the artery, spattering my face.

Jade heaved the girl forward, into me. Through her restraints, Eve took hold of her neck in order to stop the bleeding, but it was too much. Her mouth was agape, her eyes red and protruding in fear as we both plopped to our knees. She gurgled, trying to get words out.

"No!" Pea screamed from below, too injured to move from the same spot.

We both slid to the ground. She lay in my lap, her legs thrashing as I tried my best to stop the hemorrhage. My fingers slipped through the liquid as I tried to apply pressure in the form of a chokehold. She started to convulse. I held her still. She was drowning in her own blood.

Her body convulsed less and less as her eyes and body became softer in my arms.

The rebels had taken care of the Impures that had jammed Liyo. When he was finally released from their powers, he levitated. I saw what he saw. A lifeless Eve.

Instructor Skylar crawled up the hill after finishing off the last watchman. He looked at Liyo once and flinched. He grabbed Pea from the heap. "We've got to get out of here."

Liyo's eyes turned into white orbs as tears streamed from them. He soared higher and higher until I could barely see him at all.

"Retreat!" I heard someone scream.

Then everyone began running.

Chapter Twenty-Five
LIYO

Not many Europes had cousins, but I had Eve. Tate was her father. My mother's brother. Workers labored so hard that most births didn't go full term. Stillbirths were common. But during my parents' time, the government allowed two children instead of one.

They used to say that Mema was strong as a buck and carried two healthy babies to term all the way up until her water broke in the dirt. She delivered both of them, too, propping herself up against a tree and cutting the cord with a smuggled razor blade. Even afterward, she worked in the fields with a heavy baby on her back and never missed a beat. Her output never went down. She was the model slave.

They worked her so hard till every part of her palms and fingers were thick with callouses and her back had a permanent hump in it.

When I came along, my mother didn't want the same life for me. Neither did my father. They met Mama Seeya, and they joined the cause. I can't remember how exactly we evaded the Union, but we did. We were safe from the testing and the hard labor.

But we knew that the safety was short lived. That the Union would one day come for us. And they had. *Be ready,* Father always said. *Be ready.*

Just like that, as if flicking ants from a log, they took them both from me and hauled me into a labor camp.

Tate took me in, and I met a tiny little thing with hair as white as mine. She was the closest thing to a sister I'd ever had, and I made a promise to my uncle to protect her with my life. To serve the cause so that she could—would have a better life. She deserved that.

Eve deserved to play with little dolls that looked like her and not have to work in the mines doing back-breaking work. She deserved to go on a date and have her first kiss and get married and have kids of her own. Not one or two but as many as she wanted. And her kids deserved to not be caged like the ones before her.

That was my why. She was my why. Why I fought so hard to stay alive in those caves and crawled back into the depths of hell to get back. To finish what we started. See it through. Earn her freedom once and for all . . .

When her blood was spilled. When I came to the realization that all of this was for nothing. That there was no hope left in humanity. Something in me tore away. I wasn't sure if it was sanity or control or mercy or all three.

With the unwavering strength of Mema, I allowed the power to consume me as it never had before. I no longer saw droids or watchmen, or black or white. My vision was consumed with silver streaks of electricity. No matter where my eyes turned, it was there, and it burned something bad. So bad that I thought my eyes would boil in the sockets like stew.

But I couldn't stop it. I was too far gone. I was past the point of return, past the point of redemption. Everyone, everything had to pay. And I was the punisher.

With one shriek, beams of light came from every orifice. I destroyed every armored craft in the sky; every watchman on the ground was blown apart; the archways shattered; trees split. I felt everything metal explode, the uprooting of ancient trunks, and the ripping of skin and snapping of bones.

I felt it all. And all of it felt me. They experienced the chaos, the pain.

Afterward, it was all demolished. I felt a cool breeze. I wasn't sure how I got there, but I hovered over Saige and Eve. I collapsed to my knees and laid my forehead on her small stomach and just wept.

What had we done?

Wayal arrived. He instructed his team to search the scattered forest for Jade and the others. He looked down on our tangled forms, cupped Eve's face, and groaned.

Mama Seeya reached us not long after. Her nostrils flared when she saw the corpse. She shook her head once and knelt beside us. She placed her head on mine, and in my ear, she whispered, "This is why they must all burn."

Chapter Twenty-Six
LIYO

It had been mere hours. No, days. Months maybe. It all felt the same. Time wasn't time anymore. Dusk and dawn rolled into one endless ring. After the surge where I tore apart everything and everyone, my body became numb, just like my heart and my brain. I was a living automaton.

I counted my blinks to make sure that my lids still worked. My eyes were the only thing I could sort of feel, and they ached something bad. I tried to keep them peeled open, because every time they closed, I saw her. The red gash so deep that she'd almost been decapitated. The white strands from her scalp absorbing the puddle of crimson that had pooled around her head.

I sobbed often, but nothing came from the ducts anymore. The reservoir was dry, barren.

I was exhausted without even having moved a muscle. Kept awake by my own obsession. By the misery. By the vengeance. The same faces, the same scenarios of that day tumbled over one another like many boulders rolling along a steep hill, fighting to see which one would reach the bottom first. Over and over, they would rerun the echoes of what already was. What could I have done differently to cause a different outcome? I would take away one component and then add in another element, creating different reconfigurations, but it never mattered because they all led to the same result.

I was powerless even inside my own head. A prisoner trapped between the highest solid walls with no way of escaping, but that didn't stop the thoughts from showing over and over again.

One day, I was lost in my umpteenth version when Saige entered my quarters. I didn't know she was real until she placed her palm on me. When she lifted the weight of her arm, the spot ached like my eyes did. She told me that they were going to burn the body. Scatter the ashes. That I should be there. Be present.

My knees cracked as I stood upright. My bones felt like gel. I couldn't remember the last time that I'd moved from that spot. I followed her to a clearing near a hovertram passage. Surrounded by dozens of onlookers was a small, plain wooden box with garlands draping over the top and sides. Tate, her father, set the box ablaze. The fire crackled and spat sparks onto dirty asphalt. Mama Seeya made remarks, but I couldn't hear any of it. I was too captivated by the strength of the fire.

Before I knew it, I was at the side of the chest that held a charred Eve. Soaking in the heat of the flames.

This is why they must burn. Her little voice copied Mama Seeya's last words.

"I did everything I could to protect her. You did too." I hadn't even known that Tate was next to me. "And in the end—they still took my child."

He sobbed. Something in me wanted to tell him that it would all be okay. That he had done the best he could. That I had. I wanted to be there for him. Reach out and place a soothing touch on his sloped shoulder, but I was still trapped inside my own self. Unable to escape.

I felt stupid. Believing Avi. Believing that her people could accept change. Believing that I was willing to fight for Avi's affection, her approval. That we could ever be a thing that just made sense in this world. They weren't capable of goodness. They'd kill even each other to get ahead. We'd just witnessed it again.

Mama Seeya positioned herself beside me after Tate was led away and ogled the inferno.

"There's something I haven't told you because I didn't think you were quite ready," she said.

I took in a deep breath of hot air, allowing the smokiness to fill me. I wanted to cough, but I kept it in. I needed to feel something. Even if it was more pain.

"We have Avi."

My fingers flexed slightly. Why had she thought that after all that time that the right time was then? I'd just lost something that I'd never be able to get back. I was in a place of grieving and disbelief and revenge. Even though I couldn't put a finger on her reasoning, I was still curious to know.

"Alive?"

She nodded.

Another me, the former me, would've had a different reaction to the news. Would've had questions. How and why. But the mental space that I had was nonexistent, and I was too exhausted to grill her, to wrap my head around a singular thought that could make sense of it all.

"I need you to get her on board. After this last stunt, negotiations are off the table." She turned her back to the fire and faced the others. "I know how you feel right now, and I wouldn't ask you to do this if there was anyone else that I thought was capable."

Why she believed that I was capable was beyond me. I was the most unhinged I'd ever been. I finally locked eyes with her.

"Avi thinks that we're going to live together in harmony after this, but I can't honor that deal anymore," she continued. "We've tried to compromise."

That they had. We all had. The only people who hadn't held up their end were the Elites. They couldn't ever be trusted. Their schemes had cut too deep and would continue unless they were snipped at the core. Mama Seeya was right: casualties were the price of freedom. I couldn't save Eve, but how many other countless Eves could I help? No father or mother would ever have to go through what I was going through. Not if I had a say in it. I didn't need any more convincing. I was on board.

Grief had turned me into something else. At first, I hadn't known who it was, but maybe that was the person I'd always been. Maybe it happened so that I could fulfill my part in bringing it all down.

Jade and anyone who sympathized with her were going to meet a wrath that they hadn't expected, and we were going to bring it down on them once and for all.

The fire seemed to be much angrier than before.

Before Mama Seeya departed, she said, "Don't tell Saige. She wouldn't understand. She doesn't care about the rebels or the cause like we do."

Chapter Twenty-Seven
AVI

I had lost a sizable amount of blood. They'd had to perform an emergency transfusion using outdated tech with plasma donated by workers. Europe hemoglobin saved me and would forever course through my veins.

Did that, too, make me an Impure, according to the Union?

I lifted the chemise. On the right side, beneath my ribs, was a misshapen scar filled with darkened ridges spanning from end to end like meandering lakes. The tips of my fingers glided over the thick welts, the spot where Jade had stuck a spear in me.

I'd never had an actual scar before. Union physicians always had the most modern cosmetic mechanisms that would return the skin to its original glory or even better within moments. But I wasn't in the Union any longer. I didn't have access to the benefits of being an Elite, being above anyone else. All of that was in the past, and for good reason. I had chosen a side when I'd struck a deal with Mama Seeya to expire on the live broadcasts, show the people that Jade was as diabolical as I'd always known she was.

Mama Seeya wasn't the type that played the board for quick gratification. She was in it for the long haul. She'd caused issues for the Union since I was a mere seed in Father's loins. She was something like a harvester in her approach to warfare. Some flowers bloomed only once every decade. An ordinary farmer would choose plants that would yield guaranteed fruits every year. They lacked the patience that Mama Seeya possessed. Her fortitude was impeccable. She would strategically bury seeds of hope within the workers of the Subdivisions, of fear within the Upper Residents, and of doubt within the remaining Elite populace. She'd caused just enough ruckus so that the Union would pounce, snuff them out. She would then retreat again, compile data, and wait for another opportunity to study us as we had them.

I knew that type of drive from anywhere. Elite DNA was definitely in her lineage.

The rough exterior of the mark looked bad, but I hoped the smuggled tech had at least fused the innards. I hadn't coughed up any flesh clots, so I believed they'd brought me back to fullish capacity.

The scar reminded me that sacrifices had to be made for the greater good of humanity. I always needed that prompt to keep me from descending back into fear, into skepticism. It was hard not to, because although Mama Seeya had shared vital information with me at the beginning, then she tapered off. I was starting to suspect that she was using the same strategy on me. Give me something, monitor my behaviors, and then analyze the findings.

Mama Seeya kept me out of the loop. I hadn't heard from her since the duel. None of the workers would send correspondence, either, or give me updates. I was starting to feel less like an ally and more like a prisoner with each passing day, but I didn't have a choice in the matter. I was not in command there.

On the first day, I had awoken to sweat-drenched women with granules of desert pasted to their faces. We were inside a rickety tent in the middle of a sandstorm. They hovered over me. One injected fluid into an IV that protruded from the crook of my arm. Another lifted my eyelid farther back and flashed a light beam into the retina.

"Wh-where am I?" I mouthed. "What are you doing to me?"

"You're okay, Avi."

That voice sounded familiar. "Eve?"

"Yes," she said from not too far away.

When I tried to sit up, I noticed that my opposite arm was shackled to a rail.

"For your safety," a woman with a wide gap in her teeth said as she allowed my lid to slide back into place.

When I tried to struggle, they injected me with something else.

Before I passed out, I got a glimpse of a white-haired angel.

When I awoke for the second time, I was inside a storage room, laying facedown on a hard cot. My cheek on a lumpy, stained pillow that reeked of mildew and probably other embedded human secretions. My attire had been changed to a simple pair of trousers that was two sizes too big and a linty parka. My hair was disheveled, matted in parts.

I was not restrained as before. I wiped the crust from the edge of my mouth and sat up too fast. The freshly healed wound burned with sudden movement. I groaned and cupped the spot as if an organ would spill out.

I expected the door to be locked after what had happened prior, but to my surprise, it opened. I stepped into the quiet hall and gauged the area. Empty. I crept until I heard voices. I concealed myself behind stacked crates and listened for the footsteps to cease. When the coast was clear, I slunk from the other side but was intercepted by an Impure man with a red-brownish beard.

On impulse, I tried to spear him in the neck, but he was very quick and dodged the strike, while catching my wrist midair.

"I see you're awake and well." He released me. "I'm Wayal."

"Where are we?" I felt a surge of adrenaline.

"A rebel compound in a wasteland."

"I need to speak to Mama Seeya," I said. "Jade is out there causing havoc . . ."

He looked at me sideways. "Yes, I suppose much havoc could be caused in two weeks."

"T-two weeks?" I wanted to faint again. The world didn't feel steady. "I've been out for that long?"

His eyes narrowed. "Yes, your wound was deep."

Wayal allowed me to explore the compound. It was magnificent. Under the radar. Rebels worked toward one goal, and that was to secure their liberty.

He led me to a counter where a piece of bread, jerky, and water were separated into individual portions. I grabbed one and took a seat across from him. He watched me intensely as I gnawed on the protein. The way he watched caused discomfort, but I was their guest, and I had to act accordingly.

"Doesn't compare to high teatime at the Citadel, does it?" he asked, tearing into his dry roll.

I became self-conscious. I knew that he didn't think I belonged, but he had every right. I had to earn their respect.

"That's why I am here, to make it right."

He chewed slowly, deliberately. When he swallowed, his Adam's apple bobbed. "You Uppers love playing saviors. Guess that's what makes you feel better after doing exactly—no, worse than—what the Europes did to you."

I wasn't going to fall into his snare. He was bitter, but I was too.

"What I don't get is why us Impures were beneath the Europes." He added, "You'd think that even just a little bit of melanin would've saved us, but guess not."

"I did not create the system; I was brought up in it," I said. Choosing my words carefully.

"A cop-out response." His face turned grim. "You didn't create it, but you just perpetuate it."

I couldn't take it anymore. I stormed out of the area and returned to my quarters, unable to keep the tears from falling. I couldn't allow them to see my weakness. Mama Seeya's plan was to return me to the rightful position of General. How could I rule over a people when I couldn't even convince one that I wasn't like the others? What more could I do to prove to them that I was no longer a dictator in the making?

I'd just allowed Jade to gut me like mere cattle on a live stream. I put my trust in the rebels wholly. They could've chosen not to step in and bring me back to life. But as I trusted that they wanted peace, change, I needed them to do the same.

The following day, Wayal didn't return, but another took his place. The same woman with the gap. Her name was Frida, and she was one of the women who'd brought me back to the realm of the living.

I was happy to see a familiar face. I hugged her hard. She accepted. I asked about Eve, and she told me that she was ill. Before I could ask what part of the compound she was in, Frida had already moved on.

I was given a daily duty like the others. They assigned me the position of a bottom-tier cleaner. I knew it was one of the low-grade jobs that no one else wanted to do and that they were trying to humble the former Elite from the Citadel. I took my bucket and a scrub brush that barely had any bristles remaining and got to work.

In between the strenuous labor of keeping the workstations and the outhouses unsoiled, I trained at the end of work shifts. I needed to be in top shape for the battle that was to come. After training, I familiarized myself with all the old tech that they had conjured. And when it was too quiet, and I had time to think, I wondered where Liyo was, where Saige was. If they were well.

It had been weeks when Wayal returned to the outpost. I scurried to him, the dirty water splashing over the sides of the pail. A few droplets spilled on his boot.

"Apologies," I said, steadying the bucket's murky tsunami. "Were you able to get in touch with Mama Seeya? I need access to her. It's imperative."

"She's busy planning a war, cleaning up your messes." He wore an expression as if he'd just gotten a whiff of something sour. "I'll pass along your message."

He didn't give me a chance to rebut before he and the crew dashed off.

The following evening, something inside my stomach wouldn't rest. I felt the urge to expel the moldy food they'd served the day prior. On the way to the lavatory, I overheard voices.

It was Wayal, Frida, and a few of his usual team, huddled together. Frida was in tears.

"She slit her throat," Wayal explained, peering off into the distance.

A woman who I'd never seen before covered her face. "Little Eve. May she rest peacefully."

I got a sudden urge to run. I wasn't sure where to exactly. The reality was that there was nowhere to go. Each place was just as bad as the previous. Each place exploited the innocent. Each had slaughtered. Adolescents weren't even safe.

Eve . . .

I was dizzy as I edged from the shadows. Everyone stared. I was the last person they expected.

I stepped forward, fully into the dim light, shaking. "Tell me what happened, and do not toy with me."

Without meeting my gaze, Wayal said, "Your sib has taken another."

I knew that it was not the time to pour salt into the wound, but I was void of all patience, and I was not in the mood to continue the estimation game or beg for contact with Mama Seeya. I swiftly grabbed a laser gun from one of the holsters and aimed at Wayal and anyone else who moved.

"Contact her." I pointed to his wrist. "Now."

He sneered, then tapped his wristcom. "You people just don't quit."

He thought he was slick and tried to reach for his gun as the wristcom connected with intermittent *beeps*, but he was too slow, and I let off a round that grazed the top of his hand. He jerked it back with a hiss.

"I could say the same thing about you." I squinted an eye for better aim. "On the account that you carry half."

Wayal scowled at the reminder. Mama Seeya answered. Her attention panned about the room and then landed on the weapon pointed at her people.

"I'm starting to feel like a prisoner here and not an ally." I recapped, "That was *not* the plan."

"I understand your frustration, Avi." Mama Seeya lowered her gaze. "Things have taken a turn."

"I heard. Overheard." I was starting to regress back to the old me. "I do not accept being kept out of the halo. We are supposed to be working together. This will not work if we don't stand united. Wholly."

"Yes, yes." She seemed present in body but not in mind. "Someone will be there at dusk to retrieve you from the outpost. It's time."

And just like that, she ended the call.

No one stirred. Not even a muscle contracted.

I tucked the weapon inside of the band of my pants. Before retreating, I announced, "I'll be hanging on to this."

❖   ❖   ❖

I was awake before dusk. I crammed the stolen laser gun in a slimpack. I'd retrieved my last meal of jerky and bread and stuffed it in the side pocket for the journey back to the city. I knew that I wasn't going to be consuming anything once I returned.

To pass time, I kept smoothing out the wrinkles in the tattered blanket and fluffing out the pillow. I'd nearly beaten the thing to double the number of lumps.

The door opened behind me. I expected it to be Mama Seeya, perhaps Wayal ready to usher me to the transport. I turned around to find neither. My body reacted before my mind was able to. Standing under the arch of the entry was Liyo. His hair cut low; his blue eyes carried grayish bags. My knees bowed, but I was able to catch myself before leaping halfway across the chamber and into his arms.

Chapter Twenty-Eight
LIYO

She grabbed my entire face and planted her soft lips on my forehead, my cheeks, my neck, and then my mouth. The old Avi would've cared about how appropriate everything was. She was much more mature than when I'd first seen her in the greenhouse, more evolved. She was no longer a girl but a woman.

The thoughts, the memories of our short time together were what kept me going in my lowest moments. I never gave up hope that we'd find each other again.

I dreamed of the day when we'd reunite. It played on repeat. I'd hold her tight, so very tight. I'd vow—we'd vow—to never leave the other's side.

But I wasn't the same Liyo. We'd all changed. Some of us for the worse.

As the kiss lingered, the spark that she waited for never came. I couldn't give her anymore false hope that it could ever be.

I peeled my mouth from hers slowly. Her hands still cupped my jaw. "Liyo?"

I couldn't look her in the face. I kept seeing Jade.

She backed away and held her body as if I'd just walked in on her being naked. She was embarrassed. How could she have ever expected to just pick up where we'd left off after everything that had happened. Her sister had taken Eve from me.

She created more distance between us and grazed her bottom lip.

"I-I apologize. I hadn't—I was just—"

I lifted my hand to make her stop.

She wiped away a tear.

I trudged over to the freshly made cot and took a seat at the edge. She positioned herself beside me. We both stared at the open door as if it were a mediator.

She parted her lips to break the silence, but I beat her to it. "When I was cooped up in that cavern with Saige, I used to imagine your head on her body. For galaxy's sake, she was the worst cave roommate." I laughed once, then stopped. "I wanted to come back so bad for you. I knew that your father was going to punish you for treason. Punish everyone just to make a point. How dare we undermine the great Union?"

Avi continued listening.

"I was on the brink of death out there. You know what my goal out there was when I was fighting for my life?"

She shook her head.

"You. It was you, Avi. It became less about me, less about my people, less about Eve, even, and more about you."

She searched for something in my face but couldn't find it.

"And it stayed that way for a long, long time. You became my *why*."

I stood. She craned her neck to look up at me.

"I believed in your kindness, your conviction," I said. "You're a good orator, just like your father. You had me spinning, believing that equality could be reached, if we all just stopped the violence, and then your sister, an Elite, your kin, executed one of ours to prove a fuckin' point."

"Liyo—"

"She proved a valuable point for not only me but for the rest of us. Uppers will never, never change. They will never transfer power, their privilege. They will fight until every one of us is wiped out."

"That is *not* fair!" She shot up, invading my space once more. "What about me? I *am* of them, but I am *not* them. I would never hurt you."

"You're an anomaly," I yelled. "Just one."

She stumbled into the bed. "I am just an anomaly to you?"

"You deserve to know." I flexed my jaw. "The plan has changed."

"What does that mean?"

"The treaty is done. It's over."

"Let me speak with Mama Seeya."

"Who do you think sent me?" I scoffed. "Mama Seeya will lead the rebellion. She'll lead us the way she sees fit. It's only right that she gets that position. She's the reason we even have a fighting chance."

"What about the Upper Residents? What say do they get? Not all of them believe in Jade's system, my father's system," she tried to reason.

"They should've thought of that before they became complicit with the genocide of my people." I lowered my eyes. "I have no empathy for them—or any other sympathizer, for that matter."

"This is not you. This is not the man that I remember." She shook her head, trying to shake off disbelief. "An eye for an eye creates a blind society."

"Don't look at me like I'm some kind of disease," I spat. "I am *not* the disease here."

"So are you here to kill me then?" she asked, getting so close that our stomachs touched.

"I would never—"

Why didn't she understand how hard this all was for me? No one wanted to be there, doing what we were doing, feeling what we were feeling. There was nothing that I wouldn't sacrifice to have it both ways. It wasn't as if I didn't want to believe in her ability to convince her people to stop the mandates and the killings. I wanted to believe so, so bad.

"Mama Seeya has gotten into your head." Even as she spewed lies about her, she still seemed innocent. "Her plan was never to have me lead; she wanted that position all along. I was a pawn."

They always thought it was someone else's fault and never their own.

"Suit up," I told her. "We have a war to fight."

"If you won't kill me, that means that she still needs me," she said. "And if I refuse?"

I leaned on the edge of the frame. "Do what she says, Avi. Prove to her that you're useful. She'll be merciful. She's not like your kind."

That hurt her. I knew it did.

Chapter Twenty-Nine
SAIGE

Mama Seeya stood high on a podium wearing a beige bodysuit with all the extra reinforcements needed for a showdown. Underneath her armpit was wedged a shiny helmet to match. Wayal and Liyo were proudly positioned behind her, as were the rest of her telekinetic crew. Of the four, one was an albino with yellowish hair, white lashes, and Upper features. A boy with three brow cuts. A tall man with a round stomach. The last one was a girl who used an arm crutch for a bum leg. They all rocked Mama Seeya's identical battle set.

We all did.

She paid homage to the hundreds of years they'd forced us to wear dull government-issued worker bodysuits. That color had been ordinary and connected to submissiveness. No choice they'd made about our outerwear, our livelihoods was without reason. Each action was purposeful.

Mama Seeya wanted to make a statement. And now beige bodysuits would be the last thing Union inhabitants would see as their former workers cut them down at the knees.

Pea and I were in the middle of thousands of men and women arranged in rows. Their hands locked behind their backs at attention and chests pressed forward, gravitating to their chain breaker.

For me, the feeling was all too familiar. The vibration of patriotism was at an all-time high. They would do anything to fulfill Mama Seeya's objective. How many would die for the cause? How many had perished before us, fueling that same mindset? I wished I had believed Avi earlier. Supported her more. How could I have been so dumb, so misguided? It was no different from how the Elites regained power. No matter what any of them believed, we were going down that same road that led to more warfare.

Great leaders always fell short during their reigns. Tyranny never just ended with a big war. A be-all and end-all. One winning side. There would always be losers even among winners.

It was bigger than me. Much more so. I was only a meager piece of the scheme. Self-preservation and protecting the ones I loved was all I could gather. The system—no matter how much we fought against it—would always persevere. Humankind was never going to learn from its mistakes.

"I won't bore you with all that it took to get to this moment in space, in time." Mama Seeya chuckled to herself before continuing. "But for the ones who know, just know."

Jeers rumbled from the crowd like a surge.

"Old and young. Chattel and Disposable. Domestic and Impure. We have all been persecuted by the Union and all of its populaces. They've made us test tube babies. Tore apart families. They have terrorized us, slashed us down in the streets, even when we were docile and unable to fend for ourselves. They've ripped our children from our wombs." She clutched her stomach; her eyes bulged, the veins prominent even from a distance. "They plotted genocide!"

The mass began to stir, with each word gaining the energy, the hype they needed to commit more atrocities on her behalf.

"But they failed." She outstretched her hand to calm them.

After they gathered themselves, Mama Seeya closed her eyes and tilted her head back. For a long time, she remained still and allowed the sound of the wind to carry the message far and wide.

"The calm before the squall." She took in a deep inhale and then reopened her eyes. "After today, I say 'not ever again.'"

A voice from far away was faint. "Not ever again."

"We say: NOT EVER AGAIN!" Mama Seeya jabbed her finger to the back and began to take longer strides, crossing the entire length of the stage. "No more chains. No more slavery. Today's the day where we reclaim our power. Reclaim what's ours. Reclaim it ALL by any means necessary!"

The mob was riled up beyond bringing them back to ease. I pulled Pea closer just in case they started to mosh and, in the frenzy, squashed her.

Mama Seeya's palm faced up, starting at her thigh, and rose slowly above the top of her head. The soldiers behind her, like marionettes, mimicked her movement. Helmets rocketed above and whirled about like a silent symphony, creating shapes and patterns. Once the spectacle was completed, each helmet was placed onto our heads by the invisible hands of her powerful crew.

❖ ❖ ❖

We were split into units. Pea and I got the hovercraft led by Wayal. I was sure that he was thrilled about it. Liyo was placed into another, two groups down. He headed toward his assigned craft. I waved my hands overhead and called him. I hadn't seen him since the cremation. I knew he'd heard me because he hesitated slightly before vanishing into the tail of a ship.

I stood there stewing in my own annoyance. He was really going to head into battle without saying anything.

"He's just grieving." Pea could almost read my thoughts as of late. "Give him time."

I finally broke my attention from the spot he'd disappeared from. "Yeah, well, time's what we don't have."

Once we were on the hovercraft and strapped in, Wayal gave final directives.

"We've been training for this day." Not ever looking in my direction, he said, "Our goal is to take over the fortress that is the Citadel. It won't be an easy feat. They've had power of this estate for well over a thousand years. It's imperative that we gain control. Many of us will die trying, but our bodies mean nothing if they aren't free from their control. We take the Citadel, we take the city. Got it?"

The team nodded in unison.

He stared at us and only us. "Shoot to kill. Anyone who gets in the way. Children included. Sympathizers won't be tolerated and will be punished with execution. We don't have space for weak links."

He vanished into the main cabin, leaving the rest of us in the hold. The hovercraft elevated. It trembled too much for my comfort. I guessed Pea's, too, because she grabbed my hand and squeezed. Once the shaking eased, she'd noticed what she'd done and quickly returned her hand to her lap.

"Do you think they got any word from Elu yet?" she asked, trying to take my mind from her action.

I shook my head. "Probably not."

Pea remained thoughtful. I knew she was afraid. We all were.

She chewed her nail.

"What?"

She removed her index finger from her mouth. "I don't think I'm ready to kill children."

"Listen to me." I brought my face down to meet hers. "You don't kill innocent people. Okay?"

"But—"

"But my ass. You heard me. They can have that blood on their hands. Not you. And not me." I scooted back after we hit more turbulence.

"After all this is done. We do what we gotta do. You and me, we're returning to the north. Mama Seeya promised me that." She twiddled her middle finger and thumb. "Why would you want a cripple to come with you? I can't do much. I'd just be a thorn in your side. Slow you down anyways." The old me would've allowed her to sit in her own trash. She wouldn't have cared about anything other than her own selfishness. Escaping by any means. Leaving people behind. No matter who got maimed in the process. That was what got Avi killed. And a slew of others. I'd always thought that caring was a weakness, so I'd shielded myself from it. Locking away any feelings or emotions that would bond me to another. I thought for a long time that that defense would work. Carry me through life. That it was something that I could live with, with no regrets. But I had regrets. I also had choice. I could live with those regrets and sulk, or I could live with them and do something about it.

"You are *not* a cripple. You've got the best one-handed shot out there." I pulled her bony chin to face me. Her dark-pink lips were puckered. "It'd be an honor for you to continue to be that thorn in my side. I like pain, remember?"

It looked like she was going to cry.

"If I see one tear, I swear that you'll stay here."

She sniffled then wiped her nose with her sleeve and smiled.

"Any word from Instructor Skylar?" I asked. Sad time was over.

Pea shook her head and peered out the circular frame. "No, but I'm glad he didn't stick around. Things are about to get—oh no."

I unstrapped myself from the harness and pressed my nose against the chilled glass to get a better look. Rebel hovercrafts were being fired at from beyond the clouds and from the Citadel itself below. They were going down by the dozens, like birds diving for prey. We fired back and so did others, creating an opening. We entered the Citadel's restricted airspace.

The craft in front had been struck and then in turn slammed into ours. The hit knocked me to the ground. We nosedived, spinning. The pilot was able to gain control again before we fell too deep into the forest, but it was a madhouse in the skies. I was able to pull myself up as the lights began to flicker and sirens boomed.

Wayal burst through the access. "Move. Move. Move!"

The bottom of the hovercraft opened, and rebels began to propel forward. I pushed Pea to the back, wanting her to stay put. She gave me attitude, and I returned it.

"Wait here," I growled.

Against her wishes, she obeyed.

As I waited in the long line to be hitched to the connection, I watched through the window and down at the entrance of the massive estate. A body of a woman—I thought—had just landed on the ground and removed their helmet. It wasn't a pale person; it was someone who had a darker hue. They were too far to get a better look. They placed their helmet back on and continued with their weapon pointed forward as they stormed the first set of front gates.

Why would an Upper be among rebels? I had been with the rebels for a while now, and there were none among the crew. Mama Seeya wouldn't have allowed it.

Avi?

I pushed past the jam of soldiers waiting to rappel down and cut the line. I had to see for myself. Men protested, but I didn't care. I attached myself to the track and rode it down to the end.

Before the tip of my boot even hit the soil, I had already unlatched myself and raced. My arms pushed so hard that it hurt. I wasn't even holding my gun because cradling it would've slowed me down.

Something inside told me that my mind, my eyes played tricks. That maybe being back at the Citadel caused trauma to erupt in the form of hallucinations. That logical part reminded me that it wasn't her. She was dead. I saw it. We all saw it.

People didn't just come back from dust.

But then there was a feeling of something else. Delirium. Hope, maybe. That told me to keep going. See for myself. I needed closure. I'd never gotten it for Ma. For my father. Not even for Miah. I needed closure that my sister was dead for real. I knew it was stupid, but I had to get to her. If it was her. Too many times I'd turned my back on Avi, and I wasn't going to do that anymore. I was with her until the end.

Caught in my own possible delusion, I wasn't fully aware of my surroundings until I reached the head of the Citadel. Bodies of watchmen and rebels alike lay motionless outside of the double doors. More of theirs lay stiff than ours, which meant that the first unit had been successful at clearing out the entry.

The surroundings were eerily soundless. I was expecting more firepower than that. It was like they weren't even trying. I'd have thought Jade would've destroyed the place before ever letting rebels step foot inside. Something didn't line up. And if Avi was truly inside, I needed to get her out.

I began to allow myself to spin into a frenzy. My heart beat way too fast. I was light headed. Confused about my next step, my next decision. Jade could've been hiding in any nook, ready to pounce for round two. The anticipation was what got me. I used to be fearless when walking into the belly of danger, but I used to have a lot less to lose too. More groups of armed rebels whizzed past as if I were a stationary table in the way. They cleared out as fast as they entered.

Time wasn't on our side. If I was going to find her, I would have to calm down, be aware. I lifted the laser gun, allowing it to lead, and tiptoed along the long, winding halls. From behind, I heard soles scuffling, and I aimed, finger on the trigger. What I thought were watchmen turned out to be a unit of rebels who came from out of nowhere, jogging toward the next space to clear.

I stalked deeper into the familiar galleries of a place that was once a prison among many prisons for me. I came across that huge kitchen that the elder workers labored in when I'd first arrived from Head Gardner's detention facility. I remembered them slaving over steamy cauldrons and piping, blistering stoves lined with fresh breads, cooking food that they'd never have the luxury to eat themselves. I remembered how red and swollen their fingers were from their monotonous tasks of making sure their masters were nourished.

I kept moving.

Laser shots could be heard not too far away. I was closing the gap between me and the action. I stepped over more mangled and dead forms that scattered the level. A rebel was slumped over, her back held up against the wall, weeping softly with her face in her palms. I attached the laser gun to my back and knelt to assist her. I tried to loop her arm around my shoulder and lift the deadweight, but she shoved me away. I fell backward over a severed leg cut off at the thigh. She raised her face, revealing tear trails of red that straggled along her cheekbones and to the corners of her mouth, coming from two fleshy sockets. They had gouged her eyes out and left her.

"Kill me," she cried out loud. "Please!"

I couldn't talk. Answer. Nothing.

She sniffed, her head jerking to find out where I had gone. If I had left her behind like the others.

"Hello?"

I shuffled to my feet. "I'm here."

· Her head switched back in the direction that my voice had come from. She tried crawling toward me but was blocked by the lifeless lying in a heap.

"Right here." She kept tapping the center of her forehead. The place where she wanted the laser to go.

I couldn't. I wouldn't.

I pulled out a smaller gun from my ankle holster and guided her hands to it. She grabbed my wrist and gripped, looking up at me from the cavities, trying to imagine my face. "Gratitude."

She released me and scurried back to the wall, admiring the weapon with the tips of her fingers.

I left her.

I heard her say, "Long live the Brotherhood." Then a single shot. Around the bend, in the middle of a connecting hall, were watchmen tussling with a group of rebels. Mostly women. I aimed and fired. Hitting the first watchman in the neck. Blood spurted from the wound as he tried to apply pressure. I hit two more right in the helmets. The first one was practice. More watchmen loaded into the area. We were blasted by a barrage of ammo. The lasers whizzed over my head as I dodged, zigzagging along the barriers. More of Mama Seeya's enforcements took the rear and sides, and together we moved as one, taking out another hive.

After that area was emptied of live watchmen, rebels went one way, and I went the other. I took a stroll toward the General's study. A lone watchman caught me off guard, slamming the butt of his gun into the center of my helmet. The next thing I knew, he was on top of me, striking my helmet until the surface splintered. A sharp piece sliced my chin down to the white meat. He yanked the helmet off and placed pressure on my neck with his clammy fingers. I scratched at his helmet, and then when that didn't work, I clawed at his thick fists, but he had a canine lock and wasn't letting go.

He lifted my head by my neck and then slammed it back to the ground. I tried to push my hips forward, pop up, but his weight was too heavy, too solid. I was pinned.

"Impure scum," he said as he pressed harder into the center of my throat with the tips of his thumbs.

I gagged for a sweet breath that never arrived. My lids fluttered into the dark gray.

Suddenly, his head snapped to the left, and instantly, he released. I gasped. Choking on my own saliva.

Liyo stepped over his body and continued about his business as if he hadn't just saved me. I couldn't even get a word out to tell him to stop, that I needed to talk to him before he continued on. I was too weak to catch a breath, let alone grab him. The blood rushed back to my head as I rose to my feet and snatched my weapon. Before I returned the broken helmet back over my head, I spat a huge wad on the watchman. I pressed forward.

A young woman grunted from a cracked opening of the General's massive study. I placed my foot in the center and then wedged my body in between the dense sliding doors. With my shoulder, I pushed one side, and with my hip, I pushed the other until I was able to slip through. Inside, another altercation was going on. It was dark; the only light came from the slit in the entrance I'd just slithered through. In the dimness was a small-statured body encircled by a group of watchmen.

I caught only a glimpse of her back as she got into a low fighting stance. It was as if she'd choreographed every laser slug and every knuckle and every foot strike. She moved as if she'd known each exchange. She was purposeful and measured in her effort as she ducked flying ammo and disabled each watchman.

I stood in awe as she cracked arm bones over her shoulder, drove her heel into the back of heads, split helmets, and drove her knife through body armor. She moved so fast and so swiftly, weaving in and out of that sliver of light, that I couldn't make a clear shot.

As I got nearer, I noticed that she was out of breath but down to two last opponents.

"You're a disgrace to all Elites." The watchman removed his helmet and spat blood. "I want you to see my face, you traitor."

He charged her. She jumped in the air, and before he could tackle her, she spun, and the outer part of her boot nearly crushed his jaw. When she landed, he dropped, but the other one took the opportunity to drive his fist into her spine. Her back curved inward as she stumbled forward into the shade.

He approached.

I loomed silently.

He grabbed her by the back of her bodysuit and slammed her onto the General's bureau. She wiggled around, grunting, the shine of her helmet's face reflecting in the shard of light.

I heard the unsheathing of a blade yet still didn't have a clear shot.

He raised a hand over his head and then came down. She was able to slide out of the way before it penetrated. She slid the panel of her helmet open to chomp down on his thumb; he yelped and then dropped the weapon with a *clunk*. She closed it and then wrapped her legs around his torso as he lifted both of them back into an upright position. She grunted again as she pounded on his head. He moaned and twirled around, trying to get her to stop. He was able to peel her off and toss her to the side. She brought both legs over her head, and with one swoop she was back on her feet.

Before he could tackle her, she sprang up and grabbed onto a bar above and knocked him back with both boots. He went flying back and right into me, but before he could figure out what or who it was that had stopped his fall, I slit his throat and allowed him to slide down my leg to his final resting place.

I stepped into the light and removed my helmet. She mimicked me.

"Saige?" Her large eyes widened, watered.

I gasped once, almost as if the watchman was choking me again. I never thought I'd lay eyes on her after I'd left without a proper farewell back on the compound. She'd returned to me and I to her.

She came forward. Closer but not too close.

I closed the gap. I dug my face into her braids and breathed in the smell of jojoba oil and coconuts. She was tense at first with disbelief but then relaxed. The sounds of her breath shook as she held on tight.

She pulled back while still holding on, just soaking in my face as I was hers.

I shook my head. I couldn't believe she was alive. In the flesh.

My sister.

We both grinned at each other through tears and snot and slobber.

"I didn't know princesses could fight," I said, wiping my nose.

Avi let go and then shoved my shoulder. It actually hurt. She had some force behind her strikes now. "You should know. A princess to another princess." Her brow lifted high on her face.

"I thought you were—" I felt my eyes getting soggy again just thinking about the thought of losing her. The grief, the anger that I'd felt when I'd thought she was gone.

She cradled my chin. Her hands were soft despite the power in them. "I will never leave you again. You will never be able to get rid of me now. We are blood, sisters from here until forever."

Watchmen pried open the door fully, falling over one another, loading inside. Jade would've loved it if we died together at the hands of her army. She would've loved to snuff us out at once. Two birds. One stone.

Avi and I grabbed weapons from each part of our bodies and stood back to back.

"Ready?" she asked as they circled.

"Mm-hmm," I replied.

❖   ❖   ❖

We sat on the General's counter covered in the blood and grime of the watchmen we'd just slain.

"We've got to get out of here," I said all in one breath.

As I limped toward the door, she grabbed my wrist. "We can't trust Mama Seeya."

I hadn't even turned around yet. "I know."

"She never wanted me to be General," she said gravely. "And I have suspicions that she surrendered Eve to my—to Jade in order to incite violence, to sway Liyo."

The veins in my neck pulsed. "You saw him?" I pivoted to face her.

Avi nodded.

He knew she was alive. And he hadn't told me.

"He is different now," she said slowly.

Mama Seeya was a serpent hiding behind liberator's clothing, and Liyo was becoming a close second. I should've stuck to my gut. Not only did we have to worry about Jade and Head Gardner, but now Mama Seeya and possibly Liyo were on the list. Her cause was cruel. In my eyes, she was worse than the Union, because she betrayed her own. How could she have kept Avi from me? How could she have given Eve to the enemy? Her intentions were never to send me back to the north either.

What did she have planned?

Chapter Thirty
AVI

Saige tried to convince me to leave with her, that something about the coup didn't feel right, but I expressed that I had to locate Mother first. I had to ensure she was safe. Jade had made it clear that she didn't prioritize familial ties. If I knew anything about Jade, it was that she was quick to sever bonds, and that she'd probably left Mother to fend for herself. I'd already left her behind once, and I wasn't going to make that same misstep again.

I told Saige that I could do it alone, that she could move ahead and that I'd meet her at the port when I'd finished this last pursuit. She looked at me like I was mad and jumped in front, leading the way.

"Do you even know where her quarters are located?" I asked. Skeptical.

"No, but the strongest leads." She looked back and winked.

"Well, I'll have you know that I advanced with honorable mentions in the Watchmen Academy." I shot a watchman in the leg and then in the heart before he even clashed with the pavement.

Saige huffed. "Show-off."

The entrance to her quarters was already unbolted. I rushed ahead of Saige, my heartbeat intensifying with each stride. Had they gotten to her before I did? The chamber was in disarray. Bodysuits and shawls hung halfway off the slumberpod and in piles. Heels and boots were scattered in heaps on the floor. The vintage jewelry chests had been torn open and rummaged through. There was even a blood trail leading into her closet. I swallowed hard before following it, preparing myself for what was to come. Perhaps I was too late.

"Mother?" The word sailed along a single exhale.

Saige surveyed the area with me. After we'd checked each crevice, the massive closet had no signs of a body. I allowed a sigh of relief. She'd gotten away. Hopefully safely.

Saige picked up a hologlobe and held it high in the air, observing the bottom compartment.

It was one of the presents I'd gifted Mother as an adolescent for her centenary. I remembered the day I offered it to her. I waited beside her slumberpod, anticipating the timer's lapse. When the lid hissed ajar and Mother rose from the cavern refreshed, I popped up and screamed, "Surprise!" She nearly had an aneurysm as she clutched her chest. She lifted me into the pod playfully, and there I watched her unbox the hologlobe. She waved her hand over the sensor, but it didn't activate. Unsuccessfully, she waved again and again.

Finally, I told her that I had reprogrammed it to be stimulated only with a voice-relayed password.

She tapped me on the tip of the nose and called me her clever little girl.

I placed the hologlobe to my lips. "Ifemi."

The translation was *my love* in the ancient language of our people.

A hologram of a much shorter Avi running from her as she chased me in our gardens appeared. She cried. At the time, I hadn't understood why.

Now as I stood in the middle of warfare, I understood completely.

I repeated the password, and the hologlobe initiated. Instead of Mother and a tiny version of me, it was only her. I almost leaped from my own skin, dropping the sphere. It thumped and rolled into the base of the island, and from it emerged an older-looking version of Mother. "Avi." The hologram noticed me right away and moved closer. "Is it really you?"

"Mother?" I reached out to touch her, feel her warmth once more, but it was nothing to hang on to, just tiny particles. She was only a live simulation.

I dropped to my knees. She stood over me with that familiar comforting grin. She looked around her space. Unsurety plagued her, but she tried her best to conceal it.

"I am safe, my child." She sensed my worry and wiped a tear from her face. "I knew you would come back."

I lowered my chin to my chest.

"That's why I programmed this communiqué."

I looked back up at her dazzling form.

"Mother, tell me where you are. I'm coming to get you."

I heard a bang in the background. She jumped ever so slightly. "There isn't much time."

Another thump. On a door or a wall, perhaps. "Mother?"

"Within this hologlobe are the manual override codes for a Transmega. Use them to end this chaos." She gazed at Saige and then shot her an earnest smile. "You have your father's eyes. His drive too. Protect your sister." Her voice cracked.

Another knock but it was the loudest of them all. Mother became frantic. She knelt down and tried to caress my face, but her ghostlike fingers just passed through. "I love you."

She kept eyeing the unknown.

"Mother?" I reached out as she stepped back.

Her eyes darted to the side, to the source of the disturbance.

"Mother." I crawled forward.

The hologram started to glitch, to disintegrate.

It returned to the hologlobe.

"Mother?" I screamed.

I drove my fist into the island. I smashed it over and over again until the skin broke. Saige stepped in, grabbing the last strike in her palm.

She allowed me to weep in her shoulder, but I knew she was counting down the seconds. We had to leave. I couldn't help Mother if I was a mass of sentiments. If she had any chance of survival, it would depend solely on our next moves.

Saige pulled me to my feet. I wiped my already-stained face the best I could.

"Ready?" she said.

I repeated the codes, etching them into my memory. "Hmm."

"Then let's pay Mama Seeya a visit."

A message came through our comms notifying the troops that the Citadel had been officially overthrown. There were vague sounds of cheers permeating through the halls I'd once played in as a youth. Saige and I saw men and women rejoicing and running through the galleries, embracing.

The celebrations didn't last.

The tile began to rumble beneath us. Cheers turned into cries. Saige grabbed my arm and propelled me forward as bursts of fire erupted from each entryway, blowing off doors and caving in floors and ceilings. We ran as fast as our legs would take us, but an archway surrendered to the weight of the disconnected concrete, creating a cavernous hole. We both were swept in like debris.

❖   ❖   ❖

My tongue was covered in clay. When I coughed, a slew of dust exited, creating a mini cloud. I lay flat on something hard, rigid, and watched white particles drift midair. My arms were outspread like a bird's when it used the wind to glide just before flapping against gravity. There was something heavy on top of me.

Saige moaned, then shuffled around before she materialized above me. She appeared upside down.

"I'm going to get you out of there," she assured me.

She frantically patted the shattered archway that entombed my lower extremities, trying to find a ridge she could use to lift it. She used all her strength to elevate the mass, but it wouldn't budge. She then put her back on it and tried pushing. Her boots digging and dragging in the dirt, causing deep furrows.

"Saige," I called, but she just ignored me and continued to muscle the boulder with no advancement.

I witnessed the determination, that age-old stubbornness that I'd missed since she'd been gone.

I gave up and allowed her to believe that she could save me, but as time spent itself and she began cutting herself on the boulder, I yelled from the depths, "Enough."

She slid down the bulk, defeated, and pinched the bridge of her nose.

"The comms." She sprang upright and tried to initiate contact.

Static.

She tossed the helmet; it flew and smashed into something hard.

"Mama Seeya destroyed the Citadel," I said, tears rolling through my sideburns and disappearing into my scalp.

Saige rested at my side. "Are you hurt?"

"How could I have not seen the signs?" I continued.

"Can you move your toes?" She examined the parts of my body that were visible.

"She will go to great lengths to demolish everything."

"Avi—"

I turned to her with bulging eyes. "You should've left when you had the chance."

She shook her head.

"You wouldn't be here if it wasn't for me."

"I stayed because I wanted to."

"We both know that no one is coming for us." I laid my head back down, the weight too heavy to hold. "Find a way out. I'll be fine."

She scoffed. "The foundation isn't stable, Avi. The whole thing could crumble at any time."

"One dead is better than two."

"Don't. Talk. Like. That." She grabbed my face and forced me to stare into her piercing eyes. "Do you understand me?"

I frowned.

She let go and began surveying the area. "Stay put." I heard a light lilt in her voice.

I appreciated her ambition, but we both knew that the rebels had gotten what they wanted from us and that we were just pawns on a game board. Throwaways. Both sides were better off without either of us interfering in their games. Jade's explosion had worked in favor of everyone.

The first phase of Mama Seeya's plan was completed, and none of it would have happened if it weren't for me. If Father hadn't been cremated, he would've been quaking in his grave at the sight of the alleged alliance. Shame shrouded me in a way that I hadn't expected. I always imagined that taking down the system would have brought me peace, a sort of nirvana. But I felt nothing. Instead, I was unsettled. Had I inadvertently just chosen one evil over another? Those people were my own. Of my blood. I'd betrayed them.

And now I was jammed between two immovable masses. An ironic death.

I didn't know how much time passed as I wallowed in my own failures. Retracing every tread as to where I'd gone wrong. Had I been too overzealous? Had I embodied the same trait that I hated so much in Jade, arrogance, so that I hadn't even noticed the errors of my own ways?

Another light quake occurred. Saige shrieked. I heard pebbles and rocks tumble and fall. I got to my elbows and tried to unwedge myself. I screamed as I pulled and pulled, but I was only hurting myself more in the process.

"Fuck." I grunted. "Saige?"

She appeared, covered in more soot. "I'm here. I'm okay. Stop moving."

"What happened?" I relaxed.

"I found a shaft, but as I started to dig, it buckled. I have to find us a way out."

"Don't go." I seized her before she could leave again. "Please, just stay here. With me."

We idled in silence for a while, soaking in the grave condition, both minds working overtime in order to figure out the next approach. Our breaths were synchronized, and it seemed like on every other exhale the structure that held our cavern shrank a little more. It wouldn't hold for long. The Citadel would consume us like a decadent dessert on a silver platter during an Elite ceremony.

Saige started muttering to herself as she picked the skin from around her nail. Then she started chuckling, pretending to not know that I was staring.

"Care to share the pun?" I asked.

She flicked the dead membrane and set her sights on me. "When I left—escaped from the General that last time—Liyo and I took shelter in a cave in the mountains." Her eyes, her mind wandered to another place as she recounted her journey. "I hated it. Being there with him. Cooped up with nowhere to go."

"I thought this would be more of a lighthearted recollection."

She pulled a knee into her chest and leaned back. "If you can't see the irony of me being stuck in a cave with one pain in the ass and then being stuck in another with an entirely different pain in the ass, then you have no sense of humor."

I burst out laughing. She followed suit. It took us a while to come back to the fact that we were trapped.

I cleared my throat and turned my face to the jagged ceiling. "Well, there's no one that I'd rather be stuck in a cave with than you."

"How long did it take you to come up with that?" She sniggered. "You act like we're going to die in here or something."

My throat tightened as a certain reality hit.

"I never stopped thinking of you when I left," Saige said. "When I found out that that man was my father, that you were my sister, I wasn't sure what—who I was anymore. My entire existence had been a big, stupid question mark for such a long time, and I finally had a purpose, a goal. I wanted to escape so badly. Find myself in the chaos. But when the answer slapped me right in the face, I still decided to run away from it . . . I could've stayed."

In a soft voice, I reminded her, "He would've killed you."

Her eyes watered. "But you—I left you. What kind of eldest sister does that?"

I tried to lean forward to reach out to her, but I'd forgotten that I was jammed. "I was—I am fine. You deserved to taste freedom, Saige."

"Stop being so understanding," she yelled, spittle flying from her mouth. "Why are you so fuckin' pure?"

"I'm not pure," I said. "I want to be fair. I want to right the wrongs of my people, our people. I owe that not only to you but to the others."

She moved in closer. "The weight of your ancestors isn't for you to carry alone."

"We don't have that choice." I tilted my head.

"But it's not fair," she cried.

"Who's the baby now?" I grinned.

She poked me in the forehead, and I plopped back down to a full lying position.

"What else happened out there? In the north. What was it like?" I inquired.

Saige dug her fingers into the corners of her eyes. "It's the most peaceful that I've ever felt. My whole life I've been fighting and hurting, then fighting some more. I never knew there was another way. It was quiet. Still. It was simple."

I tried to imagine it. A snowy paradise on earth. I had to go against the grain of what we'd been taught in the Academy about the Northern Region and the savages that occupied it. They painted the people on the other side to be uncouth, but the entire time, it had all been a fallacy to keep us from exploring, connecting.

"I met someone there." She played with her bootstraps.

The one Head Gardner had executed. How could I have not known? Not inquired. The entire time, she was grieving an affection lost.

"Miah." I propped myself up to my elbows again as if we were inside our chambers exchanging secrets and not entombed. "I-I didn't know."

She smirked. "His eyes were the blackest that I'd ever seen. Like two shiny pieces of coal. He was kind . . ."

I waited patiently for more.

Her grin faded, as did the tone of her voice. "I fought him at first. But then he grew on me. I didn't think that it was possible for someone like me to . . . feel like that."

I nodded.

"He taught me how to be vulnerable." She smoothed her hair, but it just popped back into the same place. "And Head Gardner took him. Like she did Ma."

My heart ruptured into pieces as minuscule as the particles floating from the explosion. It was as if I'd become her, feeling everything she felt. My people continued to damage, to destroy. Head Gardner and the rest would get what they were owed. I was going to make sure of it.

Rumbling different from the previous rattles occurred. Powdery darts began to sprinkle from above. Saige covered me with her body.

Pillars began to drop, and we both melded into the other, waiting for the whole thing to crash down.

The Citadel's quivers ceased. The area went quiet. We both raised our heads and witnessed a transparent circular sphere with robotic limbs emerge from the rubble.

"There you are." I knew that accent from anywhere.

Pea's voice echoed through the amplifiers. In the next moment, she burrowed through the cavity with a drill machine built by the rebels. She used mechanical arms to lift the boulder from my body, freeing me.

❖ ❖ ❖

Before returning to the rebel hovercrafts, Saige and I agreed on keeping the codes Mother had shared secret. That information would prove useful if Mama Seeya became unruly. We would work everything by the book until it was absolutely necessary to divert course. We had only one chance at saving Mother.

Before I could detach myself from the line, Pea tackled me from the side, almost knocking me back through the hole that I'd just emerged from. She squeezed tight. I swept the thin hairs pasted to her forehead to the side.

"It's really you." She fumbled over her words. "How?"

Saige detached from her harness and smirked gingerly at our reunion.

"A long tale for another day," I told her and glanced at her bandaged limb. The arm that she'd lost because I was too much of a coward to challenge Jade right then and there.

"I'm okay. Really," she assured me.

"When this is all over, I will have a bionic arm specially crafted for you. It'll be better than the last. You have my word."

Her face beamed like a light orb. "I would like that."

Wayal surfaced from the cockpit holding a dirty piece of cloth. He was tattered, but he'd definitely won the fight. We locked eyes. He couldn't hide his disdain for my survival.

With his teeth, he ripped the cloth in half and began wrapping his sliced-open palm with it. "Next stop, the Square. Gear up for round two, rebels."

❖   ❖   ❖

The Square was not the place I remembered. It looked as if it were crumbling in on itself like a dehydrated sandcastle. Battles were happening in the air. Lasers hit buildings and blasted holes in the exteriors. We witnessed rebel crafts being struck and then going into a tailspin into a club rooftop, toppling over several floors. Shootouts were happening on topmost-floor balconies. I watched Upper Residents caught in the crossfire leaping to their deaths from penthouse windows to escape the violence. I turned my face away. I lay back and tried to ground myself, but the vibrations of explosions rocked the craft. Blasts sounded like mere firework displays, but I knew that with each eruption, lives, real bodies, were being lost as collateral damage.

How could I have not known that this was the expenditure of war? How could I have been so naive?

The craft lingered in front of a 3D virtual adaptation of Marco Grant. She held up a new fizzy drink that was just released onto the market and then climbed out of the cybernetic box that housed her. With a smirk, she reached out and displayed the glass bottle. She pulled it back in, took a swig, and licked her lips.

The image became distorted into large pixels and then reanimated to footage of Talon and Aura. Liyo was also in frame. They were located at Gardner's detention facility. With ease, they tossed watchmen hives into the air and flung them against cell bars. They blasted open doors, allowing inmates to rush out and flee along the winding staircases. The stream cut to another part of the Square. The physician's headquarters where they'd routinely administered government-approved toxins to the workers. They lined physicians and staff up in the grand white lobby and without hesitation unloaded their ammo into them.

The stream transitioned to Mama Seeya, who was alone on the monitor and in an undisclosed location. Her legs were crossed, and her arms were propped leisurely on steel armrests. Her face carried an almost bored sentiment.

"People of the Southern Region," she began, "if you didn't believe me then, then you should believe me now."

She dawdled, allowing her words to marinate in the anarchy ensuing around us.

"To each worker, displaced by droids or not, take heed to my counsel and join us." She adjusted herself further, relaxing more into the seat. "Pick up whatever weapon available to you and show your former masters the same mercy that they bestowed upon us. With each cut, with each tear that you inflict, remember that it's retribution for every castration, every aborted baby due to their population-control rubrics, every painful electrocution as punishment, each incarceration, each senseless murder."

Jade was somewhere in the region seething. I knew her too well.

"Remember." Mama Seeya tapped her temple. "Not ever again."

The live stream cut out.

Chapter Thirty-One
SAIGE

We joined the hundreds of rebel crafts parked in the core of the Square. It was void of the pleasant-seeming Uppers enjoying frozen cocktails and tossing discs to exotic spliced pets. The suburban city and the artisanal tea vendors were ashen, the sounds of chirping wristcoms with the region's latest gossip were gone, and the grass that had once been as green as an old oil painting was gray. The only thing that remained was the majestic waterfall centerpiece. It looked out of place among the ruins. Like a rose in a sea of brittle weeds.

As rebels carried the injured forward, others offed Uppers who couldn't keep their pain discreet. They dragged the bodies to the centerpiece. The water ran dark red.

The smell of death saturated the air even though we were outdoors. Avi pressed the back of her fist against her nostrils and shut her eyes tight, trying not to take it all in. I couldn't grieve for them like Avi, but I didn't take pleasure in the massacre either. Wayal seemed to have gotten off from seeing her reaction.

Avi stopped as Wayal stood over an injured young girl. With one stomp, he crushed her face, snapping her neck.

"She kinda looked like you." The sole of his foot remained on the girl's head. "Maybe a cousin?"

It all happened so fast, but I saw his hand go toward Avi. She caught it and twisted, and when he tried to strike with the other, she had already slipped his gun from his holster. The barrel imprinted into the skin on his forehead as he went cross eyed.

I called out, but she was under a spell.

Rebels from nearby all pointed their weapons at her. At me.

"He isn't worth it," I said in her ear.

My words weren't making any difference because she stood her ground, fixed in an execution position.

They started closing us in.

"Avi." My hands stayed up toward the horde.

Wayal had gone from fear to shock to confidence in seconds. They both eyed each other as if they were having a psychic conversation. She wanted him gone, and so did he to her.

"Enough!" Mama Seeya stepped onto the top of the Academy's stairs, breaking Avi's trance. "We have great things to discuss. Come."

Before Avi dropped the weapon, she brought it down over Wayal's nose with full force, breaking it almost in half.

❖ ❖ ❖

Wayal was heard howling in the hall as one of his people reset his crooked nose. He entered glaring at Avi, but then he regained his cool when Mama Seeya gave him a look. He simmered down, but I knew he'd have it out for her even more than before. But I wasn't going to say that the new bend in the bridge of his nose issued by Avi didn't make me proud. He'd had it coming for a while now.

We took our seats in the boardroom that had once been used for the Academy's Elites. I wondered where the Administrator was. She'd made my life hard when I was a custodial worker. She'd even tried to have me killed once, framing me for Avi's attempted assassination.

Liyo appeared. At some point, I'd have to tell him about Mama Seeya's involvement with Eve's death. I wasn't sure how she'd done it, but I knew she had. She'd been sneaking around the rebels' backs and been in cahoots with someone in the Union. I knew why she'd done it, but I didn't know for how long. Plus, what was the Union getting out of it?

Liyo and I weren't on speaking terms. He'd taken every road to avoid me. Plus, something told me that he wouldn't have believed me anyway.

I had to wait it out until I got more proof.

Elu had returned. With her she'd brought a dozen colony members dressed in parkas and furry boots with matching triangle tats on their foreheads. They all took a spot.

Mama Seeya's debriefing began. "My good people, the Citadel has been overthrown—"

Rebels pumped their fists, weapons high, and hollered. The leaders remained stoic.

When the chatter died, she said, "And the war has almost been won. The current General has the Elite Subdivisions still on lock, but they won't be able to hold for long. We anticipate the overthrow to be a complete success in the next forty-eight hours."

"Name's Frida, for all you newbies in the room." A woman addressed the people and then Mama Seeya. "What about the General? Has she been captured?"

"I've sent out a special ops team to track her. Don't worry, we'll get her. Her kingdom's sinking, and she can't help but to show herself for one last showdown. Uppers have always enjoyed a good performance."

A man with a thin gray ponytail and two missing bottom teeth was the oldest of Elu's group. He was long in body and controlled in his movements.

"If your so-called war is complete, then why have you summoned us to the south?" he asked.

"Cooperation." Mama Seeya intertwined her fingers, showing the room her hands. "Unity."

The man spat. Mama Seeya's lip twitched.

"What kind of unity is this?" he asked. "We are in the crux of an extermination."

The eyes of the once-collected leader of the rebels protruded. "It was exterminate or be exterminated. Don't play that sanctified bullshit with me. Not on my land."

"Your land?" he scoffed. "No one owns this land. We have more rights over it than you do. We are direct descendants of the indigenous people. You sound like one of *them*."

Mama Seeya's body trembled.

The man turned to Elu. "Why did you bring us here? For some misguided revenge attempt?"

Elu took his wrinkled hand. "You've seen what the Elites did to our colony, Yaya. We cannot give them the chance to move farther into our territory and repeat more massacres. They've tricked us once. Broken the treaty. They cannot be trusted."

Yaya motioned toward the dirty, rough-looking rebels. "And you truly believe that these people can?"

"We can no longer sit it out. They killed Miah." Elu explained, "We must unite. Both the north and the south."

"My child." Yaya patted Elu's shoulder. Maybe she was too hopeful. She didn't know that hope only took us so far in the south. He then turned back to Mama Seeya. "And what of the Jore heir?"

"What of it?" Mama Seeya didn't even glance in our direction. "We will no longer abide by the rules of the dead in the novel world."

"Hmm," Yaya noised, scanning the faces in the room. "So what does your 'unity' look like? Why did you really invite us all the way over here in the middle of mayhem?"

Before Mama Seeya could answer, the others joined Yaya, shoulder to shoulder. Unlike us, they were a united front.

"We know that your region has suffered even before this insurrection. That the resources here are dry, the lands infertile from the high-tech runoff that we warned the Elites against," he said.

Mama Seeya allowed Wayal to take over and deliver the next blow. "We will be destroying the wall that separates the regions."

As one, they stirred in protest, the lines in their markings glowing fierce.

"The new regime will be expanding the perimeter into the north."

"Over my frozen corpse." Yaya slammed an engraved walking stick on the table's frame.

"You don't have a choice." Wayal's curved nose splayed more to the left as he smiled.

"That was *not* the deal," Elu said to Mama Seeya. She turned to Liyo. "Where's your honor?"

Liyo kept his face forward, but his eyes were cast down. He was too much of a coward to answer Elu's question in front of his master.

"What is *honor* in times of survival?" Mama Seeya posed.

Elu's jaw locked. And just like that, Mama Seeya had claimed another casualty. The space quickly filled with pressure. The rebels were ready for whatever happened next. The colony sensed it. So did I.

One by one, members withdrew from the gathering. Elu was the last to go, but before she stepped out, she said, "Expect a war."

"I wouldn't have expected otherwise," Mama Seeya replied.

Avi and I tried to leave with the colony, but guards stepped in.

"What's going on?" I shoved a woman out of our way.

Mama Seeya sighed.

They rammed Avi and me so hard that we flew forward headfirst. There Mama Seeya loomed over us, her hands behind her back.

She then crouched before Avi. "We couldn't have done this without you. That's a fact that no one in this chamber can refute. You'll be rewritten in history records; I'll make sure of it, that your generosity, allyship, and loyalty to us will never fade with time . . ."

Avi's bottom lip trembled as she waited for the catch. There was always a catch.

"But loyalty only takes us so far."

As Mama Seeya rose, guards seized each of Avi's arms, while another stripped her of all weapons. Before I could react, I was grabbed and fastened into place.

"Liyo wanted me to grant you a pardon, and I sincerely put much thought into it . . ."

When I looked over to find Liyo, he'd disappeared. Fucking weakling.

Mama Seeya turned her back. "In order to have gotten this far, I've had to make the tough choices, the ones no one else had the guts to execute. I've had to sacrifice the people I treasured, held close because I knew that all of the pain, the deaths would be for a greater purpose.

"I know myself. What would I do if I'd just aided in getting all of my people destroyed? There would always be that inkling of resentment toward the other side. Resentment turns into anger, and then anger turns into action. I cannot wager on you not wanting to seek retribution toward us. I'm doing this not because I'm evil or because I have ill will toward you. I'm making this decision based off hominoid psychology. I cannot allow you to live and take that chance."

"Let her go!" I shouted.

Mama Seeya poured herself a glass of water and savored it before swallowing. "I do hope that you can find it in your heart to understand the circumstances."

The word *no* was all Avi could get out before guards dragged her out.

When Avi was out of sight, Mama Seeya set her vision on me. She took another gulp and then patted her wet lips dry. The same fate awaited me. I just knew it.

She waved her hand for the guards to let me go. I swallowed what seemed like a nugget, waiting for what would happen next.

My fingers twitched, not too far away from my gun. She knew what I was planning as we sized each other up. "I'm allowing you to live, Saige, because you're my daughter and one of us, whether you accept that or not, but if you fall out of line, even slightly stray from the track, I will snap your neck myself."

Wayal snorted.

"Tread. Very. Carefully," she finished.

Chapter Thirty-Two
AVI

Before tossing me into a dingy cell with little light, a guard struck me in the abdomen. I squirmed in a heap and wheezed. The other took the opportunity to kick me in the back, striking my ribs, and then in the face, before expelling a wad of saliva on me.

There two frames lingered, chortling, as I writhed in agony. They even slapped palms.

After the attack ceased, they closed the door to the cell and ran the bolt into its fixture, sealing me inside the darkness.

A moment hadn't even passed before the slot slid open, allowing for a thin beam of light to part the darkness.

Through the opening was the guard's rotten teeth. "We discovered a shit ton of dem Uppers hidden in a Sub's bunker. Was packed in there tight like sardines in a tin."

My heart dropped. No, no, no.

"And we found a few Elites mixed in wit 'em too." They sniggered. "We hit gold."

I grabbed onto my ribs and scooted toward the opening.

"Wanna know who we found?"

More laughter.

"Yer moms."

Before I could reach through the hole, they'd sealed it shut again. On my knees, I screamed until my voice began to crack, until my tonsils dried, until no sound derived from my larynx for the remainder of my imprisonment.

They had Mother. Having me wasn't enough, and I had no leverage to make demands, to offer a trade. I'd given them all that they needed. How could I have been so stupid to believe that my cooperation would be enough? That my fairness was enough? Saige was right: we'd never, ever change. Her wanting to escape, find some level of peace was what I should've been dashing toward. Instead, I was blinded by my own need to reset the region, to get it right. Perhaps there was no right in the universe. Perhaps it was consume or be consumed, and that was just the way the wheel turned. We were all just doomed to destroy one another, over and over and over again as time went on, as millennia replaced millennia. And every once in a while, a revolutionary, a persistent idiot like me, tried to toss a temporary block in the system and labeled it *change*.

There was no conceivable way out of what I had gotten myself into, what I had gotten Mother into. The others. All the hundreds of thousands, and soon to be millions, of lives cut short because their professed General thought that equality would be such an easier feat.

I'd gambled all those lives and lost.

I had already accepted my fate, that I wasn't going to make it out of the rebels' containment alive. I was at the end of my story, and rightfully so. I chuckled silently because who knew that I would've even lasted as long as I had. In that sense, I knew that Father would've been proud.

He always thought of me as weaker. Jade hadn't had to tell me. I knew it, and so did everyone else. I saw it in his eyes each time I'd fall, each time I'd put forth the least amount of effort, and each time I'd fail. That glint he had would diminish more and more at the sight of disappointments. He thought that I needed an overbearing man to whip me into character or that I needed to stop daydreaming in order to focus.

He thought that I would succeed if I only followed in his exact footsteps. Regimented and noninquisitive. He wanted me to solely shadow the ones before me.

Instead, I created my own trail. I took a chance. I trusted my gut like he'd always pressed on about. For that, I didn't regret the choices I'd made. The experiences I got to have. I'd lived more of a life than I would've ever had back at the Citadel.

Although it was the end, I had to be at peace with it.

Still, I feared for Saige. I thought that I'd be of more help to her. Although I hadn't grown up with her or even spent a lot of time in her presence, I knew her more than I let on. I'd picked up on all her quips and grunts during our short times together and stored them in my memory bank for safekeeping. I'd witnessed her at her hardest and at her softest. She'd revealed sides of herself that not many had had the pleasure of seeing.

All I wanted was for her to have the life that she'd been deprived of. My wish for her would be that during whatever execution that would be issued to me and the others, she used that cover to get far, far away.

But because I knew Saige, I understood that she wouldn't let it go. She wouldn't slip away to save herself. She would fight until the very end, even if it cost her life.

I pounded the ground at the thought of Saige trying to go head to head with Mama Seeya. She wouldn't stand a chance without an army.

I needed for her to forget about me. Forget about it all. Be the old Saige. An opportunist. I was not worth the fight. One of us had to survive. One of us just had to . . .

I regained composure and lay on my back with my hands on my chest, rising and falling with each inhale and each exhale, peering into nothingness, and I imagined what the world would be like with us completely gone. Elites and Upper Residents erased. We had done such a fantastic job at creating while simultaneously destroying the earth.

The Dissent

Would we just become another notch on the planet's era chain, another lost race of people who couldn't get it correct? Perhaps we all just weren't deserving of the bountiful planet, and she would reset herself and start new again.

None of us were deserving.

Chapter Thirty-Three
LIYO

I looked like someone who'd died a long time ago. I felt like it too. I was being ripped apart from the inside. I couldn't focus. I couldn't remember the last time I'd eaten. And what was sleep? Every time I closed my eyes, I heard voices. Staying awake was the only relief I got. If what was happening could be described as relief.

Rebels around me planned the execution. They'd found more Elites hidden. They dug them out like moles. Wayal asked what my thoughts were. I didn't have any. I zoned out once I heard that Avi and her mother were on the list. He noticed my distress and rubbed my shoulders roughly and told me that it had to be done. That I had done enough. That I should sit it out.

I should. That would be the thing to do, but it wasn't the right thing. Or so I thought.

I told Mama Seeya that she didn't have to do it. Avi wasn't like the others. That I would vouch for her. That if she'd even showed the slightest signs of transgression, I'd step in and take care of it without hesitation. That I'd shown a million times over that I was for the cause. Who better to trust but me?

But she wouldn't allow it.

Why? I'd asked.

She'd said that I had a soft spot for the girl, and because of that, it wasn't safe. Wasn't fair. I had already crossed the line. I had been swayed by her. She'd do it again. Try to manipulate me. That all the measures were for Eve, and that I'd feel better once it was all over.

I'd made her promise that the death would be quick, painless. She'd agreed.

That was it. I'd watched Avi being dragged away. Saige fighting for her. I knew Saige wouldn't stop until Avi was freed. Mama Seeya was never going to let that happen.

There was nothing any of us could do but go on. Live for the ones who couldn't.

I made my way to the auditorium alone. Moving against the crowd of rebels and their murmurs of excitement to get the closest spot to the show. It reminded me too much of how the Uppers watched us be executed like it was some messed-up reality show. The tables had flipped.

I was grabbed and shoved into an adjacent supply room that stored disinfectants and cleaning gadgets.

Saige pinned me to the divider with her forearm when I tried to resist. She then slammed the back of my head into the wall. She wanted to do more than that. I felt it.

She finally let me go. "Don't play stupid games."

I massaged the back of my head. It throbbed.

Saige looked wild. Crazy. Like she was willing to do whatever to get what she wanted.

"You look like shit," she said. There was a softness in her tone, even though I knew she was pissed.

"What happened to you?" She got closer.

A few beats passed, and I only stared. What could I tell her that would ease her mind?

She shoved me harder, but I didn't budge. "This is *not* you."

I was tired of her manhandling me. I towered over her. "Why are you fighting so hard for her?"

She was caught off guard. "She's my blood."

"And I *am* your brethren."

Saige looked at me as if she'd never seen me before in her life.

"You've fought so hard for her. More than us. Your own." I was pleading with her more than anything. Mama Seeya would stop her from getting in the way.

"Are you fuckin' ill?" She poked at her temple. "Avi is the reason for all of this."

"I know that."

"Then make Mama Seeya spare her!"

"I tried."

"Your try wasn't good enough."

"Saige, don't—"

Her eyes narrowed. "Just say you used her then!"

It hurt to know that was how she thought of me. "My feelings were real. They still are," I confessed.

No response.

I mustered a half grin. "Don't be a hero, Saige. I know you. Just stay out of it."

She gave me the look that said that she would never, ever stop.

I scoffed. "Stop fighting. It's over. It's done. Just submit."

"Never." She turned to walk away.

"What do you plan on doing?" I took her arm and pulled her back. "Tell me."

"What you should've done." She snatched her arm away.

"Saige, I'm begging you," I pleaded. "Do not interfere in this."

"Or what?" She was defiant, but I had to try to get through to her before it was too late.

"It has never been normal for us. it's always been fight, fight, fight. Survive the next and then the next. I didn't know that the bottom was much farther down. How was I supposed to prepare myself?" I cried.

"Prepare for them to just rip her from me."

I couldn't bring myself to say her name.

Saige didn't move. She just listened. Maybe I was getting through. I held my face in my palms. "When I watched her bleed out . . . it did something to me. Something just broke, and I want this to be over, Saige, with as many people that I care about as possible intact."

"I, more than anyone, understand, but we've got to put the living first." She whispered, "But we can't be like them, Liyo. We can't start killing the innocent."

"That's what I'm doing." I straightened. "I'm making things right. You don't want to see it because you're too busy aligning yourself with the colonizer."

She glared. "If it weren't for Avi, you'd be in some lab right now being poked and tested."

"She owed us that."

"I thought you loved her."

It was as if she'd stuck me with a blade and twisted.

We stood in silence, until I said, "I do love her, but I loved you first."

Saige wanted to tear away; I knew it. Instead, she doubled down. "You used her for Mama Seeya then. You're nothing but a fuckin' puppet, a toy for her."

I looked away, ashamed almost that she just didn't get it, didn't want to get it. Didn't care. I wasn't sure why I said it that way or what I was hoping to get from it. I should've known by then that Saige was Saige.

I finally looked at her straight on, waiting for her to say something, but she had nothing to say to me.

I returned to that flat mask I'd been wearing since her death. "Love only goes so far." I shoulder checked her on the way out. "If you try anything to prevent the inevitable, I will have to kill you."

Chapter Thirty-Four

SAIGE

My heart sank to the bottom of my bowels when Liyo professed some sort of love for me, and not in a good way. I wasn't sure what it all meant. Was it a ploy to divert me from pursuing the escape plot for Avi, was he grieving so bad that his emotions were all over the place, or was he dead serious? The big question was, What kind of love had he meant? I mean, I was a little jealous when he decided to get with Avi, but that was it. I got over whatever that was, and I moved on. He needed to do the same. Either way, what the hell was I supposed to do with that information when Avi needed my help?

He once again messed everything up. The reason I dragged him into that closet was so that I could bring up Avi's guess on how Eve even got into the hands of the Union in the first place, but he seemed all over the place. He was unstable, and I feared what his reaction would be. I had to keep Avi safe even if it meant withholding information. I mean, he hadn't even brought up the fact that he knew Avi was alive in the first place. Liyo wasn't the most trusting at that point.

I followed a pack of workers who'd just newly joined the cause. I could tell because they looked well fed, cleaner than the rebels who'd toiled in the Outskirts and Farmlands. We were ushered toward the

Academy's auditorium, where the live-streamed execution was to take place.

Sounded like a familiar way to take a life. Mama Seeya was so shortsighted that she hadn't even noticed that she had Upper blood, DNA, and that she was falling for the same dupe that the others had.

I wasn't going to allow anyone to take Avi from me again. The odds of making it out alive were slim to zero, but it was a risk that I was going to take. I knew that wherever Avi was, she was cursing me, telling me not to go through with whatever ludicrous idea that I'd come up with.

But at that point, Avi knew me better than that.

The chairs in the mammoth auditorium had been ripped from the cement reinforcements, leaving an open space for spectators to view the display upfront. The room was packed out like a bumping club within the Square. Suspended above were strategically placed holocams, ready to catch every angle of the slaying. I shoved my way through war-tattered clothing pasted on musty bodies that were overdue for washes. A few tried to push back, grimacing at my presence, but I elbowed even harder, until I made it to the very front.

One by one Mama Seeya's people filled the stage, taking their positions. Liyo wasn't among them. Maybe he'd gotten some sense from our little meeting and was plotting like I was. I could've really used his help.

Led by an armed Wayal was a line of prisoners of different sizes adorned in fancy Upper attire, shackled at their wrists and ankles and sporting the same netted head sacks that I'd worn when I was first transported to become a ward of the Citadel. Through the mesh, I heard the whimpers and cries of both men and women.

Once they were all in a row, guards started kicking the backs of their knees out, until they fell on all fours. A few even got knocked in the back of the head with weapons. The cries turned into screams, shrieks. The guards shouted in their ears, telling them all to shut it. Calling them names. Beating them more even though they hadn't resisted.

My leg jiggled with worry. We didn't have long before they got trigger happy. Where the hell was Pea?

When Mama Seeya arrived and cheers erupted, I knew that every second would move double time. The people wanted Upper blood spilled. They'd heard enough about Mama Seeya's plan of domination, and it had come to fruition. Now it was time for the finale that they'd been promised.

A small part of me understood that the killings were warranted. The payback. The executions. The Union had made our lives a living nightmare way before I was born. But what Mama Seeya was doing wasn't right. She'd lied to the people. Lied to Liyo. Aided in killing a child, and who knew who else she'd betrayed in order to have gotten to where she was. She'd gone over the deep end trying to get to the Union. She wasn't a leader that I'd trust to take anyone into the next phase. I hadn't survived that long to have one dictator replace another.

I thought about storming the platform. Telling them all what Mama Seeya had done, but they were all so brainwashed. They'd become a hive. Plus, I wasn't the crowd favorite. They'd see me as even more of a traitor, as a threat. Then I'd be right up there with the hooded Elites about to get my skull blown in from the back, execution style.

I had to play it cautious, play to win. No shortcuts.

When the applause slowed, Mama Seeya signaled for them to remove the coverings. That revealed the faces of thirteen Uppers, all Elites, some children. Among them were Head Gardner, Avi's mother, the Administrator, and Avi.

Head Gardner's face was beaten beyond recognition. The features on the left side were rearranged like clay. Her eye was swollen shut, teeth knocked out, and the bottom lip nearly split in half. They'd ripped braids straight from her scalp, leaving speckled bald patches, and her fingers had been bent every which way. Knowing her, she'd put up one hell of a fight before they took their frustration out on her.

She'd somehow found me in the swarm and bore that same grin I was so familiar with even through her bloated appearance. She'd taken Ma from me. Miah. And she'd done it with pleasure. She was even cocky enough to think that she'd get me. Now we were on the opposite sides of power. She was in my place and I in hers.

The only disappointment I felt was that I thought that I'd be the one to kill her. Old me would've leaped up on that stage and asked for permission to take her out. Mama Seeya would've granted it, but Avi needed me more than I needed my urge for payback.

My love for Avi, for the living eclipsed whatever vengeance that I'd carried for Head Gardner and the rest of those people onstage. Head Gardner would get exactly what she deserved soon.

Avi's mother looked like she'd been through the underworld and back. Although her face wasn't rearranged like her friend's a few spots down, she'd been visibly roughed up. Her hair was untidy, dark-red blood trickled from her ear, and the once-glorious velvet bodysuit that had been handmade by slaves was matted and stained.

Avi was one Elite away from her mother. She'd also been beaten. It felt like my chest was going to cave in. She kept looking at her mother. She wouldn't take her eyes off her. I knew that very feeling, that same scenario when I was a little girl and seeing Ma strapped to that cold chair. Being forced to watch as physicians stuck her with injections.

"Elites—or rather, former Elites kneel before you." Mama Seeya motioned to the holocams. "Before the region to pay for their crimes against humanity. With death."

Jeers for the prisoners roared, then receded.

"Before you are past slave masters. Take a good look at your former life, and bid it farewell." She allowed a few beats to pass. "Even the children, who will only grow old and replace their parents' autocracy. The ones who created a system of chattel slavery and bondage. Today is not the day to weep. To feel sorry. To feel empathy for these cruel, cruel vermin."

You'd have thought it was Marco Grant dropping a new single given how loud the newly freed people were.

"Today is the day where we start anew. We get it right. We voyage to fresh life as a free people!"

Chanting began. It started as a murmur but then gained strength as each person repeated: "Not ever again."

"And not ever again we shall." She receded back into the fold of her people.

Wayal stepped to the line and brandished a gun.

The leg shake had turned into a full-blown foot tap. I glanced around the ceiling, the room, all the way as far as I could to the back for a sign of Pea. I returned my attention to Wayal as he began stalking the line, deciding who would be first.

I cursed Pea under my breath. She had one job.

He put the barrel to a man's head and blew his brains out. No hesitation. The Administrator jerked as she was splattered in the face with the remains of his skull's innards. She screamed so loud, but the sound was concealed by the ovations of the crowd. Annoyed by the scream, Wayal put a bullet in her next. The other Elites tried to flee from the stage, but they were knocked back down and held in place.

Wayal searched for the next.

He chose a little girl. I couldn't watch. I turned my face away just as he fired. *Thump.* Her little body hit the floor.

Wayal waved the gun across the track of the remaining, pretending that the weapon had a mind of its own and would choose itself. It landed on Head Gardner. During the entire execution, she'd stayed in place, presenting her dominance even in the face of demise. Her shoulders stayed square and her chest elevated.

"How many of us have you killed?" He crouched down, dragging the barrel against her puffed cheek.

She took a deep breath in as if she was going to answer, but instead she hocked a huge bloody loogie at him. It smacked him right in the eye. She laughed through the small hole that was her swollen mouth. He stumbled and wiped his eye vigorously as if the spit were venom.

"Fuckin' bitch!"

"I've killed as many honks as—"

Before she could get the rest of the sentence out, he stuck the weapon in her mouth and pulled the trigger.

She slumped over, and then her face smacked the ground. *Bump.* Blood collected around her head and then began leaking from the edge of the platform like a vat overfilling with water.

I wanted to scream Pea's name. She was supposed to have been there. Had she gotten into trouble? Was the entire plan fumbled? We hadn't come up with a plan B because we barely had a plan A. If Pea didn't come through soon, then I'd have to storm the podium, but how was I going to get past all of them? Even if I managed to take Wayal out, the rest would punch me with holes, and if they didn't, then the mind-control crew would lob me into oblivion.

It was impossible.

Liyo joined the stage but stayed behind everyone. I tried to get his attention, but he couldn't or maybe wouldn't see me. He was going to allow them to kill Avi. And if they succeeded, I swore that I'd dedicate my life to hurting him too.

More bodies dropped like slimpacks filled with rocks.

Four Elites remained.

Wayal lingered over Avi with the gun resting at his thigh. Taunting her with silence. I slunk forward. I wasn't going to let him touch a hair on her head. Forget Pea. Forget the plan.

He raised the gun. Aimed. Avi remained still but looked away. She watched as I gradually got closer.

Her expression changed. It went from fear to relief. She shook her head no ever so slightly. Just once. Freezing me in my tracks.

She didn't want to be saved. Not at the expense of my life. Fresh tears fell. Not only along her face but along mine too as we both came to the quiet conclusion that one of us wasn't leaving the auditorium alive.

If I could give Avi one thing, it would be my own survival. I knew that was what she wanted from me. That her wish was for me to trust her. So, I stayed put, mixed in the mob of workers who were cheering for my sister's life to end.

I closed my eyes. Sealing them together like an envelope. Waiting for that single kill shot to ring through the entire place.

The round cracked. I felt the vibrations shake in my core. A form crashed. I heard a scream of deep, deep pain.

Avi.

When I opened my eyes, Avi's mother was partially collapsed over her daughter's lap. Her eyes were wide open. Stiff.

I wasn't sure if she'd leaped in front of Avi or if Wayal wanted a reaction from Avi. Either way, the scene was nasty.

Avi lifted her head from her mother's body, baring slick teeth. The next thing I knew, she'd leaped forward even with the shackles. Before she could get to him, the guards snatched her back.

Words didn't even come from Avi's mouth so much as snarls as she struggled against the guards and constraints. Wayal had unlocked something animalistic inside her.

"Do you see?" Wayal gestured toward her, facing the crowd. "And they call us beasts, tuh."

The people laughed, and when that faded, they were ready for more.

"Finish the Upper off!" a woman shouted.

"Yeah!" A man pumped his fist toward the stage.

"As you wish." Wayal took an exaggerated bow and then set his target back on Avi. "Hold the animal still."

There was a light throb coming through the cement base. I hadn't noticed it until a few around me began to stir, their attention interrupted from the carnage ahead to the disturbance coming from all around us.

Murmurs of confusion swept the space as the pounds became more rhythmic. Heavier. Stronger.

The floorboards in the stage began to shake. Rebels glanced around as they were knocked off balance.

Then there was a brief silence. Everyone looked over their shoulders and down below, high above. Earthquakes didn't move like that.

Two huge thumps came from the edge of the roof. Everyone gasped, backing away.

"What the—?" I couldn't finish.

A blast followed at the corner of the auditorium. Wood shattered, and hunks of brick flew. People scattered like insects to get out of the way. Whooshing toward the exits. From the hole emerged a seemingly drunken Transmega. Its thick metal appendages weren't in sync with one another. It began shooting laser blasts in random directions.

Pea didn't seem to know how to control the ten-ton beast, but she had created the diversion I needed.

Mama Seeya and Wayal had already given orders to take the mass down.

I slipped through the frenzied crowd to fetch Avi. She was way ahead of me and had already headbutted a guard that tried to stop her. I crawled onstage and struck one of the men in the mouth. Before I tossed him off the platform, I grabbed the keywand from his holster and tossed it to Avi. She freed herself.

I grabbed her, tugging at her arm as she tried to assist the others. "We've gotta get out of here," I told her. "Leave them."

"I can't," she said while continuing to help remaining Elites.

"Gratitude. Gratitude," the Upper said to me as I hauled her to her feet.

Her appreciation was short lived. A sniper shot her in the back. Blood dripped from the corner of her mouth as she skidded down my body.

Her partner screamed at the sight of the corpse and was shot through the neck. I took Avi and ducked low, trying to locate the source. It was Mama Seeya who emerged from the tangle of bodies and explosions with a pointed gun.

I stood shielding Avi's body with mine. "You killed her."

"Who?" Mama Seeya stepped closer.

"Eve," I spat. "You sacrificed her for this. I hope it was worth it."

Mama Seeya wouldn't confirm or deny it, but we both knew.

I grabbed the blade from the holster and heaved it toward Mama Seeya's head. It seemed to glide across space in slow motion. It stopped midair before piercing her head. Liyo had his palms outstretched, electricity whining as he kept the weapon suspended. He returned the knife back at me like an arrow, and it struck me right in the chest.

I shrieked from the impact as it wedged itself inside the muscle. It was in there deep.

The next thing I knew, Pea raised the Transmega's arm and blasted Liyo, Mama Seeya, and the others from the stage.

Chapter Thirty-Five
AVI

There was a constant drumming in my ear. A single sound wave of interference that stemmed from inside my cranium or perhaps my mind. It occurred after Mother . . .

I gritted my teeth as I tried to beat the obnoxious commotion from my brain, but the sound of a flatlined monitor just wouldn't end. I would surely go mad. I tucked my head between my knees and rocked to and fro as Saige bled out somewhere in the vicinity.

I couldn't stand. Let alone contribute. I was of no assistance at that moment. Any moment. We'd miscalculated everything. I'd overestimated and underestimated. All of which had led to Mother taking a round for me. For me. She shouldn't have done that. She shouldn't have saved me. I didn't deserve to be spared. I'd made my choice.

What had I done?

Mother was gone, and I'd left her on that platform inside of the Academy. I couldn't even provide her a proper bereavement ceremony. I bit hard into my knuckle so I could feel something, anything other than the grief that lay heavy upon my chest. I couldn't respire. I couldn't think. I couldn't go on.

It was all my doing. I didn't deserve to be breathing. That shot had been meant for me. Not her.

The buzzing in my head still hadn't lessened. It was the punishment that I deserved for bringing turmoil wherever I appeared. To Liyo. To Saige. Mother. And countless others. I was some kind of pestilence. No one was safe around me.

I had to leave. I had to get out of there. Should I have gone back for Mother? Found Jade? Escaped to the north? Saige was no longer safe with me around either. Wherever I went, I just had to get away from the people that I loved.

A faint noise surfaced from someplace. Poking through the static. The noise. It sounded like my name. It was vague. Hollow. It became deeper and deeper, closer and closer.

"Avi!" Pea crashed into me. In one hand, she pinched a needle, and from her mouth hung a long piece of string. "I can't do this without you."

I nodded and snapped back to the now. Saige was barely upright; blood was everywhere as she tried to apply pressure to the wound surrounding the hilt of the blade. I threaded the needle as fast as I could. Pea shoved all the items from the counter to the floor and then assisted Saige onto the makeshift gurney. The knife was still deeply jammed into the top part of her breast.

Pea glanced at me. "Wh-what do we do?"

Saige's eyes were pinched shut. She held in sobs and hyperventilated.

I had no clue what I was doing. I hadn't ever performed surgery by hand or stitched someone without a proper medbot scan, but I had taken extensive anatomy and physiology sessions.

"Avi!" Pea screamed.

I leaped back into my body. "Towels. Uh, or fabric. Curtains. Anything. Alcohol or liquor. Something to sterilize the area."

Pea nodded and scavenged the space for items.

Saige's lips were turning purple, and her face was pale as a cloud. She shivered even though beads of sweat dripped along her forehead.

I placed my palm on her face to provide comfort. The warmth caused her to stir a little less.

Pea had arrived with all the bits and dropped them into a pile.

"When I remove it, press as hard as you can." I stroked Saige's braids. "You *are* going to survive this."

Saige wasn't responsive then. She was as gone as I had been during the delirium that Pea had shaken me from. We were both in shock but in different ways.

I doused the area with liquor from a dark jug. Saige's eyes popped open with a high-pitched scream that I'd never heard from her. I tried my best to hold her down, but her arms and legs flailed.

"You have to stay still so we can get the knife out," I yelled over her grunts, but directions went unnoticed.

Saige was in shock. Nothing I said was penetrating. Disorientation had already set in.

She was too strong and knocked me backward. Pea looked at me and then back at Saige with worry.

"I'm sorry," she said. She balled her little fist and knocked Saige out.

❖   ❖   ❖

Pea and I rested on the floor in a stupor. Gore crusted underneath our nails and all the way up to our elbows. Saige was stable but still knocked out from the necessary blow.

"She's going to kill you when she awakes," I said, cutting the calm.

Pea wiped her face, transferring a trail of red across her forehead. "I know."

"What do we do now?" I asked.

"We're outlaws on both sides." She sighed. "Must be a record or something."

I couldn't help but smile.

"Gratitude." I leaned over.

Pea readjusted herself, crossing her slender legs, one over the other. "Gratitude in return for always treating me like a human even when I haven't always felt like one." She sniffed.

I pocketed her hand between mine.

Pea squinted toward the clock. She dusted herself as she stood. "It's time."

"Pardon?" I followed her through the access.

"Trust me."

I hadn't known where we were before, but now it was all coming together once we'd ventured through the dim passages and to the exterior. We were underground at the Apex again. It was empty, barren in a way that I'd never seen it. All its inhabitants had risen to the top, leaving the alternative world behind.

Outside, Elu and her people awaited. Pea hugged Elu and then dipped her head to the others.

"How's Saige?" Elu inquired.

"Banged up but stable," Pea replied. "Avi pieced her back together like a rag doll."

Elu turned back and motioned for a man to step forward. "Tyee is a healer in the colony. He will make sure she's well taken care of."

Tyee vanished into the complex.

"Come, we have much to discuss," Elu said to us.

The colony members stayed behind as Pea and I followed Elu through the once-filled row. Empty vials of Glitter crunched beneath our feet as we strolled along the winding path that had vacant pushcarts that once were filled with smuggled goods from above. Dingy feather boas and torn tinsel garlands flapped in the breeze. All the dancers, dealers, and workers had left in a hurry, flocking to get a glimpse of the fall of the Union as we all knew it. The great exodus to the top had finally occurred.

With her hands clasped behind her back, Elu paused in front of the triple holoscreens located in the center of their makeshift square.

It played the caricature version of the scenario in which Jade stabbed me in the ring.

Elu frowned then turned away from the display. "This is why we don't care much for unnecessary tech."

Tech wasn't a bad mechanism; it was humans that took advancements too far, but I understood the response.

"Seems like every time a southerner comes to the north, it's followed by destruction of some form." She sucked her teeth, producing a high-pitched sound of disapproval. "My people. They feel—they were betrayed. I was betrayed. I wanted to believe that if we took a chance on something different, a path we'd never taken before, that we'd somehow become victorious, exit from the other side as a true union."

I empathized. We shared similar sentimentalities. We were all used and dehydrated by not only Mama Seeya but the Union.

"Mama Seeya's treachery was foreseeable." She allowed that to sink in before she added, "But Liyo . . . I thought he was sounder than that. He's not the same person I was introduced to in the north. Pain and revenge have turned him into a shell of a human, hollowed in the center by circumstance, and I can't help but to feel for him even though he now sides with our enemy.

"And even though he's far gone, it's still not enough for me to lose hope. I believe that before this is over, he'll right his wrongs and find a way to unite what has been divided."

"He tried to kill Saige," Pea reminded her.

"But Saige still lives." Elu placed her hand on her shoulder.

She was right. Perhaps he hadn't meant to kill her. Either way, he was still in Mama Seeya's band and couldn't be trusted beyond the benefit of a doubt. I just hoped that what Elu predicted was true.

"We make a new pact right here, right now," Elu offered. "The region cannot afford to have another dictator for the next thousand years."

"We're listening." Along the way, Pea must've appointed herself as second in command.

"If we win, we'll keep the regions separate. The north and the south. The colonies just aren't ready for full integration. They need to see how the south fares after all of this concedes."

"I completely understand." My head hung low.

"We are a bit of a mess over here," Pea added intuitively.

Elu stepped between us. "But residents will be allowed to voyage back and forth from both regions, openly and freely. There's strength in accord and awareness. That's the future that we'd like to invest in. No more stealing. No more wars over territory. We work together from now on. There'll be no you against us or you and us. It is *we*."

Elu and her people offered us something that I'd thought I'd lost. Faith. I hadn't overcome the trials and tribulations just to break. Elu believed in the vision, and she had as much to lose as we did, but she was willing to fight for a concept that could become reality one day.

"If we win—" Pea began.

"*When* we win," Elu corrected.

"Fine. *When* we win this, who's going to rule over the region?" I inquired.

They both scrutinized me.

"I'm not the General anymore. I was never the General." I massaged my upper arm, suddenly feeling a sense of embarrassment.

They both glanced at one another as if that was the incorrect response.

I backed away. "Saige is the eldest blood. She can take her official position once we've handled Jade and Mama Seeya."

Pea toyed with an empty vial with her boot. "Maybe we should wait till Saige gets up to have this conversation."

Elu stuck her forearm out. "Do we have a treaty?"

I took her arm in mine. "We have a treaty."

Chapter Thirty-Six
SAIGE

My vision was blurred as I regained the most basic motor functions. Short attempts at half blinks. Rolling my tongue. My pec ached, throbbed. The spot where Liyo had tried to kill me, protecting that witch. When I mustered enough strength, that boy was as good as dead. He'd made his decision. We were no longer bound by history, loyalty, siblinghood, whatever the fuck he claimed we shared. He became my enemy as soon as he decided to side with Mama Seeya and almost took my life.

A familiar tune was hummed by whoever was in the room. I couldn't quite place where I'd heard it before, but it softened me. Invaded my body and my heart, almost causing me to float with a calmness that I hadn't felt in a while. The words I couldn't make out initially, but then every so often, I would hang on to one or two syllables. It was a different language.

The form chanted softly and lit strong burning incense. They swept it over me, from head to toe and then back again. The heat from the fiery stalk warmed my face, my hands, my feet.

"Miah," I mumbled, managing a grin.

"No."

The grin faded. The awoken dream spent. My vision was mostly back, and I could see that the man was not him. Miah was dead still. And as for me, I was still very much alive.

"Tyee." He came into full view. The man looked like he could've been a close relative.

"Sorry." I inhaled the deepest one yet. It was stupid of me to have even thought that he was there.

"Miah. He was my brother." He must've sensed the connection. "You knew him."

He helped me sit up. My entire body felt like a Transmega had stepped on it and then tried to scrape it off like shit.

"Yeah." I could barely move my arm to scratch my scalp. "A little bit."

"Hmm," he noised as he rubbed a paste onto my wound.

He began wrapping a long binding around my shoulder and chest.

I figured I had nothing to lose. The world was going to shit anyway. I wanted to at least go out knowing the little details of Miah's life before I'd come along. What his favorite animal was. What he liked to eat for breakfast. I wanted as much as he was able to give.

"Do you think you could tell me a little more about him?"

Tyee rested in place, the dressing in the same spot as he visualized all the memories that he and his brother shared. He chuckled a sad one but then started rewrapping again. "Where do I start—that boy was such a handful growing up . . ."

❖ ❖ ❖

Avi, Pea, and Elu were in the center of a smoke-filled room sprawled out on the floor like children playing an intense board game, going over drawings and maps of the city as they were surrounded by colonists busying themselves by preparing weapons and waving around incense to cleanse them before battle.

"Saige," Avi and Pea called in unison. Their eyes as big as owls'. Pea smashed into me, causing discomfort. When I cringed, she sprang back with apologies.

"Good to see you are awake," Avi said formally.

"Good to be awake," I said panning over the wrinkled charts. "So, what's the plan?"

"Colonists are here, and hopefully more are coming to aid in the warfare." Avi's voice dropped at the word *warfare*.

"I know you didn't want it to go like this, but we don't have any other choice," I said in hopes of bringing her some comfort.

She looked off to the side. "More people are going to die."

"Then let's not let their lives be lost in vain."

Although she was unsure, she put on a brave face. She squatted and showed me the setup and explained each role as she pointed to the darker-shaded quadrants of the map. "We will go for Jade first. She still hasn't been located, but what we do know is that she's exhausted most if not all the Union's army trying to subdue the rebels. She is the weakest right now and the easiest target." She sighed as if they'd gone through all possible plays and couldn't pinpoint a foolproof one. "Then we deal with Mama Seeya."

Elu chimed in. "I've sent communication to all the colonies."

"How many are there?" Pea asked what we'd all been wanting to know.

"Hundreds," Elu replied modestly, "of thousands of colonists."

"When do we leave, then?" I hoisted myself up with a groan.

"Saige, you're still injured." Avi stated the obvious.

I turned my back and began surveying which weapon I wanted to use to kill.

"Excuse me." Avi trailed me. "I *am* speaking to you."

She was starting to become that mole growing on my ass again. I unwrapped a double-tipped spear from a thick cloth covering. She hurried to the front, stopping me from moving farther.

"You aren't the boss of me," I said simply.

With her arms tightly crisscrossed over her chest, she said, "I understand that fact, but what if something happened to you." Her lip started to do that shaking thing again.

"Oh, come on!" I threw the good arm in the air. "You're going to cry like that before a battle?"

"Because you are *not* listening."

"I am," I yelled at her like a temperamental child. "And I cannot allow you to go into battle without me. I can't do that. Not again. So just stop asking me to risk your life for mine. There. That's settled." I picked up a glossy whip with a piercer on the end and held it up for her to inspect. "Should I use this or a gun? This one looks really cool."

❖ ❖ ❖

At the top of the Apex, thousands of us stationed ourselves side by side, shoulder to shoulder. Fearless. Wild. Skylar had pumped us up with something he called "battle berries." It was supposed to unleash the feral part of the human. The fierceness that allowed some of us to leap across fires and climb the tallest peaks without ever looking back, releasing fear and inhibitions. I'd taken a palmful, allowing the tart dark liquid to trail down the back of my tongue, but I didn't feel any different from before. I needed whatever magic to kick in before shit hit the fan.

We marched on foot to Subdivision Eighteen. This subdivision was one of the most desolate. Watchmen were rarely ever seen patrolling the place. People came to do anything and everything. Mostly real messed-up stuff. Torture. Dumping bodies. It was hard to imagine a place worse than the Underground.

Even though the space was open, it smelled like heated waste because of the number of overfilled bins. A pack of strays with patches of fur missing crossed the street, hunting just as we were. The sidewalks were decayed. Vacant lots were filled with weeds as tall as me.

Who knew what bodies hid beneath them. Streetlights leaned, almost uprooted from the asphalt with wires hanging down. Overgrown vegetation sprouted in weird places, and algae and graffiti covered the sides of damn near every brick wall.

Elu held her hand out. Everyone stopped. "Station yourselves inside of those windows."

She pointed to twin dilapidated buildings across from one another, facing the street.

Her people didn't hesitate. A good number of them began hiking to each place, and instead of using the doors, they began to climb up the walls like kinkajous. They climbed fast, using the small sills to hoist themselves to several different floors.

"Are all the colonists that dexterous?" Avi watched in awe.

"We come out of the womb climbing." Elu laughed. "You must see our mountains one day."

"One day."

When our enemies came, the colonists hidden in the cubes would let them have it from both sides. We had an advantage. At least one. That was as much as we were going to get, and I was grateful because Avi, Pea, and I would never have been able to do as much by ourselves. At least I knew that we'd fought tough until the end. And I would do my best to keep Avi, Pea, and Elu safe and alive for as long as I could. That was my goal. Although I was terrified about what would happen next, I had to focus on surviving, winning. No matter what.

I'd have to face fear another time. Maybe that was the berries working their magic.

My grip tightened on the handle of the whip that I'd chosen from the colonists' stash. It was long and slender. It looked almost like a metal spine that had little electrode hairs on it that sparkled even though the sun wasn't out.

The metal was glassy, and it gleamed in the daylight.

Some had bows that could hold three arrows, while others had sharp spears double tipped with obsidian.

"The ore is distinct to the region," Elu explained. "It cuts through anything."

Both enemies had access to spyware, bots that scanned the region. They knew exactly where we were. So, we waited for them to show.

Who'd arrive first between the rebels and the Union was unknown.

The day got brighter as time passed. The clouds seemed to have moved away, and the sun beamed down on each of us. I knew that the colony was sweating something heavy in all their custom pelts and furs because I myself was drenched, my own tension pouring down the sides of my neck.

The rebels were first to arrive. They didn't hurry but kept a steady pace filing through the wide alleyway. They weren't going to put on a showy entrance like the Union. They'd seen lives lost. They knew death inside and out. They wanted a fair fight so that they could tell their children and their children's children how they won it all back with no gimmicks.

Wayal led the army of roughnecks. Only one of the Tele-Impures was present. Mama Seeya and Liyo were missing in action. What would be more important than taking us all down at once? Something was going on.

Wayal glared. His people at ease but holding weapons and shields, and just twitching to use them.

We held firm. No one was going to make us back down. We'd been through too much shit to give up.

But something had to give.

A shadowy form flew over us too quickly to catch what it was. Heads leaned back to observe, watching for the figure again, while others clutched their weapons closer to their torsos and kept steady.

A whistling sound.

The western building was hit.

Someone yelled, "Get out of the way!"

It began to collapse. People scurried out of the area. Colonists started to jump from the windows and smash into the ground. Avi pulled me out of the way of a falling stone. Pea used the Transmega to hold up the side of the tilting building so we could get to safety.

As she held it so people could climb down safely, the Union arrived in full attack mode.

"Get into position," Elu commanded, lifting her spear.

We all moved into tight ranks. Ready.

A solo hovercraft came into view. Probably where the missile had derived from. It hovered low. Still, nobody moved.

The hatch was lifted, and from it came three people in watchmen battle gear. They hoisted themselves onto the top of the craft and looked down on all of us before removing their helmets.

Two of Jade's telekinetic sellouts and Lieutenant Butler took in the scene. It was just like an Upper to do the most. Everything was a reality broadcast for them. With Head Gardner gone, it was his chance to step up to the plate. That battle was the moment where he could finally show the Union that he was able to snuff out the flames before they became a mighty inferno.

If he won, beat both of us, he would go down in Elite history as the one who finished what his people had started, had always wanted. Complete genocide. The stakes were high, and they were going to bring everything they had on us. There was no time for mistakes or hiccups.

I should've offed him in the Cube when I had the chance.

All at once, dozens of hovercrafts emerged, joining Butler. Figures ziplined down. The ones on the ground level looked like vermin from afar moving in waves.

"Get into position!" Elu called.

When the first line of offense was close enough, we grasped the grips, pulled back the strings, steadied the arrows, and turned them upward like sunflowers facing the sun.

Their army came at full speed, as I could make out individual watchmen. All strapped and all loaded with lasers and flames.

My heart blew nearly clean out of my chest, as Elu still hadn't made the call for us to release. Something told me to let go, start lighting them up. Take out as many as I could.

Beneath Butler's feet, the craft fired two more missiles, but that time at the rebels. All of them flinched but Wayal. He stared the floating rockets in the face as the Tele-Impures held them. They struggled to keep the masses in place, but together, they hurled them back at Butler's craft. One of the sellouts tried to hold the ticking missiles back. The other took Butler and leaped. He wasn't strong enough to hold them, and the things exploded, pieces of craft raining down on the war.

Seconds felt like eons as we waited for Elu's word. As watchmen closed in, she tightened her fist, and arrows sailed before that breath was over. The arrows were like thousands of thin lightning bolts. I watched as many as I could hitting their targets. An arm, a head, a thigh, a neck was penetrated by obsidian tips. The first and second row of watchmen went down like mannequins. The third and fourth lines of defense still hadn't gotten the play. Another rainstorm of arrows hit their marks. And another and another.

"They are shooting from the buildings!" Butler was still alive after the jump.

I thought he was ordering his watchmen to go for the buildings, but then their Transmega appeared and began blasting lasers into the cubes.

Colonists were hit and dropped like fiery comets from the windowsills.

Pea was already on it and tackled the machine with hers. The mammoth machine was caught off guard. Its arm flung around, and it knocked over lampposts in the process, live wires spraying sparks everywhere. Pea went in for another ram, and this time, it tumbled to the ground. People hurried out of the way, but some got crushed as the whole ground quaked.

All three groups clashed on the streets, the alleys, in nooks, and inside of the halls of what was left of the buildings. Hovercrafts shot more projectiles, and Tele-Impures flung more crafts into the abyss.

The watchmen finally closed the space. The archers retreated, and the spear holders switched positions. Avi, Elu, and I gripped the shafts and sprinted into the madness.

Lines of lasers zipped past my ear, hitting their enemies in the chest. Arrows and spears soared like eagles. Colonists snapped the necks of rebels. The smell of casualties grew more and more pungent as the body count grew.

I breathed too hard, my lungs burning, working at full capacity as I chopped and sliced and butted my way to nowhere in particular.

"Saige!" I saw Avi pointing.

It was too late; a watchman carried a flamethrower, and he sprayed blue flames into everyone's faces.

Blue flame singed the fur of my hood. I instinctively shut my eyes as tight as I could. It was so close that I tasted it. I was on fire.

After a few beats, I hadn't felt the burning sensation that I expected. When I opened my eyes, the flame plume was motionless in space. Dice had paused it. Saving her people as well as me. We caught eyes.

"Only this one," she said.

I nodded and scurried away before her people tried to choke me out.

A loud bang. Something splintered. I ducked, landing on my face.

Someone came up from behind me and wrapped thick twine around my neck, dragging me backward. I scratched at them. They finally let go. A foot stomped on my back so hard that I fell flat. They turned me over, yanking my arm so hard that I felt it would've dislocated with just a little more force.

Butler.

He slammed his fist into his chest twice and grunted. I scooted back, but he put his foot on my chest, grinding the sole and causing the fresh wound to throb.

I screamed.

"I'm doing what none of them could." He stuck the barrel of the gun in my mouth. "You should've perished in the Cube."

Elu stuck a spear in the back of his head. His face froze in horror or shock. Maybe both. "Why do they talk so much?" She then ripped it out, kicking his body to the side.

As she held out a hand to help me up, a crazed rebel without a shirt tackled her. As they tussled, I came from behind and cracked her neck. I shoved her off Elu, only to find out that she'd stabbed her in the side. Elu noticed the wound and started choking.

"Come on." I scooped her from beneath her underarms. The clumsy legs of Pea's Transmega almost stepped on us, but I wasn't letting her go. I wasn't going to let the same thing that happened to Miah happen to her. Together we wove through the stumps, and I dragged her between a broken fence and a dumpster.

I ripped cloth from my bodysuit. "Here. Keep pressure on it."

Elu wasn't breathing.

"Hey! Look at me!" I brought my face to meet hers. "You gotta breathe. Nice and even."

She began to sip and shiver.

"You're going to make it. Do you hear me? Just keep pressure on it."

She began to weep. "I-I failed."

"No."

"I did." She nodded over and over again. "I just wanted to save my people from the Union."

"And they *are* going to be."

"Promise me that you will guide them?" She touched my face with a bloody hand, leaving a smudge.

"I'm not making you any promises." Her face turned sour. "Because you aren't going anywhere. You *will* lead your people. It's what Miah would've wanted. Survive. For him. Got it?"

"Okay," she said softly.

"Where's Avi?" I scoped out the area from our little hiding spot. I didn't see her.

"Sh-she was right beside me, and then sh-she wasn't."

I cursed. Everywhere I turned appeared to be a different cluster of butchery. Folks kept getting in the way of once-cleared sections. Avi could've been in any of the scuffles. All I could see was that we were losing. We'd been overwhelmed by our enemies. Our Transmega had been knocked down, pulverizing the street and whatever unlucky bastards were in a fifty-meter radius with a loud *thwump*. Pea was trapped inside the machine's head, banging on the panel as the other Transmega tried its hardest to pummel it to fragments.

We weren't going to make it.

I squeezed Elu's hand and lied. "Everything's going to be all right. Just stay here."

Pea was too far, but I had to try. I ran. As fast as I could. My strides long and quick, almost gliding over all the bullshit. A rebel swung; I ducked. Kept going. A watchman tried to tackle me. I dodged and kept going.

"Saige!" Avi called out, fending off two people who were much faster, much larger.

Pea banged on the screen. As I went back and forth with myself, I wasted time.

I went to Avi, hoping that the Transmega's titanium skull held up for just a bit longer.

I flew into the rebel hovering over Avi about to go in for another strike. I grabbed a piece of misshapen asphalt thanks to the degraded streets and bashed him in the face with it until his skull cracked, and I didn't stop until everything was caved in.

"Saige," Avi called out, but it wasn't a call for help. She was fine, but I was not. We were in over our heads. We weren't equipped to fight both the rebels and the Union. We didn't have enough fighters. Enough weapons. We had the heart, but sometimes that just wasn't enough. Luck wasn't on our side, or time. We'd just signed our death pact.

I was tired of the fighting. The blood. The killing. Us against them and them against us. Them against each other. I'd never wanted any of it. All I'd ever done was fight, and it was time to accept that maybe it wasn't meant for us to win. Maybe I was never meant to be free. I'd tasted it, and that was good enough for me.

"Avi, it's over," I said.

"No." She laughed through the word. "Look."

Clomp. Clomp. Clomp. Mammoth-size claws tore into the ground as an entire pack of armored PolarWolves skidded to a stop. Colonists were balanced in the grooves of their backs and used their scruffs as reins. The animals came in different colors: black, white, gray, and reddish. There was even an albino one with red eyes and fangs the size of my arm dripping with saliva.

Like the PolarWolves, I felt the heaviness of boots through the tremors as an army of Uppers draped in different-colored battle body-suits cut down anyone who approached.

They were led by Instructor Skylar, Commander Chi, and Jemison.

The war was still nowhere near won, but the fight wasn't over just yet.

Rebels and watchmen were hurled backward as their beasts tore through limbs and stomped on torsos and heads.

"Are you seeing this?" Avi was almost in tears.

The watchmen began fighting harder after seeing their own turn against them. One had a bazooka. He aimed and fired, but a PolarWolf used its hind legs to kick the barrel in the other direction.

We both stayed idle, just taking in the panorama of death, destruction, and disorder blanketing us. Intestines flew from stomachs, heads were crushed in with boulders, with boot soles, with mallets, crumpling under the pressure like a black hole. Soldiers being disintegrated with single blasts. Lasers burst through space like holographic confetti. Brain matter and skin fragments and blood droplets and ash from who knew where showered us like a snow blizzard.

We were so small, so insignificant in the grand design. It was hard to not lose courage at that moment. To forget why we were doing any of it. Would things truly get better after we'd weathered the typhoon, or was that sight, all that we saw in real time, the only thing that humanity had to look forward to?

"There." Avi grabbed my shoulder and used it to pull herself up.

A group of watchmen stopped fighting after receiving a message through their comms. A second later, they began retreating to a nearby hovercraft. What could've been more important than immobilizing the enemies? Avi was on the same page. We removed watchmen helmets from the dead and listened in:

"*Get us to Gardner Subdivision. Now,*" a watchman ordered the pilot. "*The op has taken the bait. Let's move!*"

We reupped our artilleries from the corpses, and then Avi slunk her way to the tail end of the entrance. We pressed our backs against the exterior of the hull, making ourselves as flat as possible, until it was time to strike.

The mechanisms sizzled, sputtered as the pilot tried to rev her up. The craft had been hit pretty bad. Through the comms, the head watchman cursed and ordered mechanics to get the craft in the air.

Avi bowled to the opposite side and took a quick count of how many watchmen were in the access.

She extended three fingers and then pointed two forward and then made a fist to hold.

I watched intently for her command. When she moved, I moved.

As soon as the engines purred and the inner extensions pulsated, she pointed a finger forward and advanced. She hit one. I hit another. The third one leaped out of the way. The craft lifted with a jolt, knocking gigantic cargo bins and Avi to the ground. As I hung on to one of the seats, waiting for the ground to level, the watchman that had gotten away took his opportunity while he saw Avi was down.

Before I could get to either of them, the others heard the commotion and started to file from the pilot's chamber with guns gushing rounds without direction. I dodged the first wave, firing back, and took cover behind a downed freight container. They lit it up with more lasers, filling it with cavities on top of cavities.

In the midst of them trying to end me, they stupidly damaged one of the thrusters, and the ship dipped on one side, bringing everyone down with it.

"Hold your fire!" a watchman ordered once he'd noticed what damage he and his swarm of dummies had done. "And turn off your comms. They can hear us."

The pilot was able to jerkily pull the ship back to a seminormal altitude, but we were still cruising on a tilted axis.

On my belly, I wiggled to the next area and peeled open crates to find something that I could use. Avi was on the other side, still tussling with the solo watchman as the others proceeded to deal with me.

I found a box of grenades, but that was too harsh. We'd all drop from the atmosphere like bricks once it went off, blowing a hole in the heart of the base. In another container were fume bombs. The gases wouldn't affect them because they wore helmets, but it could be used as a cover; then I'd pluck them off one after the other.

I let off over a dozen and flung them into the center. They hissed in harmony as they emitted vapors.

When the area was full of fog, I grabbed the first watchman from the back side. My knife sliced through his neck like lard. Two emerged from the swirl, and I handled them too. Then two more arrived. One from the front and one at the rear. I jerked my head back, striking the one in the helmet. The other I front kicked and then pounced on his breast, slicing into his chest. The other took the opportunity to place a chain around my neck and yanked me back. We struggled, knocking into walls and bouncing from toppled metal cases. He wore me down, as I exerted all my energy without creating a dent in his force. Instead of his grip loosening, mine did as my fingers slid from his grasp and dangled at my sides.

"Eeeeee!" he slurred as I choked.

A single shot was discharged, and the pressure of the chain eased.

Avi took my hand, hauling me up like gear as I gorged on air. She lurched forward and made her way into the pilot's area, gun drawn. Focused like a laser.

Before he could grab anything, Avi put a bullet in his hand and then his head. She kicked him over and took position of his station. Her eyes and palms glided over the control panel. She pulled up the location. A red dot pulsed over the holoscreen.

We were headed to Jade and Mama Seeya.

❖ ❖ ❖

We'd already known that the watchmen who were sprawled out on collapsed cargo had already sent out a distress signal. Whoever was on site knew that we were coming. Maybe they didn't know how many of us there were, so we had some sort of surprise element. But in reality, it was just us two with no real plan of attack. No backup because the real battle was behind us. We were on a one-way hovertram to a wolf lair.

Avi and I were going in blindly. Bullets would fly, though. I knew how she rolled, and I was going to stick beside her. Even if it meant that one of us, or possibly both, wouldn't make it out.

Her back was straight in the pilot's chair as she manually navigated the craft. The umpteenth blast that the transport had sustained had fried the autopilot's mainframe. Her hair was almost matted to her scalp; wounds spoiled her face, neck, and probably the parts concealed by the bodysuit. Her gazed remained forward, steady, and thoughtful as she watched the fog skirt past the blood-spotted display.

Her face had changed so much since I'd first met her back at the Academy. The roundness of her chin had tightened and become sharper. Less baby cheek and more adult angles. Although she was still petite, I'd noticed that she'd put on weight, some muscle during training. She moved with surety, with a confidence that I'd never seen. She wasn't that same naive kid that I'd loathed seeing on the propaganda commercials they'd play before the Administrator's clock-in. Her form was that of a mature person. A determined adult.

She wasn't my little sister, solely. She was a woman.

My throat burned as I tried to swallow the flames as it all hit at once.

I couldn't save her, us from what was to come.

It must've been the same thing that Ma had felt when we were captured and tossed in that cell. She'd felt for me more than she'd felt for herself. She sacrificed for me to exist. To live. And although Avi wasn't my offspring, she was the closest thing that I'd ever get to it.

I wasn't good with words. With feelings. I wished that I was comfortable being vulnerable. Being open. And although I knew that Avi would never make me feel weird, I still didn't feel comfortable leaking my guts. One would've thought that balancing on the edge of death would've made things easier, but it didn't. Not for me. I wanted to tell her so many things before we landed in the mouth of the devil, but I didn't want to break her focus. The last thing she needed was to be bogged down by my last words.

I ransacked the drawers in the hatch, looking for a reader. When I found one that had a little charge left, I began to record.

❖ ❖ ❖

"Saige!" She screamed from the cockpit, but before I could react, a huge *thunk* hit the flank, knocking the reader from my grip.

In the cockpit, Avi used all her strength to pull the gear outward, toward her stomach, to keep the hovercraft from nosediving. I got behind her, and together we pulled. The gear trembled so hard that we both shook with it as she tried to regain control. We were hit again, and then there was a whistling sound coming from the back. That last blast had torn a part of the ship off.

"We're not going to make it." Avi tapped buttons and zoomed in on what was attacking us from the ground. "Buckle up."

Once we dipped below the clouds, I saw the luxe green pastures of Gardner Subdivision. It seemed to be the only part of the region unscathed by the anarchy. And the perfect spot for Jade to camouflage herself.

"It's them." Avi transferred the image to my monitor.

Nadia was on the ground, trying to guide us off our airpath with her hands like a conductor.

Avi's directions got quieter as I grabbed a missile gun attached to the craft and sprayed where she stood. There must've been hundreds of lasers. She dodged the rounds, and, with her palm outstretched, she rose slowly about a kilometer from the earth. With a brush of her hand, she caused our craft to spin out of control.

Avi couldn't regain power manually, so we both popped on our helmets and braced ourselves as we plunged from the atmosphere.

Chapter Thirty-Seven
LIYO

Mama Seeya sent everyone to fight in the war and at the last minute requested that me and a few others remain at her side. And that was it. I walked beside her in the Gardner Subdivision. I wasn't sure where to exactly. She'd refused to give me anything helpful when I asked. I sensed apprehension in the way she moved that I hadn't noticed before. Her strides were quick like she was late to an important meeting. Who would've been that vital to get to when her people needed her in the final battle?

The farther we ventured into the Elites' sector, the more worried I became. Was there some truth to what Saige had claimed about Mama Seeya? Had I been blinded by loyalty, by revenge? Had I wanted to destroy the Elites, Jade so bad that I'd forgotten what path I was on? *An eye for an eye creates a blind society.*

I was getting closer and closer to believing that I had done the unthinkable. I'd turned my back on the ones who needed me most. I'd stabbed Saige in a fit of rage. I was going to allow Avi to be executed. There was no coming back from all of it, no redemption for all the hurt I'd caused.

Mama Seeya finally stopped. I followed her gaze to the top of a slender structure.

Jade stationed herself at the edge, glaring down on us, on everything that the Elites owned.

Without hesitation, I stepped forward. I was going to get Jade, make her pay, but Mama Seeya grabbed me.

"Let me go." Her arm almost got ripped off.

"I'll handle her."

"No!" I said. "She's mine."

Mama Seeya pulled her shoulders back and got in a don't-mess-with-me stance.

We both heard explosions from where we'd initially come from. I turned around and saw a lone hovercraft being tossed around like a toy.

Saige and Avi. I knew that they'd figure out a way to survive, to track Jade down. I also knew that Mama Seeya wouldn't forgive Saige for the stunt she'd pulled during the executions.

"Go help Nadia and get rid of Saige and whoever else is on that craft," Mama Seeya said. "I'll handle Jade."

I waited for her to give me more, but more never came.

She blinked slowly. "For Eve."

I obeyed Mama Seeya, but I was having a hard time keeping the doubts under wraps. Had she already known Jade was going to be there? How had she gotten in contact with her? Why had she been so secretive about it before?

The biggest question was, Why hadn't Mama Seeya allowed me to take care of Jade? Eve was my kin. I was supposed to be the one to avenge her. That was the fair thing to do. She owed me that after all my loyalty, all my sacrifices. I chose her over Saige, Avi. I thought I was her chosen son, so why was I feeling more like a mere soldier?

I looked up and saw the hovercraft spiraling. Nadia had let go and allowed gravity to do the rest. I held out my hands and guided the craft so it'd look like it had crashed but wouldn't land hard enough for them to perish.

I owed them at least that after what I'd done.

I jogged to the area of impact and hid.

Voltage popped and sparked at the wreckage site. The smell of burnt fuel and hot metal scratched inside my nose.

Saige was on the ground. The cloth of her leg on fire. It took me everything to not jump in. Help her. Help them. But I knew they'd think I was the enemy, only there to hurt them like Mama Seeya had ordered. Like I had done.

Saige's eyes shot open as she tried to kick and slap the flames out. She'd burn alive if I didn't step in.

Just as I was about to leap forward, a blackened Avi smothered the flames.

I returned to the hiding spot.

"Argh!" Saige wailed as she peeled the singed fabric away from the wound.

With shaking hands, Avi rummaged through the wreckage, probably trying to locate a medkit.

Saige pointed to where Mama Seeya and I had been before. "Avi."

Avi rummaged through debris. "I'm kind of busy here."

"Do you see this?" She pointed at their sister.

"Yes!" Avi had located a medkit. "This will do."

"It's Jade."

She paused and squinted in another direction. "Watchmen are coming in from the west."

Avi spilled the contents of the packaging and sifted through the tools and casings.

"Go." Saige took her arm.

"Go?" She snatched herself away, causing Saige to groan.

"Get out of here." She shoved her. "I'll hold them off."

"We go"—she stabbed her in the thigh with probably adrenaline and anesthetics—"together."

Although part of her leg was raw, the meds must've worked because when Avi tossed her a weapon, Saige caught it and checked the magazine. A haze of lasers flew in their direction. The place was crawling with watchmen.

"We've got to split up." Avi breathed hard, peering over a short white fence. "We'll cover more ground that way."

"What happened to the 'we go together' bullshit?" Saige reminded her.

She pointed the nozzle of her gun upward and glided along the divider. "You're right. We need a diversion."

"And what do you—"

Avi had already gotten up and started moving toward an Elite's estate. They stumbled into a perfect avenue lined with manicured bushes and buildings that looked like crystal monuments.

I couldn't see them after that.

"Hey." Nadia snuck up on me, causing me to jump. "You okay, boss?"

I gathered myself. "Yeah. Fine."

"We got a incoming hive." She looked around. "Have you seen them?"

"Who?"

Nadia raised a brow. "Saige and Avi."

"No, no." I shook my head. "They probably died in the crash."

"I searched the wreck." She eyed me. "No bodies."

"So, we should go look for them then."

"Yeah, I guess we should." She got up before me. I followed.

Chapter Thirty-Eight
SAIGE

Avi dashed across a lawn as watchmen fired. I kept the rear protected as she used the butt of the gun to knock out the glass window and gain us entry into a palace.

The place was picturesque. There was a clear blue pool smack dab in the middle of the foyer with heavy fish and seaweed floating around at the bottom. The background music was a sad piano concerto, and it smelled of earth and salts. Everything was white, and clear, and clean, and ordered. Almost like no one had ever lived there at all.

Avi and I left a trail of the muck that had attached itself to us through the past few hours along the shiny crystal floors like slugs. There was no sign of life the farther we ventured. Maybe the family had escaped to a bunker, anywhere but there, to protect themselves from the mess that their government had created.

When I let my guard down, we were met with firepower. Avi dove one way, and I dove the other.

I concealed myself behind a statue of an embalmed extinct species that was the size of three hovercycles stuck together. The estate owner blasted again, wanting to send the message that they were not to be fucked with.

"Is this what you wanted?" The person seemed to have spoken through clenched teeth as they let off more rounds. "Mutts running amuck." More bullets.

Through the reflection on a shiny-surfaced mantelpiece, I saw that it was someone from Avi's class. I just couldn't remember the girl's name.

"Whose place is this?" I called out.

More ammo unloaded in my direction. "Tell her, Avi."

"The Gardner estate," Avi chirped.

I bit my knuckle until marks of my teeth remained.

"You killed—murdered my aunt, and then you have the audacity to break into my manor?" That time she allowed the shots to strike only Avi's guard.

"Blair," Avi began. "Head Gardner was a tyrant, and you know it."

Lasers.

"Maybe less provoking, Avi," I offered.

Avi spoke with intent. "I am going to come out now. With my hands up. You aren't going to shoot me. We will talk about this like adults."

Bullets.

"Kill them," another much older, shakier voice ordered. "Avenge the Gardner family."

"I am offering you a chance at redemption, Blair," Avi said.

Blair chuckled and gradually approached where Avi was hidden. What was Avi planning? I didn't have a clear view of the other person in the room. Odds were that they had a weapon fixed on me.

"Redemption?" Blair sang. "Why would I need redemption from a honk-loving defector like yourself?"

The room went quiet. Not a good sign. I had to act. Avi and I rose simultaneously. I saw only the back of Blair's body. She pulled the trigger, but it only clicked and then clicked again as she took the weapon and shook it in frustration. Avi took the weapon and slammed it into Blair's nose. She collapsed, screaming as blood oozed from her face.

Avi stepped over her and approached the elderly woman sitting in an AirChair who wasn't armed with anything more useful than a blade.

She swiped at me, and I knocked the weapon from her papery hand.

Avi pointed the barrel in her face. "Comply or die."

The woman shivered, wetting herself in the process.

"Take me to the weapons bay," Avi ordered. "I know there's one here."

From the ground, Blair pinched her nose. "Don't tell them shit!"

I put my foot on her head, pushing her face farther into the pretty tile.

Avi's nozzle was a centimeter from Granny's forehead. "Don't make me ask again."

The AirChair pivoted, whirring as it floated along the hall and past the galleries. The place looked like a museum. We'd come up on an entry that initially looked like a wall. For the last time, Blair pleaded with her grandmother to not obey. I struck her in the ribs. The grandmother's chair elevated into an erect position. The control panel scanned over her irises. The plate glowed green, and it unlocked, revealing an entire stockroom of weapons.

"Explosives?" Avi examined the area. "Where are they?"

The chair had returned to its original position. "There." The woman pointed.

"Strip," Avi ordered the prisoners.

The grandmother clutched her chest. "I beg your pardon."

"You heard me."

The woman went from a frightened old lady to having a stare that would kill if they'd been fit with lasers. "You are a disgrace to your lineage. You are running around with some gutter rat. How dare you turn your back on your people. In the name of what? Freedom? Equality? The very people you protect are the ones that will stamp out your entire existence. Silly girl, have you not learned that history always repeats itself? You are on some mission to overthrow the government. Our government. Have you forgotten where you've come from, who you are?"

I could tell that Avi felt some kind of way. That this woman had probably been a part of their family. Attended Avi's ceremonies. Gifted her with luxuries that I could never imagine.

"I have not turned my back on my people. They have turned their backs on me," Avi began. "The person standing next to me is General Jore's daughter, whom he consummated with a Lower Resident to create but hid from the region, hid from Mother, from me."

"Lies!" she exclaimed. "How dare you make up such a thing?"

Avi pretended to not even hear her. "He had the mother of his child executed so no one would find out. Pinned it on another man. Had him killed too. Head Gardner and Jade both tried to kill me. And the worst of it all was that in the end, my own sister actually succeeded in killing our father for power, control."

Blair looked confused, almost sorry as Avi recalled her truths.

The old wretch not so much. She was probably stuck in her old ways of keeping family business on the down-low. Never to speak of it. Sweep it as far under the rug as possible.

"So I know exactly who I am and what I am to become," Avi finished.

"And what is that?" The woman seethed with a certain Elite arrogance that I had grown used to.

"A leader. A fair one. That won't kill you even though your crimes have certainly earned you both executions." Avi's expression had gone from hopeful to serious. "Now, you will remove your garments. You will put on ours. Both of you will walk toward the watchmen stationed outside, slowly, and then we will blow up your home."

Avi's plan worked like a charm. The watchmen were aggressive at first but then got confused by the floating chair. Once we were at a safe distance, she detonated the explosives. The blast shook the ground beneath the subdivision as flames plumed high into the sky. The Gardner estate burned something fierce. We'd made a little mark in the peaceful suburb.

We darted through the buildings as watchmen rushed to the scene of the explosion.

"I think it's clear," I said to Avi, waiting on her response. "Avi, how's the back look?"

When I turned around, there were Liyo and Nadia, standing not too far away. I immediately aimed, but Nadia had already slammed me against the wall, knocking the wind out of me.

"Why are you protecting her?" Avi asked him.

"Liyo, what are you doing?" Nadia held me down. "Our orders are to dispose of them."

"Stay out of this," he said to her.

She sneered. "I knew you were a traitor."

Liyo turned to her. I felt her grip loosen.

His eyes crackled as he tossed her over a fence.

"You don't get it, do you?" He came closer, but Avi stepped back, almost losing her footing over a garden ornament.

Her fear seemed to have upset him, hurt him even.

"She's controlling you," Avi said.

"No one's controlling me." His eyes were bloodshot red as if he'd been up for too long or crying nonstop. Maybe both.

"This isn't you," she cried.

"This is me, Avi."

"I don't believe that. I *won't* believe that." She shook her head.

"You have always seen the best in situations. In people." He reached out and stroked her face with his energy. Her eyes closed as she took it all in. A moment they'd shared together. Maybe the one I'd seen at the creek in the woods when they'd first kissed.

"They stripped me of my humanity, Avi," he said. "I can never get that back. We can never go back."

"Tell him," I told her as I held my ribs in place, struggling to get back to my feet, "the truth."

His eyes bulged. "What's she talking about?"

Avi lowered her gaze. "Jade—she got Eve from Mama Seeya."

"Liar!" He stumbled as if the earth had quaked.

She continued, "At the outpost, I saw Eve. She was there, and then she just . . . wasn't."

"No."

"Mama Seeya needed something to incite the—"

Avi began gasping and scratching at her neck.

"You would say anything to pit me against the cause." Around him crackled electricity.

"Put her down, Liyo."

"Or what?" His voice was distorted.

A barrage of lasers caught his attention, breaking his connection. Avi dropped. Watchmen rounded the bend. I wasn't sure what happened next, but I snatched her, and we jetted toward the structure where we'd seen Jade. We didn't have much time. The watchmen wouldn't be able to hold Liyo for long.

❖ ❖ ❖

We'd made it to the lower level of a double monument building that resembled a twisted stalk. Avi tried to pry the door open, but it was bolted. She kicked it repeatedly as I scanned for another way in.

"Over there." I pointed to an adjacent structure.

"That's not the same building."

"I know, but they're attached." I took a deep breath. "We'll have to jump across."

Under normal circumstances, Avi would've called me crazy. Detested the idea. Instead, she jogged ahead and went inside.

"Stairs?" She waved, out of breath.

"You know the electricity still works here, right?" I rolled my eyes and pushed the button on the partition.

We waited anxiously as the elevator pinged on each floor of the complex before arriving at the lobby. The doors shut on us and then ascended.

The elevator was made entirely of mirrored glass. She leaned in closer, surveying scars.

"You could use a dermabrasion facial when this is all over," I teased.

She giggled with a split lip. "It hurts to even smile."

The doors went ajar. Avi spun around and stepped outside of the lift and onto a lofty roof garden with a floating cubed ceiling. Well-manicured trees and bushes lined the crosswalk. Robobees pollinated flower beds. We skirted past mini ponds with floating waterlilies until we got to the threshold.

Avi positioned herself on the edge and observed the distance below. I joined her, barely able to make out the spot that we'd come from. The drop was at least half a kilometer. If we fell, we died. The distance across was long but doable. Avi started to run, but before she took off, I grabbed her.

She looked offended. "Sorry to interrupt, but is there a plan that we should go over when we get over there?"

Avi began to pat herself down. "Do you have any weapons on you?"

"No, your ex disarmed me. Remember?"

"He is not—" Her cheeks turned a deep shade of red. "We have bigger things to worry about right now."

Watchmen had found us again and busted through the shaft with guns burning. There was no more time.

Avi and I got a running start and sprinted as fast and as hard as we could. At the ledge, we pushed off, and together, we hurdled across. We hit the pavement on the other side hard and rolled a few times before halting far behind Jade. In front of her was Mama Seeya. The gusts of wind were so forceful.

Mama Seeya yelled over the noise, "Tell your watchmen to stand down. It's over, Jade."

Jade paced with her hands behind her back. "And for a mere trice, I thought we were partners."

"I would never be partners with the likes of you."

"The likes of me? Even I have my limits." Jade chuckled. "I wasn't the one who sacrificed a child."

"You killed your own father."

"Touché." Jade poked out her bottom lip. "The reason I asked you here—"

"—is because you're losing really, really badly," Mama Seeya finished.

"No," Jade offered. "I wanted to see if you would be open to a treaty. You have your region, and we have ours. We would never have to mix or mingle or see each other ever again. How's that sound?"

Avi looked at me with some kind of hope that her sister had had a change of heart, but I knew that it would be short lived. Neither of them could be trusted. It was all or nothing.

"How's that sound?" Mama Seeya mocked her. "You *would* like that, wouldn't you? Another chance to re-up and enslave us again. I'd be a fool to believe that the Elite would ever consider such an offer."

"That's very disappointing." Jade sighed. "Something told me that you weren't going to accept my truce."

"And something told me that you didn't invite me here not to kill me."

"You know me too well." Jade revealed her arms. Attached to them was some sort of machinery. Electricity sizzled over them.

Talon and Aura dropped in behind Mama Seeya as Jade revved up her new tech. Aura guarded Mama Seeya as Talon handled Jade.

Waves of power surged through his body, and his hair flapped as the current created a strong draft. Jade leaned more into her power stance, welcoming the attack. As the ghostly energy traveled to its mark, Jade crossed her arms over her head like an *X*. The mechanisms seemed to have absorbed the energy. Once it was powered, Jade thrust forward, throwing back the power on its owner. The guy appeared to be fried by his own abilities. His body shook aggressively; his tongue thrashed as his eyes began to bleed. Volts leaped around his being until he was a smoldering heap.

Jade shivered in elation when she witnessed her toy in action.

Mama Seeya's eyes went large. "What are you waiting for?"

Aura trembled at first, seeing what Jade had done to her partner. She started to harness her abilities but then stopped midway.

She knew that she wouldn't be able to fight Jade with her abilities, so she charged at her instead.

Avi whispered, "We can take her."

I nodded.

Jade snapped the girl's neck after toying with her for a few moments. "Is that all?"

She motioned for Mama Seeya to step forward, whistling like she was signaling a pet. "Let's really see if the master mutt is as mighty as she claims to be."

Mama Seeya took the bait. She pulled out a knife and began swiping at Jade's face and neck. Jade was fast. Blocking each attempt at connecting with her bionic casts.

Liyo appeared like a tornado, busting through the barricaded entrance to the roof. His arm was limp.

"Come on." Avi tugged me forward. "We've got to get to him before she does."

His blue eyes locked on Jade, and he blasted her without hesitation. Holding Mama Seeya at bay with one arm, she absorbed Liyo's assault with the other. She was able to discharge a wave that hit him in the chest and blew him back.

Avi darted to him, and as for me, I chose the path toward violence. It was time to finish the both of them. Mama Seeya, Jade, and I embarked in a three-way fight. I wasn't sure what Jade was on, but it seemed like none of the hits fazed her. Jade brought her entire elbow down on Mama Seeya, striking her unconscious. She socked me in the face, causing me to twist and stagger. Then she delivered a blow to my spine. Something had to have split. She grabbed my shoulder, spun me back to face her, and administered an uppercut that caused me to see red mists with bright-colored floating dots. I hit the ground hard.

She spat out a bloody tooth and knelt to face level. For a moment, it looked like she was admiring my face, studying it as Avi had when we'd first met in the archive. Perhaps in another time, another place, I could've been her older sister too.

She scoffed as if I'd responded to her nonsensical thoughts. "I do appreciate your fight. Your drive. Even though you grew up in the slums. Had you been born pure, perhaps you'd have made an earnest General."

I blinked rapidly, wondering what madness she'd do next.

"But you were not. You were born to a miscreant that my dull father unloaded seed in." She laughed once and then became stern. "And I have to right his wrong."

She raised herself. I waited for a kick to the face, for her to bash my skull in. Finish me off. Something.

Instead, she said before skipping off, "I want you to see me kill her before you meet the same fate."

My vision was blurred as I used tears to blink the blood from my eyes, but I could still see her form slinking toward Avi and Liyo. I couldn't move a limb. I couldn't make my mouth work. Had she broken my spine?

I screamed Avi's name over and over to warn her, but she couldn't hear me. No one could. The attack appeared in fragments. She grabbed Avi by the nape of her bodysuit. Liyo swung. Avi got a hit in. Liyo and Jade scuffled. Avi was smashed in the chest. She cried out. Liyo was down on the ground.

I closed my eyes. Real tight. That was not how it was supposed to end. Not like that. Flashes of Ma separating my toes, calling each one little piglet. Her smell of warm birdseed. Liyo and I holding hands. Spinning as fast as we could in the Outskirts until we both fell from dizziness. Snickering until our insides hurt and we could no longer feel our cheeks. Avi as she allowed me to paint her face for her stupid date. The way she trusted me too—the way she gave me a second chance at being, feeling human again before society devoured me whole. She allowed my heart to soften after being hardened for what seemed like a lifetime.

Miah materialized when I cracked an eye open. He was almost too bright to look at.

He caressed my face. I shuddered from his touch. He beamed. My mouth quivered at the beauty of his aura.

He lifted my cheek from the crushed asphalt, and with it came my head, then my neck. My shoulders peeled from the concrete and then my chest. My stomach and then my hips. I was on all fours as my head swung between shaky arms. I couldn't do it. I couldn't move any more than that.

Miah took my hand. He didn't smile, but I knew he was happy. I wanted to tell him that I was sorry that I hadn't gone back for him. That I'd messed up. That the one gone should've been me, not him. That he hadn't deserved that end. I wished he could've made it. Us together. We could've spent the rest of our lives in the north. I hadn't cared doing what exactly. Doing nothing but existing. Safe. Free.

To no surprise, I was crying again. Mourning a version of life that almost was, and one that could never be.

He pulled me the rest of the way until I stood tall.

I loved him. I never thought that was something that I'd say, feel, do. It was a different kind of love than I had for Ma or Avi. One that I never thought was possible for me. And even though he hadn't said it, I knew he felt the same. He showed me a part of myself that I didn't think I deserved, and I'd hold that forever. I was lucky to have met Miah, even if it was for a little while.

He backed up, little by little. I followed him, dragging a foot.

Even in death, he was still pushing me, making me push myself.

Closer and closer I got to him before he was too far away for me to catch up.

Miah.

I reached out, one last weak attempt at catching him. But he had already dissolved.

I wobbled, trying to catch my balance after being pummeled by Jade, by life. I wasn't sure if I had anything left to give, but I was damn sure going to try.

In the spot that Miah had vanished was a pipe that had been separated from the building during the energy blasts, and in front of that was Mama Seeya, peering over the ledge. I wasn't sure what I was thinking, but I charged. I swung the weapon against the back of her head so hard that her face whipped in the other direction.

She dropped, and so did the pipe, with a *clunk*.

I leaned over the ledge. Liyo and Avi hung from the pipeline of an unstable ridge.

"Here!" I reached as far as I could for the both of them. "Give me your hands."

Avi grabbed one first, and then Liyo took the other.

I wasn't sure how I was going to pull them both to safety, but I'd figure something out. I always did. I wasn't losing anyone else.

The extra weight tore at the muscles in my shoulder, my back. I felt them rip and then lock as I drew them in centimeter by centimeter. Avi kept looking down, her feet dangling, and Liyo's soles scraped at the building's brick as he tried to crawl up.

"You can't hold us both," Liyo said.

"I can." I slobbered, teeth grating as I used my lower half to hold all of us steady.

Avi's grip relaxed as she shrieked, causing me to almost tumble over the side. I slid forward, dropping them lower than before.

Avi squealed as Jade yanked her down. I hadn't known that Jade had also fallen over. I couldn't hold all three.

Avi was slipping, her grip becoming moist. I was more than halfway over the sill as their heaviness made me lose balance.

My feet were now off the ground as I fought to hold Avi by just our fingers.

"I can't . . . ," I said, "hold on."

Liyo and I locked eyes for just a moment, but it felt long. I knew what he was going to do. He was going to live up to his nickname. The one that I hated so much. The Savior. I shook my head, but his mind had already been made up. Liyo had had such an awful life, and I hadn't made it any better. It had to come down to real life and death for us to get it right. For us to see one another as brethren.

I cried even more when I hadn't thought more was possible.

He looked like a lost puppy. He was that kid I'd known on the Outskirts, innocent and kind before the Union, his people, had turned him into an instrument of destruction. Like me, circumstance had made us who we were.

He mouthed: "I'm sorry."

All the things I wished I'd said before, could've said . . .

"Don't." My eyes protruded.

Before I could say no, stop him, he released himself from my hold. I fully grabbed onto Avi.

He threw himself onto Jade's back. Together they tussled. I had Avi but I still couldn't hold onto all the weight.

"Liyo?" Avi called.

He dug his fingers into Jade's bad eye. She wailed, then lost her footing on Avi. Both Jade and Liyo dropped.

"Liyo!" Avi kept searching over each hip, her legs dangling, to look for a sign of him. But there wasn't one.

"Pull yourself up, Avi."

"But Liyo, he-he's—"

"Avi," I said. "Pull yourself up!"

I planted my feet back on the roof and slid her body over. She fell on top of me.

I felt the urge to scramble over to the ledge and just check and see if he was still there, but my body felt like hot rubber, and I couldn't catch my breath. There was no way he'd survived that fall. I sobbed harder than I ever had. Liyo was gone. I could feel it somehow.

Avi moaned. We embraced. I smoothed down her hair, trying to make something presentable out of the mess. "Are you okay?" I grabbed her face.

Both of us were barely able to stand. "I think we made it."

"It's over. Okay? It's all over." I smiled. "We did it. We—"

I hadn't noticed it. There was a shooting pain coming from my back. I wiped the dribble from my mouth. It was blood.

Avi's face went from joy to concern to fear as I reeled forward.

"Saige?"

My hand rode up my back, and when I felt the hilt, my knees became weak. I collapsed.

Chapter Thirty-Nine
AVI

I didn't remember the next few moments too lucidly. It was like splinters of memories playing out in a hellish dream. In and out. In and out. All I saw was red and black in between Mama Seeya's bludgeoned face. Red. Me on top of her. Black. Bashing the back of her head on something solid. Red. Her eyes rolling to the back of her skull, becoming white. Then black.

When the colors subsided like rain clouds making way for the sun's rays, my body was anesthetized. The only thing I felt were fat veins pulsating in my temples. My hands shook as I crawled back to Saige, who was spitting up blood. I sat her halfway erect and softly rocked her as she choked on her own gore.

I cleared the stray hairs from her face and tried to get her attention, but she was falling into unresponsiveness. "Somebody! Help! Please!"

Saige tried to speak, but it only caused her a great deal of stress.

"Shh-shh." I shivered as I put my forehead to hers, continuing to rock her like a newborn. Keep her awake. Present. "You will not die here. Do you hear me? You cannot leave me here."

I started to weep. Her eyes flickered as tears squeezed from the corners.

"Saige, do not leave me. I need you. I need you to stay with me, right here. We've made it this far. Together."

Her lids stayed closed more than they opened.

I shook her. "I can't be here by myself."

I sensed her gradually leaving this realm. Her soul creeping further away. "No, please. Please. No. No. No."

She looked at me one last time and then slowly wilted, melting into my cradled arms.

"Saige?" I put my hand on her heart and then on her pulse. "Saige?"

A voice from deep, deep down inside emitted from me as I howled into nothingness. It started in the pits of my being, the hollow of my stomach, and echoed throughout the subdivision, permeated through each human on the battlefield and spread through the south and the north and the unknown regions beyond that. That day, the entire galaxy heard my cries.

Everything faded to the obscure.

❖   ❖   ❖

"Avi?" Voices seemed far away like my entire head was submerged underwater. "Avi!"

There was urgency in their tones.

Arms grabbed at me. I was slumped over Saige's body. As they carted me away, I noticed that her lips were purple and her once-dewy skin was a bluish hue. Her eyes were closed like she was taking a pleasant slumber and having the most delightful dream.

Instructor Skylar placed two fingers on her neck and shook his head. Pea turned to stone.

He looked around the crumbled rooftop in a frenzy. "Where's Mama Seeya?"

I was too fatigued to answer. Too drained to think or even care about her whereabouts.

Pea broke from her trance and made her way to me. I laid my heavy head on her chest; even that was an arduous task.

"They're all waiting for you," she said softly in my ear.

I didn't have to ask what that meant. The Union had taken a pause after witnessing continuous anarchy. The leaders that they had fought so hard to please were all gone. There was nothing left but me. The survivors. They had no choice but to follow, or what we'd just bloomed from would continue to happen until there was no more left to obliterate. I knew it. They all knew it.

We took the elevator down to the bottom. Pea and Instructor Skylar aided me to the steps. There stood bloodied colonists, injured watchmen mixed with remaining Elites, and hunched-over rebels alike. I wasn't sure how they'd all gotten there. If they'd witnessed the deaths. Someone told them. Perhaps it played on the holoscreens, and word caught wind.

I took my time scanning over the faces: each gash, each burn, each laser wound, each knife laceration. I witnessed the pain in their expressions, their sorrows. I saw the loss that each had sustained and would never fully heal from. That kind of pain would always linger. Even with time.

"No more," I said.

The crowd began to murmur, confused by my first words.

"No." That time my voice rebounded, searing each set of ears and making the crowd still. "More!" It didn't even sound like my own voice.

I hobbled closer to the top of the steps. Pea tried to assist, but I held my hand out for her to stay put. Although woozy, I needed to address the nation on my own. Holocams came from out of nowhere.

"This is what happens when we"—my voice cracked, ached—"believe that we are better, higher than the other."

I teared up again. Remembering Saige. Remembering Liyo. Jade. Father. "Not one of us is above the other. Do you understand? We all bleed the same blood. Grieve the same loss. Mourn the same dead. It stops now. N-no mo—"

I twisted in hopes that Pea would grab me, stop me from collapsing, but instead the people behind caught me before I smashed into the concrete stairs.

I was somewhere in the middle between alive and dead. Awake and exhausted. Lucid and nightmare. I felt each finger, each palm, slowly slide me over the throng.

"No more," someone yelled from the distance.

Then another. And another. A group of them. Dozens of them. Hundreds of them. Then thousands droned. *No more. No more. No more.*

Chapter Forty
AVI

Since the Gardner Subdivision was the most untouched sector of acreage, we decided to set up a working city center there until we were able to fully rebuild the remainder of the region. According to the estimates, the Union's economy, its former landscape, wouldn't fully recover for the next few years, and even then, what would the new constituency look like? I couldn't dwell on the assessments. Its form couldn't be valuated yet, but I was up for the long task. I didn't really have a choice in the matter. I had brought these people there, and I'd see it through even if it'd cost me more than I'd already lost. There was no option remaining but to travel onward.

Gardner Subdivision also had the detention facilities, which we decided to use as residential centers until we could rehome people section by section. It wasn't the most comfortable design, but it was a start.

Without my knowledge, one of the advisers ordered a crew to clear out the former watchmen's offices and create a secured General's quarter for not only my privacy but for my safety. The area was so large that it could fit at least a group of forty, and we'd already had people sleeping on thin bedspreads in the entries. I rejected the makeshift space against a strong recommendation and ordered the crew to fill the space with as many bunks as they could.

"Aren't you afraid that one of—of *them* might kill you while you slumber?" Commander Chi urged.

"They are not *them* any longer," I reminded him once more. He was having a hard time integrating, but I understood that he came from a different time, a different place. Where we currently resided was unfamiliar territory. "*We* are all Southern Residents—former workers and former Elites alike."

He grimaced; the familiar lines in his forehead deepened. "But it's just a precaution, General Jore."

I took his hand in mine. "I will continue to earn the trust of the public. No separation. We have to learn to have confidence in one another. I will survive sleeping in a cell with seven others. I've been through much worse arrangements." I offered him a reassuring grin.

I appointed Commander Chi to head of Renewal and Subdivision Restoration. He took his position very seriously, but I believed that he was just content to be operational again after Jade had stripped him of his rank.

"Affirmative, General." I expected him to go about his business, but instead he just ogled.

"Is there something else you'd like to add?"

"You—your parents"—he hiccuped a bit—"would be so very proud of the General you've become."

My cheeks tingled. I parted my lips to give gratitude, but only a huff emerged.

He turned on his heels and ordered the mixed crew, "Fill it with cots. Let's get a move on now. We've got a region to reconstruct." I watched as men and women carted rusty frames and clumpy cushions inside the quarters.

I left the area feeling lighter. More competent. Commander Chi had stood by my father's side since the beginning and always looked out for him, as my father had done for him. He'd been with him through battles and during births. They were not only comrades but brothers, and I was honored to have him aid in shaping the region. His knowledge would be useful.

A congregation was scheduled. The assembly chamber was modest. Space was limited. It had a heavy round table that had been salvaged from one of the abandoned buildings and then paired with mismatched wooden stools that pupils had built in their workshop lessons. They were excited to be helpful to the cause, and every able resident had to do their part.

Inside, Elu, an array of colonists, Instructor Skylar, Admiral Jemison, Reba, Tate, and his appointees joined the symposium.

Just as I took my seat, Pea dashed in, the last as usual. She was cohead of Defense and Security along with Instructor Skylar. Her sharp bob thrashed behind her, a piece of bread hung from her mouth, a beaker was in one hand, and in her bionic arm was a reader. She skidded onto her stool like a slider in a spaceball game.

"Score," Instructor Skylar said under his breath with a chortle.

Pea spat out the loaf and smoothed the sides of her hair back into place. "Present."

I shielded my mouth at a half attempt at hiding the amusement.

Reba rolled her eyes. "May we begin?"

Pea sat up very straight and interlaced her fingers. "We may."

"With the resources that still remain, we have yet to locate Mama Seeya," Instructor Skylar began.

The vitality of the room fell.

"It's like she vanished into thin air," Pea added.

Reba tried to boost the vigor. "Maybe she died somewhere in the Outskirts."

The room semiagreed, but I knew she wasn't gone. She could adapt to any climate. She was a resourceful woman, and she was somewhere recovering, plotting. Taking Saige from me wasn't enough. She wanted everything.

"Ugh, hello," Pea called out. "General Jore?"

I was brought back to the present meeting and blurted out anything that might've suggested that I was listening. "Yes, yes. I'm aware."

"Well, then we shall keep a lookout for her and her remaining factions until further notice," Instructor Skylar finished.

"Very good." I nodded.

They waited for me to say more on the matter, but I wasn't ready to have her name disgorge from my lips. Mama Seeya wasn't dumb. She'd never struck on impulse. She'd waited many years before she struck the Union prior. We had nothing to worry about until it was time to worry. Whenever Mama Seeya chose to show her face on this land would be the day that I'd rain upon her all of my ire.

"What's next on the agenda?" I inquired.

Reba tapped on her reader. "Internal conflicts among newly integrated populaces have lessened by two percent this week." I'd put her in charge of the Conflict Resolution Department.

"My people fight for fun." Pea snorted and squared up. She started shadowboxing. "One time, all the adults made this makeshift ring right in the middle of the Farmlands. People wagered whatever they had: corn, shiny rocks, sugar cubes. The fighters beat the crap out of each other. I'm telling you, it was a bloodbath."

Reba frowned and tossed her head back like a debutante. "Well, Eli—southerners aren't used to that kind of violence . . . for amusement."

Pea's mechanical fingers rapped on the tabletop. "Says the people who used to live stream public executions like it was another grand evening at the cinema."

Reba scowled, but before she could say anything else, I almost went airborne. "Enough!"

Some recoiled, while others remained still, already expecting that my tolerance had been running thin.

"We must remain cohesive." My tone leveled. "You don't have to love one another, accept the other's oddities and differences, but you will work together while you are under this jurisdiction. Is that clear?"

Pea's and Reba's heads bobbed vigorously.

I uncurled my fingers. "Assembly adjourned."

I exited the chamber in quick, long strides. I no longer wanted to be referred to as a General, a leader, a head of anything. My chest was starting to tighten. I needed air. I needed to breathe. The little attacks had turned into bigger ones whenever I worked myself up. After Saige. Liyo. That never went away. I hadn't been given time to mourn. Lament. Everyone had their hand out and rightfully so. They looked to me for the answers, for the solutions. When the truth was, I wasn't as prepared as I assumed I would be.

I'd believed that Saige would be right there beside me. She would've been the voice of purpose. A pillar that couldn't be swayed. She'd be the General. Not me.

Perhaps I wasn't cut out for it. Father had known it. Jade had known it. One needed more than a vision to lead people to it. Was I going to be able to lead the region to that vision?

During my distressed stroll, I found myself sedentary in front of a massive shrine in memory of the fallen. There were thousands of holographic pillars that continually played the faces and names of those who hadn't made it. I touched the silvery surface, and it turned a snowy white.

"Number 3299," I muttered. I'd memorized his work number. A lot of workers hadn't been given last names.

Liyo's face materialized. There he was, immortal. I'd never, ever forget him. What he'd taught me. How he made me feel. I kept replaying what would've happened if I had escaped to the other side with him instead of Saige. Would it all have just ended the same? One thing I knew for certain was that I wished I could've had more time with him.

What I'd sacrifice for just a mere minute.

In the end, he'd saved my life. He told me that he hadn't believed in my dream for the Union any longer, but I knew that was Mama Seeya speaking through him.

The Liyo I chose to keep in my heart was kind and helpful and loving.

"Number 7612," I commanded.

My reflexes were quick as I reached out and touched the holomonitor before I could convey to my mind that it wasn't real. Like Liyo, Saige was eternalized inside that mechanism.

Whoever generated the system utilized the photo she'd taken when she'd advanced to an official watchman. Although behind the scenes of that moment—she was plotting an escape—there was still a glint of accomplishment in her appearance.

She hadn't deserved that end, and that was something that I would never get over. I placed my forehead to the screen and allowed the dull colors to wash over me.

"General," a teeny voice peeped.

I twisted my body around.

Pea stood before me with two readers. One was almost pulverized, and the other was a newer model. A cable linked them together.

"You can still call me Avi," I said.

"I know, but General just sounds a lot cooler."

I scoffed. "Cool sounding but not so cool in reality."

She bit her lip. "I know it. You have a lot on your plate. I just came to apologize for what happened at the assembly. You're right. We don't have the time to bicker. It'll never happen again."

"I shouldn't have yelled." I pinched the bridge of my nose. "I've just been under an immense amount of pressure, and I'm not sure if it'll cause a break."

"It won't."

"How do you know?" I looked away.

"Because you won't let it." She sounded so sure.

One of the readers indicated that a download was completed.

"Good." Pea disconnected the wire and handed a reader to me.

"What's this?"

"This was found in the rubble by one of the crew members. It was the one from the hovercraft that you and Saige took over."

"I-I'm not following."

"Well, as my newly appointed position as head of Defense and Security, it's my job to decode the former Union's data securities." She continued, "And, umm, I was hacking this one, and I found something. A message from Saige to you."

I pulled the reader screen into my chest and looked into the sky before charging Pea with a hug.

"Gratitude."

Her face had started to redden. "I'm going to get going then. See ya back at base." She ended with a salute before disappearing.

Skidding down the monument, I crossed my legs once I hit the gravel and began to view her manifesto:

"Avi, I'm not even sure where to begin." Saige was in a discolored nude bodysuit in the back of the hatch. Her face full of contusions just like I remembered on the day of the battle. I blubbered and touched her face on the screen.

"You're seriously in GI mode right now. You're so focused and somehow still poised. I'd like for you to teach me that skill one day. I'm a lot of bit rough at the core, but you probably already know that by now." Her eyes watered, so she kept looking upward to keep tears from surfacing. "Time isn't really on my side—our side right now, but in case I don't make it, I wanted you to have something to guide you across the bullshit that's going to happen. And by no means can I give you General-y advice, but I can be your strength from wherever I am, even if I'm not physically by your side.

"I really, really wanted to be by your side, Avi. I swear it on everything that's good and shitty in the universe. But sometimes, we just don't get to have it all. Sometimes, we just have to survive it and go through the motions until something pops off. Until we find that stupid little thing that brings us joy.

"I never knew that kind of joy existed until I tripped into you. It's funny, because I used to hate you so much. Seeing you and your family on those propaganda commercials they played at the Academy. Seeing how perfect and happy you were since I was just a little shit. I thought you had it all. I wondered why I couldn't have what you had. I guess you could say that I was kind of jealous, and I blamed all the bad things that had happened to me on you." She sniffled. "None of this was your fault, even though you feel like it is.

"We both were born into a system that was unfair from the get-go. Both of us should've had the chance to be exactly who we wanted to be.

"I know that you carry the weight of the world on your shoulders, but that can't be your entire life. Let the people who love you, care about you, help. Let them lighten your burden. You can't do it alone, and you shouldn't have to.

"Stop blaming yourself for what happened. We all chose our routes, and wherever the destination ended was already written in our stories.

"I'm sorry that I was nasty to you. Rude. Calling you names and shoving you around. You aren't as flimsy as you look." She chuckled to herself.

"Well, I guess I'm saying this to say that it's hard expressing what I feel because . . . you know I'm not used to saying nice things to people." She cleared her throat. "I love you. My sister."

The hovercraft was hit because the cargo in the background toppled. I heard myself calling out for her.

She laughed at the me who manned the ship and spoke quickly. "I'm sorry it took so long for me to say it, but I feel like you should kinda already know that I do because I've saved your ass like so many times. Like more times than there are fingers on my hands.

"Avi Jore, you will make the best General there ever was, and I hope that I'm around to see you do that. Do what you said you were going to do. And well, if I'm not, I hope that whatever sacrifice I've made gets you one step closer to it."

I hadn't noticed that the reader was buried so deep into my chest until it started to hurt. My sister's last words, her final thoughts. She still believed in me from beyond when I didn't. I needed them more than she could've ever known. I sobbed when I thought there were no tears left to cry because I'd wished—I'd hoped that we could've done all of it together. I would take her essence, her spirit with me and infuse it into the future of the Union.

I wiped tears from my face, dusted my knees, and stood tall. The people were depending on me to pull them forward. And forward was where we would go.

As I made my way back from the memorial, I sensed energy. Something charged in the atmosphere. It was a familiar feeling that I felt when . . .

The reader fell to the ground. I, myself, almost collapsed.

My being stiffened. My breaths stopped. I felt as though I was suspended in the margin.

Liyo had somehow materialized. It wasn't my imagination. He wasn't an apparition. An illusion or fantasy.

When he said my name, I knew it was all real. That he was right there with me.

He'd survived the fall.

I ran as fast as my body would take me. He waited with arms out-stretched for the impact. When our forms made contact, I was engulfed in a sphere of electrical currents that permeated through every vein, every cell and filled me completely with warmth.

Perhaps I didn't have to do it alone after all.

ACKNOWLEDGMENTS

I kept going over who would I thank, who would I acknowledge for *The Dissent*. Writing the second installment was a bit of a blur. Like I remember writing for hours and hours each day and then taking forty-five-minute naps in between because my mind needed to rest from the plot twists and the world-building and the major cuts and additions.

During the development of this book, I was sexually assaulted. Something I hadn't known how to process. Writing this story was top priority for me, and I got derailed in the last leg.

I wanted to dedicate this story to the victims, the survivors of sexual abuse. In book one, *The Union*, I dove into topics like sexual abuse and exploitation. I even made Saige a survivor. A badass who didn't take anything from anyone.

I just wanted to carve out a section for people who've been affected, silenced, derailed from abuse. I see you. I hear you. You are valid. We are forever warriors.

Secondly, I want to take the time to acknowledge the readers. I couldn't—we couldn't do this without folks that wholeheartedly dive headfirst into stories. The ones who breathe life into them, make them real.

I can't express the joy I feel when readers send me messages about the characters or how they devoured the book in a sitting or two. I am that kind of reader, and I appreciate when others are just as passionate.

I have to acknowledge my New York–based friends. The ones who made sure I was still being a human during the writing process. The ones who took me out for drinks and yoga classes and forced me to take breaks even when I obsessed over deadlines and plot points. They always have my best interest and that right there is invaluable.

To my big sister, she knows who she is, who listened to me bitch and moan through FaceTime. To my online community sending messages and posting funny memes after I posted cryptic posts about wanting to never write another story again. I see you and I appreciate you greatly.

I can't forget about the team that made this all happen. Not once, but twice! My agent, Penelope Burns, with Gelfman Schneider. We did it again! To Melissa Valentine at 47North for believing in not one but two of my books. Much love. I am forever grateful. To the entire team at Amazon Publishing, thank you a million times for setting the bar high for more inclusivity in the book world and giving this fat, Black, and very Muslim author a chance to share her work with the world.

Let's keep the momentum going.

ABOUT THE AUTHOR

Photo © 2020 Maryam Saad

Leah Vernon is an author, a body-positivity activist, and the first international plus-size hijabi model. During her double master's program, she started a blog about being a fat Black Muslim in Detroit and experiencing everything from eating disorders to anti-Blackness. She's been featured in ads from Target to Dove, and she even made it to the *New York Times* and *HuffPost*. She currently resides in New York City. Connect with her on Instagram, @lvernon2000, and on her website, www.leahvernon.com.